A TREE OF BONES

GEMMA FILES

VOLUME THREE OF THE HEXSLINGER SERIES

CZP

ChiZine Publications

FIRST EDITION

A Tree of Bones © 2012 by Gemma Files
Cover artwork © 2012 by Erik Mohr
Cover design © 2012 by Samantha Beiko
Interior design © 2012 by Danny Evarts
All Rights Reserved.

LIBRARY AND ARCHIVES CANADA CATALOGUING IN PUBLICATION

Files, Gemma, 1968-
    A tree of bones / Gemma Files.

(Volume three of the Hexslinger series)
Issued also in electronic format.
ISBN 978-1-926851-57-0

    I. Title. II. Series: Files, Gemma, 1968- . Hexslinger
series ; v. 3.

PS8611.I39T74 2012   C813'.6   C2012-900395-6

CHIZINE PUBLICATIONS
Toronto, Canada
www.chizinepub.com
info@chizinepub.com

Edited and copyedited by Sandra Kasturi
Proofread by Chris Edwards

Canada Council   Conseil des Arts
for the Arts   du Canada

We acknowledge the support of the Canada Council for the Arts which last year invested $20.1 million in writing and publishing throughout Canada.

ONTARIO ARTS COUNCIL
CONSEIL DES ARTS DE L'ONTARIO

Published with the generous assistance of the Ontario Arts Council.

Printed in Canada

To Steve,
whose contribution grows greater
with every new book:
partner, support, love.

And to Cal,
who keeps my hours full
and my intentions honest.

Otherwise: Elva Mai Hoover, Gary Files,
my surprisingly large roster of friends,
plus everyone else who has found themselves
developing a sneaking taste for
blood-soaked gay porno black magic horse opera.

The story is never over.

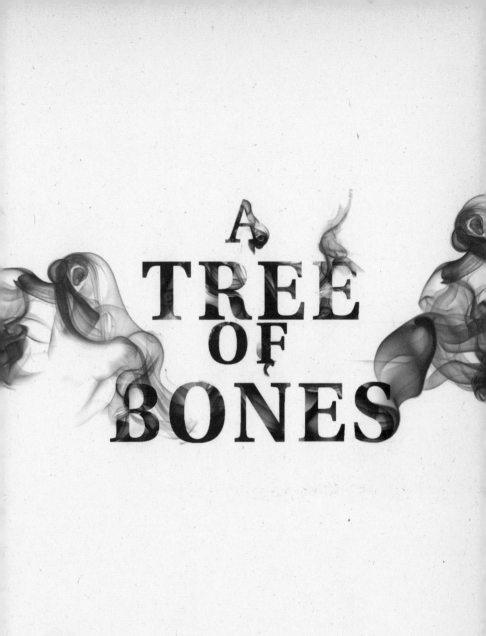

A
TREE
OF
BONES

Out there in the large dark and in the long light is the breathless
Poem,
As ruthless and beautiful and amoral as the world is,
As nature is.

In the end there's just me and the bloody Poem and the murderous
Tongues of the trees,
Their glossy green syllables licking my mind (the green
Work of the wind).

—Gwendolyn MacEwen

Poor fool, you are divided at the heart,
Lost in its maze of chambers, blood, and love,
A heart that will one day beat you to death.

—Suji Kwock Kim

TABLE OF CONTENTS

PROLOGUE

From a missive sent by former Pinkerton Detective Agency man George Thiel from the Texican "ghost county" of Perdido—abolished in 1858—to fellow ex-agent Frank P. Geyer, whereabouts unknown. To save paper (and create a crude cipher), sentences are cross-written, first from the bottom left-hand corner to the upper right-hand, then from the upper left-hand corner to the bottom right:

My dear colleague,

I write you this from the shelter of Texas, where fresh disputes w. Mexico *are hotly brewing. Though we cannot be sure, repts. indicate a great host ready to march on N. Mexico* at the whim of Emperor Maximilian. Said host is composed of Imperial soldiers, Carlotta colonists (who *would have ever thought any American, defeated secesh or no, likely to change his citizenship on* promise of undisputed slave ownership alone? Yet it has happened, it is happening) and other, even less *desirable elements. A second Schism seems almost imminent, and all because cultists conflating Hex* City's devilish doyenne with Mary, Mother of God are streaming up over the Border and making their *way to throw themselves at her bony feet, there to gash themselves with stones.*

As one might expect, the Hapsburg considers this hexacious

seduction of his citizenry further *aggression from the United States, moving perilously close to an outright act of war. The Carlottas, in turn, have been ghosting up through Texas to* catch and return as many as they can, which doesn't make *our allies happy. Thus far, President Johnson has gotten 'round it by claiming Hex City no longer part* of the United States *per se*, thus implying he has allowed it to secede from the nation—which perhaps *explains why he sent Capt. Washford and his Negro brigade down to help Pinkerton in the first place; i.e.*, so as to not encourage other only recently reintegrated parts of America to backslide. Texas, *for example, where civilian government was only restored two scant years back.*

One way or the other, our former mutual boss knows neither what he sows nor what the country *at large will yet reap, as a consequence. The Texicans, a hot-headed race (to say the least), are poised* to meddle, but without information, I fear this would be a fool's game. So please tell me soonest what *has come of your own quest, and address if you will all correspondence to the home of mine* inestimable host, Texas Ranger Leander McNelly. Since I have no notion of where you presently *reside, I send this via Apache scout. Awaiting further word, I account myself yr. most obt., etc., etc.*

From Frank P. Geyer to George Thiel, one week and three days later:

George,

Since Pinkerton's war on Hex City still rages apace and all notion of intelligence gathering seems frankly to have fallen by the wayside, I write to you directly. I am still wandering the wilderness like Elijah in exile, seeking after those ladies I told you of earlier—Mrs. Marshal Kloves (née Experiance Colder), a Spiritualist of some degree, plus the renegade squaw known as The Night Has Passed and that phantom shamaness she calls "Grandmother" or "Spinner," who returned from the dead during Sheriff Love's final battle with Chess Pargeter at Bewelcome.

Rumour has it that the Celestial sorceress "Songbird," once Pinkerton's confidante, may also be in their camp, making it the fullest roster of hexation-inclined females we might possibly hope to encounter. But since those same rumours imply she may yet be suffering from what other hexes fallen subject to Doctor Asbury's vampire methods call the Little Death—i.e. been emptied of her reserves, down to the dregs and after—the prospect of her participation in any sort of revolt against our former boss may be considered moot.

As previously discussed, we have engaged a source inside Bewelcome itself to make contact with Ed Morrow, and possibly gain his observations from inside Camp Pink (since, loyal as I know him to be by nature, I suspect his true allegiance may lie elsewhere). While I fear the man in question essentially unreliable, I yet trust utterly in his ambition, as well as his skills at rhetorical politicking. I will retain his name for now, 'til next we meet in person.

Meanwhile, for all that Chess Pargeter remains supposedly dead, his influence—like that of his former paramour, Reverend Rook—seems to have infected the very landscape around us, altering it almost beyond recognition. Each night and morning, the weather witches of Hex City brew storms, lashing Bewelcome like a second Deluge; monstrous rumours abound, trumpeting creatures unrecognizable by any report. The Red Weed, too, still ranges apace, impinging on settlements with hideous results. What steadholders remain have resorted to routine self-exsanguination in order to drive it back, which in turn only serves to further establish the presence of that *thing* currently wearing Pargeter's shape: Lady Ixchel's sibling and rival, a black god which styles itself our whole world's Enemy.

This entity roams the battlefield, appears in dreams to voice cryptic warnings, even pops up here and there to "help" one side or the other (its aid, like hers, bought always at the price of fresh-shed blood), before making itself once more scarce. Yet just as its overarching goals remain mysterious, its thirst for the same substance that powers the Lady's soul-hungry Machine renders the very notion it might be somehow more trustworthy, laughable. Tezcatlipoca is, after all, the god of Chaos, Night, and Magic . . . as much a hex as any other, though writ so much dreadfully larger.

Reverend Rook and his kith aside, George, we are rolled like toys between two opposing devils—one angry, one amused. And increasingly, I cannot any longer begin to decide whose victory frights me more, as a prospect.

Your friend and ally,

Frank.

From a representative agglomeration of newspaper headlines recently filed by San Francisco Californian correspondent Fitz Hugh Ludlow for his series *Notes on a Tenth Crusade: At the New Aztectlan Front, with Allan Pinkerton and the 13th Louisiana Regiment of Infantry (African Descent)*—

THE HEXACIOUS—THEIR LATEST DEPREDATIONS EXPOSED
Fresh and Exciting Report
of how a Combined Battalion of Pinkertons and Negro Troops
Liberated, at Great Personal Cost,
23 Captives of No Magickal Skill,
Enticed and Enslaved by the Hex-Horde!

HORROR IN THE MOON-LADY'S STRONGHOLD
True Testimony of Victims Reveals
how Men, Women and Children of all ages, all races
Continue to Suffer Imprisonment, Assault (and Worse).
While Pinkerton and his Compact struggle
Vainly against Incalculable Odds,
Innocent Americans still fall Victim to the
Barbarous Old Mexican Practice of
Human Sacrifice!

FRESH NEWS OF THE HEX-WAR'S MAJOR PLAYERS
Agent Edward R. Morrow, Fully Reinstated
After his Flirtation with Outlawry,
while Professor Joachim Asbury,
Pinkerton's Witch-Finding Weapon Master,
is even now Employed in Discovery of
New Anti-Hexological Methods;
In Bewelcome, Widow Sophronia Love makes no effort to
Disguise her Disappointment over the Sad Fact that
Mrs. Kloves, Vigilante Murderess of Sheriff Mesach Love,
Remains, as yet, Un-apprehended.
Pinkerton's Response: *"We have more
Pressing Matters to Worry Over."*

And finally, a notice published in Bewelcome Township's own *Daily Letter*:

All citizenry to assemble as of Four O'clock Sharp at the Nazarene Hall for Town Meeting; grievances aired and debate heard.

Resolutions to be voted upon accordingly.

In attendance: Mrs. Sophronia Love (Widow), Reverend Oren Catlin, Mayor Alonzo H. Langobard, with testimony on recent breakthroughs in all matters arcanistric from Doctor Joachim Asbury.

(Though most probably unable to join with us himself, Mister Pinkerton has promised at least one more high-placed representative of his organization will also be in attendance.)

To-night's reading: *Proverbs 2, 20 to 22—*

Walk in the way of good men, and keep the paths of the righteous.

For the upright shall dwell in the land, and the perfect shall remain. . . .

But the wicked shall be cut off from the earth, and the transgressors shall be rooted out of it.

BOOK ONE:
RAIN-OF-FIRE WEATHER

November 11, 1867
Month Fifteen, Day Thirteen Eagle
Festival: Quecholli, or Treasured Feather

During Quecholli, prisoners dressed as deer are hunted as sacrifices to the god Mixcoatl, Cloud Serpent, Lord of the Milky Way. Since Mixcoatl was the first to strike sparks from flint, and is also a god of war—though not on the same scale as Huitzilopochtli, the Lightning-Bearer—this may explain why war is known as *in atl in tlachinolli*: "the water, the fire," a flaming rain.

This Aztec *trecena* (or thirteen-day month) is ruled by Itzpapalotl, the Obsidian-flake Knife, first of all *tzitzimime*, those female warriors who have been honourably killed in childbirth. Itzpapalotl reigns over Tamoachan, the heaven for dead infants. Here grows the Suckling Tree, which bears over 400,000 nipples; here children can rest, nourished and safe, until they feel ready for reincarnation. She stands for purification through sacrificing that which is most precious.

By the Mayan Long Count calendar, today is governed by Xipe Totec, who provides its shadow soul. It is a day dedicated to Huitzilopochtli, Hummingbird on the Left, sometimes known as the Blue Tezcatlipoca—Lord of all warriors, those who willingly lose their lives in order to keep the current age, the Fifth Sun, moving forward. A good day for action, a bad day for reflection; a good day for invoking the gods, and a bad day for ignoring them.

CHAPTER ONE

SQUINTING UP AT FULL gallop while the rain pelted hard into his face, cold and raw as judgement, Ed Morrow almost thought he saw Heaven open, as on the final day, for: *behold a white horse; and he that sat upon him was called Faithful and True, and in righteousness he doth judge and make war. His eyes were as a flame of fire, and on his head were many crowns; and he had a name written, that no man knew, but he himself.*

Digging his knees in, he wished that that particular passage didn't remind him quite so much of the red beast earlier in *Revelation*, with its seven heads and ten horns. Let alone that the bulk of his Bible knowledge after Sunday School didn't come from such a very . . . *specific* source.

Then thunder detonated, haloing Bewelcome's pitiful excuse for a Main Street in a glare that flashed from blue-white to red to purulent green. As what looked like a blast of lightning whip-struck past, Morrow threw himself free, hitting the mud with a squelching slam that punched the wind from his lungs; as his horse ran on, unconcerned for any safety but its own, the spell-missile he'd just dodged went sizzling through the rain above him to strike one of Captain Washford's hapless soldiers full in the face.

Yet no shriek or blood spray resulted: instead, a greyish-dun mass like some wad of dough smashed flat by an angry child sealed tight over the bluecoat's head, a horrible flesh-bag snapped tight. He threw up arms and legs alike, rifle gone flying, and collapsed—a landed fish flopping, so disoriented he barely knew where best to claw.

With no breath left to swear and his bad knee screaming, Morrow scrambled to the other man's aid, careful to stay flat as possible throughout, so's to not present a tempting target. He pried his fingers under the thing's clayey edge (blood-hot, damp and rubbery to the touch, like flayed muscle) and yanked with both hands 'til it peeled back just a titch, revealing one eye rolled up and a wrist-thick tendril shoved deep 'tween the man's gagging jaws, bloating his neck's dark flesh obscenely. Revulsion stomach-punched him, loosening his grip; the death mask snapped immediately back into place, *writing* as it did.

Oh no you don't, *you Christ Jesus-puking piece of foulness—*

Digging so hard into his breast pocket that the thing he sought fair leapt to his palm, Morrow soon came up with a familiar device, just about the size and shape of a pocket watch. He wound its fob frantically 'til it burst to shrill, buzzing life, then slammed its flat glass face into the wriggling mess, and bore down. A mindless shriek ripped his eardrums under the torrent's drumming, fierce, yet so high-pitched as to be barely audible—then cut off, sharp as a snuffed candle. Simultaneously, the spell-chunk he gripped commenced to shrivel, gone so fast its dust had washed away almost before Morrow could let go. In its wake, the soldier jackknifed over, retching fit to dump his guts.

Poor bastard.

Apparently, however, this one was an old hand—experienced enough to get himself under control within a few whooping breaths, if nothing else. "Th' hex . . . one who threw this . . ." he gasped out, casting 'round for his lost gun. "Where'd she . . . ?" Bolting back upright, just as fingers met stock, to holler: "*Hind you, Pinkerton man!*"

Morrow hurled himself clear, Manifold punched up like a tiny shield 'fore he even had a chance to register who "she" might be.

Only instinct and speed, along with the device's last few whirrs, saved his life as another lit cannonball of hexacious smother-flesh struck like a haymaker, knuckle to knuckle; it put him over with his wrist on fire, either broke or paralyzed. The Manifold, caught in between, burst outright, taking the spell with it—greasy shreds and gears sprayed everywhere, pattering down into the muck, while impact knocked what was left of his weapon from his hand, leaving him defenceless.

Morrow rummaged for his pistol, praying 'gainst all hope he'd somehow managed to keep his powder dry. But his eyes stayed on the girl, similarly froze maybe ten feet away, rain skittering clear of her like she was galvanized: no more than twenty, tall and lovely, her hair a braided mahogany crown. The ragged hem of a once-fine green dress mended with thread of living light just brushed her ankles, disclosing bare feet sheathed in black mud.

Poised to attack? No. Might be she didn't understand his Manifold was gone, or had actually never before seen one at work, in close quarters. Might be she was an essentially gentle girl in bad circumstances, unfit for fighting, except at self-elected Hex City general "Reverend" Asher E. Rook's beck and call. One way or the other, however, and with all power disparity momentarily set aside—in that same throat-catching shared heartbeat, she seemed almost as terrified as they were.

The instant Morrow finally got his gun free, her horror flashed to panic like lucifer-lit touchpaper. She flung one arm skyward, calling out to someone unseen: "I'm threatened, can't see my way clear—help me, sissy!"

Was that flat-vowelled accent of New York extraction? *One of Hank Fennig's wives, then,* Morrow thought, only to have it confirmed when the answer came back from high above—feminine likewise, but well-touched with County Cork, its hoarse musicality worn thin by shouting above the storm.

"Berta? I see you, *acushla*. Now *stay still!*"

The girl—Miss Schemerhorne, the files named her—nodded, and shut her eyes.

All at once, the air seemed to twist 'round her, lariat-style; a black whirling strand of wind and dust lashed down, falling neat into one hand as any rope flung to some drowning man. Skilfully, she whirled her forearm in the cyclone-cord to wrap it tight, then leaped; it caught her up and bore her high into blackness, beyond the range of sight.

Prone in the mud, Washford's soldier stared up after with eyes gone silver dollar-sized, their already vivid whites set in stark contrast with a face the same shade as Bewelcome's freakishly arable new earth. "You all right there?" Morrow asked him, gently.

The man shook his head first one way, then the other—a cleansing shake, chased with a grim nod. "Me? Hell, I'll be fine enough if you gimme a slug an' a minute, or maybe just a slug, t'wash the taste of that damn thing out my mouth. I'm workin' for the Kingdom, sir, like all the Captain's people; ain't got time to die." He pushed himself to his feet as thunder boomed once more and retrieved his well-worn bummer's cap, canting it so icy rain would splash off what little brim it had left. "Gotta wonder, though—are these the End Days come to pass, way some say? Fallen angels walkin' the Earth, Devil's children like that gal there runnin' wild?"

Getting up cost Morrow more than he'd thought it would, so much so he had to spend a few hacking breaths fighting not to cough up a lung before he could reply. To say this weather didn't agree with him was understating things substantially, considering how it'd left him with a gasping ague that all too often kept him from what little sleep he could afford, and his bad joints—the knee, particularly—in near constant misery. "Might seem that way, I'm sure. But you can take it from me, Private—Private . . . ?"

"Carver, sir. Jonas Carver."

". . . good to know you, Carver; Ed Morrow's my name." If Carver's eyes widened further still at this disclosure, Morrow affected not to notice. "All spectacle left off, these folk're human as you or I, and a bullet *will* drop them, so long's you catch 'em with their guard down."

"That ain't all too easy, from what I seen."

"No, sure ain't. But it can be done."

The two men exchanged a species of grin, equally wry. Briefly, as he watched Carver start to reload, Morrow thought about telling him what Doctor Asbury'd promised him those fresh shells in his own gun might be capable of, if put to the test. However, he decided against it; there was no time, and the risk of false hope was too high.

"Seems like thankless work on the face of it, I know," was what he said, instead, scanning the mud for any trace of his Manifold's empty casing—ah, and there it was, right by his boot-heel; he knelt again to snag it, then heaved back up, with a painful huff. "But Christ knows, we in the Pinkerton camp're all glad enough to have you backin' us up."

Around them, the rain pelted Bewelcome township ceaselessly, unseasonably, much as it had almost since the morning after Chess Pargeter's sacrifice and Sheriff Mesach Love's murder—too cold by far for fall, let alone for summer, and hard as a bruising kiss. Behind this latest tempest, meanwhile, Allan Pinkerton's endless assault on Hex City ground on: rocket-trails of spells and spell-passage alike could be glimpsed 'cross the sky like ball lightning, throwing off icy sheets of green, blue, purple which wavered groundward; just like every other night this week, the earth shook intermittently too, probably from shelling. Above, even the traitor moon—Rook's dread wife's symbol, through which popular rumour had it she could spy on whatever luckless creatures slept beneath—hid its face at the sight of such rough work.

On every side of the rut-puddled cow trail the Bewelcomers claimed was called Love Avenue, the land was now all torn to hell with constant skirmishing, an indiscriminate churn of muck where nothing grew but the Red Weed that came in the Enemy's wake, and graves. And the rain, unnatural itself, brought far more natural threats in its wake: fever, rats, plus a palpable fear of flash-flooding through nearby canyons, producing an artificial river strong enough to wash the whole village itself away.

"Naw, sir," Carver continued, yanking Morrow back from his reverie. "My troop an' me, we're *glad* to be here, never you doubt that. When we heard the witch-folk was slavin' folks on top of everything else, even after the War seemed to leave all that over and done with . . . well, none of us was too keen to leave the job half done. Though I can't lie—there *was* a few here 'n' there said how turnabout might be fair play, once we heard they wasn't just puttin' the chain on Negroes, this time."

He followed this remark with a look, cool and level, as though assessing whether or not Morrow would take offence. But Morrow was far too tired to bother, even had he been so inclined.

"How they do it's called layin' a geas," he said, turning to limp into the wind; Carver followed along, seemingly genuinely interested. "It's a sort of a spell, goes without saying, but a love-working, more'n anything else—kind that hooks 'em deep and ties 'em tight, makes 'em *want* to come, and want to stay."

"That don't beat all."

Morrow shrugged. "Well, they got a fair bit of practice doin' it by now, since it's how the Rev and Lady Ixchel bind 'em to themselves, and the City. Only makes sense they'd start to tinker 'round with it after, I guess, the hexacious being who—what—they are."

And then there are the others who come and stay, those bound by something deeper, Morrow thought, but didn't add. For far too many of the Hex City host, blood tied tighter than magic: men following after wives, women after husbands, children all too aware that having a hexacious sire or dam would ruin their name no matter what, even if it later turned out the power didn't breed true. Like the girl last month he'd watched dump whole buckets of lime off New Aztectlan's North Gate wall, six years old if she was a day and pale-faced with effort, teetering on the barricade in a tight-tied pair of ladies' high-buttoned boots. She'd paused to giggle at the way the Pinks below scurried, rabid to avoid burning their skin or eyes—'til somebody (he still didn't know who, and hoped he'd never learn) had pocked her straight through the forehead with a long-range rifle.

Oh, the Rev might've planted the first seed and Dread Moon-Lady Ixchel made it grow—sure and foul, like a cancer—but Hex City was only half theirs now, maybe less. Others had built it up since and would die to maintain it, without being asked, let alone compelled.

Yet it *would* fall, if Pinkerton and the rest of the compact had their way: the Agency, Bewelcome, Washford's brigade. That was their task—to make it so, or die trying.

"But like you saw, the Manifold can break any chantment, you happen to get a strike home with it in hand—ah, crap." Having flourished it out only to drop it again, Morrow bent to scoop it back up; Carver peered at it over his shoulder, wincing when another lightning flash showed the broken glass face and sprung gears inside.

"That's one of 'em, huh? Doc Hex's Manifold?"

"One of the original models, believe it or not—*was*, anyhow." Morrow stuffed the useless item back in his waistcoat; least it wouldn't be galling him with its obsolete clatter, anytime soon. "Where you headed?"

Carver wiped rainwater from his face. "Captain sent me to scout southward. All activity's been to the north; he had it in mind might be a distraction."

"Good thought, but wrong approach." At Carver's half-raised brow: "Washford's thinking like an officer facing others, Private; Rook's a hex, leading hexes. We've already seen how they move, in ways we sure as hell can't stop 'em from going—all's we can do is try and predict where they'll light down next, and be there waitin'. Which means, if this was a distraction, it'd be from . . ." Morrow cut off, like he'd been slapped. "Oh, *shit*."

"Sir?"

Morrow weighed his options, mind buzzing. "Private, I can't trump Captain Washford's orders, but I can tell you where you're *really* needed to intercept the enemy." More lightning roared past above, screams drifting back from what would have been the township's limits, had the posts once indicating it as such not been either washed or blasted away. "Does your boss trust your judgement? And if he does, do you trust mine?"

Carver's jaw clenched. "Lead the way, Mister Morrow."

They pounded down the next swampy half-mile. As always, war's affray made for ghastly accompaniment, all the more so for those eldritch elements woven among the usual tumult of gunfire and dying men's shrieks. To their left some invisible creature gave out a wounded minotaur's bull roar, while from elsewhere there came the sizzle of fried bacon fat cut with a monstrous rattling hiss and ponderous, slurping footfalls thudding hard enough to be felt. Half of it, Morrow suspected, might be nothing but sheerest illusion, yet no less deadly to terrified, armed men, for all that.

Determined to outpace the pandemonium, he turned down a side lane, Carver on his heels, heading for Bewelcome's main meeting hall—and just as he did, the sky itself exploded, seeming to crack in half and hammer down, blowing the building's roof apart. Morrow flung himself sideways into Carver, flattening them together as lethally sharp, still-burning fragments pincushioned the mud, hissing into puddles around them. Fire and smoke billowed up, high as Babel's tower. The hall's front doors burst open to expel the citizens who'd sheltered within, who fled, screaming.

Shielding his eyes with one arm, Morrow squinted through the black spots in his vision, gut clenched in dread. More to come, he well knew it. Like always.

Seconds later, a whole new torrent of *words*—silver-black and sparking, writ in crabbed Bible print, their capital points sharp as just-forged ironwork—began to fall through the clouds toward them like burning debris, touching their upturned faces with an awful light. And they'd've been considerably harder to read had an all-too-familiar voice not been heard rasping along, while the demonic text spiralled down:

WOE TO THE CROWN OF PRIDE, TO THE DRUNKARDS OF EPHRAIM, WHOSE GLORIOUS BEAUTY IS A FADING FLOWER, WHICH ARE ON THE HEAD OF THE FAT VALLEYS OF THEM THAT ARE OVERCOME WITH WINE!

BEHOLD, THE LORD HATH A MIGHTY AND STRONG ONE, WHICH AS A TEMPEST OF HAIL AND A DESTROYING STORM, AS A FLOOD OF MIGHTY WATERS OVERFLOWING, SHALL CAST DOWN TO THE EARTH WITH THE HAND . . .

AND THE GLORIOUS BEAUTY, WHICH IS ON THE HEAD OF THE FAT

VALLEY, SHALL BE A FADING FLOWER, AND AS THE HASTY FRUIT BEFORE THE SUMMER; WHICH WHEN HE THAT LOOKETH UPON IT SEETH, WHILE IT IS YET IN HIS HAND HE EATETH IT UP.

Isaiah 28, one to four, Morrow thought, numbly. And watched the next disaster take shape, clear as the Devil's own hand. Five more black tornado-strands, a figure clinging to the end of each, whip-striking down through the torn roof. Three were women, one heavily child-laden; one a slim young man, gangster-fashionable, his eyes hid behind smoked-glass spectacles and clutching a cane, the digits on his scarred left hand having been violently reduced to two fingers and a thumb.

Hank Fennig and his ladies, the full complement, which was surely bad enough, by any standards. But then there was that house-huge fifth figure—one Morrow hadn't seen in almost half a year, but would recognize 'til the day he died, and maybe after. *He* went clad in black, a preacher's frayed collar round his neck, and under that collar was a scar—the hanging rope's kiss, his dreadful lady's marriage token. Painful toll paid for his passage from faithless secesh preacher to hexslinger, outlaw, administrator supreme of all New Aztectlan.

Yeah, that's right. And now . . . now, we're well and truly *fucked.*

Morrow hauled Carver back upright, spitting mud, clapped him on the shoulder. "Get to Washford!" he bawled, over what he suspected were both their equally ringing ears. "Tell him the Rev is *here*, Private! Reverend Rook is *here!*"

Carver's eyes widened; he saluted, turned, and ran.

Morrow swallowed, wishing with all his heart—disloyal as he knew the impulse was—that he could go with him.

SEVEN DIALS: ONE

This is where the Gods killed themselves, to make the sun and the moon come up.

CHESS REMEMBERED.

His first time—down here below everything, where the blood-fed calabash bloomed and bone dust and black water mixed to breed a nightmare river of mud—he had stumbled through stinking water, naked in all senses of the word, goaded by pain inside and out.

He remembered the Enemy peering down at him off that wall of skulls, white eyes crinkled in a pitch black face, amused by the dim, obsidian mirror image of Chess's flayed agony, drawling—

Ah . . . not sweet sister Ixchel's **ixiptla,** *after all. Who does that make you, then, little king? Little sweetmeat?*

And him, snapping back in turn through all-nerve lips, each word a fresh spray of red: *Chess Pargeter, motherfucker; you really ought to've heard of me.*

THAT HELL WAS WET he'd known already, through hard experience. But not how *dirty* things could be when coal and other infernals were involved. The well-earned grime of a hard day's ride was only dust and sweat sometimes cut with blood, half inconvenience, half seasoning. Here, all things bore a layer of ground-in scum, each touch leaving black smears; the walls 'emselves seemed dingy, porous, weeping grey.

So Goddamn cold.

Through the glass pane, so muck-crusted it looked like a rotting grave cloth stretched flat, he was still somehow able to see the looming column beyond. Crowned in sundials set shimmering in the constant soft downpour, its shadow reached out in every direction at once, like one of those blood-daubed stone images of Tezcatlipoca Chess had glimpsed before, in other visions.

K'awil, "God K," Night Wind, Possessor of the Sky and Earth, We Are His Slaves. He who in red, white, blue and black aspects fuels every part of the Machine. Red Xipe Totec with his nude eyes flaring, facing the east . . . blue Huitzilopochtli gathering lightning from the south, so bright he cannot be looked on directly . . . white Quetzalcoatl rising from the west like a feathered vision-serpent, drawing blood from his own penis to bring the last dead world's bones back to life. . . .

The steel hats heard how my brother refused human sacrifice, red boy, the Enemy's voice told him, without warning. **They thought to twin him with their White Christ, claiming him as proof that fate brought them to our shores. As though he did not already have a twin of his own! But then, they rarely kept quiet long enough to learn the truth of things, even when they claimed to be interested.**

Chess felt his empty hands flex and looked down, yearning for gun-butts to fill 'em, let alone a target to train 'em on. *Couldn't've known he'd drowned at least one of those other dead worlds himself, I guess,* he thought back, *and outta pique with you, no less. Or do I got it wrong? 'Cause, you know . . . when you tell me this shit, can't say as how I'm always listenin'.*

No. But if such observations distract, then I will leave you here, red boy, to your own devices . . . all alone.

And then there was only silence, once more.

So now he sat ensconced in the snug of some particularly rancorous varmints' drink-groggery—called the Clock-house, he'd been told—watching the human tide eddy past. All 'round him, stinking ghosts spat and fought and roistered, so many that Chess could see the bilge-water which passed for whiskey in the phantom glass he gripped tremble with their movements. They jabbered as they elbowed 'round each other, Limejuicer voices shapeless and hoarse as crow-caws, blank gazes never quite meeting.

And all without a word thrown his way, staring right on through him, like he wasn't even worth the hip-check needed to squeeze by.

No Ed to keep him company down here, in his despond. No Rev. No widowed Yancey Kloves, even, that calm grey gaze of hers just a lid ill-set over a hate as hot as his own. Only Chess's own limping thoughts, slow as freezing, while he sat and shivered amidst the throng, utterly unmarked on.

Why can't I feel Ash Rook, at least? Always could, before.

Like an absence, a wound, that was all. A fallen God-botherer-shaped hole.

'Cause he thinks you're dead, is why, something told him, shortly—not the Enemy, though equally unsympathetic. Maybe even grieves you, in his fashion. *But clever as he is, he saw you die and somethin' else rise up wearin' you like a coat; knows it was all his fault, too, if he's halfway honest with himself. That's got to leave a mark.*

And everybody else?

There damn well isn't "anybody else" down here. Just you and the dead folks, and him, *and—*her.

"Talkin' to yourself again, I see," "English" Oona Pargeter's shade observed from where she sat, a few arms' lengths past where his elbow rested—just beyond reach, yet far too close for comfort.

"Yeah, well, might be I got friends you ain't privy to, woman," Chess shot back, "which'd be a sight more'n *you* could ever claim." A grin, gap-toothed in her raddled face, was her only answer. "Ain't you got some other place to be?"

"From the look of fings, I'd guess not."

If he had one last straw left, this was it. Chess threw back his chair and shoved his way out onto the cobbled streets outside, where he couldn't even muster sufficient dismay worth snarling again to find Oona already standing there in the rain, waiting for him.

Fuckin' perfect.

YOU REALLY OUGHT TO'VE heard of me, he remembered telling Tezcatlipoca, his first time in Hell. *I mean, seein' how you're the Devil himself.*

And now that very phrase rang in his ears yet, mockingly, as proof of his own naive assumption that every bad thing in every bad place existing should surely be aware of him by name or reputation. Worst moment but one in Chess's entire life and he'd been so *certain* he was still somebody's nightmare, Goddamnit, a skeleton strung with lit nerves tearing ass through the underworld, undebatably bad and unrepentant with it, too. With a cocked gun fisted in either raw-meat-on-bone hand, ready to fire at will.

But he'd been wrong about that in the end, like so much else.

Ripping his own empty chest open in the name of self-sacrifice— or pissiness, more like—aside, he sure hadn't ever expected to find himself here again, buried alive in one more dark place beneath the world's skin. The Sunken Ball-Court, the Place of Dead Roads, and now—*this* crap-hole, named by his Ma as *Seven Dials* for the same teetery column they stood beneath, from which seven streets radiated, all alike in the awful unending dark. Just a din of muck and yammer cut with a cacophony of clanks a-boom in the middle distance, like faraway ordnance.

Almost enough to make a man miss 'Frisco, Chess thought.

"Gone, that is, in London true," said Oona, staring up at those looming dials. "Long 'fore I drew a breath, let alone got big enough to—"

"—screw your way clear?"

"That's right. Always did fink yerself a cut above, though, didn't you? Too good for the likes of anyone else."

"Never claimed to be 'good,' woman, or anything like it." Chess stuffed his hands inside his coat, trying futilely to warm them while wondering if the truly dead at least got to sleep; felt like he'd been up for days, maybe a week or even more. "Whatever I am, though, I know I'm a damn sight better than you."

"What, 'cause you was born wiv that piece 'twixt your legs?" And that *note*, that sneering scorn, going straight to his gut. Fifteen years fell away. "All you *are*, old son, is lucky. Only wish to Christ you *'ad* been born a girl, so's . . ."

"So's you'd know what best to charge, I expect," Chess snarled.

Only to watch her spit, and snarl back: "*No.* 'Cause then I could've made you suffer like I did, *just* like, and not no different. The *exact bloody same.*"

"I suffered enough," Chess said, turning his back. And strode on, boots clopping through the rain, with his spurs trailing a-scratch on the cobbles like a dead man's fingernails.

Though he might have walked for hours, the stones underfoot did not change, and every wall looked like its neighbour; even the ceaselessly moving crowds had nearly vanished. So when the dry voice came back into Chess's mind, at last, he was lonesome enough that he didn't even flinch.

What do you plan to do now, red boy?

Leave this damn place. Kick your damn ass.

Laughter like a desert gust, sere and hot and swift.

You appear to have your work cut out for you.

Suck my dick, you spectral motherfuck.

Chess took a corner at random, followed by another, and another—then abruptly found himself back in the sundial column's square, meeting Oona's eyes yet once more, and clenching both empty fists at her smirk.

"Shouldn't've given your irons away up top, you wanted t'stay armed," she agreed, as if she could read his mind. "But then, you never could plan ahead for bollocks."

"Stay the hell outta my head, bitch. Got more'n enough company in here, without I add *you* to the mix."

A snort. "Ah, but ain't nothin' real *but* what you fink, down 'ere." She jabbed a finger at his gun-poor belt. "Them guns of yours is gone 'cause out of mind, out of sight—and since you never gave nuffin' away you still cared about, must be you don't care no more, except for 'abit. But as for the rest . . . well, *look* at yourself."

Grudgingly, Chess checked himself in the same muddy window he'd given up trying to stare through, not all so long ago: red beard well-trimmed to the touch once more, clothes their usual tailored purple. Hell, even a number of his scars'd been pruned away, though the curlicue strand under his jawline Oona herself had given him was still there—and as his fingers traced it, the knots binding his rage began to give way.

"*Such* a peacock, you are, same as you ever were. Such a gilded bloody prancer." Oona clutched her shawl to herself, scowling. "And always the 'ardest done by, ain't ya? Well, fink on this: bad as I was t'you, let alone myself, *I* never killed nobody."

"Not for lack of trying," Chess pointed out.

"Oh, I ain't sayin' that's not true. But you, you're the curse made flesh, little boy, ain't ya? Everyfing you touch bleeds."

The knots burst. Chess screamed at her: "*You think I don't know it?*"

"I know you *do*. So what's the remedy?"

Woman, he yearned to snap, *if I knew that* . . .

Before he could think of doing so, however, Oona'd already seized him by the coat, hands knit in his lapels. "All right, playtime's over. You need to *listen* t'me now, you great whingin' molly—"

"Fuck I *do!*"

"—shut the 'ell *up!*" She slapped him, hard enough to shock; from the tone of her hiss it'd hurt her as well, but Chess barely noticed. Her screaming face pressed huge 'gainst his, plus the sting of flesh on flesh—how could it still terrify him? Chess Pargeter, killer of hundreds, hex and god alike?

"Ain't but one way t'leave any place you comes into feet-first, boyo," she continued, unheeding, "an' you ain't doin' that wivout me. Look at these last few years on your own go-by, and just try an' tell me different. Every choice you got 'anded you made a dog's breakfast of. What makes you fink findin' 'ell's back door'll go any better?"

Chess moistened his lips. "Difference is," he managed, at last, "*this* time, if nothing else—I can sure as hell shut *you* up."

"Sonny boy, I'd like to see you try."

No you don't see, bitch, Chess thought. *But you Goddamn will.*

"All right," he said, out loud. And threw his hand up, palm out, same way he'd done at least a score of times since Rook had made him something more than human, flinging open the floodgates to rain down a tide of greenish-red Flayed Lord power 'pon her.

Nothing happened.

Chess's gut froze, skin crawling agonizingly, as if bracing itself to be stripped away once more.

"See?" Oona whispered. "No guns. No witch-tricks. Not even a bloody knife left over, wiv a blade the exact size o' your Johnson." Leaning close in, to put her wormy lips right beside his ear: "Just gotta do fings up close 'n' personal now, and take your chances, like the rest us. But that's a gamble you ain't 'ad t'risk in some long time . . . and if you can't *kill* no more, then you're *nuffin'*."

"Might be I don't need to *kill* you, just to stop your damn tongue."

"Ooh, la! Listen t'*you*, fancy boy. 'M I s'posed to be impressed? Very well, yer 'ighness—I'll just drop you a curtsey, shall I? As befits your bloody station."

Which she did, bobbing ridiculously, and adding a pantomime air-kiss for emphasis. At the sight of which, that knot behind his jaw jumped, sparking—sheer revulsion gave way, bursting into rage the way flashpaper touches off dynamite. Without thinking, he reared back and pasted her one, with all his strength behind it.

Torque set her neck sidelong, so hard it cracked outright—was that her jaw he heard go, in one mutton-bone crunch? At the same time, something flew from between her lips in a bloody spume-haze: her own tongue tip, severed on contact, ground like chuck between two uneven rows of grey teeth.

Oona hit the cobbles face-first, then propped herself back up on both elbows, shaking her bruised head. And grinned a wide, red grin, blood painting her chin.

"Oh, I fink you can probably do better than *that*," she spat out. "Can't ya?"

Chess got up. "Let's see," he replied, and kicked her, full in the stomach.

This is your mother, *fool*, some voice in his skull's back cavity warned him, like he couldn't've figured that out himself. *So what?* he snapped back at it, kicking her yet again even as she doubled over, one spur raking 'cross her gasping cheek. *What-all's that s'posed to mean to me, exactly, given the little it ever seemed to mean to* her?

Oona's ghost jackknifed on the filthy stones at his feet, eyes level with his toes. Her hair fell down like a veil. And Chess loomed over her, poised to give fresh hurt for a lifetime's worth with righteous rage still filling him tip-to-toe with gall, a lifetime of spoiled seed suddenly come to crop.

She gave you life, is what, the voice said, simply. *Kept you alive, when she could barely keep herself.*

Chess shook his head, eyes suddenly blurred. *'Cause she needed a whipping boy, someone to take it all out on.*

You were all she had.

Fancy that. Must've been why she sold me, right? Why she drove me away with both hands, screamed the shame of what I am at me in the street, stuck a knife in my Goddamn neck?

You came out of her . . .

Like a turd, yeah. Again, fuckin' so?

She's half of you, Chess.

Wasn't for her, you'd be—

Somebody else, entirely.

Whose *was* that damn voice, after all? Not Rook, not Yancey. Not even Ed, reasonable as it sounded. No one he knew. And yet, and yet, it seemed so very . . . *familiar.*

Oona had turned over on her back, coughing wetly. She tried to hump herself away, dress a rag sweeping the rain-slick cobbles; Chess set one boot's sole on her flat chest and pushed down, pinning her. "You stay *here*," he ordered.

Maybe it's your *voice, fool. Ever thought that?*

"I . . . I got . . . nowhere else t'be," Oona managed, and gradually Chess realized her hacking spasms had curdled back into some parody of laughter. "Go on, son. Drink your fill. Used to tell you that, when you was on the tit." Her head lolled from side to side. "'Urt me bad as you want, long as you want. Don't make no difference, not t'me."

To me, or you. Or nobody else neither, accordingly.

What sort of shit-heap life would somebody've had to live, he wondered, if even death held no possibility of change?

And with that thought, all Chess's simple rage swelled to something far beyond fury: something vast, something brilliant. So pure it almost felt like mercy.

He knelt, cupping Oona's head in his hands, almost tenderly.

"How 'bout this, then?" he asked. And twisted, hard.

AFTERWARD, HE SAT STILL there beside her body, letting the cold rain plaster clothes to skin, a second sodden hide. He knew she wasn't really "dead," obviously, considering where they were, but by God, it'd seemed the only way to shut her up . . . and since it seemed to've worked, he wasn't about to question his own logic.

Without knowing why, he found himself recalling the first hot wash Oona had ever bought for him, alone; whenever they could afford to previously, she'd always opted for cold and gone in with him to save coin. That day, she'd sent him to the brothel's tub-room by himself, water steaming already like it was set to boil laundry; he'd stood chest-deep in the great copper upright, with soap and a tin mirror set handy, so smooth you could actually see yourself undistorted, to a point. And new clothes to put on, after. The shirt had been white, not purple, but he'd buttoned it clear to the collar and smiled at his reflection, proudly.

Within the hour, that shirt had been trash, torn off by the man who'd been his first customer. The pain had been coring, but the memory of what he could look like with enough coin, and left to his own devices—the charms others would spend on, given opportunity—had been almost worth it.

Chess glanced again at Oona's body, brow furrowed. He'd expected . . . more, somehow; satisfaction, if not glee. Or was this flat numbness a species of peace, in itself? He'd never had much hands-on knowledge of the phenomenon.

Three times I wrote you off as dead, bitch, he thought. *Once when I left Songbird's opium den, knowing the undertakers was on their way; once when Rook told me he could kill you for me, and I told him to go ahead if he wanted . . . and now. And at no point, I only just now realize, did I ever really start to believe it.*

He turned away, pushed himself to his feet, and picked a direction at random. Any path that'd lead away from this column, and his mother's corpse beneath it.

Hadn't gone ten yards, though, 'fore an earsplitting *crack* rang out; light flashed behind him like a thunderbolt touching down and he spun, dropped battlefield-ready to one knee, arm already up to protect himself from shrapnel.

Panting, he slowly lowered his sleeve back down. The circular pattern on the cobblestones, charred and steaming now as rain struck home, did look something like a lightning strike. Scattered over it was a slurry of burnt and torn rags, frayed on every edge as if burst apart from inside—and not all of it fabric, either; Chess recognized that yellowish hue, that raddled texture. Nausea kneaded his guts. He pulled his gaze upward, with effort.

She stood in the centre of the blast, naked and pale, girl-slender again—not quite his same height or make, being curved at hips and breast with red hair rain-plastered back over a narrow fox-face, thatching the junction of her legs in a slightly darker triangle. And when she smiled, her teeth were crooked yet but *there*, bright, sharp and clean—porcelain, almost, like the whites of those green, green eyes. . . .

"I'll be Goddamned and go to hell," Chess Pargeter said, out loud, knowing exactly how stupid those words must sound. But Oona's new-made grin just widened, almost to her back molars.

"Come now, lovey," she replied, voice a silver bell soaked in sour wine. "Nuffin' comes from nuffin'. Didn't fink you was the *only* 'ex wiv my name, did you?"

More damn *fool me*, Chess thought, *for thinkin' there's any part of me don't have her thumbprint on it already. For thinkin' I was* special.

"Okay, then," he said. "Let's damn well hear it."

CHAPTER TWO

THE NIGHT BEFORE she'd dreamed Ed Morrow held her in his arms again, warming her all over, and counted herself lucky. But in the morning Yancey Colder Kloves woke cold and stiff as usual, eyes narrowed against the unforgiving sky as it rose purple over what Grandma and Yiska called *Tse Diyil*, Old Woman Butte, a massive outcrop of stone stacked in concentric rings jutting up from sand and furze that cast its shadow on a seemingly endless series of lava drifts making their way from horizon to horizon, uneven as some badly laid road.

I hurt, she thought, too much in pain generally to be more specific, even if she'd wanted to. *Wouldn't it be nice if we could do that in life, one day, 'stead of always touching with only our minds? Or would that really be too much to ask, considering the circumstances?*

Beside her, Songbird stirred, unhappily. "You think too loudly, innkeeper's daughter," she muttered. "This is what comes of some talent and no instruction."

"That's really the way you feel about it, then maybe it'd be best to stay out of my brainpan."

The Chinese girl-hex hissed. "I would if I could, believe me! *Waaah, chi-shien gweilo, cho ya-de, cao ni zu zong shi ba dai* . . . to think I find myself stranded *here*, caught between two savages and a long-nosed ghost—I, who am the product of a thousand years of breeding!"

It is not to be borne, this disgrace."

While Yancey thought back, each syllable pitched uncharitably loud, since she now knew Songbird could hear her: *Yes, yes, you great bleached baby.*

The band had been squatting for weeks in a spattering of caves hollowed from the butte's side, telling time by the sun dagger's track as it eked its way across the spiral petroglyphs carved into three separate south-facing sandstone slabs. They'd made their way to this refuge sidelong, now hiking, now riding—and occasionally using what Yancey had come to call the "punch-a-hole" method, with Grandma and Songbird pooling their resources to move instantaneously from one place to another. A vortex would gape open in the air—the "Bone Road" Yiska had travelled to meet them at Bewelcome—and they'd all plunge through it. Grandma in her bone relict-suit, shaking the ground with each creaky step; Songbird eddying along behind just a foot or so up off the ground, jerked like a kite by one long sleeve; Yiska and the rest of her bravos on horseback, taking the jump at a steeplechase gallop and ululating as they did, while Yancey clung on for dear life with both white-knuckled hands 'round the Diné boy-girl's hard, flat waist.

Each such trip, however, began with Grandma and Songbird going at each other like cats in a bag as they argued points of procedure. The shamaness's ghost would loom threateningly above her spindly little companion, berating her for not yet being fully recovered from whatever damage Doctor Asbury's bracelet had done her, while Songbird in turn clenched her delicate hands (their clawed golden finger-sheaths long since removed, relegated to Yiska's saddlebag) and scowled as though contemplating evil she obviously felt still ill-equipped to deliver.

"You have bad habits," Grandma told her, "this is your trouble! And being stronger than your teachers has not helped to break you of any of them—it has only made you slow to regain your power, because you so much fear being weak."

"Unlettered barbarian, old mountain sow—you, who could not read your own spells, even if you knew how to write them down!

What do you think you know that I, educated by Imperial tutors, do not?"

"Better than you, not-yellow yellow girl, especially here on my people's land, where my people's ways work best. *You* let an old man rob you of everything, gambling he was too entranced by your helplessness to take advantage; *I* brought myself back from the dead."

Songbird's face screwed up, pale gaze full of poisons. "*Not entirely.*"

"I balance on the threshold, yes. Will *you* be the one to push me one way or the other?"

The question seemed to take Songbird aback, which might have been the point—the China-girl was still enough of a child to be much more tractable when thrown off balance. As the silence stretched on, however, she narrowed her eyes at the giant bone-puppet carrionette, waiting in inhuman stillness. Yiska and her riders watched too, keen attention in their eyes setting Yancey's nape hairs a-tingle.

"Perhaps I will not have to," Songbird said, at last. While Yancey exerted herself to rein in a shudder, as her mother's words came back: *It behooves us to know how to spot them, the hexes—so we can run the other way.*

And I should have, shouldn't I? she thought, watching the two work their castings in synchrony, prying open the Bone Road's door once more. *Should've told someone straightaway I knew Chess for who he was, or else never spoke to him—or Ed—at all; it's sheerest hubris I didn't, considering the cost. Just . . . couldn't stand not having a hand in my own fate, I s'pose.*

Now here she was, a killer herself, by commission as well as omission. A maker of orphans and widows, just like Chess, and Mesach Love, too.

Was it such a crime, to refuse the place that the world had made for you? And was the price of that refusal, ever after, to never find any other place for yourself at all?

She still hadn't found an answer to either question, but then again, pondering them over while stuck on *Tse Diyil* probably wasn't helping matters much. Though the sheer age and silence of this place would have been exhausting by themselves, for anyone, from the very moment Yancey had touched the butte's topsoil, shallow over stone, she'd also known that there was far more to reckon here than simple history. The air atop the upthrust megalith smelled of a lightning strike; when she took off her boots, the rock itself tingled beneath her bare feet, seeming to hum.

Like Bewelcome, in other words, this too was a thin place— another point on the endless "Crack" in the world that Grandma was always going on about. And even though she now knew just as well as any hex how often things mystical had to be understood more poetically than literally, Yancey had to admit she'd still half-expected it to be some kind of physical chasm, a tangible rift in the earth. It wasn't until reaching the butte that she'd finally understood the sheer scale of the damage, a winding, miles-wide line of hexacious force which bestrode the land from north to south.

"Web of the Spider," Yiska had called it early on, one night around the cookfire. "Warp and woof of Changing Woman's loom. *Bilagaana* Rook's witch city lies on it, as does the salt-man's Welcome-town reborn, and this place too—even the Mexica capital, that place your red boy wrecked when he first came up. It is all the same." She'd snorted then, not unkindly, at Yancey's appalled look. "What, dead-speaker? Did you think our task would be as simple as finding some big rock, and stuffing it into a hole?"

"...no."

"Oh yes, you did—you *bilagaana* all think that way, just as the White Shell Girl's people think in circles, devious as *coyote*. But if things were so easy we would not need both of you, nor the Spinner as well."

"If it's all the same, then ... why here, 'stead of anyplace else?"

Yiska shrugged. "There has always been much power here, a spiral that hides us from Rainbow Woman's sight; it should help the little ghost to heal, too, if she ever unstiffens her pretty neck enough to accept the Spinner's counsel. Just as it helps the Spinner stay ... in Balance."

Was that the exact right sense of the word, though? Yancey's gift might help her understand much of the Na'isha tongue, but some concepts still eluded her.

"Besides, here we have long sight and fresh water, game to hunt if we are sparing. And most of all, here it should be easiest to send out the Call," said Yiska.

"Call . . . to who?"

Yiska had only stared steadily at her, not needing to make her thoughts loud, or think at all. Yet "saying," nevertheless: *You know who.*

THE CHACO WASH flowed northward within walking distance of the butte's foot, running unseasonably high and fast. Yancey went to bathe there most mornings, not letting the water's increasing frigidity as months wore on deter her from her ritual cleansings— and "ritual" was the proper word. They had become a touchstone, a reconnection with the flesh, a grounding, calming process which washed away most—if never all—of the bone-deep weariness of her work.

For similar reasons, Songbird performed her own set of daily ablutions, though usually much later on and in hiding, with water Yiska brought her. Unused even to dressing without help, she had at first tried to beat her embroidered red satin outfit clean against the cavern walls until it began showing signs of wear and tear, at which point she'd given up, and gone silent and filthy. When Yancey tried to help she'd spat at her, claiming that when she regained the full extent of her magic, she would punish all interfering white ghosts accordingly.

By mid-July, a month into their stay, the realization she *still* wasn't yet strong enough to reweave her outfit from its own decaying components—and didn't seem likely to recover such strength anytime soon—finally sank Songbird into despair, prompting Yiska to take charge. The war-shamaness began to bring presents, some probably traded for on provision-gathering trips, others made, with painstaking skill: a pair of deerskin breeches and gartered leggings, neatly stitched, to replace her worn-through pyjama-pants; moccasins beaded in red and white, with rawhide soles; even a "squaw-dress" woven on a blanket loom with sides and shoulders laced together, leaving room for armholes and a poncho-style neckline. A full blanket, once added overtop, made for far better shading than Songbird's original scarlet silk wedding veil—and provided a stylish accoutrement, too, 'specially when fringed with a hundred pierced abalone shell slices that rattled as she walked, announcing her queenly tread.

At first, the hex-girl greeted these overtures with grumbling, sarcasm . . . what sounded to Yancey like outright insults, for all she was careful to keep to her own language for those. But as time wore on, persuaded that tolerating Yiska's aid was her only hope if she wanted to stay presentable, Songbird finally allowed the woman to touch her long enough to braid her white hair back into two tight plaits, then coil and pin them into a bun at the back of her head, protecting her delicate nape. She settled into the game, appearing to accept such tribute as her due. Adopted a murmuring, musical tone, gave compliments, even favoured Yiska on occasion with an occasional flirtatious glance from under bleached eyelashes.

These gifts were a form of courtship, as all involved well knew; hell, Yancey recalled receiving much the same treatment from (the late) Marshal Uther Kloves, though his love tokens ran to colourful store-bought frippery, the kind her Pa'd probably assured him all young maids dreamt on. He'd hoped to gain her hand in the bargain, with her heart following somewhat after—not quite the same sort of outright transaction Miz Songbird was no doubt used to from her time on San Francisco's Gold Coast, but not so very far away from it as Yancey might've once been comfortable to think, either.

Marriage for money's not but one step away from outright whoredom, in my opinion, Chess Pargeter had told her in the desert outside Splitfoot's, just before she'd pasted him one 'cross the chops. Back then, it'd seemed like deadliest insult; now it just rang like wisdom, hard-won, hard-worn.

According to fled Pinkerton Frank Geyer, Yiska had a reputation for being "like" Chess—a lover of fellow women just as Chess's own urges leaned only to other men, which suggested a fairly good idea of what the martial squaw hoped to gain from whatever bargain she and Songbird might negotiate. Seeing them together at close quarters, however, Yancey found she wasn't so sure. Her own upbringing hadn't kept her overly innocent, after all. Lust she knew, well enough to recognize, but love as well, in several varieties.

"This Old Woman in the rock we squat on," she heard Songbird say now, sponging herself clean with the remaining length of her veil, while Yiska leaned on guard against the canyon wall, carefully angling her gaze to keep the girl's modesty intact. "Is that this Changing Woman of yours, the . . . *Ash-da Nah-lay*?"

Yiska shook her head, black mane swinging. "*Asdzaa Nadleehe*, Three Ages in One, the woman who is transformed time and again—this is somewhere she watches over, yes, like all thin places. But *Tse Diyil*'s Old Woman is another thing entirely, to be feared, not worshipped. Almost *Anaye*."

"A ghost, then."

"Perhaps. When I was young, my grandfather told me no one was allowed on top of the butte, or even allowed to lean against its sides. A long time ago, they used to say a lady lived there, called She Who Dries You Out. Every so often she would go to a nearby canyon and fill her jug with water, then carry it back. Sometimes, she would take a man up to the top of the butte with her. Next morning, her beauty would be gone; she would be old and ferocious, very hungry. The man would be tied up in the sun, dry and dusty, and when he asked for water she'd piss into a bowl instead, telling him to drink it. Soon the man would make his way back down the butte, get thin, and then die."

"Ah, so she is a *jiang-sh'i*, beautiful suck-blood demon: a corpse who never withers, with only its lower soul remaining. We also tell this story, but better."

"Since Ch'in stories are always better, uh?"

"You are learning, barbarian." Done with her toilette, Songbird squeezed out the last of the water, tucking her silks away once more into her narrow bodice. "And was she very dark, this Drying Lady in your grandfather's tales, the way you and your men are—like something carved from wood, or cast in copper? Do you still fear to meet her, having disobeyed his advice and occupied her home?"

At this, Yiska smiled, wide enough to show her eyeteeth. "In fact, I had always heard that she was fair, White Shell Girl," she replied. "Like the moon, or a cow's hide without one flaw, brushed until it shines. And no, I do not fear to meet her, or her reflection. I dream on it."

Songbird sniffed. "Thus proving only that you are as foolish as I have always thought."

"One more idiot barbarian savage," Yiska replied, nodding, "in a nation of long-nosed ghosts. Is that the way this song goes?"

"You have said it, not I."

"*You* are the one who says it over and over, trying to make it hard for me to like you. But when have I ever let that stop me?"

With a hiss, Songbird snatched up her blanket, wrapped it so as to leave only her eyes visible and flounced forth, striding into the morning sunlight with her fringes all a-jangle. Yiska just stood and watched her go, still smiling.

"Has trouble with saying thanks, that one," Yancey spoke up, after a moment, "and more trouble yet with feeling grateful. Or needing someone."

"I have noticed."

"Seems to me she got raised to think pretty much every way people deal with each other is just . . . business. People like that— they don't tend to treat any kind of affection too gently. They can be hurtful, whether or not they mean to be. And *very* hurtful, when they do mean it."

"Is it the little ghost you describe, dead-speaker, or your friend the red boy?"

"How you think I came to figure this all out?" Yancey shot back. "Songbird's got way too many scars for a girl as young as she is, and she's way too used to power. This . . . she . . . isn't *safe* for you, ma'am. Or any of the rest've us, something goes awry."

The Diné woman's smile went lopsided. "If I liked only safe things, the track of my life would not run where it does. All I know is that some wounds cannot heal, if left on their own."

"Or some people, either?"

Yiska rolled her eyes, snorting—but whatever she was about to say next was lost in a sudden ripping *crack* like a tiny thunderclap, followed by a high-pitched scream that jerked her 'round. "Ai-eh, *now?*" she snapped, grabbing up her spear, and bolted back up the path; barefoot and weaponless, Yancey tore after her, on sheer reflex.

They rounded a curve behind a rise in the rock, and stopped, gaping. In front of them, something like a dog bounded back and forth—but no dog stood near as tall as Yancey at the shoulder, nor clawed at its victims with leathery five-fingered hands like an ape's, ruff of black glass spikes bristling with every growl. Around it, dozens of deerskin- and wool-clad albino Chinese girls shrieked as they ran in all directions, crab-walked backward or stood paralyzed, hands to hidden faces. The creature took the head off one in a single vicious swipe, only for both head and headless body to burst in a damp cloud of ectoplasmic mist and vanish; it sent up its own cry of cheated hunger, an unnatural soprano yipe.

Illusion! Yancey thought, throwing the word straight at Yiska's mind. She focused her Sight, struck through hexation's layers to find the real Songbird perhaps ten feet away, backing just as slowly and silently away from the monster as she could. A damn good plan, in Yancey's opinion. But you couldn't say any shred of the Enemy was without sense, and maybe realizing Songbird's intent was enough to draw attention to it, for the dog-thing paused, hunkering down—cocked its head and shifted, nostrils flared wide, dragging in deep, snorting breaths, ignoring the ghosts in favour of the girl's real scent.

Without thinking, Yancey found herself leaping forward, waving both arms wildly. "*Hey!*" she screamed. "Here, you son of a bitch! *Here!*"

The thing whirled, drawing bead on Yancey, and she went still—not in fear, so much, as sheerest concentration. Danger slid her senses to their highest pitch, so far she could see lines of power like greasy tendrils running from beast to the Crack and beyond, from whence it came. Even if she had no hexation herself to smite it with, those power lines she *could* seize . . . could, and did.

Contorted in mid-leap, the creature crashed to earth, flailing at her feet with those inhumanly human hands while its soul pressed hard 'gainst hers, tight as any lover. Yancey shook with effort, alternating blasts of rage and hurt lighting her mind with dreadful images: Chess Pargeter and Sheriff Love in full array, tearing at each other hopelessly; the reborn Sheriff under her gun, his skull bullet-hollowed, wife screaming his name like she had Uther's. Ed Morrow sprouting claws and fangs, savaging her. The creature hunched itself closer, flooding out hunger so fierce it was its own agony. Yancey tried to step back but found herself paralyzed, her grip on the spirit lines slipping.

The monster began to rise—then slammed back down as Yiska drove her spear hard through the back of its neck, pinning it to the earth, before dodging away. Ear-scraping squeals drowned to gurgles; it writhed, spewing gushes of stinking black blood Yancey avoided only by inches. Songbird's many selves winked out, leaving a single version, striving hard to seem unimpressed. And when Yiska saw that she laughed out loud, triumphant—wheeled back, poised to count coup, eager to show off in front of at least one of them.

But it wasn't to be. Without warning, a massive foot made of dirty bone crashed down on the thing, flattening it to silence in a single stroke.

Angrier looking than she'd seemed at any previous point, Yiska glared up at the only vaguely human figure towering over her and Yancey. "You broke my spear, Spinner!" she shouted, fists on hips. "Am I to slay the next foe with my knife only?"

Grandma looked blankly down without speaking, then turned, trudging back up the slope. Yiska grimaced and muttered under her breath; Yancey couldn't catch the sense of it, but felt a hint of fear under the anger. Which, given how little fear she felt from Yiska generally, was worrying enough.

"Hell was that, anyway?" she asked her.

"*Huehueteotl*," said Yiska. "Tools of the Enemy, when he wishes; more dangerous still, when he gives them no orders." To Songbird: "A good tactic, White Shell Girl. You remembered what I said."

"Which was?" Songbird called back, shrill and breathy, arms wrapped 'round herself with the blanket fallen from her white face.

Yiska's smile returned, wide as ever. "If you can't be strong, be clever."

Songbird opened her mouth to refute this, but found Yiska half-gone before she could—slipping past Yancey, shattered spear already snatched up, following in Grandma's wake to meet her braves, who'd come running down to "help." She yelled something raucous at them, earning laughs in return.

Songbird stared after her, face shaded, yet bewilderment plain.

"SPEND HALF OUR TIME killing whatever comes out of that damn crack," Yancey complained to Songbird, later. "Dogs with hands, fish walking, snakes with a head at each end, what's it gonna be next? And for all the . . . stuff . . . comes out of that Goddamn thing, you'd think it'd be easy to send one thought halfway *into* it, right? Well, no such luck. Like trying to cast a fishing line through mud."

Instead of snapping, Songbird actually cast her an amused look. "Are you *sure* you have not yet contacted English Oona's son? Your imitation astonishes."

Against her will, Yancey found herself laughing—and was surprised as all hell, after a moment, to find Songbird had joined her.

"As for this-all with . . . Yiska, and you," she said, finally, "I just hope . . ."

Songbird bristled. "Hope what?"

". . . you're not taking advantage, that's what. Not trifling with her affections, such as they are, since she's treated you well in harsh circumstances. That you'll consider how she's an honourable creature, in her way, and act the same, if you can. But I've said my piece, so that's where I'll leave it."

Schoolmarmish in the extreme, Yancey chided herself; *she'll never fall for it*. And indeed, the albino first stared at her askance, before having the grace to seem just a touch guilty.

"Look at me," she said, at last. "This place . . . I am hardly suited to it, or anywhere else. I have spent my whole life in a box, surrounded, always a possession; I cannot take care of myself. I *must* have a protector, especially now, and—she *wants* that role. Shall I deny her?"

Though Yancey could hardly object on moral grounds, she nevertheless heard herself say: "Might be kinder." To which Songbird only laughed again, this time more bitterly.

"Do I seem *kind*, to you?" she demanded.

"You could be. Could *try* to, anyhow."

Songbird nodded slightly, as if to say: *I know it.* "Yes," she agreed.

CHAPTER THREE

THERE WERE NO CLOCKS in Hex City, no more than newspapers, so what information Reverend Asher Rook got on the outside world came mainly from the mouths of dying men with a side order of illusory infiltration and spying-by-proxy, since there were those to hand who could throw their consciousnesses up and peep through passing birds' eyes, or cast 'em down into the narrow minds of a whole stealthy hoard of creeping things. Or cough out bits of 'emselves to fashion fetches from, tiny jewel-eyed sickness-bugs they'd let loose to float across to Pinkerton's encampment, there to gather what intelligence they might before being spotted and squashed.

Every night, darkness beat the sun down like a hammer, reddening the horizon with its blood. Yet every dawn it struggled back up again, eager for similar punishment.

Even with Chess, Rook had woken to an otherwise empty bed or bedroll as often as not, yet that fact had never troubled him, no more than when a housecat leapt from your lap, tired of caresses. Most times, he could crack open an eye, roll to one side and find Chess crouching sentinel by the fire's ashes or sitting in a chair cleaning his pistols, green eyes bright in the gloom. Never far, with something always left behind—some heat, some scent—to hold his place 'til he came back.

The bed Rook slept in now, in a vast stone room midway up the Temple's side, was the grandest he'd seen west of the Mississippi: down-filled pillows, silken sheets, rich dark wood ornately carved as any Continental throne. And if it might've been nothing but deadfall and grave cloth before the Lady set her power to it, that hardly mattered, for once fixed in shape, the sybaritic softness was real enough. But however many nights Ixchel shared it with him— fewer and fewer, of late—no warmth ever lingered in its hexaciously self-cleaning sheets. The limestone walls held cold silence, as if jealous of the favour their maker showed him; the chalky flint of the floor stung his feet, and shadows sulked in every corner. Rook almost wished he had his Bible back, just so's he might find words enough to express how deeply he'd come to hate it.

But a room amongst the people did not befit the High Priest-king of New Aztectlan—and hateful though it might be, Rook had to admit, this chamber did have its advantages: wards fierce enough to keep anybody but Herself from entering without his say-so, for example, or wake him if anyone tried. So when the Mexican girl, Ixchel's pet—Marizol, her name was, one of the blood-cult's get— walked in, Rook snapped instantly alert, cold and tense, a literal curse on his lips.

"*Jefe?*" Her accent, so like that of dead Miz Adaluz—Ixchel's unfortunate first vessel—slurred liquid yet higher-pitched, diffident and breathy. "Forgive me—the Lady, she said I could come. That you could . . . use me."

Use you? Well, that was mighty nice of her. Like how, I wonder?

Rook felt the urge to laugh and a surge of anger, but managed to fight 'em both down, hopefully unnoticed. This job certainly was good for his self-restraint, if nothing else.

"Marizol," he rasped, scrubbing a palm 'cross his bristles. "I'm sure the Lady must have . . . a sight more useful things for you to do than wait on me. Could be you're needed at services, maybe? In the Moon Court?"

Marizol shook her head. "No, *jefe*, please! I don't want to go back—you don't know, I think, how bad it's gotten. Terrible things are done there. Terrible . . ." She seemed a mere shadow herself, face unreadable. "Lady Rainbow, she knows I like it here, far more than back with *mis padres, los Penitentes*—I'll run errands, do whatever's needed. Anything. So if you truly have no use for me, maybe just send me on to someone who will . . . Mister Glass-eyes Hank, or his 'g'hals'?"

"Darlin'," he said, as gently as he could, "I'm sure you mean well, but—the Missuses Fennig are hexes, you understand? *Brujas.* Can't think what-all you might do for 'em that they couldn't get just as easy from each other, or almost anybody else."

As he'd assumed, Marizol had no answer for that one. Just stood still, biting her lip, while Rook let his mind wander back to the rest of her group, whom he rarely saw; they lived sequestered in Ixchel's throne room, that raw stone hole she'd taken to calling the Moon Court, pouring the juice of themselves out like water for her to feast on—and died, too, the most tapped-out amongst 'em conveniently content to stagger to the window slits and throw 'emselves out, so's not to stink up the place. But then again, there always seemed to be more where they came from.

That the cultists' faith bolstered Ixchel's power was undeniable— but in a way, it was equally good for everyone else, as well; kept the Machine fed, so nobody had to bleed for it who didn't want to. And though the Americans had resented the "lottery" system which chose victims at random, these Mex enthusiasts were downright *happy* to contribute, volunteering with a smile, instead of being tricked or taxed into it.

Not all of 'em, though, he guessed, looking into Marizol's frightened eyes while she stared on, mute pleading writ large in every line—older by far than when she'd first arrived, if only in spirit, her slender figure bent with the weight of that moonstone-laden trinket Ixchel'd clasped 'round her throat like some thrall's collar.

"Please," she repeated, without much hope. As though he could do anything about . . . anything.

Goddamnit, little girl, you're come amongst nothing but monsters and bad men here, even the ones you think you like. If you've any hope of survival, you need to grow the hell up.

"Your parents know where you are?" Rook asked her, finally.

"*Mi madre, mi padre* . . . they stay with Her, always." The implied capital rang strangely chilling. "They don't need me. *She* don't need me."

Repeating it like a rosary, in fervent hopes that if she said it enough times, it'd make it so. When the truth was, Ixchel *did* have a very specific use for this girl-child, as the gal herself probably well knew. With her current body withering, held together only by magic and sheer awful will, the dread goddess needed a new one to cram herself inside, and was grooming Marizol for that express purpose—the way her Enemy-brother Smoking Mirror had with Chess, maybe, after Bewelcome's resurrection left him bled out and on the point of dying. Trying to make her *want* to submit, aspire to nothing so much as to be Ixchel's *ixiptla*, her sacrificial anchor in this world . . . the carrion-fed human tree from which all her grand schemes might finally bear their stinking, blood-soaked fruit.

Rook remembered walking in on them together, in the Throne Room—Ixchel balancing Marizol on her bony knee like an uncomfortably large child, extolling her loveliness while stroking her up and down. All but counting down the days to Marizol's "flowering," the very instant she'd be mature enough to consent, while simultaneously trying to ladle boiled-sugar sweets into her with both hands.

Dear child, hold still; have more, if it pleases you. Tell me that you love me—that you hold me in your heart, as I hold you in mine. Oh, what a pretty thing you are!

In his mind's recesses, Rook heard Ixchel's deeper dream-voice murmur, as it once had to him alone: **This well is full of bones, and all of them have "been" me, little king . . . all of them, and none.**

Sometimes she made the girl thorn-rope her own tongue, dragging each prickly link through in turn, while her cheeks glazed with tears. Then kissed her deeply, spreading the blood between them both like rouge.

Rook shut his eyes on the image, just for a breath. Choked down a sliver of bile, and tried to cast his mind elsewhere—only to have it slide back to Chess, and all the harm he'd done him, in the process of trying to "save" him. As the God he'd abandoned only knew, Rook had spent some long, numbed time after that last skirmish thoroughly convinced that by struggling to turn Chess's Hell-bound trajectory Heaven-ward once more, he'd done nothing but get the one man in all the world he'd ever cared for killed outright. But even though he'd since had ample proof to the contrary, he still didn't believe that the *thing* wearing his hide "was" Chess, not where it most counted. For nobody could meet that black stone gaze, in battle or out of it, and truly think they saw any part of Chess Goddamn Pargeter staring back . . . not if they were intimately familiar with the original, at any rate.

Chess, however, had gotten no forewarning of Rook's perfidy—while Marizol, far as Rook could figure, understood at least a bit of what Ixchel had in store for her, and shunned it. For much as her parents might worship the Lady, this girl had been dragged here, threatened with abandonment and damnation every step of the way. What few charms Hex City held for her all lay outside Ixchel's quarters, back in the sunlight, amongst people who'd only died once—thus far.

"Please, *jefe*," she said again, "don't send me back there. Not yet."

Did she truly think he could do anything about her lowering fate? If so, she was a fool. Ask anyone and they'd tell you just what Reverend Asher Rook's role was, in this whole affair: to stand by Ixchel's side, take her orders and do her will. To watch and wait, raise his hand whenever she voted, and—above all—be silent.

Rook sighed, and sat up. "Get my boots then, gal, and walk me down to the council meeting—that's where you'll find Fennig and company, if nothin' else."

As Marizol ran jackrabbit-quick to obey, gratitude bright in every line of her, Rook felt it sink deep in his side like Longinus' spear, and twist: *Christ's wounds, stigmata, the old Catholic heresy. As though such as I was pure enough to even imagine such pain, let alone feel it—to hang a second's tick on His bright cross even in mockery, when merely to contemplate the very idea is error, if not sin outright.*

He shut his eyes one more time, shook his head emphatically, as though to clear it. And swung himself out of bed, joints cracking prodigiously, to face yet another day of war.

THE COUNCIL MET most mornings, always in the same place: that very adobe-walled house, overlooking the Temple, on whose roof Rook had once raised the shade of dead Kees Hosteen, his friend and fellow outlaw. Inside, watery sunlight trickled through the slotted windows, nowhere warm enough to dispel this dull November chill, seeing last night had brought snow in feathery drifts. Someone should've already gone 'round the walls, lighting dish-lamps full of stolen oil . . . and would've, he supposed, had the group already there not found 'emselves so deep in conversation.

"I can help?" Marizol asked, at his elbow, looking longingly toward the table's end, where Three-Fingered Hank and his ladies sat—and as though cued, dark Eulie Parr looked up just in time to catch the girl's eye and grinned, beckoning. Marizol's face coloured prettily, a lamp unto itself. Sketching a quick curtsey, she knelt to lay her head in the youngest Missus Fennig's lap while Berta Schemerhorne reached over to stroke her hair comfortingly, and Clo Killeen continued to whisper away in Hank's ear, her hushed tones typically ferocious.

Happy to give little Marizol and her troubles up, Rook conjured a brief flicker between his fingers, and set himself to bringing light out of darkness. The dishes themselves were hex-free; likewise, the splintery table, mismatched chairs and benches had all been brought to the city as they were, without any touch of magic, while the hut itself was one of the few buildings sufficiently well made to stand without active spell-work.

That was the irony of it—in a city of hexes, where the innate hunger of hex for hex made every flare of power perceptible to any who cared to look, the only way to hide was to disdain hexation. In New Aztectlan, anti-scrying cloaks were nothing but black blankets in a white room—there was no spell another hex couldn't pierce, given patience or luck. As with so much else, therefore, the best way to avoid detection was to simply never prompt anyone to look, since the only truly unprovable lie was one you never spoke at all.

But then, we never do have to speak, out loud, we don't want to—not so's you'd notice. Ain't that right, Rev?

Rook nodded, acknowledging the sly twang of Fennig's mind-voice, before casting his eyes back over to where his unofficial right hand slouched comfortably, all three of his "wives" chatting away with Marizol, as Eulie and Berta balanced the extremely *enceinte* Clo precariously between 'em. Rook raised an eyebrow at the Irish girl's bulging belly, then directed a half-reproving glance to Fennig, who shrugged.

Can't get her to do nothin' she don't want, Rev, anymore'n you can get her not to do whatever she's set on. I'm sure you know the type.

Clo, keen enough to catch the exchange—at least in abstract—went red to her ear-tips. "Something ye want to say, Reverend?" she demanded. But Rook, knowing better, refused to be drawn—he raised his palms, which counted for enough of a surrender that Clo let herself slump back, still scowling, into Berta and Eulie's supporting grip. "'Tis only that walking's more labour than once 'twas," she said. "But I have as much right to a place at this table as any other, caught short or not, as I'll thank ye to remember."

Rook fought the urge to smile. "Yes, ma'am."

Oh, but he could see why the other three loved this girl, difficult as she was, defiant and fiery to the very last. But here remembrance closed his throat once more, crushing it, a second hangman's noose.

At the same time, a grey-haired, mahogany-skinned woman whose muscular frame spoke of too much labour and not enough food, rendering what her Maker might once have intended as womanly curvaceousness with unforgiving strokes, was taking her seat on Fennig's other side. "Brazier and coals still not ready to hand, Rev'rend?" she drawled, passing out a kerchief-wrapped basket of rolls stuffed with meat, peppers and cheese.

The Rev shook his head. "There's too many would remember

such an odd request, by far. So if these gatherings' purpose is to remain private . . ."

Sal Followell shook her head. "Secrets like snakes," she grumbled. "Hard t'hold onto, no matter the circumstances—and they *slither*."

"Got *that* right," Fennig agreed, glancing 'round. "So where's the Honourable himself, old Mister Chu?"

"Ain't comin'," Missus Followell replied. "Him and the Shoshone been up all night on war party business, so they sends their regrets—talkin' 'bout dragons under the earth and such, how best they can entice 'em out t'help us. Well, Chu thinks it's dragons and the Shoshone thinks it's spiders, but I ain't minded much which of 'em's rightest, so I left 'em to it."

Clo had already finished her portion, devouring it like a feral dog. Rook gave her his too, earning a brilliant smile from Clo and a glare from the old Negress, who snapped: "You ain't too much hex to need to eat, *Reverend*."

Fennig took a ginger bite, with rather less enthusiasm. "Much obliged for the thought, Missus F.," he said, "but, ah . . . exactly what's this we're eating, again? Wasn't just *conjured*, was it?"

"An' what if it was, Yankee man?"

"Pax, Missus F.; truce. No insult intended. It's just that me and the g'hals, we tried that, travellin' here. Didn't yield much pleasantness."

Rook remembered a hex-crafted cob of corn, melting to slimy decay in his mouth, and wanted to spit. "True enough," he said. "Well, ma'am? Have we come to that pass?"

Followell sighed. "Stores is tight," she admitted. "With Pinks camped all 'round the outside walls, we can't take no small-folk on raids anymore, and there ain't many strong enough to wind-walk over them, or side-slip beyond. If we weigh our stocks careful, and ain't too fussed 'bout what we eat—not like *some*—we can go 'nother four, six weeks. Longer, we get some more strong hexes come to join us."

Fennig cleared his throat. "Yeah . . . might not be much cause for cheer on that front, neither." As Rook motioned him to continue: "Since you delegated Oath-takin' duties to me and the g'hals, Rev, you probably ain't had opportunity to notice, but we ain't been gettin' much new blood for some weeks now. Stragglers, mostly— and they're weak, too. Some of them's still gettin' pressed by the Pinks, sure, but . . ." Fennig doffed his smoked-glass spectacles a moment, rubbing at the marks they'd left on his nose. "I'm beginnin' to think how maybe the well's just run dry."

Never so many of us in one spot before, his mind-voice echoed, unheard by any but Rook—or was that true? Probably the Missuses could listen in to that particular telegraph line too, they cared to bend their will to it. Yet still it struck an intimate chord, a note of desperation Rook couldn't ever remember having heard in Fennig's roguish waking speech. *What if the Call's finally brung all there was to bring? What if we're all there's left to feed—*

The Machine, Rook completed. *To feed the Machine.*

They were all still predators, however much the Oath kept them from each other's throats. Perhaps Fennig thought Rook had forgotten that . . . or perhaps, in his Utopian blur, he'd all but forgotten it himself.

Still, the one thing left he couldn't afford was for any of the rest to *think* him afraid.

"I've been advising the Lady to stop the Call for some weeks now," Rook lied. "Obviously, it's done all it can; just swelling Pinkerton's ranks more than our own at this point, anyhow. Once it's no longer drawing power, meanwhile, the Machine's . . . appetite should diminish, enough to give us time enough to find another source."

"Source of what, exactly?" Clo asked. "Feedstock?"

"*Sustenance*," Rook corrected. "All cities are gluttons on their own flesh. New York any different in that respect, Hank?"

"New York's got close on a million lives to spare, Reverend," Fennig replied, "whereas if we've topped five thousand, it's news to me. How many hexes die a day on the Moon Court's altar? Six? Eight?"

"Used to be, sure. Less by far, since the Mexes turned up."

Leaning forward, Fennig's three-fingered hand jabbed the tabletop. "'Kay, then: let's say, without the Call, the Lady don't *need* more'n one or two. Anyone care to wager on her choosin' to settle for what she 'needs,' 'stead'a whatever she damn well feels like takin'?"

Rook's voice hardened. "We've *all* gone that bet, Henry," he rumbled. "All staked our lives on her bein' wise enough not to waste what she can't replace yet, not before we've won for good. You're lettin' your fear run away with your temper, and this ain't the time."

Fennig held still a moment, but subsided, his breathing harsh. "Not like we don't have options, either," Rook added, "unkind as they might strike certain tenderer ears amongst us. Auntie Sal—in your informed status as Midwife General, how many of our hexaciously inclined female citizens are currently about to bear progeny, 'sides from the obvious?"

Followell sniffed. "Marse Followell an' all his kin dead now these good four year, Reverend, which means I don't have to be nobody's 'auntie' no more. But as to your question—three score, just about, with ten to fifteen ready to drop within the fortnight."

"So many?"

"All witches work a charm to keep their childbed empty, but some gave it up after comprehendin' they could survive havin' a hexacious babe, here. Still, since most've 'em never expected to keep a babe anyways, they got about as much fine motherly feeling as alley cats—give you whatever you want, probably, long as there's money or privilege in it for them."

"Just you wait one damned moment, Reverend Rook." Clo fought her way to her feet, bracing on Eulie's and Berta's shoulders. "Are you telling me you'll *order* our womenfolk to rip their own childer from their breast, render 'em up to be boned like fishes on that Hell-shat slut's altar, just to keep this City alive another month?" The rage began to spark off her hair, spontaneous flares of magic crackling from fingertip to scalp, actinic-bright. "Anyone tries the same wi' *me*, an' I'll—"

"Not one of us will take any babe against its mother's will," Rook assured her. "But *you recall your Oath*, Clodagh Killeen." He touched the name with power, enough to still her where she stood. "Disobey

Lady Ixchel, break your word, it's your life *and* your babe's, with nothing I can do to stop her—not me, not Henry, not your sisters here. That what you want?"

Chest a-heave, Clo sat back down, heavily, into Eulie and Berta's arms—a four-arm hug, half embrace, half restraint.

"If all else fails," said Rook, "the Machine *can* be fed with the blood of the non-hexacious, as it was by Her worshippers of yore; them Mexes ensconced in the Moon Court alone prove that, as Miz Marisol could tell you. Which ain't as potent, but means that even if we don't have as many such as we'd like, we *can* still do what they did: take prisoners." He tried to smile. "And fortunately for us, we just so happen to have a literal army of potential donors encamped outside these very walls."

"The Pinkertons?"

"Who else?"

Fennig nodded, ruminating. "Cert, I see it now. Like back home, when they swelled the constabulary with any man-jack could stand a beatin', no matter if he'd been gang-bound before—or stayed so, after."

"Exactly. The strength that army gives us, once taken, will give us the strength to take *other* armies . . . any, however many are sent, whosoever sends them, each victory making us all the more invincible. Go forth to meet them like the Israelites of old, with Ixchel's banner before us like the Ark before Moses."

"Conquerors," said Fennig, voice suddenly gone flat. "That the way of it, Rev?"

"Moral qualms, Hank? You never struck me as a man scared to do what needs doing."

"When it does, and t'protect my own? Hell, no. But I—*we*—didn't come here with it in mind to become no new Alexanders, neither. Just to rake our plot, raise our seed and *live* like we never could, back in the Five Points." He reached out a hand, not even looking to see if Clo, Berta and Eulie would all put theirs atop his, which they did; as always, Rook envied his easy trust in their affections, so much it almost made him green.

"That Goddamn Oath," Clo growled. "Times like these, I wish I'd plucked me own tongue out before uttering its first word."

"You had, you or your babe'd most like be dead, by now," Followell pointed out. "An' don't you glare at me none, miss—but seein' you don't know my tale, I'll tell it. I come on late, didn't flare up with my bleedin', so I had three babes laid in to suck who died on me and never knew why, not 'til I woke up ravin' with fever, too delirious t'see I was so strong now, I'd already brung myself back from the dead.

"Even then, when I did know, could I stop? No ma'am. I went on an' killed my own boy, ate 'im up like candy. Was after that I finally broke an' run, for fear Marse Followell'd try to keep on breedin' me—he was just the sort of fool gotta have all his dogs and niggers be top merchandise, and wa'nt 'bout to quit the idea just on my account. Not like he could stop me, though, once I got my mind made up. And that's why there ain't no Marse, no more—no Followell Plantation, neither.

"So. Say the Machine stops, and the Oath falls to pieces—you pondered much on that? A thousand hexes, all turned on each other at once; you an' your babe, your sisters—yes, your man, too! 'Cause love won't help, as I've lived long enough to know, Miss Clo." Her voice roughened. "Think on why 'mages don't meddle,' an' you'll find the truth right quick. Without the Oath, we're all of us naked to our own hunger, just meat served up for judgement. Myself, I'll do whatever best be done, to keep *that* day from my door . . . and you—will—too."

Such eyes that old woman had! Rook found himself fair melting under their regard, worn away like soap, reduced to a seat-shifting boy. Knew the others must feel much the same, considering how their own gazes fell, guiltily, to the tabletop. Soon enough, however, the spell was broken by a voice he'd frankly never hoped to hear within these precincts—soft yet horribly present, as though it sprang full-blown from the brainpan of every hex there.

"Well put, my dark daughter. Your wisdom is admirable—your loyalty, also."

And in stepped the one woman-shaped thing none of 'em would have ever conjured on their own, given the option: Rainbow Lady Ixchel, the Suicide Moon herself, who came melting through the wall like all the chinks between bricks were one door split in à thousand pieces, each opening only to her command. Then hung there by Rook's side with the exposed bones of her feet barely scraping against the floor, while her dragonfly cloak swarmed in to meet her—wrapping her close 'til nothing remained of that half-flayed corpse-face but a shimmering veil disclosing just her eyes, her too high brow and an inexplicable glimpse of purplish-dark lips strained back over teeth rendered wolf-long by her gums' retreat.

Catching a view of Marizol cowering in the corner, half-hid behind Berta's skirts, she smiled; Marizol sketched a sort of answering grimace back at her, then scurried over, head hung low, when Ixchel snapped her claw-tipped fingers, and re-took her kneeling place at that dread queen's side.

"*Señora . . . mi reina,*" she brought out, tight and high, as though stomach-punched. "*Yo te saludo.*" While Ixchel just grinned all the wider, carding those too-sharp implements carefully through the girl's hair.

"I have missed you, pet; you did ill to flee me so soon, without any word where you might have gone." Adding, to Rook, with a creepish airiness: "And you too, of course, little husband. How seldom we see each other, these days, you and I!"

"Business of the War, ma'am," Rook replied, deadpan. "But I do s'pose as how it's necessary, much though I might feel the lack myself."

"The War, yes. Whose direction I have thus far left to you and yours—Mister Fennig, or whatever others you might accord similar trust—since, as my brother Lightning Serpent proves, this is a matter men excel at."

"And I'm grateful for the opportunity, that goes without saying. Was there something you wanted, wife?"

A bit too off-hand for her liking, perhaps; Rook certainly heard almost everyone else present suck in a gasp, soft as they tried to keep it. But thankfully Marizol, already deft at trying to draw her attention away, chose this very moment to volunteer—"Apologies, señora . . . it was remiss of me, I know. *Lo siento mucho, mi dama celestial.*"

Ixchel chucked her beneath the chin, drawing blood. "Ah, child! You are so young. I understand—you meant no disrespect. How could you possibly know how very much you mean to me, and why?"

How indeed, Rook thought, seeing Marizol shake under the Lady's touch, a discreet tear streaking from one eye. *Goddamn yet one more time this bed I made, let alone the filthy butcher-shop diablerie I have to practise, daily, in order to stay here!*

This was just what came of being a hypocrite, though, he guessed—a faithless preacher, sworn to false idols. *Chess* never would've stood for it, in any of his forms, for though ass-kissing was an art he'd excelled at (literally, at least), the mere grinding repetition of paying Ixchel homage would've bored him so senseless it'd've set him off like a lit fuse long before now, 'specially seeing how he was naturally immune to her mixture of cock-raising glamour and accelerant decay.

Always did make him dangerous to sit still too long—that was one thing she never understood, 'bout Chess. That, along with so much else.

And once things'd come to a head . . . well, that'd've been a fireworks show for sure, fit to rock the whole stinking world from horizon to horizon. Something Rook would've paid good money for, to watch, and to clap at.

But you are not him, husband, Ixchel's mental voice told him, **as we both know. Conquistador dream of "one flesh" aside, you never were . . . nor will you ever be.**

You know what I'm thinking? Ridiculous as it was, he couldn't stop himself from forming the question, though it held its own answer.

Of course; I know everything you do, little king, always. And why.

Sal Followell had both hands shading her eyes, like she found Ixchel's visage too fierce to consider directly, and Rook could tell how much that pleased the goddess by the way she preened, her grim cloak hissing. But in the far corner, Hank Fennig had once more pushed his glasses down so's he could survey her over their rims with narrowed eyes—taking measurements, perhaps, or tallying some list. Rook made his own mental note to ask him which it was, later on.

"These ideas of yours amuse me," Ixchel told the others, meanwhile. "I approve—you may do what you must in order to keep the Machine going, just as I will do what *I* must, in order to use its power to its fullest. Thus it is that will we triumph, in the end, together."

The clear implication being: *I will suffer sedition in speech, if not in deed. For nothing you plot is secret to me, or any sort of threat; you live only at my sufferance . . . even you, my husband.*

"Should we expect you along for tonight's raid, then?" Rook asked. To which she bent her head, regally, fixing him with eyes whose softening ligaments had already started to make them cant in different directions.

"I would not miss such a chance," she answered. "I have spent too much time in the Underworld lately, to far too little effect. I must show myself to the populace, that their terror may swell and spread."

Fair enough, Rook thought.

Besides which, her mind-voice told him, *I have a new plan which needs must be rehearsed under conditions of battle—a gift for you, of sorts. A terrible weapon, one which will sweep our enemies away before us.*

That so, sweetheart? Or do you mean just the ones whose names don't start with "The"?

Behind Ixchel's back, the dragonflies snapped and hissed, angered on her behalf. If any of that annoyance reached her, however, it didn't show; sucking day and night on those Mexes of hers really was altering her, he guessed, making her colder, more dispassionate. Bringing all her most unnatural inclinations to the fore.

He cast his mind back to when Hex City's foundations were first laid, and she'd at least pretended to care.

Remembered telling her, after they were two weeks and fifty hexes deep in kowtowing, barely able to stroll from here to there with stumbling over some prostrate supplicant: *These people are here at* your *say-so, madam—left everything behind like they was fleein' Egypt, on nothing but the Call and some bad dreams. Least you could do is walk amongst 'em and grant a few damn prayers beforehand, 'stead of always goin' straight for the pound of flesh.*

She'd nodded, as he recalled. And told him, face so straight it might as well have been the jade chip-scaled mask it sometimes seemed: *But . . . this is what I have you for. Is it not?*

Original plan was, you'd wake a few more of your relatives and get 'em up here, on our side, he thought at her, back in the here and now. *What happened to that idea, exactly?*

The barest hint of a shrug. *Things change, husband. As ever.*

Conversation disposed with, Ixchel turned back to Marizol, still frozen in a dumb-show of acquiescence. Telling her: "Now, child, you have spent enough time away from Court. I need you to take up your seat at my side once more, as is your ancestral charge and right, and . . . feed me."

Marizol bit her lip even harder, for all the world as though she were trying to make the skin tear. As though she wanted to bring the red flowing freely, if only so she wouldn't have to make use of the thorn-rope again.

"*Si, señora*," she managed, through her pain.

"*Good* girl," Ixchel said, laying a half-fleshed hand to her forehead. And with a concussive flash, they were gone.

From Fennig's side, Clo Killeen let out one long-held breath in a fit of coughing; Berta embraced her from the side, stroking her chest soothingly, while Eulie—typically the most gentle of the three—squinched her pretty face up, and actually spat.

"She's gonna kill that girl," she remarked, to Rook, sounding like she hoped he'd deny it. "Ain't she?"

"I think so, yes."

"Goddamn it all to hell, then. She's—good, that one, even if she ain't hexacious."

Rook nodded. "A few more like her on either side, and maybe we wouldn't be in this fix."

From her place in the corner, Missus Followell shook her head. "Pure foolishness, and y'all know it. 'Nice' that gal may well be, but she ain't never gone be one of us—no way, no how. Whereas the Lady, awfulness and all . . . *is*."

"She's a monster," Clo whispered, lips barely moving, so fast Berta didn't have time to clap a hand over her mouth. But Followell merely turned her too-calm eyes back on the Irish girl, replying, "And we ain't?"

CHAPTER FOUR

"FROM MY VANTAGE, those who do not consider themselves entirely committed must, of course, feel free to move on," Sophronia Love said, voice even, though still loud enough to fill a close-packed room. "Each of you must seek grace in your way, as your understanding of the Lord's word prompts you, since I believe we all share the sure and certain knowledge that each man's path is his own business."

The small group of supplicants before her—disadvantaged by a good three feet of extra height granted the woman most simply called "Widow," along with Bewelcome's other town elders, by virtue of the stage on which they sat—shuffled where they stood, leader shifting his hat from hand to hand. "Ain't like we *want* to go, Missus Love, what with the town still under fire. But . . . our families . . ."

"Mister Trasker, if you truly feel your family better served by cowering upon your land and hoping to be overlooked, then by all means—go ahead and cower. I'll note, however, that this same strategy entirely failed to save either the Harmons' cattle, the de Groots' breeding studs, or those men who died in guarding them." Her eyes flicked sidelong, to skewer a man uncomfortably tapping one boot in the front row. "And you, Mister Russell—Hiram? Did a similar policy save your daughters, when Satan's servants came to carry them away?"

"You know full well it didn't, ma'am."

"Well, then."

From the back of the hall, Morrow and Doctor Joachim Asbury watched this spin out, in silence. For the sin of arriving late, they'd been forced to seat themselves next to a frantically scribbling Fitz Hugh Ludlow, whose Palmer Method shorthand was as unintelligible to Morrow as his overtures of friendship were unwelcome. A yellow journalist of some repute in first New York, then 'Frisco, this fashionably dressed fool had been touring the area writing exposes on Hex City when Pinkerton began his assault, and stayed to play war correspondent—from a safe distance, naturally. He had a way of smiling that barely reached his eyes, and a vulture's keen instinct for the unwary quote which made Morrow almost loath to open his mouth wide enough to spit, whenever he chanced to find himself in the man's company.

"She's quite the fearsome virago, our Missus Love," Ludlow murmured, admiringly. "A true Madonna-in-armour, equally suited for battle and worship alike. And pleasingly buxom, too; that boy of hers is a fortunate young man, indeed."

"Sheriff Love sure wouldn't've approved of you saying so, at least within his earshot."

"Oh, no doubt. How lucky for me, then, that my arrival in this town chanced to fall *after* that inestimable gentleman had already been dispatched to his reward!" Ludlow turned, hand still scratching away unchecked at his note-tablet. "But I'd almost forgotten: you were there that day, weren't you, Mister Morrow? Quite close by, as I recall—though the mysterious Missus Kloves, naturally, was closer. Perhaps you might see your way clear to relating the story of that adventure to me, one of these days, in detail. . . ."

"Sir, if you'll excuse me, I really am trying to listen."

Sophy had already returned her attention to Trasker, who seemed increasingly spooked, while the dignitaries sharing podium space with her—Mayor Alonzo Langobard, his bulk more fat than muscle, white shirt already sweat-stained in the stuffy hall; Captain Washford, looking somewhat embarrassed to be so elevated; young

Reverend Oren Catlin, not half the Nazarene Sheriff Love had been, who'd nevertheless taken up the town's vacant ministry under the apparent conviction that an easy smile and clean-cut good looks were all a new pastor needed in order to thrive—stirred in a milder form of discomfort.

"We will miss you, of course," Sophy told the man, "you, and all you take with you. But I will have no compelled soldiers in my husband's army."

Here Mayor Langobard cleared his throat and sat forward, perhaps hoping to regain control by sheer force of bodily mass alone. "Widow Love . . . much as I hate to be indelicate, your *husband* has nothing to do with this."

"He was Sheriff here, sir. He founded this town, along with its militia—swore in each and every man-at-arms who defended this place against iniquity in its infant stages, long before Mister Pinkerton or Captain Washford made their appearance, on this very Bible." She tapped the tome, drably bound in practical oilskin, which even now rested close by her right hand, where her gurgling son could play with its well-worn edges. "My *husband* is the reason Bewelcome exists."

"For which we all thank him, and kindly. But in case you hadn't yet noticed—he's dead."

Reaction to this ran through the crowd like a ripple, and Morrow watched face after face turn Sophy's way, studying her steel façade for any sign of a crack. None came: the woman was immaculate, grief-hardened like stoneware. Even with her youth, bereavement and stern beauty sentimentally leavened by the baby balanced on one knee, Mesach Love's former bride might as well have been a corpse herself, her coarse black weeds and implacable regard erasing any hint of allure.

"Are we so quick to forget our Gideons, then, when we have so much need of them, if only as examples?" the Widow asked. "The Sword of the Lord may be wielded by anyone, Mayor, so long as the fight—and the warrior—be righteous. It says so here, in *Judges*."

At this, Catlin raised hand and voice together, in all-too-polite objection. "Now, Sister Sophy, I'm not *entirely* sure that's the correct interpretation to place on—"

"Sure does," someone behind Morrow confirmed; "sure does. She's right about that."

Sophy knew her audience. The ripple grew, became a general agreeing murmur.

"Sheriff taught her himself, and there wasn't no one better'n him for Scripture."

"Or bravery. 'Member when he stood toe-to-toe 'gainst Reverend Rook, with nothin' but the Lord for backup? Devil won that round, but only halfway; even Satan himself couldn't keep them two parted, or let young Gabe there stay bewitched."

"And so what if he went down later on, still fighting? All flesh turns grass, eventually—way of the world. Yet it was God himself told the first Zealot: *Peace be unto thee, thou mighty man of valour; fear not; thou shalt not* altogether *die.*"

"That's enough!" Langobard thumped the tabletop, face reddening. "Missus Love, there's courage, and then there's plain foolhardiness. The Harmons and the de Groots were *told* not to take lots so far north, and suffered the consequences. But I'll not strip every field of able bodies, 'specially this close to harvest, and in this weather! If these men have an honest need to tend their lands—"

Sophy drew herself up, suddenly ablaze, shifting Gabe to her hip. "More delay!" she shouted, uncowed. "You have done it again and again, since your election. Indeed, I begin to wonder if we shall *ever* be ready to march on Hex City, upon *your* say-so!" Morrow watched as a group of some dozen townsfolk—all with faces he recognized from the aftermath of Bewelcome's resurrection, that day Ludlow so yearned to pick his brain on, and all well-armed—assembled at the stage's far end, gathering 'round Sophy like Templars to the Ark. "The people of this town dare not wait forever—"

"The people of Bewelcome voted *me* Mayor, Missus Love, not you!" Langobard bellowed back. "I won't be dictated to, not by a mere female grasping at power she has no right to—earthly, or otherwise!"

"I repeat: this is my husband's town, with Gabriel his only heir. What small influence I have here I hold in trust, for them both."

"And therein lies the rub. For this is still a democracy we inhabit, madam, one in which your son has yet to attain his age of majority, let alone be elected to any sort of public office."

"*Be* Mayor, then, Mister Langobard." Abruptly, Sophy was all ice once more; Langobard rocked back on his heels, nonplussed. "Fulfill the charges given you. You know as well as I do that Bewelcome is over-billeted with Mister Pinkerton's operatives and Captain Washford's soldiers—we cannot feed them forever, much less endure the riff-raff, provenderers and Hooker-girls trailing in their wake. As for the newcomers who've helped to settle our God-blessed land—His kindness be with them all, but a growing population is a distraction we can ill afford, one which renders us daily less united in our purpose."

"You were less displeased with our success when the depot station went up. Without Mister Pinkerton's influence, it might well have been years before we saw a rail line out here—"

"And Captain Washford can well speak to the problems *that* caused," Sophy went on, inexorably. "Or am I wrong, Captain, in thinking that the supply-line trains have been consistently preyed upon by Reverend Rook's forces, since they finally began regular runs?"

Washford rose, his stance more uncomfortable than ever. "Raids've increased, yes, like we knew they would. Still, they serve to draw the hexes' attention away from Camp Pink, where Doc Asbury assures me he's developing new measures to counteract the enemy's resources—"

"Yes, yes, all right." Langobard cut Washford off with a peevish wave, ignoring how the other man's eyes flashed. "To recap, Missus: though your points are taken, you must now take *mine*. I am in charge here, not you, and I don't aim to see us all go the same way as Mesach Love himself, solely 'cause you've lost patience for justice."

An underhanded strike, but one which seemed to hit, and deeply. For a moment, Sophy looked down, studying the table, as though in search of an answer—and as the blue granite of her gaze softened, Morrow got a sudden sense of the pain which lay behind it: still jagged as the moment after Yancey Kloves' bullet met her man's skull, these long months later. A hurt which had burned away everything in her that once rang gentle, purifying through calcination to leave nothing behind but commitment, cold as any butcher's blade.

And this image, in turn, sent his mind careening back toward the woman who'd spawned it. Lost Yancey, whom he'd known so briefly, at least in the flesh, yet thought on so damn often. For a man to yearn after a woman he barely knew was more comedy than tragedy, prime as any vaudeville. But it was a hard thing nonetheless, to find himself so lamentably haunted by somebody who, he could only assume—could only *hope*, devoutly, fervently—probably wasn't even dead.

He had a fair idea that she probably still rode with the man-squaw Yiska and her renegades, yoked to the will of that undead harridan, "Grandma." Stranded amongst savages, with Pinkerton's former pet sorceress Songbird her only "civilized" companion—was that any place for her to heal, even with her own bitter vengeance already accomplished? Or was she changing yet further, so much they'd be unrecognizable to one another when next they met?

Those few nocturnal reveries he'd had of her since, however, sweetly fleeting as they were, seemed so damn *real*. Even now, shutting his eyes, it was like he was there: the taste of her skin, the feel of her in his arms, that scent he could never recall on wakening, yet knew he'd know for hers under any circumstances. They lay abed, tracing each other like a pattern while she let down her dark hair, a curtain shutting them away from the world; in between bouts, she quizzed him on subjects he liked to think might give her aid or comfort, wherever she found herself.

Where are you? He'd asked her, once.

Only to watch her shake her head, sadly, and reply: *Can't tell you that, Ed. Too dangerous, for both of us. We're working at a disadvantage, after all.*

I miss you, he told her, to which she shaped a smile, already fading:

sweet, just the way he remembered, or thought he did. For there was much about her he found slipping away likewise, worn down by time and distance—and all the time meeting only in dreams probably didn't help much, on that score.

Of course, there was another ghost held tenancy in Morrow's brainpan, too: someone also still upright, at least bodily, who he tried his best to avoid musing about at all, and mostly failed.

For awake or sleeping, Morrow intermittently felt Chess Pargeter's touch, heard his voice, his sly laugh, the punctuational double-cock of his guns. He saw red hair glint under every hat, read Chess's rooster-proud strut in a thousand passing walks. Thinking, as he did: *This must've been how it was for him, with the Rev. . . .*

"You mistake me," Sophy Love replied, at last. "No person in this room knows more keenly than I do that Law is the only certain cure for lawlessness—Mesach preached on that very subject many a time, and though he knew he might never live to see it truly flower, we held it worth the price. For Law is the future's currency, Mayor, and once established, it *must* be defended. Tooth and nail." The knuckles of her hands, folded primly before her, were white. "But if our enemies are not defeated, all Law will fall before them. Therefore do not count me so much impatient as afraid, lest all of us should lose what slim chance at it we have."

The room was shamed to silence. And Morrow, caught in admiration, could only marvel at those stupid enough to think "mere" women unfit to rule.

It was the mild, reedy voice of Professor of Experimental Arcanistry Joachim Asbury which broke the spell first, declaring: "Missus Love, your position—though eminently moral—remains strategically unsound, in almost every respect."

Langobard peered into the hall's recesses. "That sounds like Doc Asbury."

"Indeed," Sophy agreed. "Once again, I see Mister Pinkerton has chosen to delegate his leadership duties." Her eyes moved to Morrow, now rising to join Asbury, as the older man made his limping way down. "And Agent Morrow, as well—good to see the

Agency represented directly by someone, at least. *You* are always welcome."

Morrow cleared his throat. "Widow Love, Mayor Langobard, Captain Washford." Adding, hesitating a scant beat before reflex overrode distaste: "Reverend Catlin."

"Agent Morrow!" The pastor projected a blitheness so unflagging Morrow was hard put to figure whether it sprung from profound idiocy, incalculable self-confidence, or some admixture of both. "God bless and keep you. I take it your latest errand was successful?"

"Thank you, Reverend—we can deal with the niceties later, if you please." Langobard leaned forward, table creaking under his weight. "But for once, Agent Morrow, I find myself and the Widow in full agreement. Where *is* Mister Pinkerton? Are we not important enough to receive our information from him at first-hand?"

Asbury shifted. "No, no. Mister Pinkerton wanted to come, I do assure you. But . . . circumstances . . ." He shrugged, helpless, as the crowd fell back to muttering.

He's fighting a return of his old complaint, the old man had told Morrow, at the depot. *It does seem to continue flaring up; the symptoms worsen, as well. Though I remain confident I shall find a true solution soon*, he'd added, far too quickly to reassure.

For his own part, Morrow did not care to imagine what Pinkerton's unnaturally imbued hex-hunger—like that of a born magic-user, yet somehow more venomous, eroding his very humanity along with his health and strength if not constantly fed—would look like, after "worsening." He was only grateful he hadn't yet had to find out.

"What the Professor's tryin' to say," he interposed, "is how Mister Pinkerton's needed particularly close to hand in camp these days, 'specially in times of war."

"Huh." Langobard leaned back, with a disgusted noise. "'Tween honest folk and hexes, war's like men versus little red ants on a hill, with them the men in this equation."

"Not so." This last came from Captain Washford. "They've power, sure, but comparatively few have imagination or the discipline enough to wield it optimally, whilst we have numbers and persistence. Plus, we know full well what *we* fight for: Our entire world's survival."

"Oh, Hex City's Lady don't seek to destroy *that*," Morrow remarked; "it's hers already, by her lights. And she'll need us, too, after—as fuel, for that Machine of hers."

Catlin said hopefully: "Yet, to paraphrase *Matthew* 7:12 . . . if we leave them alone, might be they'll leave *us* alone?"

"Uh huh. And might be pigs'll learn to live shit-free, but I somewhat doubt it."

Langobard scowled. "Gentlemen . . ."

"No, Mayor; Agent Morrow's right, impoliteness aside." Sophy's mouth twitched, shaped a ghost of a smile. "Those to the north won't let us be, not so long's they do the Rev's bidding, or he does hers."

"Exactly." Morrow glanced from the Widow to Langobard, then Washford. "All of you have a chunk of the truth, and we need to parse it out proper. Though we don't dare wait much longer to take the fight toward Hex City once again, we can't afford to do so unarmed." He gestured to Asbury, who opened the heavy hide rucksack slung at his waist. "Now, the Doc here's worked hard preparing the tools we need, in order to steal at least some hope of victory. So, with your permission . . ."

Asbury cleared his throat, turning the glass-faced device he'd withdrawn from side to side, so all could see. "This, which you may have already heard of, is the Manifold," he said. "I shall not waste time explaining its construction, save to note that its clockwork incorporates gears of magnetized metal and a silver-iron-sodium alloy." He twisted the fob several times, setting its gears a-whirl. "Once activated, the interaction of these kinetic-magnetic energies with the arcane conductivity of the alloy creates a field capable of disrupting hexacious input. While active, this device may be used as a shield against witchery and a weapon to dispel standing enchantments—merely strike the object or creature in question, and its efficacy will be dispersed."

"Very clever, Doctor," Langobard began. "Yet I fail to see what use one gadget might possibly be. . . ."

Here he trailed off, however, when Asbury upended the rest of his baggage onto the stage with a great cascading metallic clatter. Dozens of Manifolds slid out, shining in the light of the hall's lanterns, and the crowd's manner—hitherto that of bemusement—sharpened, with electrical fierceness, to an excitement so palpable it made Morrow grin.

"One to any who think they need one," Asbury declared. "A charitable donation to our Bewelcomite fellow travellers in the War on Hex, care of Mister Pinkerton . . . and myself, of course."

"Amazing." Washford rubbed his chin. "Delicate mechanisms, though, Doctor, am I right? Not amenable to direct impact, grit in the gears—or being dropped?" As Asbury flushed: "Not that I mean to belittle your contribution, but we must know its limits. Will this truly work on *any* hex? Even ones such as Reverend Rook, or his Lady?" Adding, with a sidelong look at Morrow: "Or that other demi-deity we all know of . . . can we speak *his* name aloud, without inviting his participation?"

"Chess Pargeter's no part of this," Morrow replied, perhaps a bit too quickly. "Not anymore."

"But reports put him all over the battlefield—at its edges, in the thick of the fray. He's been seen at the station, watching trains come in. Hell, he's been seen in people's *dreams*."

Here Catlin shook his head, smiling stupid-wide. "Wouldn't place much trust in *those* tales, Captain—we're none of us Daniels. People dream of what they fear."

"And they *fear* what they have reason to. Don't they, Mister Morrow?"

Suddenly, everyone was looking Morrow's way.

Knowing Asbury in particular awaited his reply, he took the time to draw breath, before allowing:

"It's true enough that *something* wages a campaign 'gainst the Rev and Herself, wearing . . . Pargeter's shape, then turns the hammer 'gainst us, whenever we interfere. Take it from me, though—it ain't him. I've been close enough to tell." People fell silent, embarrassed by the implications. "For my money, he died in your town square, bringing y'all back from Beyond."

Looking to Sophy, he was obscurely heartened to see her nod, albeit reluctantly. But Washford, who—like all the newest arrivals—hadn't witnessed that particular anti-miracle for himself, stayed sceptical.

"The point still stands," he said. "Regarding our biggest guns, and theirs—"

"Doc might have a thing or two to say 'bout that," Morrow replied, looking to Asbury, who nodded.

"At Mister Pinkerton's request," he began, "I have improvised a mechanical analogue to the Hex City Oath, which—according to our information, gleaned mostly from deserters—apparently prevents those hexes who consider themselves its citizens from parasiting each other and yet still allows them to use their powers individually, though not against either the Lady nor her sworn consort, Reverend Rook. I had previously thought to shield our former ally Miss Yu Ming-ch'in—or Songbird, as she prefers to be called—from contagion by giving her a prototype version of the neutralization bracket we now distribute to all Camp Pink hexes. In her case it proved ineffective, but not in any way through the item's own fault."

Nope, Morrow thought. *All that was on "Mister" Pinkerton's head, for breaking it off her and swallowing the pieces, 'fore they had the chance to take permanent effect—chawing 'em down like jerky, to suck up all the sweet hex-juice inside. 'Cause when the fit's on him, he can't keep himself in check at all . . . and seein' how you were one of the last to see him that-a-way, Missus Love, I'd say it's no longer a great mystery why he shuns your company. Since he can glimpse the shadow of his monstrous self in your eyes, same way he does in mine, he keeps us both at arm's length, dealing with us through middlemen; simply happens I'm the one in the middle, this time.*

As though his words were bleeding over, Sophy Love's clean white forehead wrinkled prettily. "And this restrains any secret hostility they may harbour toward the Pinkerton Detective Agency, as well? For with so many hexes under his command, I don't doubt but Mister Pinkerton must sleep with one eye open, always ready for attack—"

"Oh, the Thaumaturgical Law of Replication sees to that," Asbury assured her. "All our brackets are cast from the same mold as Miss Songbird's first shackle, with that close-held by the boss— Pinkerton—himself. And he who holds the master prototype may also use it to reverse the flow, de-powering every bracket-wearing hex who thinks to stand against him."

"So you do keep your wild dogs leashed, then—that's a mercy. For lo, *One of themselves, even a prophet of their own, said, the Cretians are always liars, evil beasts, slow bellies*; Titus, 1:12."

"More collared than leashed, ma'am. But accurate otherwise, to a point."

Morrow shut his eyes, unable to dismiss the immediate rush of memory: saw witches and warlocks, volunteers and prisoners alike, lined up knee to knee to wait their turn at the striking iron; with each fresh collaring a groan went up, along with a blast of heat, the slight smell of singed hair or flesh, the wince and stamp of pain. After which the blacksmith's apprentice would douse their necks in a bucketful of water and move them to where the healers stood, charged hands already outstretched for a mighty laying-on, with the raw assault to everyone's spiritual dignity left completely untreated.

Though Morrow hadn't had occasion to sit down with their mutual "boss" for some time now, he found himself nevertheless already convinced of the scenario Asbury had occasionally let slip hints about, late at night, in his cups. For the idea that Pinkerton's ultimate goal might be to make the Agency the States' predominant outfit of internal control, sole wielders of the only arcane branch of technology allowing mere humans to police and identify hexes— to break them like horses, groom them like dogs, put them down like sick pets if and when they exceeded their purviews—was both a truly horrifying one, and all too easy to believe.

Strange how it'd taken the War, that dreadful upheaval pitting neighbour 'gainst neighbour, culling an entire generation at one swoop, to convince a divided America that centre-driven unity was better by far than state-to-state autonomy. In a way, it had become their own version of the Oath: a commitment to Missus Love's Law, instead of that wild, God-given justice the first colonists had supposedly fled England in order to regain. And now, with the constant spectre of fresh Division hanging low over all their heads, Pinkerton was right in thinking how any nation who could use hexes like tools instead of having to deal with them like weather might expect to write its own ticket from now on, both at home and—eventually—elsewhere.

It could never be forgotten that staying within siege distance of New Aztectlan also kept Pinkerton close to a source of hexation he could sample at will, distilling it like the tinctures Asbury had once used to fend off his curse-pollution. Which might explain why all his strategic decisions hitherto seemed to suggest his aspiration was to take the city wholesale, thus enslaving the largest concentration of hexes in America—magicians already used to working together, if only under an oath of loyalty so stark that to break it would kill them outright.

To do so, he would have to dispose of Ixchel, Rook and probably the Enemy as well, a triple coup of spectacularly crazy proportions. Yet Morrow could well imagine that in his hex-juice-drugged state, Pinkerton might think this ambition more easily fulfilled than not.

ASBURY DRANK A LOT these days, for a man so patently unused to doing so; did it late in the night and early in the morn, with little pause for full recovery in between. His pleasure was gin, poured into a teacup with the pinkie extended, then chugged straight down without wincing. Sometimes he probably cut it with other things— Morrow'd heard tell that laudanum in red wine would give you horrors so bad you'd think you saw a woman's nipples wink at you, and as manager of Pinkerton's medical stores, the Professor sure had access to that. But for all Morrow could really prove, he might've been rolling the Red Weed and smoking it the way he claimed those old Mexes used to, or chewing it up like peyote buttons.

Didn't much matter, either way. Though Asbury's hands seldom shook and his voice remained slur-free, he did keep himself well-lit. From where he was sitting, for example, it was obvious to Morrow he'd already had a few nips today; luckily, no one else seemed to recognize this fact except perhaps for Langobard, who was probably willing to let it slide on account of being in a similar condition. And once past a certain point in his routine, Morrow'd lately had cause to observe that if you asked Asbury something straight out—no matter what, or what about—he'd just go right on ahead and answer it.

"That first bracket, the bracelet I made for Miss Yu, wasn't right," he'd told Morrow, a week back. "Untested. To lock it on a mere girl, in such primitive conditions . . ." He shook his head, sadly. "What right have I to call myself a scientist, after that sort of behaviour?"

"Much right as any here, I s'pose. More right than most, still."

Asbury shook his head. "Pinkerton's idea. Wanted a demonstration of its efficacy; demanded I use it just as soon as opportunity presented itself, and on Miss Yu too, if at all possible. Left to my own devices, I would never, but—he insisted. And . . . circumstances were exigent, at the time."

"No doubting that," Morrow had assured him.

"Yes. Grateful as he was to reap the rewards, though, he was equally quick to inform me that the effects fell markedly short of his true ambitions."

Morrow forced a laugh. "What'd he want," he made himself ask, lightly, "for it to make him turn hex altogether *and* rule America, like Rook and Chess might've planned? Or be President, then, after he'd made short work of Johnson—hell, what about *king*?"

Asbury muttered something into his collar, the only part of which Morrow thought heard sounded like "uh guh"—followed by another long swallow, to compose himself. After which he eventually managed to eke out: "No. For Pinkerton, you see, wants more. Desires, in short, to be . . . a . . ."

And here things took on a far darker filter, like looking through a pebbled storm window. Because what the word in question turned out to be was *"god."*

After all, if Asbury's theories held true—which they certainly had, thus far—even the "gods" of Old Mexico were once no more than hexes, just as all hexes were once mere humans, thus suggesting that any human charged with hex-power could (in theory) become a god. How, though, exactly? This was the question Morrow most dreaded, hoping devoutly to never see it answered—yet fearing, more and more, that he was doomed to do so.

"Can't be done," he'd replied. "Right?"

Asbury regarded his booze-filled teapot, bleakly. "Such a transition requires sacrifice, obviously, from what we saw happen to your Mister Pargeter—that the applicant himself be sacrificed, in point of fact. Yet sacrifice is simply death, placed in special context. And when we speak of creatures as powerful as Lady Rainbow, let alone that Other, are we even really speaking of *death*, per se? Disruption alone might suffice, if it lasted long enough. The resultant backwash of released mantic energy, horrifyingly strong as it would have to be . . . I see no reason why Mister Pinkerton might not use it to elevate himself to their power status, if only temporarily."

Temporarily'd be bad enough, Morrow didn't have to say, since he could only suppose they were both thinking it. And a few minutes later, Asbury put his head down on his folded arms for "a short rest," never lifting it up again 'til morning.

And here I am, stranded right in the middle of a pile of shit, just like effin' always, Morrow concluded, his long musing over. *Sure hope Yancey and the others have found the* real *Chess by now, wherever the Enemy might've stashed him—that they have a plan to go with that idea, too, if and when . . .*

UP ON STAGE, Langobard raised "his" new Manifold to the light, admiring its shine. A second later, however, he almost dropped the thing as though burned—for it had begun to twist in his hand, buzzing waspish, mercury popping like it wanted to escape.

"The hell—?" was all he had time for.

Outside, the thunder cracked like God's own whip, shaking Nazarene Hall to its foundations. And between them, on the table, a noise rose up that Morrow'd hoped never to hear again: ticking and chattering, magnified by fifty-odd. The Manifolds themselves, rattling like bees in a sack.

". . . what?" This from the Reverend Catlin, still left off to one side, pathetic in his lack of practical understanding. But the rest of them knew better.

"Hexation," was all Sophy Love said, folding her little boy close. While Morrow just shifted back into fighting stance, one hand automatically going to his gun.

It's on, he thought. And ran for the door.

CHAPTER FIVE

ATOP HEX CITY'S southernmost ramparts with Fennig at his elbow, Reverend Rook looked down on a four-foot-wide bowl that had been made by hexation-gloved hands digging up the stone like wet clay, tossing it pell-mell over the edge to shatter. Then filled by bucket after bucket hauled laboriously up from the city's wells— that part had to be done *without* magic, the man who'd designed it had told them, or the reflections it cast would be false, and therefore impotent.

The water must be a mirror, the mirror an eye, without flaw or artifice. It is known, barbarians. Everywhere, it is known! All civilized places, at least.

Have you truly no system of traditions here, in this empty pigsty of yours, this bone-kennel? Do you not at the least strive to educate yourselves, knowing no one else will do it for you?

The voice in Reverend Rook's mind didn't much sound like Songbird's except in terms of tone—that damnable Celestial arrogance, a thousand years of Chinee witchery made literal flesh. For the Emperors and mandarins had done with both their ancestors what Auntie Sal's Marse Followell had only dreamed on: in- and out-crossed 'em generation after generation like any other owned creature, culling their bloodlines for potential, power and amusement-value deformity—as pets and slaves, equally. Living weapons used 'til they broke, then bred again and again 'til their children outstripped them, or died trying.

And here he was now, the man himself—the Honourable Chu, squatting over that same pool like a snapping turtle. He was short and broad, black eyes narrowed, the water below him rippling in red circles as he stirred it with a handful of long yarrow stalks. With his frayed black cotton pyjama pants and callused bare feet, he looked most like what he'd once masqueraded as: a scholar reduced to beggary, escaping his inherited yoke by slipping on the uniform of a simple railway-labour coolie. One thing alone marked him out as maybe more—the tatters of a royal blue silk tunic, faded almost lavender.

When Chu spoke, threads of light writhed in that silk like the worms which had birthed it, showing him for what he was: New Aztectlan's war-master, born of a culture with millennia invested in the arts of battle *and* hexation. No matter how worn the garment became, Chu never removed it, and answered no questions about how it had been ruined. But Rook, thinking back on his own black-covered Bible—long gone now—and of Songbird, so trapped in her sacred whore's gilded red lacquer cage that the earthquake he'd called down on her must've seemed less a disaster than a freedom-spawning miracle, thought he could guess.

Next to Chu, another man crouched, taller and browner though equally broad, his cheekbones flat as copper axe blades. "See it yet?" he demanded, raking his long hair back behind one ear, while the beaded pectoral covering his chest rattled like an abacus. "Spinning its web, under the earth's skin . . . there, and there. If you can't, you must be going blind, old idiot."

"There are no spiders here, fool. Only dragons, rulers of weather and water—Ying-lung, who brings rain and floods, whose name we have called every day this week. Will you never learn?"

"Day I need to 'learn' from you, yellow man, I'll lay myself face down in this pool and try breathing water. Who was here first, uh? Your people, or mine?"

"More of mine left here than yours, you dung beetle, even *with* the quota. As for lying face down—that must've been the extent of your strategy, when the *gweilo* came. The sage Sun Tzu says, *Confront them with annihilation, and they will then survive; plunge them into a deadly situation, and they will then live. When people fall into danger, they are then able to strive for victory* . . . but he never met any Shoshone."

"Oh, go eat a buffalo liver, you miserable creature."

Chu replied, without turning: "Seeing there are fewer shaggy cows roaming these hills now even than Shoshone, that would be difficult. So, are you ready at last to assist me, or do you need yet more time to complain, like a woman?"

The Shoshone snorted, sounding somewhat like a buffalo himself. "*Aiweape-ha*," he said, to the air. "Crazy person, wandering free. You'd think you had no family to look after you . . . oh, *wait*."

Chu flipped water at him, without looking, which the Shoshone avoided effortlessly. The droplets fell on the pool's dusty rim, smoking slightly, before resolving themselves like mercury, then sliding sideways to rejoin the rest.

"Think them dames'll stop squabblin' anytime soon?" Fennig inquired, watching the scene.

Rook sighed. "Probably not, without I tell 'em to."

"Well, we I on a schedule, or so Herself says. Interesting, though, how she wants to tag along just now, when she never did before. . . ."

"Who of us knows her mind, really? And don't say me, 'cause flattering though that might've once rung, these days you'd be wrong."

Now it was Fennig's turn to sigh, casting a glance behind him, to where his three women sat arm in arm, laughing, their legs hung a-dangle over the abyss. "Morts is all somewhat mysterious by nature, Rev," he observed, as though Rook hadn't already noticed, "no matter who, or how big the size'a their hex-bag. Believe you me, I should know."

"'Morts'?" Rook repeated, cocking a brow.

"Ladies, I mean. Females. Them as ain't men—or she-hes, neither."

Nodding, Rook looked down, recalling when he and Chess had stood atop that ridge outside Bewelcome, surveying it like Lucifer and Jesus with all the kingdoms of the earth laid out before 'em. It'd been a spectacularly deadish place back then, with points north and west a veritable painted desert of wild green shale and furze, points south and east a barren scree studded with long-dead sea creatures and shadowed by arroyos dried near to crumbling; what little Sheriff Love's bunch had managed to wrest from the earth had come up small and mean, fed by rigid faith, paid for in the sort of blood that didn't reap crops worth speaking of. Not much magic to be found, one way or the other.

Now the same area was soaked in it, and the landscape lay utterly transformed.

Two months ago, as Pinkerton's forces began trickling onto the surrounding plains, Ixchel had stood atop Her temple and spoken to the earth, which answered by thrusting great walls of granite and sandstone up 'round the city in a perfect circle. Those dwellers caught outside, their houses not within the walls' arc, had scrambled fiercely to get back in—and strangely enough, not all had succeeded, exploding when they touched the wall-wards. She'd called that cull a Flowery War, its lost citizens martyrs to their cause . . . but what she'd really been after was the blood they left behind: tribute, tithe, tool. A red ring which was then met and matched by just as many "volunteer" lottery sacrifices on the Temple's top, Machine-grist sent flowing down to sink into the soil, causing a forest of *ceiba* trees to blossom as a second defensive ring, tight enough that there was barely a handsbreadth left between brick and bark.

The *ceibas'* close-set branches had leaves sharp as obsidian, sap smoking and venomous, and whenever anyone tried to slip between they were met with swift-strangling vines that snaked out to lasso unwary scouts, dragging them off in pieces. The City folk on the wall had cheered to watch Pinkerton's men die, until one had overbalanced and fallen; his magic was enough to break his plunge safely upon the ground, but not enough to save *him* from the trees, either.

Maybe a mile beyond the forest, meanwhile, a wide swath of

fires and lanterns eventually began to appear as the sky darkened, sketching the outlines of hundreds of tents and a few new-raised buildings, all raw plank and whitewashed adobe: Camp Pink, meeting place for Agency and Army alike, with old Doc Asbury running interference between—yes, and that traitor Ed Morrow too, if rumour spoke fact.

Ed hadn't been anything but a toy tossed between competing currents, though, if Rook forced himself to be charitable; a good man torn between bad people, put in untenable situations mostly by the Rev's own hand, and acting as he saw fit. Hell, Rook couldn't even really resent him having shared Chess's bed, not when he'd sent him there himself—for if he did, he'd soon be forced to scour the whole West for other men he'd be similarly constrained to waste his precious time killing.

Doesn't matter, anyhow, a thin voice whispered, nastily, at his inner ear. *All that with you and Chess, the epic tryst? Gone, never to return. One thing alone he ever asked of you, and you, you son of a bitch, went on ahead and left him.*

He won't forgive you now, no matter what. Not if you tore your own damn heart out and gave it to him, still beating, to plug up the wound where his used to be.

"Nor should he," the Rev said out loud, to no one but himself.

"What was that, Rev?" asked Fennig, from behind him.

"Nothing, Henry."

Rook turned back, encouraged to see Chu and the Shoshone engaged over their work once more. The yarrow stalk bunch discarded, both mages wove their fingers in opposing cat's cradle patterns across the pool, rolling energy back and forth like they were carding wool. Soon enough, its surface began to dance and dimple, slopping up 'til it sprouted a funnel the size of a wine-ready goblet, above which a storm-cloud bloomed—bruise-dark, small but intense, rotating at a slow tilt. And *growing.*

"You must wait for it to swell further, before letting it slip," Chu ordered. "Not too soon! Let it reach the size of a small dog, or a large child."

"Who d'you think you're talking to, railroad man? I was making rain before you ever knew this place existed."

"Making *water*, perhaps. But a storm, large enough to destroy whole towns—this is different."

"You don't stop flapping your tongue sometime, it'll split in two and fall off. And wouldn't *that* just be a shame."

A bit further down, Fennig's three Missuses watched the hex-whores from the Blister shaking sand, salt and rice in a great glass bottle, patiently raising dust devils into tornados, then knitting the results together to release them, sending twister after twister sidewinder-shuddering 'cross the plains toward Camp Pink. The principle was basically the same, for all Chu and the Shoshone seemed to think they had an all-male lock on something twice as fierce.

"Won't be long now, looks like," Rook told Fennig, who nodded, then pulled his glasses down his nose, scanning the courtyard behind them. Ixchel was emerging from her seclusion, shadow-wrapped 'cept for where the largest of her insects perched here and there on her like living jewels, their wings throwing off minor rainbows. All around, a veritable tide of self-flagellating Mexicans eddied, lashing themselves with thorn-studded dried gut whips; in her wake, Marizol—already bled a shade or two lighter—padded glumly along like the world's least happy bridesmaid, holding her mistress's train up out of the dust.

"Explain it me again," Fennig said, to Rook, his sharp eyes never stirring from that dread form. "How she got herself out of Hell, exactly."

"Cannibalism, of a type. Theophagy. She ate other gods, like hexes eat hexes."

"Yeah, that's what I thought. And that'd be why she has a plug in her back, right *there*, 'tween the shoulder blades—a hole she can't fill no-how and with nothin', I'll venture. 'Cause takin' a bite out of them took a bite out of *her*."

"I don't follow."

"Don't you? Where do any of us get our power *from*, Reverend?"

Rook considered that question a while, crossbreeding mythology and metaphor with observed fact. From what-all he'd seen, there seemed to be a strain of magic all hexes could tap, perhaps the same universal flow drove Songbird's *ch'i* or required Grandma's Balance—inexhaustible, hard-won and hard-wearing. Yet this was cut with two other streams, one bolstered by hex-vampirization, one pure dream-stuff, bastard child of fantasy and will. A sort of poetry made flesh, living or dying on the hex's own confidence in the innate truth of whatever they could conceive of.

"I've seen her gulp witch and wizard alike down like an after-dinner shot," Rook said. "So've you—remember? Looks aside, she don't seem to be hurting much, in that direction."

Fennig clicked his tongue. "So why don't she fix herself up, at least, or skip bodies into that girl of hers, 'fore bad gets worse? Ain't natural for any female to let her appearance slip so, even if she does derive some extra mojo from seemin' an object of fear."

"Needs Marizol to love her, apparently, or the trick won't take. That takes time."

"Hmmm. And she can't push *that* part along any faster, either? All it takes is a word and a drop of blood, her hair and yours tied up in a knot—a damn honey-cake baked with her name on top. Didn't they cast no charms in old Mexico?"

Rook simply shrugged, thinking: *But it's not her hair, just like it's not really her body. And anyhow, as we none of us should forget—she's different.*

"Wouldn't bet on her forbearance being a sign of weakness, myself," he warned.

"You told me to look—I'm tellin' you what I see when I do, is all. She has limitations. And that's more'n we knew, even if we don't know what, or why. Or what best to do with it, now we do know."

Rook felt those black doll-eyes shift his way, and hissed through his teeth, projecting: *Shut it, Henry.* Felt her alien intelligence stroke his brain almost affectionately at the same time, before moving on—too busy, or bored, to bother probing deeper.

"She knows everything," he said, at last. "Told me as much. So I don't see the point of plotting, let alone anything else."

Fennig's spectacles were already back in place, rendering gaze and expression equally opaque. "Wants you t'think she does, more like—got her consuming interests, just like the rest of us. And contrary to popular belief, she *can't* be everywhere at once, neither. I've checked."

"Henry—"

"I'm a big boy, Rev. I slip up, I'll gladly pay the price; g'hals can look after 'emselves, if they have to." A thin grin. "Not that I wouldn't miss their sweet company, from across the river. Still, once we get this War put to bed, we can . . ."

. . . rebuild, branch out, found schools and hospitals, do all the things necessary to make this means to an end permanent. That's what Fennig wanted, like most've the rest—this haphazard experiment was a paradise to them, or close as they thought themselves ever like to see. Whereas Rook, like Ixchel, saw the edges blurring as New Aztectlan became a portal from one future to another, and knew what was coming would wipe out everything in its path regardless . . . that in the end, the Hex City crowd could either join it, get out of its way or be borne away, accordingly.

Can't help them with that, though. I'm all hers, bought and paid for. Can't help anybody, with anything.

Chu and the Shoshone, having gotten the storm where they wanted it, had spun it free and let it expand, eating what was left of the twilit sky. Now Fennig's ladies stood with arms still linked, thrilling to the thunder's rumble as the first intimations of lightning swirled around them; Clo was already starting to drift up a tad in sympathetic response, her swollen belly lit from within, the other two just managing to keep her anchored.

Ixchel, meanwhile, was somehow already halfway out atop the cloud itself, which parted to let her pass. Her train and cloak formed a second funnel, sucking up a dose of darkness that spawned yet another roiling energy ball between her own hands, charge concentrated enough to lift the bulk of her hair by sheer galvanization.

With a tiny kick, she swam upward still, turning toward the

east, where a dry riverbed snaked through two miles of canyons. And even without her mind touching his—not so's he could notice, anyhow—Rook nevertheless thought he began to see what she might have in mind.

Time to go. To lay her vengeance down on Bewelcome—could've been anywhere, Rook supposed, but he could see why that place in particular held a certain charge, seeing how it was the last place she and that "brother" of hers had thrown down—and watch what rose to greet it, then crush that thing in turn with all the force of a dead pantheon, a living yet absent God.

At his elbow, Fennig still watched Rook from behind those lenses, twisting his cane—like he hoped for some sort of elaboration, but understood if none was forthcoming.

So Rook made himself look up, and tell him, lightly enough: "Best not to rely on me too much, maybe, when all's said and done; not with your women on the line, and your child likewise. As the Lady's own property, I'm hardly trustworthy."

This time, the dapper New York gangster didn't even bother to nod. Just replied, equally nonchalant, "Oh, no more'n any of us, Rev, I s'pose. But more so than Herself, by far."

Rook inclined his head, reaching to rake up an appropriate verse from deep inside: *Job* 27:21, *The east wind carrieth him away and he departeth*, perhaps. Or *Psalms*, 83:15—*So persecute them with thy tempest, and make them afraid with thy storm*. Either would do.

Yet hearing in his head simultaneous, as mocking echo, a few more of those Celestial war-wisdom adages Honourable Chu liked to quote: *All war is deception; to win one hundred victories in one hundred battles is not the acme of skill—to subdue the enemy without fighting, that is the acme of skill; if ignorant of your enemy and yourself, you are certain to be in peril.*

"Let's to it, then," the Rev said. And stepped off the ramparts with Fennig and the Missuses trailing behind like a kite's tail, blown straight into the storm's beating heart.

CHAPTER SIX

THE TOWN HALL'S ROOF came off like kindling, as if the storm'd turned one big mouth, opened wide, and took itself a bite. Rook came drifting down inside what was left with the rain still pelting 'round him and Fennig a mere half-step behind, bringing the Word along as well, in silver-black clumps: *Isaiah* 13, 6 to 9:

> HOWL YE; FOR THE DAY OF THE LORD IS AT HAND; IT SHALL COME AS A DESTRUCTION FROM THE ALMIGHTY. THEREFORE SHALL ALL HANDS BE FAINT, AND EVERY MAN'S HEART SHALL MELT:
> AND THEY SHALL BE AFRAID: PANGS AND SORROWS SHALL TAKE HOLD OF THEM; THEY SHALL BE IN PAIN AS A WOMAN THAT TRAVAILETH: THEY SHALL BE AMAZED ONE AT ANOTHER; THEIR FACES SHALL BE AS FLAMES.
> BEHOLD, THE DAY OF THE LORD COMETH, CRUEL BOTH WITH WRATH AND FIERCE ANGER, TO LAY THE LAND DESOLATE: AND HE SHALL DESTROY THE SINNERS THEREOF OUT OF IT.

The place was gutted, chairs and pews flung every which way, smashed to sodden flinders. A stage took up the back half, uneven now, as though it'd been stamped on—and that was where he found what was left of the elders' council: some fat man with a broken leg, sprawled with a Manifold clutched to his chest like he thought it could ward off heart attack (Mayor Langobard, probably), plus a roster of other notables, similarly stricken—including a dapper fool Rook could only assume, with a twinge of nasty amusement, must be the town's new preacher: no Mesach Love, that was for sure. For though this man's lips moved feverishly, Rook could barely sense enough faith in him to light a lucifer, let alone ward off evil.

In the corner crouched Doc Asbury, managing admirably to not quite cower; might be the last few months had finally inured him to the shock of seeing his theories turned fact. While nearby, half-hid behind a tangle of fallen furniture, a man with similar taste in fashion as Fennig crouched with tablet out and pencil busy, scribbling frantically, as though he aimed to preserve all he saw for posterity's sake.

But even as Rook took note of them all, they paled to invisibility in the face of his true target, who crouched above Langobard with one hand laid soothingly on his sweaty brow, clutching her baby close with the other: Sophronia Love, the Sheriff's woman, moral heart of Bewelcome's resistance. The figurehead all the rest rallied behind.

For a year in the salt, she looked uncommon good, even dressed in black with her hair plastered dark by the downpour's vigour. As did that fussing boy of hers, whose healthy lungs sent up counterpoint music, loud enough to be heard over the storm itself.

Strike her down, this town dies with her, lit and fig. Strike her down, and victory follows.

Easier said than done, though, he suspected. Since *this* one's faith was so pure it all but sparkled, even under these circumstances.

"Ma'am," he addressed her. "As you know, I knew the Sheriff briefly, in both his guises. Are you sure he'd really want you to risk your life, let alone his only son's, by staying here?"

She met his eyes straight on, without fear. "In the town my husband founded? Where else would I go, Mister Rook?"

"Well . . . many places. There's a seat left open amongst *us*, for example, for every outcast." And here he indicated Berta, Clo and Eulie, just settling down behind him. "My intelligencers inform me you're scorned, accorded not even half the respect you merit—but we've more women than men in *our* councils, Missus Love; hell, we're *ruled* by a Lady, and a most powerful one. We'd grant you authority fitting your mettle."

"You're ruled by a devil in woman's shape, whose laws designate any without witchery in your city as no better than slaves . . . though even those *with* witchery seem like as not to wind up on her altar, sooner or later." Switching her uncompromising glare to Fennig and the girls, she continued: "Those in Satan's service meet only one end, however long it takes: They're eaten by their master, body *and* soul. Are you sure you're all far too useful ever to be made a meal of?"

Clo's eyes flashed. "Ye little limb!"

Berta and Eulie, meanwhile, had turned their mutual attention on Catlin, who was scuttling backward with hands flung up, calling (predictably enough) on *Leviticus*, 20:27. Eulie gave a girlish laugh. "Cute, ain't he, sissy? Like somethin' off a band-box!"

"A real wedding cake swell, all right—doll-faced little fake priest, playing at toy soldiers. But we've no time for diversions, do we?"

"Just as well . . . for him."

Sophy blinked at Clo, just noticing her condition. "God Almighty in Heaven, you foolish girl, did you actually bring yourself out on a mission of war while *great with child?*" The surprised indignation in her voice was so sharp that Clo actually flushed, putting one hand over her bulging stomach as if to guard it, even as her temper touched up the higher; her hair lifted, lighting from inside, with greenish St. Elmo's fire.

"And what's that there in your *own* arms, woman?" she snapped back. "Fine place for a mite like him, on the very line of battle!"

"The Lord is my buckler, sorceress, just as He was for Mesach—Gabriel's, as well."

"Oh yes? An' it's *my* man can see where best t'make that buckler crumple, he only cares to look for it; can't ye, Hank Fennig? Well?"

But Fennig, after staring Missus Love up and down, just shook his head. "Can't see a thing, not where she's concerned—there's somethin' in the way. Though as to whether it's divine in origin . . ."

"It is."

". . . she's covered. Looks like the ball's back in your court, Reverend."

Sophy nodded. "If your business *is* with me in primary, then let be done, and go. You and yours are not welcome here."

"Unwelcome, in the very town of Bewelcome itself? Some might call that a hypocrisy, ma'am." Folding his arms, Rook cocked his head to one side, "Tell me, though, for I'm curious . . . do your Mayor and your new Reverend—hell, anybody in this town, save those keeping silent out of loyalty—happen to know how you and the Sheriff weren't actually *married* yet, as such, the first time somebody killed him?"

Sophy Love coloured, furiously, and though Langobard—who'd finally managed to sit up—seemed too flummoxed to grasp anything of what he'd just heard, the little band-box preacher whipped 'round to shoot her an absurd glare, so offended it made Rook want to laugh.

Face bright red but voice icy calm, the Widow wrapped her child—who seemed to register her agitation, his sobs skipping an upward key—yet closer, and replied: "We were bound in God's eyes, as you well know, having seen inside of Mesach's head. But perhaps such distinctions are lost on the faithless."

"Without doubt. But then again, God don't really get a vote, come election time—you either, I'm guessin'. So . . ."

From behind Rook, by that heap of splinters where the town hall's threshold had once lain, a third voice intruded. "Whatever you're 'bout to say next, Rev, I'm fairly sure Missus Love don't want to hear it. And that's why I'd step away from her, if I was you."

It was a deep voice gone somewhat flat with all too rational fear, yet steady as any soldier's under fire, and Rook smiled to hear it.

"Hello, Ed," he said, turning to greet his former employee, who looked about the same, if wetter. Beard no longer neat-trimmed, his muttonchops bristled, almost reaching his duster's collar; rain sprayed from shoulders and hat alike, while Rook and the others stayed bone dry, safe within their intersecting power-bubbles.

"Heard you got reinstated," Rook said. "Pinkerton see fit to forgive you your many sins?"

"Probationally."

"Ah, yes. That do sound like the Law, don't it? For they sometimes feign to forgive—but *never* forget." Eyes homing in on the vague flash of grey barrel-metal, then, he asked, "Ain't a gun you got there, though, is it? I only ask out of concern for your health, which prompts me to warn you how those don't work too well, on me. Or could that be something the Professor over there dreamed up?"

"It might."

"You don't say! Tested it out, as yet?"

Morrow swallowed, sights kept admirably steady on Rook's midsection. "Nope. But I'm favouring trial by fire, right about now."

"Enough," Sophy Love chose that same moment to interject, drawing herself up. "God alone knows my fate, *Reverend*. If this be my day and hour, then it will be His decision—not yours. And while you may have the power, you will *never* have right on your side, for that too is His to apportion."

"Little lady, what makes you think there *is* any right?"

"If you truly believe that, sir, then strike me down this moment and do not hesitate; I fear no judgement. You?"

Fennig's brows raised. "Stargazer's got sand, ain't she?" he muttered to Rook, who merely shrugged; the quality of Missus Love's courage had never been in question, at least for himself. Still, while her willingness to throw her own life away might have no limit, did that willingness extend equally to others' lives? *Like, for example*—

"*Your* day and hour, maybe," Clo Killeen put in, unexpectedly completing the thought. "For a Jaysis-jabberer like yerself, I'm sure that's of no moment. That *boy* of yours, though—"

—young Master Gabriel—

"—how would he feel about bein' bargained away with only Heaven's promise as a get-out, if he was old enough to know better?" As Sophy's face whitened: "Don't tell me you haven't thought on it, woman."

"That's none of your concern." But Sophy's free hand had clenched to a fist, and she turned her body in blind reflex, shielding Gabe as best she could. Clo grinned, as lightning flashed above with the rolling boom of field cannon.

"All right, then, since logic doesn't seem to appeal . . ." Rook raised his voice, through the thunder. "Look out there, Missus Love! See what's comin', and ask yourself if you wouldn't rather remove you *and* Gabe from its path."

He flung out one long, black-clad arm. All heads swerved together, as though magnetized. And there on the horizon, just where the canyons gave out onto what had once been flood plain, Rook watched the clouds and rain alike twitch apart, one huge, liquid curtain. To reveal—

—Ixchel, Lady of Traps and Snares, the Goddess of the Rope, suspended there between sky and earth like Juno enchained. Looking genuinely eerie in the storm's shifting light, an icon shadowed with tarnish like gangrene, lambent skin slightly fallen in over the moon-sharp points of her black-spiralled cheekbones, her chin, the sunken orbits of her eyes. Somehow visible in clear detail to them all, despite rain and distance; as angels and saints were said to be, in legends. Yet not even the reaping angel of Egypt's firstborn could seem so dark as this.

The new preacher muffled a tiny squawking sound; Asbury's jaw dropped and Langobard gaped. Sophy's face slackened in the first thing resembling true fear Rook had ever seen from her. In her arms, Gabriel screamed on and on. Even Rook's hexmates were silent—Fennig audibly swallowed, and Clo crossed herself in what must be sheer childhood habit, the gesture giving Rook a sudden pang. Only Morrow did not turn, though he tightened his eyes near to slits, as if fighting the pull with everything he had.

"Did you really think," Rook asked Sophy, "if I decided this job was big enough to come in on myself, that she wouldn't come in on it with me?"

"As I'd heard, was *you* she once trusted, to do her dirty work."

"Oh, that's still true, in the main. But actually, it was her idea to pull Bewelcome back down, in the first place—let many waters quench Love, in literal as in figurative, and make a clean sweep. And in this, as in all things, we are her creatures."

"That's nothing to boast on, Reverend."

"Ma'am, I don't disagree." Rook sighed, suddenly sick of this game. "You and I know that even such a deluge as this won't end this town completely, not so long as its people have you to look to, for inspiration to rebuild—so I'll make no more false offers concerning *your* life." He willed more power into his shields until they blazed, looking to fend off whatever attack Morrow might mount in return. "Instead—surrender, let us end you clean here. I'll guarantee young Gabriel grows up safe and sound. Swear it on my power itself, if you wish it—and there's more happens when a hex breaks an oath than you know." He extended his hands to either side; Fennig took one, Clo the other, their force-bubbles bleeding together into a single crackling halo, hissing with rain-steam. Behind Clo, Berta and Eulie put their hands on her shoulders, adding their strength to the moil.

On the horizon, the raindrops around Ixchel turned to swarming dragonflies, their buzz rising up in a deadly drone even through the thunder; light rippled beneath her, horizon turning fluid. And below that, a rumbling, more felt than heard.

Rook held Sophy's gaze with his own. "Missus Love. Please."

If she'd reacted differently, Rook was to think later—turned to rage, broke in pleading for Gabriel's life, or tried at the last to bargain or persuade—he might've acted faster. But Sophronia Love only cuddled her screaming baby close, stroking Gabriel's head. Face calm with a serenity he had never known, she looked up over his head, dismissing Rook entirely.

"The Lord is my shepherd," she began, quietly, yet bell-clear. "I shall not want. He maketh me to lie down in green pastures: He leadeth me—"

"Stop it!" It was Clo shouting, angrier than Rook had ever heard her; startled, he felt the sudden nauseous *shift* of power through his gut as her fury wrenched control of the conjoined hexation away. "Shut your hole, ye Protestant hoor! *Shut* it!"

"—beside the still waters. He restoreth my soul: He leadeth me in the path of righteousness for His name's sake—"

Above the prayer, Clo screamed on. "I'll have your tongue out by the roots, yeh rotten mab!" The power spit and flared, sliding out of Rook's grip entirely, as Fennig, Berta and Eulie all shouted unheard pleas. "I'll wear your guts for garters! *Stop that!*"

"—though I walk in the valley of the shadow of death, I will fear no evil, for Thou art with me; Thy rod and they staff, they comfort me—"

Clo drew back her hand, then flung everything all five hexes had gathered at Sophy Love in a single roaring blast—but in the instant before it struck, light burst outward from Sophy's arms, enveloped her and vanished into nothing, taking her with it. The fire blew through the empty stage, sending Langobard sprawling and the preacher diving to either side, leaving only a broken pile of smoking planks in its wake—but nothing of either mother or child. Clo's scream took on a new note of cheated indignation.

Rook had enough time to think, *I . . . didn't do that!* before three thunderous cracks of shotgun shells shattered the Irish gal's howling. Lulled by the same automatic disdain for gunfire they'd all learned long since, he turned to slap Morrow down, just a hair too slow—and saw Fennig twist away, narrowly avoiding death as his specs blew off his face in a burst of wire and smoked-glass shards. A second shot whined past Rook's ear like a hornet. He felt the third shot before he heard it, first punching straight through his own shields, then in a searing slice across his shoulder.

A skirling shriek cut through his brain: distant Ixchel, sharing his pain through their bond, blind with the hot hate Rook himself was too stunned to feel. Instead, he flung the crudest hex possible in Morrow's direction, sending chairs and benches scattering, but Ed hurled himself backward, out into the rain and the dark. A buzzing surge of amazed, shocked delight caught from *Asbury*, of all people, washed over Rook at the same moment, resolving spark-fast to some sort of psychic memory echo, perhaps from Morrow's experiences in Tampico.

As any wire of iron or steel grounds the galvanic energies of lightning, or similar phenomena, so a certain alloy of silver, iron, and sodium in its metallic form serves to ground magical energies where they manifest, conducting them away to discharge harmlessly. . . .

Flipping, magic-lantern-like, to another image: Asbury on the war-bought train depot platform earlier that day, handing Morrow a small box of gleaming shells. *These are experimental, Agent, too expensive as yet for mass production. But they should pierce any conjured barrier, though the side effects of disrupting particularly powerful castings may be somewhat . . . unpredictable. . . .*

Meanwhile, he saw that Ixchel had already let loose the flood, sending waters pouring down the valley and racing across the plains. Rook heard screams rise up from the townsfolk outside, frozen where they stood while doom came thundering down upon them, and felt Ixchel's rage like his own, inhumanly ancient, monstrously deep.

Remove yourself, little kings and queens, for this city ends now— now that they have dared to thwart My wishes, to strike at My high priest.

Not a moment's concern in that sending, though—no care for him, for Fennig or the girls, for how close they had all come to death. As Berta went to support Hank while Eulie staggered under Clo's weight, pulling her back from the stage, Ixchel stayed safe inside her vortex, not reaching out even a tendril to pluck them from harm's way. Simply trusting they would save themselves, or deserve their own deaths.

Join me in the heavens, therefore, to watch our vengeance.

Rook fought down the pain with a groan and flung out his power to seize all the others at once, hauling them up into the sky: ten yards, twenty, thirty. High over Bewelcome's rebuilt steeple, the five hexes clung to one another, watching the massive torrent boil and roar toward the town, and then splash *upward*, slamming into a barrier that ripped out of the earth on all sides in a single thick wall of hot-pulsing life like a vast bank of flayed muscle encircling Bewelcome, guarding it. More great slabs of the stuff—*the Red*

Weed, Rook realized—slapped upward like giants' hands, sending massive gouts of water into the sky to arc *over* the town, spraying wide and harmlessly. And in the town square beneath, another crack of lightning revealed a figure Rook knew had not stood there a scant second before, a figure he could barely see and yet knew in an instant, without needing to: small, slim, hair fire-touched in the hissing light as it looked up, grinning.

Chess—

"REV, *LOOK OUT!*"

Fennig's yell came too late—a huge surge of water had already struck the group, knocked them all spinning sideways, snapped apart. Rook saw poor Clo slam heavy into the church's steeple, breaking bones and wooden beams alike, even as instinct told him to break his fall by grabbing at the air itself. He hit the town square's mud in a roll, breath knocked from him with a thud, and lay still a moment, fighting for his wind. Then rolled over with a grunt of effort to find Fennig kneeling by him, face oddly young and naked without his specs.

"Henry! You harmed?" At Fennig's headshake: "Then *what in God's name happened?* Was it *you* smote the Widow, before Clodagh could?"

"Not me and none of us, 'cause wherever she's gone, she ain't been harmed—I'd'a seen, she was!" Grabbing Rook's shoulders, the younger man leaned in close: "That boy of hers, though—I saw him *flash* as it happened, like bottle lightning."

"Meaning?"

"He's a hex."

Jesus! That young? Could it even happen? Well, Clo's belly shot out sparks whenever *she* got going. . . .

But here solid, squelching footsteps broke Rook's daze as Morrow strode to them, shotgun levelled. Certain now of its efficacy, his eyes were steel-hard. "Rev, Mister Fennig—stand down, if you please."

Rook looked round. From the wrecked main hall, the young minister—Catlin, his name was, Rook now recalled hearing—and Asbury had emerged with Langobard balanced between 'em, that

New York fop with his notepad right behind, still scribbling. Catlin had purloined the mayor's Manifold, which was chattering in his hand, frenzied by the hexation hanging thick in the air. Around them, blue-coated soldiers had materialized, all of them Negroes; their guns were levelled too, though Rook felt confident only Morrow bore a weapon of any import. One of the soldiers might've been that same young man he'd seen fleeing at Morrow's side, just before they'd ripped the hall's roof off. Beside him, a taller officer wore the epaulettes and stripes of a Union captain: *Washford*, Rook remembered from the intelligencers, *Isaiah Washford*.

The young soldier whistled, admiring Morrow's work. "Like to get me one of *those* shells, sir, you got any spares goin' beggin'."

"You'll have to talk to Doc Asbury 'bout that, Private Carver," said Morrow.

Gathering what dignity he could, Rook slowly regained his feet. "Gentlemen," he said, in his deepest voice, "the Professor's devices notwithstanding, you still cannot hope to resist my Ladyship's power. . . ."

But his sonorous declamation trailed off as he looked skyward, to see—nothing. Only the rain and the black night sky.

Fennig, following his look, clenched his jaw. Blue light blazed in his eyes.

"Bitch up and left us," he observed, unnecessarily.

On the meeting hall's wrecked front steps, Catlin suddenly began to laugh, hysterically. "See!" he cried. "The Devil abandons his servants, at the first good show of righteousness! I told you all we had to do was be strong in our faith, and—"

Even Asbury looked disgusted. But the speed and fury of Fennig's reaction caught everyone flat-footed; he turned with a glare, sending that same blue glow arcing straight at the idiot. Reflexively, Catlin flung "his" Manifold up; the light smacked into it and locked fast, discharging harmlessly into its whirring gearwork.

Agape, Catlin burst out into the same maniacal racket. "For behold, my God is a righteous God!" he choked, as Fennig sent ever more power at him, the Manifold's buzz rising higher while Morrow,

Washford, Carver stared on, mesmerized. "I shall fear no evil, not while I walk in His sight—"

"Mister Catlin!" Asbury shouted. "Reverend, sir, you haven't the training to—you don't, you can't—" Abruptly shoving Langobard at the notepad scribbler, he didn't wait to watch them hit mud before flinging himself backward, with a yell: "*Everyone, take cover—!*"

At which point the Manifold, overloaded, exploded in Catlin's hand, blowing most of it off. He sat down hard, blood gouting from his left wrist's wreckage.

With one forceful sweep, Rook smacked Morrow backward into the mud, sending the gun flying; two more tumbled most of the soldiers like ninepins. He pulled Fennig back, sprinting toward the steeple base, where Berta and Eulie were hauling Clo up. All three were sodden and filthy; Clo hung with her legs spread wide, and Rook's heart clenched to see a dark stain spilling inexorably between them. Face bone white to the lips, her huge stomach glowed, swelling and pulsing, a swallowed star.

Eulie clung to her, weeping. "Sissy, sissy—oh, God! Don't give up, now. . . ."

"I don't feel well," Clo replied, voice small and bewildered. "Is it . . . s'posed t'be like this?"

Rook's throat clogged up. *Damn Ixchel*, he thought, not caring if he was heard. *Damn all gods and monsters. Like us. Like me.*

Then, wounded shoulder burning, he glanced around, wondering if any of the soldiers had regained their feet, or Morrow his hex-killer gun . . . and locked eyes straight on with the figure standing in the mud not ten feet from them, clad all in purple shreds and lightning.

This close, in the awful light from Clo's stricken, labouring womb, the blue tint to his skin glowed like alchemist's venom; Weed twined up and down each limb, a mesh of skull-fragment armour hung with old ivory shards, red flowers like jewels swivelling to hiss at Rook's approach. And when Rook took a single, truncated step more in his direction he smiled, revealing teeth like obsidian flakes chipped triangular, the hungry malice of it *so close* to what Chess's smile had once been that Rook felt his groin clench and his pulse leap. Yet the eyes, the absinthe green eyes, were . . .

No. Not him, at all.

And— whose fault is that, exactly?

Rook's arousal died. Behind those empty eyes, something inexpressibly weary pressed its unnatural weight upon the earth.

I raise a mirror to you, priest-king, his Enemy said, softly. *Do you see yourself?*

To which Rook only shuddered, bursting head-to-toe with cold, and grabbed for Fennig's hand to connect them all again. Ripped the air open headlong, bridging the miles back to Hex City in a single spasm of shared pain.

Thinking, at the same time: *Oh Chess, oh darlin'. What the hell have I done?*

No answer seemed forthcoming, if there even was one.

MORROW TRUDGED STIFFLY toward the Chess-thing, shivering himself as it turned to fix him with that horrifying, black-glass grin. Barely aware of Asbury stumbling up behind him, he bowed his head, and rasped: "Thank you."

It chuckled. "So polite. This, I hope, puts paid to any notions you may have that I am allied in any way with Reverend Rook, or the Lady Ixchel? For as I have said, many times before: I am their Enemy."

"Ours, too," said Morrow, through dry lips.

"You remember, soldier! Yes, yours too. Everyone's. Which is why I will not tell you where your Missus Love has gone." Then, as cheerful-flirty as Chess himself might, it winked at him—while to Asbury, it simply gave a cool: "A clever working, Professor. Very . . . interesting."

And sank back down through the ground, leaving nothing behind but lightning twisting itself dark in the mud, a wet mess of fuses.

Asbury stared at the spot, blinking. "Why—would he *do* that?" he asked, presently.

"Why's it do any damn thing?" Morrow sighed. "'Cause it's what we wouldn't expect."

He trudged to what was left of the church steps and sat down, too tired to stand another minute. Couldn't hear Catlin's screams anymore; whether that meant he'd died or been helped, Morrow couldn't tell, and didn't much care.

Asbury followed, looking dubious. "You know him best of all of us, I suppose, Mister Morrow."

"Chess, maybe. But like I said . . . that ain't him."

He broke open his shotgun, ejected the empty shell casings and began to wipe the mud from the stock and barrel. And froze, Asbury along with him, as a soft but undeniable voice echoed up through both their skulls:

Are you so sure of that, **conquistador?**

CHAPTER SEVEN

DOWN UNDER THE BLACK water of Mictlan-Xibalba, sinking deep and deeper, to truly unreckonable fathoms. That was where Yancey glimpsed Chess Pargeter, yet once more: sitting next to a woman she could only assume was his mother, red-haired as himself but wasted from the inside out, who either squinted up at Yancey sourly or gave an occasional broke-toothed sneer of secret knowledge, like she was reckoning odds. While the little pistoleer, on the other hand, simply looked right through her, when his gaze chanced to fall Yancey's way at all—then sighed, took a shot of not-whiskey from his phantom glass and turned to stare glumly out the window once more, watching Seven Dials' ghosts pass by.

Made no difference at all how Yancey called and yelled at him, not even if she broke down and begged outright; Chess might hug himself a little, like he'd felt a draft, or a goose walking over the grave he'd never yet lain in. And then Yancey would feel Songbird and Grandma reel her back up by the silver cord she'd come down on, vaulting levels 'til she thought her chest would crack and her eardrums burst. 'Til she emerged at last from the latest inconclusive session atop Old Woman Butte, sweat-drenched and head banging, only to look up and see the hexes scowling down on either side of her again—equally annoyed (in their very different ways) by her consistent failure to make Chess even register her presence, let alone communicate with him directly.

Crossed legs all pins and needles, Yancey unfolded herself with a grunt of pain, fighting the urge to vomit. The fire had long since died to ashes, leaving them only shapes and sketchy gleams in the starlight.

"'Dead-speaker,'" Songbird spit out, scornful. "How *polite* you are! Inefficient, as well; ghosts need a heavier hand, a master's voice. When you travel through the Ten Thousand Hells you must threaten, not wheedle."

"Don't notice *you* stepping in for a turn," Yancey replied, face gone hot.

"That is because she cannot," Grandma said, shaking her ponderous head and levering herself up as well, every part of her creaking, as though that reliquary she'd made for herself was 'bout to bust apart. "Or me either, much as we may risk ourselves to protect *you* on these fishing trips. Dead-speaking is not the white one's gift, while I—a ghost myself—am just one more shade to those Below, indistinguishable. Thus it falls to you . . . and you do not deliver."

Songbird nodded. "Yet you claim to be his friend; that was supposed to help, was it not? Perhaps you do not mean so very much to him, after all."

All at once, for some reason, this seemed to be the proverbial back-breaking straw—Yancey found herself rounding on her, using whatever inch-and-a-half of height difference there was between them to try making the younger girl feel small. "Me or any other woman, is that what you mean? Well, you can stop talking like you *know* him, Little Miss Hex-no-more, just 'cause the two of you were shat out on different sides of the same sewer!" As Songbird hissed like a scorpion, a fizzing pyramid of sparks rising from her left palm: "Yeah, and *now* you've got juice enough to slap at me, don't you? Better go on ahead, then, 'fore it all goes trickling out the other end!"

"*Ai-yaaah*, daughter of dogs! I will lay you out and fill your mouth with corpse-vomit for such insolence, see if I do not—"

"*Quiet!*" Grandma roared, her shadow suddenly large enough to chill them both. "You disappoint equally, and for far too long! Are we fools, to waste time on such trifles?" At her shout, Yiska came running, only to halt in dismay near the dead fire, uncertain how best to interfere. "Truly, if my dreams had not told me we *must* bring the red boy back up in order to have even a hope at victory over the Lady of Traps and Snares, I would gladly knock your heads together myself 'til they cracked!"

For one half-instant only, Yancey felt like snarling back: *If you're dead, and I'm the dead-speaker, seems I don't have to let you do* nothing *I don't like!* But the words rang in her head like something Chess Pargeter would've never hesitated to throw out, and that alone pulled her up, a sharp jerk of the rein. Face still burning, she clenched her teeth, breathed deep and forced the words of an apology into order, but never got them out.

Screeching something in Chinee, so fast and guttural even Yancey's talents couldn't translate it, Songbird flung the gush of pink-green sparks in her hand straight at the two shadowed pits serving Grandma for eyes; they struck and sizzled, throwing off steam. For the first time since Bewelcome's resurrection, her feet left the earth and she floated up into the air with her white braids stiff as snakes until she was on a level with the giant stony corpus's head—a pale and monstrous spectre, lit only by her own power.

In response, Grandma just shook her huge head like a dog throwing off water, reached up with one massive hand and seized the current mid-stream, roping it taut. Then lunged out, defter than Yancey could've ever believed, and smacked the other palm-first into Songbird's body. The spread fingers (only three of them plus a thumb, Yancey saw in numb bemusement) spanned the girl's whole midsection. Then Grandma yanked on the stream, hauling hard.

Songbird threw her head back, jaws straining wide in silent agony, as something *tore free* from her in a single wrenching yank: a naked ghost image in rose and viridian of the girl herself, hex-power spun from its navel like an umbilical cord. It held its shape in mid-air for a moment before dissolving, disappearing into Grandma like spilled ink being absorbed.

"Yes, *little ghost*," Grandma told her, viciously—either unaware or uncaring how Songbird used that term only as insult, applied to every white person who got in her way. "The hunger is still there, even now. Always. And you too will try to feed it if you can, given opportunity, after *your* death . . . to chew its brief warmth down and revel in the taste, no matter how briefly. *No matter what the cost.*"

Songbird collapsed, dropping limp. Her slant hazel eyes bulged wildly, rolling in terror, as her remaining breath huffed out while the stone giant's grip tightened on her waist, flint and granite knuckles swelling. Rock grated in Grandma's throat—a snarl, bestial, rabid.

"Such *children* you are," she said, as to herself. "Headstrong, stupid. You know *nothing*. You *are* nothing."

"*Loose* me, damn you," Songbird barely managed, though Grandma didn't seem to hear. "Uh, aaah . . . *aaah*, it hurts! For all gods' sake, *please* . . . let me *go!*"

It was more panic-edged courtesy than Yancey'd ever heard her use previously, to anyone. And Yiska just stood there throughout, staring up at the tableau with fingers clawed, face rictused—probably racking her brains for some way out that didn't involve her throwing down with the strongest hex of her tribe, and getting either of them killed, in the process.

She does love that old monster, Yancey thought, amazed. *And that young one, too.* Strangely, it was this last that spurred Yancey's next shout, surprising herself with its force, not just for volume but also for the eerie *weight* of the cry, as if the words had tangible physical mass shooting from her lips. "She *said* put her the hell *down*, Goddamnit!"

Grandma's hand jerked open, on purest reflex; Songbird fell hard to earth, whooping out one great sob. Yiska rushed to her side and gathered her up, cradling her like an infant, and Songbird clung to her in much the same way.

Again, Grandma did not appear to notice. She had switched her glare to Yancey, a sickly yellowish-blue light dancing about her. What little heat there was left in the desert night air dropped out of it; ice touched Yancey's bare face and hands, freezing the sweat in her clothes. The menace trembled above her, a weight so massive it would crush her if it fell upon her yet so perfectly balanced a mere finger's jab would send it the other way—if she could jab quick enough, precisely enough.

Don't test me, lady, Yancey willed at her, silently, not looking away. *Said yourself how you need my skills, even if they're not up to your idea of snuff; meddle with me, whoever wins, we all lose.*

But it was Yiska who broke the silence, this time. "Nothing more can be done tonight," she said, Songbird still pressed face-first to her vest. "We need rest, all of us. I will take her down." Then paused, to point out: "Consider this, though—if either of you hurt the other, tomorrow night's work will be made the harder. And our task seems hard enough to me, as it is."

Yancey's head dropped, shamed; she was about to finally voice that apology, and mean it. But before she could, Grandma replied— so little heat in her "voice" she might've been chatting about the weather, for all the coiled menace in every inch of her hulking stance gave that the lie, "She could not hurt me, even if she tried. But she should not try, either." *Or you, granddaughter.*

Yiska nodded, then walked away—quickly, without glancing back. And when Yancey finally had the heart to look Grandma's way one more, she found her gone, as well.

Somehow, Yancey let herself sit down, and if it was faster and weaker-kneed than she wanted, at least it wasn't a fall. She covered her face with her hands, making herself breathe slow, forcing back a thick-throated wave of wanting, badly, to weep.

Goddamn, these women could be difficult. Songbird with her ridiculous airs, Grandma, held together with spit and will; Yiska, that proud oddity, monster-slaying when circumstances demanded and hounding after what had to be the worst possible option every other hour of the day. Hell, she'd be better off going sweet on Yancey herself, but for the fact it wasn't as though that version of the story'd end up anyplace *more* joyful.

Rage and fear at last subsiding back to manageable levels. It only now occurred to Yancey that in her whole life thus far, the only people she'd never lied to about herself—who she was, what she was capable of—were Chess Pargeter, Ed Morrow . . . and them, her kidnappers turned companions, fellow prisoners of the Crack. Those who stood beside her now at the very edge of the Underneath, squashing whatever came welling up while trying to suture it shut. That alone had to count for something, surely.

Didn't it?

THE NEXT NIGHT, roasting corn and squash 'round the fire with Yiska's braves while Songbird pouted up in their mutual "sleeping chamber," Yancey caught the war-squaw sidling off and rose as well, claiming she had to go do her business. Instead, she followed after— tracing that supposedly fatal track back up through the butte's coils, to where Grandma kept sleepless vigil on top of the Old Drying Woman's own seat.

"I need speech with you, Spinner," Yiska told the hex-ghost's broad back, sitting down cross-legged with palms on knees, eyes calmly trained on the mismatched exposed bones of her spine.

"Huh," Grandma huffed. "Because I spoke harshly to that girl of yours?"

"She *is* difficult, though not 'mine.' But no. This is something else, more important."

"Tread carefully, then, granddaughter."

"As you say." Yiska straightened her own spine, and said, "Spinner, when you anger yourself thus you risk losing control, knowing that to do so is to set your foot upon the Witchery Way. You risk Becoming what you fight—*Anaye*. And who will it fall to, then, to deal with you, as you hope to deal with the *bilagaana* blackrobe Rook?"

"Is it The Night Has Passed, scalper of Pinkertons and burner of ranches, who warns *me* against risks?" Grandma sounded half amused, half annoyed. "There *is* no safe choice for us, granddaughter. We face too many monsters. Like all of us, I do only what I must to fight them."

"*Anaye*-power used against *Anaye*." Yiska shook her head. "How is this different from the Reverend and his bride?"

"You dare ask me that, who lost my body at Rook's own hands? Since I have shed no undeserving blood to return here, I have earned the right to restore that Balance myself—"

"—a Balance that cannot be restored so long as you *stay* here," Yiska rejoined, unflinching. "'The dead are dead, and must move on.' You told me that yourself, Spinner. What would you have done with Yu Ming-ch'in, had Yancey not stopped you? Tell me plainly she was never in any danger—that you sought only to frighten her, if you could." The fact that Yiska knew Songbird's true name was only slightly less startling than the honest pain in her voice. "Truly, Grandmother, I would hear that from you. Please."

Grandma's golem-body neither breathed nor stirred of itself, when not wilfully moved by its rider, and though it didn't slump, the long silence that followed made it seem empty as a dropped puppet. Yancey held her breath.

"I cannot slacken," said Grandma, at last. "This city is Rook's dream, and I will see it fall."

"*Her* dream," Yiska pointed out. "How often have you said that *Hataalii* should find a way to band together? Now look—here are *Hataalii*, a whole city of them! It is *their* dream, too. What better revenge than to help them take it from Rook and the Lady, to make it ours . . . and *theirs*?"

My God, Yancey thought, forgetting entirely to mask herself, so stunned was she by the very idea, which had frankly never hitherto occurred to her. *Could that* work?

"I see no reason not, dead-speaker," Yiska replied, without moving, as Grandma's "head" slid 'round, grating in its socket. "It seems to work well enough for them now, even under Rook and Lady Suicide's reign."

Hex City as destination rather than obstacle, then: a refuge for all hexes, if events saw Rook and Ixchel removed. As already proven, it could certainly sustain itself; once Oathed to each other instead of the Lady, its inhabitants wouldn't feel the need to parasite on newcomers, or even on the non-hexacious. In fact, so long as that Balance Yiska and Grandma were always chawing over stayed preserved, it might go even further than accepting "just" hexes—considering how well-defended and powerful such a place would be, Hex City could provide a refuge for all peoples who felt themselves not part of "the Union." Natives, for example, starting with these two's own tribes. Freed slaves, Chinee 'scaping 'Frisco's immigration quota; Jews, like Yancey's Pa; gypsies, like her Ma. The two-spirited, even . . . hard women and frilly men, like Yiska, or Chess. Any-damn-one.

No one would feel they had to hide themselves anymore, to take a false name or put on a false face. No one would feel they had no place of refuge, no Promised Land to flee to.

"They do not know what we know, most of them," Yiska told Grandma, "that *Hataalii* are everywhere, always—part of the Land's plans, and thus to be neither feared nor avoided, any more than one may avoid weather. But we can teach them a better way, you, I and the dead-speaker here . . . and Yu Ming-ch'in as well, if she is amenable."

Grandma seemed to look down, contemplating her nailless, mitt-like hands.

"You want me to solve the whole world's problems," she said, "when this thing I call my flesh, containing neither flesh nor blood, is coming apart like a seedpod."

Again, Yancey heard her own voice reply, without knowing it was going to: "All the more important, then, for things to be done quickly . . . and *right*."

This time Yiska did glance back, long enough to give her a single firm nod of approval. To which Yancey could only think back, a trifle flustered: *Thank you kindly, sir—ma'am, I mean; oh, that doesn't sound right at all. No offence meant, Yiska. I'm a* bilagaana *fool.*

But Yiska simply shrugged a bit, one hand making a dismissive flutter. As Grandma allowed, slowly, "Something is happening in that city of Rook's . . . his city, and Hers. I did not see it coming, while in my body; it was as yet hidden in time's creases, even when looked at through the weave of Changing Woman's own loom. But now I am bodiless I see far more clearly, knowing in my soul my vengeance is less important than the seed these two have sown, without even knowing they did so. There is something growing, alive and unforeseen, and though it galls me to say so, it must be preserved."

A high laugh cut the air behind them. Yancey didn't have to turn to know that Songbird had slunk out of her hole once more and climbed to listen as well, standing there with her blanket-shawl wrapped tight against the night wind, her hair—unbound for sleep—blowing like snow.

"Fools," she said, though less scornfully than usual. "Even if I had my full power once more, these are *gods* we trifle with—they cannot be killed, and guard what they consider theirs jealously. As Pinkerton will discover soon enough, should he overstep himself. And how I shall laugh to see it, when he does!"

Yiska shook her head and *tsked*, as if disappointed.

"No," Grandma told her, equitably enough. "Whatever they are now, Suicide Moon and her Enemy were once only as you and I . . . as this ghost-speaker here, even. *He* proves it, that red boy we seek after so desperately. Gods sleep within us all, waiting to be prayed alive, or bought and paid for with blood. And gods can kill other gods."

They all took a moment after that, sitting and standing, in the moon's bright light. 'Til suddenly, a fresh new thought struck Yancey full force 'tween the eyes, and she gasped out loud. "I really am a fool," she said, to no one in particular.

Yiska's eyes sharpened. "How so?"

"Because—we've been trawling down through Hell-that-ain't for how long, wasting our time trying to get Chess Pargeter to hear me, and all 'cause I'm a dead-speaker, right? But see, thing is . . . he's not *dead*."

Now it was the three other women's turn to look her way in unison, with the same sort of stare you'd give some idiot.

"We know this already," Yiska reminded her. "But what can we ever do to remedy it except try again, and harder?"

"Well, I don't know. Talk to his Ma, maybe, who *is* damn well dead? 'Cause considering I see her sitting right beside him most of the time, I'm thinking that might be helpful!"

And if not, given all she'd heard about Oona Pargeter, from Chess himself . . . well, there were dead people everywhere in Mictlan-Xibalba. And now she'd remembered it was so, Yancey could just as easily speak to any one of them.

Might be I'm getting better at this, she reckoned, giddily.

Grandma nodded, satisfied—looked first to Yiska, then Songbird. "See, granddaughter?" she asked the warrior. "I *told* you there was merit to bringing them both."

"Hmp," was all Songbird gave back, by way of a reply.

But when the bleached girl saw how Yiska was smiling again, Yancey almost thought she might have seemed pleased.

SEVEN DIALS: TWO

All worlds begin, and end. All worlds begin again.

Here is a flower, watered from a skull. Here is a seed of blood. Here is the tree that grows from it—yaxche, tree of heaven, with leaves like hair and roots like veins, anchored deep between this world and all others. A tree of bones.

Here is where we tossed the husks and silk of eaten lives, that new lives might grow once more, rendered up in joy to feed the ever-turning Blood Engine. And always, new lives came, new hearts blazed in fire, new blood washed the stone. As it had been, ever would be, world without end . . . until it ended.

IN MICTLAN-SEVEN DIALS, Oona Pargeter's revivified spectre showed her teeth once more and laughed, shortly, a sulphurous rasp to its undertone, creepily reminiscent of the Rev in his sin. "Wish you could see yer own face, sonny, truly," she replied. "First real tin bath I've 'ad in months."

"First what?"

"*Laugh*, you prat; can't 'elp it if you don't know your proper flash jabber, can I?" But here she tossed her hair back, dismissively. "Well, s'pose I *could*'ve, 'ad I been so inclined. But what good it'd've done you in San Fran, the Devil only knows."

Chess shook his head and took a sodden half-step back, running his eyes up and down this slim spectacle before him, clad only in her witch's mane: this flirtatious, sharp-witted creature whose words rang simultaneously too familiar, and not at all. But as he did, she stepped lightly to him, advancing while he retreated, fighting the urge to back away further—bold as polished brass, her movements lithe and easy, as if she'd never ruined her joints with cold, or her guts with gin.

"Awful nippy out 'ere, though," she observed. "Care to 'elp a girl out?"

"You ain't no girl."

Oona rolled her eyes, vivid as his own. "No more'n you're a gentleman, given 'ow I raised you. But you're still the one wiv the coat to spare, ain't that so?"

Nonplussed, Chess found she'd already slipped one of his purple sleeves half-free—so he gave up, letting her tug the whole rest of it off his shoulders, trusting she'd use it to wrap her off-putting nakedness away once more. Which she did, shivering delightedly.

"*Much* better." Looking up through lowered lashes, then, she winked, lasciviously throwing one hip out toward him like it was a magic trick . . . as though that swinging dick of his meant he was just one more john to hook, with every trick in her arsenal. "Fanks, *ever* so."

"Don't do that, Goddamnit. Ain't—"

"Right? Proper? Never knew you t'care too much over either of *those*."

"*Jesus*, Ma!"

"Well, 'ave it yer own way, then. I'll lay off the treacle, so long's you agree to 'ear me through—*wivout* the beat-down, this time."

Chess paused and spat, mouth all of a sudden sour. For it was all so *wrong*, and horribly so. The unpersuasive croon he'd hitherto known only as a hundred shades of lying mockery gone suddenly playful, cheerful . . . *real*, and painfully so. The misremembered source of every saucy trick he'd practiced in his own turn, and rendered horrid for the comparison. For who had he been imitating, after all, each time he'd turned the flare of his attention on some hapless sap—the Rev, Ed and countless others—but *her*, apparently?

At the very thought, his gorge rose up again, only to find itself crammed back down, with all the considerable will at his disposal.

At the sight of his repulsion, Oona's smirk took on a savage edge. "Takes some gettin' used to, don't it?" she murmured. "The very idea that I was ever young, like you—fast, like you—fresh and pretty, fit to 'ave any man fool enough t'meet my eye, I wanted 'im, 'fore cuttin' 'is purse and movin' on. *Just like you*."

"Fuck, no." Chess made himself straighten, regained what little height he had on her and used it, staring haughtily down. "Ain't no single part of me comes from you, save for the trappings."

"Oh no, 'course there ain't—just the parts what like to 'ook a man deep and string him 'long for as far as you can, for the fun of it. Just the parts want what they want, and 'ooever gets 'tween them and their desire dead. Or aches t'frow 'emselves at men won't do nothing for 'em but fuck 'em 'ard and walk away, smilin'—"

"You're talkin' out your well-worn backside!"

Oona raised a brow, gold-red as his own. "Never did tell you much 'bout your Pa, did I?"

"Never asked you to. Then again, I misdoubt you know which he was, let alone *who*."

Her smile softened, making his stomach churn. "Ah, but there you'd be wrong, for 'e wasn't the sort you forget—an educated man, wiv quite the 'ead for hoity-toity God-botheration: Malcolm Devesstrin, what sailed from Dublin to New York City and took up with the gangs, standin' mage for the Might of Eire 'gainst every roisterin' jack in the Five Points. Said 'ow 'e'd been a monk once, which was why 'e called 'imself Columcille, after the saint." It came out *Collum-kill*, and here Chess felt another odd twist in his gut, something turning, a keyhole *creak*. "And Christ knows, I didn't 'ave no cause to doubt 'im. But that was all put paid to, when 'e stole some mouldy book and took off runnin'." She glanced back over her shoulder, then, lashes lowering flirtatiously, to add: "A fine, tall man, big as a 'ouse and broad as a barn and ministerial in 'is declamation, wiv a powerful love to 'ear 'imself talk. Sound familiar?"

"You're a lyin' whore."

"Oh yes, always, but not about this. Why bother? Bastard's dead any'ow, from what I heard; struck out in the streets, five years after you was born. Was some Nativist battle-witch they calls the Widowmaker what laid 'im low, probably 'cause 'e tried to pull the same trick on 'er 'e did on me, but she *was* wilier. Or just luckier."

Chess shook his head, muzzily. "What . . . *trick*?"

"Fink a minute on it 'fore you dismiss anything I got to tell you out of 'and, just 'cause it's *me* 'oo's talkin', Cheshire Pargeter—for that's your full name, as it 'appens, and did I never tell you *that*, neither? *Sorry*." Her voice dropped, sweet giving way to rough, as the rasp crept upward. "Named you for a county, one I fought my own Ma came from, once upon a time. But that don't matter much now."

"Keep on talkin', bitch, 'fore I paste you another, story or no story."

"All right. Say a man 'as hexation, powerful bad, and meets a woman 'e's drawn to, on account of the power *she's* got locked up inside; say she's drawn to 'im the same, enough to let 'im 'ave 'is way and trust 'e'll do right by 'er, for all every scrap of experience tells 'er that's a load of old rope. And say one day she misses 'er courses, knows she's taken short."

"Any of this got a point, beyond the obvious?"

Display, that's all it was—his only weapon left, used without compunction. But it made Oona's eyes light up, same way he knew his own could, or had—shoot genuine sparks like tears from either corner, kill-flash bright, which scarred her cheeks on their way down before healing themselves anew, flesh knitting back together in their wake.

"Point *is*, you berk," she gritted, "that everyfing you 'ave you owe to 'im an' *me*, more'n you ever knew. Fink I was conjured out of nothin', wiv you already stuffed up inside? I 'ad fourteen 'ole years before you ever existed, and damn, if I didn't make 'em count! I could've done anyfing, I'd only come into my own, wivout *you* to 'old me back."

She clapped her hands and whipped them apart, blue-white arcs of lightning writhing between her palms, their spitting light painting her face. *"Anyfing,"* she whispered, whites of her eyes gone sodium-bright.

Chess shuddered, then shrugged.

"Gonna need more than that to make a mark, Ma," he ground out. "That little crackle wouldn't set me back none even if it was real—Ash Rook was ten times any hex you might've been, and I'm ten times the hex *he* was. 'Sides which, you already told me—down here ain't nothin' but dreams. Shadow shows." He thrust his hand straight into the lightning field, and saw it pass unscathed. "I'll say it again: I ain't you, and you ain't me. Never were."

Oona closed her hands, making the lightning vanish, but didn't lower her eyes from his. "No," she agreed. "Glamour I 'ad, enough t'get me shed of *this* place, but I wasn't no true 'ex, since my full power 'adn't yet come to pass." A pause. "Your preacher-man—'e tell you what 'appens to witches carry witchlings?"

"How the whelp comes out dead, or the mother dies, or they both die?"

"That's right." No smile, now. "Could feel it movin' inside me, right along with you. The craft I'd yet to grab 'old of, close as my own blood. I felt it pullin', each and every day; felt *you* pullin' *on* it, fightin' me for it. "That was when 'e came back, your Pa. And when I saw 'im again, you jumped inside me like you was tryin' to bust out right then . . . and I knew. Could see in 'is eyes that 'e knew, 'ad known all along, 'ow this would go."

Nothin' worse in this whole world, darlin', Ash Rook's Hell-deep voice told Chess, mildly, *than a bad man who knows his Bible.*

"'E laid it out for me," Oona went on, "told me there was nought to be done about 'ow fings would end, unless . . . 'e tried something."

Chess's brows contracted. "And you *let* him? Some ex-monk hex you didn't know from Adam, savin' he'd had his tackle up in your box, and left you like to die of it?"

"'Adn't much bleedin' choice, did I?" Oona snapped. "And 'e . . ." Surprisingly, she flushed. "'Ad a way with 'im, Columcille did. Made me fink it was—I was—*important*. That we'd learn something, if everyfing worked right; that if fings went wrong, there'd at least be no pain in it, far as I was concerned."

"Bet he lied about that one, though."

"Oh, 'e lied about all of it, from first to bloody last. That was just the topper."

She looked down, red hair falling curtain-long once more, wrapping her profile away. And as Chess's gaze followed, instinct-driven, he saw her fold into a squat, balancing on those small bare feet, toes already black with mud. Watched her dip the fingers of one hand through a rut puddle, yet more light trailing in its five-fold wake while shadows bred inside the brightening water, a cloudy mirror full of images he struggled to decode.

This same younger form she wore now stretched out in some foul tenement bed, held down, her mouth wide. A dark man crouched watching, one big hand cupping her jaw, the other stroking her sweaty brow. Gas hissing in the sconce, blue flames pin-pointed in her pupils; the beat of a heart, two hearts, a doubled pulse ebbing in and out.

Give it t'me now, girl. My lovely Oona, my hunger's bride. Just as you promised, as you want to, along with that brat of yours, poor little sweetmeat. Poor, puling little mage-bred sacrifice.

Reminded him of nothing so much as Dame Ixchel, swimming in blood-drool and other hot juices. Suicide Moon Ixchel, taking his lip between her teeth and grinding ever so slightly, like she meant to tenderize him just a touch, 'fore throwing him on the grill. Or eddying alongside as Rook puppeted him stringless through Mictlan-Xibalba's rainy corridors, telling him that dying for gods you didn't even know, making 'em a raw meat meal, wasn't so much dreadful as *glorious, flowery,* **beautifulbeautifulbeautiful**—

So sons of bitches ran in his family, apparently. No great surprise, given.

"Sly as the bloody Pope, that one," Oona spat, one fingertip tracing the dark man's regal profile, erasing it with a ripple. "So I'm turnin' inside out from the pain of squeezin' you clear, feelin' the 'exation in every part of me ready to pop the exact same way *you* was, an' I 'ear Columcille call out somefing . . . Jew cant and church-talk all mixed together, what 'urt the ear t'listen to. And it all just *tore*, ripped clean away, so fast I didn't even feel you drop. Nothing left behind 'cept a hole, raw and sick and covered over in scab—"

Her voice broke, startling Chess, one thought crystal clear in every rigid line of her: *No more man, no magic, no promises of love— just me, alone, like I'd fooled myself I wouldn't be. Positionless and street-bound, with one skill only t'my name, 'less I wanted t'swing for thievery; all that, nothin' more.*

Except, of course, for . . . you.

Chess didn't want to tell her he knew what that was like—to be took up and dropped, have the whole world pulled out from under you like a rug, by one you thought you'd gladly die for. Shouldn't *have* to tell her, anyhow; could just go on ahead and read his damn thoughts like any other dead person, if she was really interested.

Instead, he cleared his throat. "I never heard of anybody could do that—take a person's hexation from 'em, without killin'."

"'Cause you know so much about it, eh?" Oona didn't look up, staring grimly down at the puddle's fading picture show. "But no, wasn't like 'e *took* it, as . . . made it so's I couldn't catch 'old of it—so's it just flowed in one way and out the other. Closed fings up inside me and fused 'em shut, like any back-alley angelmaker."

"What the hell'd be the point of *that*?"

"'Oo knows? A give-and-take, maybe, for some bigger reward on 'is own end—'e 'ad ambitions in that direction, though it wasn't like 'e'd discuss their particulars wiv the likes of me." Another shrug. "Or maybe 'e was just a bastard."

More'n likely, Chess thought.

"Saved your life, though, not that 'e was finkin' of it—'cause by makin' such a mess of me, 'e made sure I couldn't feed off of you, even if I wanted. And believe you me, I *wanted*."

"What makes you think I don't believe you?" Chess asked.

A silence fell between them then, dull as any unhealed break. Chess let it pass without remark, being used to the sensation—pain run through him like a tide, out and in and out again once more.

Though it did surprise him just a tad to see Oona wince slightly, for all the world as though she *felt* it, too.

"So," she continued. "There I was wiv *you* and not enough glamour to light a candle, after I'd been bankin' half a year on the day it'd all change." A ghastly smile. "Oh, sonny, you don't know how many times I almost frew you overboard on our way down the coast, or drowned you in the bath like a kitten . . . not since you were cause of all my sorrows, so much, but just since you were close to 'and. And 'e wasn't."

Now, *that* he could almost believe. Same way he'd ended men for not being the ones he really yearned to kill, or fucked 'em for much the same reason.

"And I was the one set you to whore and smoke, too, I s'pose; neat damn trick, with me still on the tit. Next you'll be sayin' the Devil made you do it."

"Was Columcille I'd've blamed, like I said, if there was anything to gain by it. You I kept alive, much as it cost me . . . but ask yerself this: given 'ow much I wanted to get rid o'you, why d'you fink I never actually did?"

"'Cause baby killers get the gallows, they get caught? 'Cause I was worth more sold than thrown away?" Chess spread his hands. "Both or neither, don't even matter, considering how little of a fuck *I* give."

Yet here another voice came back to him, this one light and clear, pleasantly absinthe-softened, betraying no hint of the steel he knew lurked behind it. *Babies die, Mister Pargeter. Happens lamentably easily. . . . She'd really wanted you dead, you would be.*

"You really *'aven't* wondered, 'ave you, all this while?" Oona cocked her head, disbelief writ wide on every line of her too-young face. "Why I kept on at you, put you straight into 'arm's path a thousand times over—consider what you know 'bout your father now, 'bout me. Then tell me you really can't see the why of it all."

The why of it all: half his life, to this point. That same life had made his double purpose escape and vengeance, without even a hope of prosperity, after. Just hit the ground running and not look back, or fill any motherfucker got in his way with lead.

But yeah, he finally did know what she'd wanted all along, now. So simple, from *this* side of things. So impossible to guess at, from the other.

"You *wanted* me to turn hex," he said, and coughed up a sick laugh. "Go up like a blow-stick, take the whole show with me when I did—that about the size of it? Christ, no wonder you got more and more pissed, every time I never turned the trick!"

"Contrary to the last, you bastard. You really must be the toughest little shit alive."

"No thanks to you. But then again . . . how dumb *are* you, woman? In any of the stories I heard tell of, only thing makes a man-hex bloom is threat of death! Ash Rook *swung*, for Christ's sake, and he had to take my damn heart out to make me what *I* am—what I always was. You telling me that for all the neck-stabbin' and pimpery, there was never one time you thought of just slittin' my throat in my sleep and seeing what might happen? Or . . ."

He trailed off. She didn't answer.

Didn't have to.

Because—oh God, it was already creeping up like he'd been born saturated, a poison-knowledge tisane, waiting for the right hand to dunk him in boiling water and brew the truth right out of him. The bitter truth, too disgusting for anyone—even him—to swallow.

'Cause . . . if you'd done it wrong, all I'd've been was dead, and . . . no.

"No," he repeated, out loud. "You do *not* get to say that to me, Goddamnit."

Oona simply stood there, green stare level, now he was the one unable to meet it. Chess shied like a horse, swung away, stormed a few paces off, spun back. "Bitch, *no*. You . . . you don't get to . . . to even *start* to say . . ."

Appalled, he felt a lump thicken in his throat, and fought the temptation to finish his thought, furiously as he'd ever fought anything. But though she herself showed not the faintest flicker of expression to confirm these traitor words in his head, it was too late—even unspoken, they hung between them, like the stink of powder after gunplay.

You do not, not ever, get to tell me you really did love me, after all.

Took near a minute of the silence that followed for Chess to realize that the everlasting "London" rain had finally stopped, along with the noise of that threadbare, cycling crowd. Hugging himself hard, he turned a slow circle, blinking. Down all seven streets, from here to their vanishing points, the Dials were empty but for him and Oona: every fellow phantom gone, every building hollow and silent, every laneway glinting slick. No rat-skitter or pigeons' coo to break the stillness; no footfall over the grey rooftops, pavers dull as teeth below, shingles like scales above. The black sky held no stars.

For a moment, the entire scene seemed to *ripple*, no more than a hastily sketched picture on threadbare black silk curtains, stirred in a cold breeze.

"What's it matter, any'ow?" Oona asked, finally. "Don't know why I put myself out. You're dead now, same as me."

"I am *not*. My body's still up there, still alive—"

"Occupied, too. Which means you can't do nothin' wiv it, don't it?"

"Well, I ain't about to stop tryin'!"

She gave him a long look—and smiled again, finally, with far more warmth than last time. "That's different, then. Now, you ready to get out of 'ere, or what? 'Cause I sure am, and I'm thinkin' it'll take the both of us."

"Be one fancy piece of work if it did, seein' as how you ain't even a hex no more."

"You neither, cully—not down 'ere. But I'm sure we can figure out *somefing*."

Chess's lips drew back. "Fuck 'we,' *Ma*. Might'a slipped your mind how you ain't ever been exactly reliable—for me, anyways."

Oona slid one small hand out from under his cuff, considering her fingernails as though they were little horn mirrors, nonchalant. "Oh, I could be, wiv the right incentive. 'Sides which," jabbing a thumb skyward, "them lot upstairs been droppin' lines for weeks, trawlin' for your attention, and *you* can't even see 'em. Can ya?"

Christ, how Chess loathed this feeling of being just a step behind, that glee some so-called "smart" people took in changing subjects too fast for him to follow: Oona, Songbird, the Enemy. Hell, even Ash Rook'd talked down to him at first, though—give the big bastard his due—he'd also been the one person ever tried to break himself of that habit, if for no other reason than Chess had told him to either do so, or get reacquainted with his own right hand.

"Seems not," he said, between clenched teeth. "Can't even say I know which 'lot' you're talkin' on, unless—" But here memory broke past anger. "Yancey," he breathed.

"That's her name, then, Miss Table-tapper?" He nodded. "Well, la di da. Strong little missus, ain't she? She's been yammerin' away at you for donkey's years, wiv never a bit o' joy. Which might be why she's suddenly decided t'talk t'*me*, instead."

Chess's hackles rose. "Right now?"

"Says 'er friends are layin' a trail for you, to take you up an' out. Which makes sense—this place's been flush wiv silver, the last few days. But you don't know why that is, do ya? 'Scuse me again, for not rememberin' you don't know nothin'.'"

"And whose damn fault is that?"

"Patience, boyo. The way a call from Up Over looks down 'ere, it's like a silver thread you catch 'old of, then tug at it t'follow it up." She plucked something from the air alongside the dial-column, traced it, as though running her fingers up an invisible wire. "And that's where you'll need *me*, to show you the way. The show you where any one of 'em *is*."

"You been' . . . seein' these call-threads. All the time. Since I got here."

"That's when they started, yeah.'"

"And you never told *me*."

"Didn't fink you'd be amenable. Was I wrong?"

"More like 'cause you already tried to tug on one yourself and didn't get nowhere, is what I'd guess."

Oona let her eyes drop. "'Course," she admitted. "Can't expect you to trust me now, though, can I? Not when I always did leave you to pay the butcher's bill whenever I could, 'cause on the pipe, it's take what you can and keep it, wiv barely any room for anything else. No changing it now. But I never did nothin' to you I wouldn't've took myself."

"Oh, no doubt. And that's what taught me to reckon my own price higher."

Oona nodded, face rigid, silver gleam of the rain-drenched streets reflected in her downcast eyes. They stood there a moment, long and longer. Chess would've reckoned it by heartbeats, if either of 'em had had one.

"Maybe it's that I 'ad to be like I was," she offered, at last. "So you'd turn out like *you* are. Like you 'ad to be."

Raw as he was feeling, the guffaw that burst out of Chess at this last piece of ridiculousness caught him by surprise, but he was grateful for it all the same.

"Oh, fuck *that* horse-crap," he said. "You 'had' to ruin your life just to ruin mine, 'cause soft don't win the race? Makes it sound like Rook's Book without the poesy. At least that Hell-whore Ixchel and the Enemy got a bit of patter to go with *their* craziness, even if it's all in some palaver I can't speak. So apologize or don't, but save the excuses, 'cause I don't want none."

"Little boy. You don't want none of nothin' . . . never did." Oona shook her head once more, half rueful, half malicious. "But you're gonna get it."

Then, catching hold of what Chess could only assume was that phantom cord again, she reached out for him, fingers flickering impatiently. "Now—shall we?"

Chess let out his breath, more than half minded to say *No*, just to see the look on her face. Then thought, amazed: *But my friends are waiting.* And wasn't it sadly strange how easy that word came to his lips now, as if he'd had friends all his life, 'stead of only learning what that meant a tad too late to be worth the education?

Even natural perversity wasn't enough to keep him *here*, though.

"Let's," he said, shortly. And took her proffered hand.

BOOK TWO:
SAVAGE WEAPONS

November 13, 1867
Month Fourteen, Day Six Crocodile
Festival: Still Quecholli, or Treasured Feather

Day Cipactli (Crocodile) is governed by Tonactecuhtli, Lord of Nurturance, as its provider of *tonalli* or Shadow Soul life energy. Cipactli is an auspicious day, ruled by energetic work signifying advancement and honour, good for beginnings. But this *trecena*, which starts with day Cozcacuauhtli (Vulture), is ruled by Xolotl, god of fire and bad luck, who sometimes aids the dead on their journey to Mictlan. It therefore signifies the wisdom and freedom of old age, representing the path of the setting sun—and while the way of the warrior points to the primal relationship between predator and prey, this sign points to the Third Way, which is neither.

Accordingly, these thirteen days are set aside to perfect the Way of the Scavenger. While the young heart must strategize between offence and defence, the old heart floats like the clouds, stooping to earth only to take what no one else wants. These are good days for disengaging; bad days for participating.

By the Mayan Long Count calendar, today is governed by Piltzintecuhtli the Youthful Lord, who is the planet Mercury—the sun's little brother, that planet visible just before sunrise, or just after sunset. His wife is Tlazteotl, filth-eater, who redeems through lust and may be invoked during childbirth. He is the third Lord of the Night.

SEVEN DIALS: THREE

This is where the gods killed themselves to make the sun and the moon come up.

Down here in the dark, in the house of dust. Down under the black water, deep and deeper. At the very farthest point, the great taproot, where the crack in all worlds begins. This is where a thousand catastrophes lurk, waiting to be rediscovered—where a million apocalypses slumber, waiting to be recalled. Where the end of all things lies fallow, hoping to be summoned, to fulfill its purpose: to complete itself, and everything else.

In truth, there is no denying that all of our ancestors knew that just as the world began, the world must end; on this point, there is never any debate. The only valid consideration is neither if, nor when—but how.

For the Mexica, first came Nahui-Ocelotl, the Jaguar Sun, whose inhabitants were devoured by wild beasts. Then Nahui-Ehécatl, the Wind Sun, whose inhabitants were destroyed by hurricanes; Nahui-Quiahuitl, the Rain Sun, whose inhabitants were washed away in a rain of fire; and Nahui-Atl, the Water Sun, whose inhabitants died by flood—except for those who became fish, as well as that single man and woman who escaped alive, only to be transformed into dogs.

After Nahui-Atl, Quetzalcoatl himself went down to Mictlan and stole the bones of all previous races from Mictantecuhtli, skeleton lord of death's kingdom. These he then pulverized and used to create clay, blending it with divine blood shed from a wound in his own divine penis, through which he had threaded a penitent rope of thorns. And from this clay was moulded the current world's population, baked to life in a furnace powered by Quetzalcoatl's heart, the glorious morning star.

This, therefore, is why we mutilate ourselves, give all we can afford (and more) in our worshippers' service, improving their too-brief lives on the assumption that they then will be glad to die—perfect, happy, knowing themselves loved—for us, in our stead.

To keep this pain-born orrery we all occupy turning.

THROUGHOUT THE LAST PHASE of his short life, Chess had seen wonders enough to flatter himself whatever miracle might manifest now as he gripped his mother's hand, reduced by circumstance to childish dependency, he'd take it in stride. Mind-wrenching shifts, vertigo and displacement, convulsive transfigurations of earth and sky with everything washed away under foot—he'd endured all that, and more. Nothing could surprise him.

What would it be like, though, this time, when the world around him peeled back to let whatever lay behind unshuck itself? *Couldn't be worse than here,* he'd've snarled, once—but experience suggested otherwise.

But I've fought my way clear of Hell before, Chess thought.

Oona smiled—and yanked hard on the unseen line of tension in her other hand, *twanging* it bowstring sharp. The recoil pulled 'em first skyward, predictably, as a hooked fish's tug will set the line whipping. But they didn't go too far in that direction, instead finding themselves dragged headlong a bare few feet up off the wet black street, kicking up slime and trash; Oona went first, red hair flapping like a torn flag in a windstorm, her grip on Chess's hand just hard enough to haul him in her wake.

By the time he'd recovered, nonplussed, they were halfway down a narrow crevice between buildings previously near-invisible in the gloom, staring at a blank, crumbling brick wall. Rancid puddles pooled between the flagstones, mud squelching beneath Chess's boots. Oona bit one dirty knuckle and considered the wall, as if she hadn't expected it.

"What's the deal?" he demanded. "Thought we were goin' *up*, not side-a-ways."

"Well, I fought the same," she snapped back, "so if I knew, I'd damn well say. The thread, it definitely goes in *'ere*, after all that; right dead-centre of this brick I'm pointin' at, neat as a whistle. But—" She stepped forward and began to probe the wall, hands spidering lightly over the bricks; her brows knotted, peering still closer. "—after that, I dunno."

"No way through?"

"Not as I can ken."

"And I'm s'posed to just take your word for it, am I?"

"'Ow many other choices you got?"

She had a point, there. But hell if it didn't scrape Chess's craw to have to rely on her sense of something so completely invisible, 'specially when she didn't appear to be doing anything with it.

"Step aside," he told her, shortly. And moved close enough to the brick to think he could taste his own no-breath, reminding him how long it'd been since he'd even pretended to eat.

"Punch our way through, maybe," he said, more to himself than anything else. "Or—blow it down? The two of us together, should be easy."

"Fink so, wouldn't you?"

Chess swung 'round, immediately on guard, with steam beginning to wisp upward through his tight-clenched knuckles. "What's that s'posed to mean?"

"Means 'I don't bloody know,' is all. This place ain't a shooting gallery—it was, you'd've already flown the coop long since, without any 'elp from me. So maybe each step of the way out's less about 'oo's got the sand to pound 'ard as it is gettin' answers; finding the *right* path, not just the easiest."

Her tone, surprisingly, rang convincing enough to make Chess flatten his palms against the wall, close his eyes and lean his head down, the stone rough but damply soothing 'gainst his throbbing forehead.

I'm no good with this shit, he wanted to say. *Ain't no book-smart intriguer like Rook, or even a Pinkerton-trained puzzle-solver, the way Ed had to be; my grand ideas at Hoffstedt's Hoard came straight from little Miss Yancey's brainpan, and they all went south quick enough, once Sheriff Love got involved. Shoot it if it stands and cut it if it runs, that's my strategy's extent. I can barely plan out my morning meals, let alone solve a Goddamn riddle designed to keep them that's Hell-locked from making their escape. . . .*

"I don't know either," he found himself admitting, at last, as despair lapped up over him.

To which she sniffed, and replied: "Then give up, why don't you? Just like a bloody Adam! Well, it's like I always said—"

That phrase alone, however, was enough to sweep him away, borne off on a dirty tide of similarly bad advice. The wisdom of a life spent facedown, with only your own blood left to spit at the world that'd kicked you; Oona Pargeter's rule-book, each chapter beginning exactly like the last, with these same, cheerless words: *My Ma always said—*

—Get the fawney up front. Never dish out what you can't take. Don't never beg; rave and curse, go down fightin', 'cause them that folds easy gets the boot. Now get out o' here, you skin-waste, and sing for our bloody supper. My Ma always said: What are you, a ponce? A bloody molly-coddle? Go cry to 'eaven and see 'oo answers, you flamin' soft-arse nancy. My Ma always said: Nothin' comes for nothin' in this world, boy. Sell for as much as they'll pay, and charge more, if you can. And if they won't fork over, then do the only fing makes you different from me . . . and kill 'em. . . .

I loved her a good long time, missy, he remembered snarling at Yancey Kloves, when she'd pressed him. *And then I learned better.*

But he knew now, oh, how he knew—that he never really had.

"'Cause all men are dogs, huh?" he asked Oona now, out loud, voice deceptively even.

She nodded. "And pigs, and rats—vermin of all descriptions." Then paused, eyes softening slightly: "But then, you ain't really a *man* at all, are you? No matter 'ow you look."

He almost thought she might've meant it for a compliment, of a sort. But even so, it made him snap upright once more, too angry to even reply 'til he'd took a deep breath, blew it out.

"Yes, I damn well *am*," he told her.

"All right, then. Do what a man does, supposedly—look, and *see*. Your Pa was a bastard, but 'e knew 'is works, by God. So fink on it, 'cause it's *you* this Call's meant for, not me; might be it's you needs to take a gander, wivout all your jaw, and ponder it through in ways I can't. Bloody *fink*, for once!"

Chess's hand throbbed, a literal phantom pain. He squinted down at the raw-scraped smear it left behind on the wall—only to watch light bloom from his palm. Oona's shadow leaped up, towering on the bricks behind her with a sizzling power-crackle. And framing it, visible now under Chess's personal footlight, three rough lines sketched out a brick rectangle, some open door backlit by the sun beyond.

At shoulder level, the red ghost of Chess's blood still shone, the only true colour in this entire pocket world.

With more gentleness than he'd intended, Chess pushed Oona out of the way, stepping into her place; his glory-hand's light faded, plunging the alley back into darkness. But now that Chess had seen the cracks, he couldn't unsee them. He drove fingers along their length, scrabbling for the hidden catch or trip-switch, tearing his own no-nails. The pain galvanized him to punch brick over and over again, hooking it from left to right and back to left once more, as if trying to bust nonexistent hinges. His knuckles shredded, dripping blood hot enough to steam, which the fissures drank up in turn. And again and again he struck, smearing that blood along every inch, to what damn end he couldn't've begun to reckon, even if you'd asked him.

Without warning, the wall's blood-delineated portion simply disintegrated, collapsing with an outward-bellying *whoof* of dust and mica. Chess and Oona jerked back, shielding their eyes, and lowered their hands to see—nothing. A gap of absolute black, not even reflecting the chill gleam of Seven Dials' rain. Yet Chess *knew* that darkness, down in his gut. Had glimpsed it before, inside the

Enemy's empty ribcage and the bottom of Her Goddamn Rainbow Ladyship's grinning black eyes, as she stared down into his while riding him: the darkness of a crack in the world, the place where the light bled out.

Oona seized him by one hand, blood notwithstanding, and didn't leave go. Chess's throat felt like sand and glass when he finally spoke. "So . . . it's in there, I guess, or stay here. Forever."

Beside him, his mother's too-young shape only nodded; didn't need to turn to see it, not at all. Not with her shoulder's muscle popping slightly and their no-pulses hammering in unison: her dead heart, his long-gone one.

Chess closed his eyes, and groaned.

"Fuck it," he said, finally. And leaped, pulling Oona with him.

GRAVITY SEEMED TO SLOW. They stepped through, touched down over the threshold, the lintel between. And just as promised by that first glance, all that rose to meet them was nothing: an absence, delicious in its way, airless and sere.

There was something under their feet, though, if noiseless and unforgiving—something making bleak walls on either side, too, with scarce enough room for Chess's shoulders to pass between, his arm turning in its socket to lead Oona through in turn. He felt a wrench of panic at the idea that they might forge forward only to find themselves trapped in a gradually narrowing space, eventually lodging too fast to go either way, and for a bare second, the still-open portal back into Mictlan-Seven Dials shone like sanctuary.

Oona's fingers clutched at his palm, waxy-cold, sticky with sweat. Not looking so much to comfort her as simply to hurry her up a bit, he shifted his grip to her thin wrist and pulled, hard enough to feel the bones grate.

"Let's get a move on, old woman," he told her, not looking back. And set his teeth, stepping straightaway into a blast of pressure that blew neither hot nor cold but horizontally, bruisingly stiff. Yet though the force of it rattled his teeth, flapped his lips askew and numbed his tongue, he bladed through setting heel to toe, heel to toe, snarling soundless, indomitable. Dragging his mother along with him until they broke free with an audible *snap*, a broke-pelvis crunch, into someplace entirely other yet again.

Dust on dust, a wilderness of it, buff and granular. And light, too, for all Chess couldn't tell where it came from—sifting down or welling up, extruding through the walls' pores, slicking everything with distinction. On either side, a doubled fall of what might be curtains receded, muslin-thin, static, aside from those shadows flickering intermittently behind.

"Chess—" Oona began, pressing against him.

"I see 'em, Ma."

"What are—I mean—are they *followin'* us, them fings? Or just followin' along, general-like? I'm tryin' t'see 'em clear, but I, I . . . can't . . ."

"Me either, Ma, and I'm sure they'd like to keep it thus. Hush up, now."

Got no real weapons to fall back on, nothing but myself, and her. So might could be we'll just have to think *our way out of this, as well . . .*

Years since the War now, but all the various instincts of *fight-flight-fuck 'em all* came ratcheting back in a single skipped breath. Chess pulled Oona along at a rapid, semi-hunched lope which ate ground steadily, angled even further sideways. Concealment being out of the question, he thought it best to opt for speed; the pursuing shadows had a bestial feel to them, a carrion heat like the breath of battlefield-scavenging dogs—running outright would only mark them as prey. To left and right, meanwhile, a twisty skein of grey un-walls stretched out endless, growing ever dimmer as the no-light failed.

Fifty steps on, marking the shadows' encroaching rate of advance, Chess dropped to his knees, pulling Oona down along with him. He pitched his voice low yet urgent, sibilants slurred for quiet, demanding: "Can you see it still? The Call, that thread?" She kept on staring back, eyes wide, rigid; Chess gave her a shake. "*Listen* to me, Oona: I need you mean and sharp, like usual. I need the bitch who raised me."

Blinking, she searched the dust. For a second, he found himself making study along with her, as though some clue might leap out at him, he only squinted the fiercer. This thing which supposedly came with his name attached, an invisible invitation, but one he had to rely on *her* to track. . . .

"There," she said, finally.

"Get in front of me, then."

"Oh, you fink? Chance'd be a fine bloody—"

"*Oona!* I ain't got time to jaw on it. *Something's* afoot, and one of us needs to have the way out scouted, you take my meaning?" He pushed back, deliberately opening a way between her and the nearing threat. "Or would you rather fight?"

Her answering swallow was so quiet it might've gone unnoticed, he hadn't been listening.

". . . believe I'll watch the door, fanks ever so," she decided.

"Thought as much."

All at once, Chess jumped upright and turned, hands coming alight. Dark pressed hard 'gainst the blaze, force balancing against force before the sheer mass of it began to overwhelm, pushing him back. One fist Chess held braced against it while he simultaneously side-stepped, knotting the other *into* the no-wall so it rucked up like heavy silk. In the light's backspill, he thought he could see black shapes thundering toward them, low-slung and brutish.

Before they could reach them, however, he'd already heaved with all his strength, ripping what lay between like a rotten curtain. Piercing shrieks rose up all 'round, blind and senseless as the wails of dying bluebellies, crushed beneath Captain Coulson's artillery. Shutting them out, Chess hauled the ruptured membrane across the passage and slammed it straight into the other wall, sealing them off. A forge's worth of sparks showering from both hands now, he ran his palms up and down the seam, fusing the wall together.

In seconds, it was done. Chess backed away, watching the membrane distort, throbbing and bulging under the thudding blows of whatever now lay trapped behind.

"Didn't know you could . . . still *do* fings like that, down 'ere," said

Oona, from his elbow—impressed, despite herself. He could kick himself for the way his spirit lifted, just to hear it.

"Me neither," Chess admitted, panting. And looked over to see her stock-rooted again, with that white, strained look around the eyes; was like the woman'd never been under fire in her life, he thought.

With an irritated jerk of his head toward what he could only assume was their destination, he reminded her: "Oona? Exit?"

"Right," she repeated, collecting herself, and turned back, eyes on the ground. Now it was her turn to lead, she made the most of it—and as she pulled him on, the seal-wall shuddered as their pursuers continued to slam themselves into it. By some paradox of the light it was still visible, if distant, when Oona at last turned to the left and stopped by a particular point, indistinguishable from any other. "This's the ticket—now open it, 'fore they catch back up."

"Ain't gonna have to cut my hand to shit again, am I?"

"Don't fink so, just . . . yeah, 'at'll do it. Press 'ard, 'ere." With a crooked grin, Oona slipped her fingers between two folds of mist-curtain, lifting 'em back like one of the hangings on Selina Ah Toy's walls. Smoky red light stirred and breathed beyond; Oona gestured, a grand ballroom sweep. "After you."

Chess might have hesitated, if the air behind 'em hadn't just that second given off with an awful *tearing* sound, nauseatingly fleshy. He whirled 'round just in time to see upright shapes pouring through a torn gash in the seal, coursing down the passage toward them: a thick wave of shadow with long, cowled forms mounted on the same dark flood, mouths open so wide as to unhinge their jaws, rattlesnake-style.

Sick dread froze him in place. Once again, it wasn't the innate monstrosity of this vision itself; he'd seen worse, by far—done it, too. But even in this empty place where all should have been equally unrecognizable, he somehow knew these things: not nameless monsters, random Hell-harrowers. They were the dead.

His dead.

I've killed a lot of people, boy, he remembered telling one of them, once, impatiently—dead whore Sadie's little defender, back in Joe's, before he and Ed became better acquainted. Before the Rev brought home that night-shiny new "wife" of his and let her have her way, driving a stake through their concord's heart a good twenty-four hours before she tore Chess's own ticker out bodily and ate it, right in front of his eyes. Back before he himself had tasted the grave's so-called delights, and therewith been transformed without hope of repair—become the awful object he was now, chased by a horde of kills too many to recall, or regret.

"*Chess!*" Oona screamed, slapping him 'cross the chops. And with that all-too-familiar pain, it at last became her turn to haul *him*, fast as humanly possible, straight out of one Hell, and headlong into another.

CHAPTER EIGHT

WHEN NIGHT'S HOUSE grew up and the Crack gaped wide, all other things fell silent, as if made suddenly aware of their own danger. But then again, this was a dangerous world, or at least far more so than ever.

Outside New Aztectlan, things gathered in the darkness, waiting. While inside . . .

THE BABY CAME OUT blue, in pieces. Rook had seen birthings go wrong before, 'course; when the doctor failed, next one you sent for was always the preacher. But it'd been a long time. On some level, he'd hoped—expected—never to play this part again: bearer of tidings so far beyond bad they approached a sort of dire grandeur.

By any lights, tonight should've marked an uncontested victory. Bewelcome they'd left humbled if not destroyed, reminded once again just who, and what, they dared to squabble with. And they'd achieved a goal of near-equal importance, for Sophy Love was gone, at last—if not dead then surely lost beyond any expectation of return, and without their personal Joan of Arc, the Bewelcomites could only be a spent force. In his experience, a wound to morale was often deadlier than the greatest bloodshed, and harder to heal.

But here was bitter proof of the same maxim wreaked on them, by fate's cruel hand. Indeed, were Rook's own faith yet intact, or he'd put more credence in the Widow's invocations, he might suspect judgement of an even higher type.

He'd brought the raiders straight back to his own sleeping chamber, laid Clo down and left her there with Fennig gripping her hand, while Berta and Eulie wept. Then he'd conjured Sal Followell in and himself out with another wrench of power, an expenditure so great it left him exhausted—too weak to shield himself from the flood of images he'd thought to escape, magic lantern-projected directly into his brain: Clo screaming, lips white; Auntie F.'s strong mahogany arms, gloved to the elbow in blood. A flickering light cupped inside Clo's bulging stomach, red-gold glow dimming to anoxic blue, like a torch strangling in mineshaft air. The opaque disks of Fennig's hastily conjured replacement glasses, still as two dark moons in the unlit gloom.

Those tiny limbs slipping out on a flood, bedsheets darkening beneath—broken, pallid, yet twitching with the last few jerks of life. That tiny face, mouth barely open enough to cry before it turned aside, gave a single gasp, went slack.

And on the wall behind, a shadow, rearing up—tall, curvaceous, with just a hint of exposed bone for ornament—to watch it all without comment, enthroned in cruel contemplation. *Waiting for . . .* something; just what Rook didn't know, or want to.

Staggering down through the Temple's dark stone halls, he emerged at last into the square and slumped to the snow-streaked ground, as empty of magic as of hope.

Too much power in flux to have any chance of hiding what had happened. Cautiously, people began to congregate, some dressed for bed, others barely decent. A nightshift-clad Marizol ran up, little feet bare against the cold ground, only to stop in horror when she caught sight of Rook's face. At the same time, two more figures came lofting in over her head on a carpet of solid air, thudding to earth: Honourable Chu and the Shoshone, both grim-visaged, battle-experienced enough to recognize the flavour of pain pouring hexaciously from the Temple.

"Clodagh," said the Shoshone, in visible dismay. "How?"

"Enemy," Rook replied, voice flat. "Lady tried to drown the place, and failed; Chess . . . her Enemy, I mean . . . thwarted it, so she left us behind, and the back-burst knocked us all to perdition." He pressed his hands to his forehead, sticky with Clo's cooling blood. "Sal's in with her now."

"For what good that will do," Chu snapped. "Did I not *say* it was foolish for the girl to go?" The threads of blue light crawling in his tunic illuminated him eerily. "In a bad birth, the child's *ch'i*-hunger will be at its worst. We may lose them both now, when we can ill afford losing even one."

"Think we already have," the Rev couldn't keep from saying, even as not-your-Auntie Sal's voice whispered at him: *Ate that boy of mine all up, without ever even wantin' to.*

The Shoshone's face fell. "That does it, then. They're bound together tight as ticks, the Fennigs, from long before they took the Oath; lose one, it as good as guts them all—in their hearts, *and* their hex-strength."

"A ridiculous theory, as always," Chu scoffed. "You have no idea—"

Neither would have a chance to argue the point further, however. Chu's tunic suddenly dimmed mid-word, a lamp guttering out; the Shoshone swayed, bonnet's feathers rising like a lizard's frill, and almost fell. All over the crowd, onlookers jackknifed, faces turned sick, grey, hollow; some collapsed on one knee, or retched outright. Rook took the punch of it deep in his own gut, ice-needle cold spiking through every vein. The power bled out from all of them, spurting toward the Temple in hot, shimmering, invisible jets.

Death, Rook realized, through his pain. Worse: an unsanctified demise, not given willingly on *any* level—a rejection of the Oath to its very core, sending the dying hex's power uselessly outward rather than channelling it back into the Machine. Such Oathbound-wide bouts of weakness hadn't happened since the City's early days, when ill-made Temple sacrifices sometimes went to waste, before the population had grown numerous enough to shrug them off. That everyone felt it now—apparently without exception, and so *strongly*—might be grim testimony to the thinness of Hex City's resources, or bittersweet evidence of how beloved Clo had been, in her hellion Irish way. Or . . .

Something else, something hidden, impenetrable and ancient. Something with his lady wife's increasingly fleshless fingerprints all over it.

The sickening pull went on, and now it wasn't only hexes that fell. On one side of Main Street, the diamond cube of Cordell Arkwright's chirurgery suddenly shattered, resolving to a pile of glass-clear shards; on the other, the huge vaudevillian façade that Luca de Belfort had conjured for his groggery-saloon crumpled to the ground like a theatrical scrim cut from its rigging, revealing the ugly crude-hammered plank walls behind. In every direction, hex-built structures collapsed, hex-woven garments shredded, hex-forged tools and objects came apart, or resumed their former mundane shapes.

Rook's heart stuttered in his chest; an awful pain shot up his left arm like a bolt. With a cry of fright, Marizol flung herself into his arms, clinging close.

The scream which rang out from Rook's balcony high above was raw with agony, holding a heartbreakingly defiant note even to the last: "*Ahhhhh, Christ, shittin'* Jaysuuuuuuuss—!"

But there it stopped, snapping to silence, a new-broke bone. The pull vanished with it. Still holding Marizol, Rook straightened far enough to signal Chu and the Shoshone with a finger-snap: "Check the defences—the rest we can rebuild later, once we don't have to worry whether Pinkerton knows what's happened. Those wall-wards, though . . . they have to stand."

The two of them nodded, and left on the run. A fresh wave of sickness threatened to capsize him. At his elbow, Marizol whispered: "*Jefe*—you are all right? You *must* be. For them." She nodded to the stunned crowd. Shamed to realize just how much of his considerable weight Marizol had actually been supporting, Rook drew himself up straight—permitted himself one hand only on her shoulder, and smiled down at her, as he did. She returned it, shyly.

"Holy *Christ*, Reverend, what was that?" shouted the first hex back on his feet—Arkwright, as it happened. "Look at my friggin' shop—the whole damn *city*! Ain't felt anything like that since . . . well, since the last time some fool tried to . . ."

He trailed off, hoarsely, as Rook completed the thought for him: *Last time anyone tried to feed on you—or last time She fed on us all, puttin' down trouble? Too bad the woman herself ain't on hand just right now to take questions. . . .*

Sucking in a breath, he recalled his old preaching techniques— breath control and dialectic, nothing fancy. "Friends," he began, "we won a victory tonight, striving against Bewelcome's witch-hunters and He Who Cannot Be Named himself, and this . . . was all part of the victory price, in ways I can't detail just now. But I promise you, once the Lady—"

Uncertain how to proceed, Rook paused to clear his throat, and realized that none of the crowd was looking at him, Marizol included. Instead, she was staring back over both their shoulders at the Temple, face fixed as though she'd spotted a rattlesnake nesting exactly where she was next about to step.

From the shadows within, Ixchel emerged. Even at this distance, she stank like rotted flowers, her borrowed flesh gone drawn and leathery, a bad imitation of dead Miz Adaluz's luscious curves. But beneath the jade-chip mask, her eyes glowed with a heat as fierce as an open cook-stove. Behind, Fennig made his slow way out into the starlight as well, looking like he'd gone seventy rounds with a pugilist who'd somehow managed not to break his spectacles. To see sharp young Hank so dazed and stumbling gave Rook a start, fresh pain skewering his breastbone straight where that burnt-out lump he called a heart resided; when he opened his mouth to commiserate, Fennig only shook his head, in mute misery.

"Mother *and* child?" Rook asked Ixchel, who gave no reply. So he went on, reminding her: "As I recall, before we left, you promised us a terrible weapon—and if you'd delivered on that, ma'am, then Clo might've lived. Might be they *both* would've."

Those knobs where her eyebrows should've been twitched

upward, as if on strings. "Ah, but she died a warrior's death, little king," the goddess said, and Christ, even her *voice* was different—its liquid music gone to a harsher timbre, more in keeping with that high-breasted ghost-girl from his first visions. Yet entirely the same, in all other essentials: remote, cold, disdainfully amused. "A *hero's* death, taking a baby in battle, at great cost of blood. And now, while her child hangs on the Suckling Tree, she too will live again . . . as that very same weapon."

Beyond the Temple's gates, the blackness remained impenetrable, no matter how Rook stared. Fennig turned to look as well, but either his vaunted interior sight was failing him, or there was simply nothing to see. Until bare feet scuffed rock floor and the darkness parted, to show—

—Clo, standing there. Upright, if not alive.

Strips of torn parchment were woven through her tangled hair, Aztec characters sketched in smeared blood upon 'em, spelling out God alone knew what. A leather cord hung from her neck, strung with gristly lumps and irregular twig bundles that proved, on closer examination, to be shrivelled human hearts and hands. From her own limp fingers black talons protruded, shaped more like a rose's thorns than a beast's claws. Strange tattoos like eyes or stars circled every joint Rook could see, while more blood had been used to paint the stylized shapes of skull and crossed bones on her ruined dress, whose skirt hung thick with bone-bell shells. Her pert Irish miss's features had drawn in so gaunt upon her skull that for a moment, Rook actually thought her face had been flayed.

Her eyes, meanwhile, were—gone, entirely. Only a cold blue radiance filled their blown orbits. And when she turned to fix Rook with those orbs, smiling, he saw her teeth had become a hundred jagged bone needles, densely packed as tiny spears.

Fennig took one stumbling step backward and fell right on his narrow behind, all dignity shucked, scrabbling for his dandy's cane against the flagstones. Marizol screamed and buried her face against Rook's side, shaking; Rook watched Clo's smile widen at the sound, lips parted, as though savouring fear's ozone-stink. He thought of

Chess's glee in those seconds before lead began flying—that *look*, presaging chaos and ruin, which said, *Finally, we're doing what* I *like!*

The world changed for Rook in that instant, with no marker other than a silent, almost resigned thought: *Ah, shit.*

"So," he said, to Ixchel. "Seems like you managed to get at least one other relative to join the party, after all."

She shook her head. "Alas, no. My brother, loath as I am to admit it, is right. They who sleep Below will not rise, at least for me. Which is why I have shepherded our Clodagh to another gift, different from that you and I gave to your lover, yet nearly as great—brought her into our ranks as *tzitzimihtl.*" The word had a rattlesnake sting, scarring the eardrum. "Because of their courage, those who die in childbirth may ascend the *tzitzimime's* roads, travelling the deep dark between stars until the day comes for the Fifth World to die. And what will happen then, daughter?"

Clo spoke, startling Rook badly; her voice sounded shockingly like it had in life, though her Irish lilt was slurred by fearsome dentistry. "Then, mother, we will descend from the night sky in our thousands, rending every human left living, so all the empty world is drowned in blood."

Ixchel clapped her hands, affectionately. "She is young yet," she told Rook. "At her full power, you shall need a *maguey*-fibre mask to view her safely. But she is strong and fast enough to lay waste to our besiegers with only teeth and talons, nevertheless—faster than any spell-breaker bullet may be aimed, or magic-eating wheel-work brought to bear. So, husband— are you not satisfied? Can you say I have done ill?"

At their feet, Hank Fennig stared silently from behind his spectacles' smoked-glass protection—stiffened his long spine by slow degrees, like the man was bracing himself for something.

"Thought you weren't too worried over Pinkerton's armaments, last time we spoke on it," Rook observed.

"I have revised my opinion. Is such not the prerogative of a queen?"

"Mmm," Rook agreed, raising his voice a trifle, to make sure all the City-folk within range could hear. "'Stead'a the whole god-passel, then, what we get is one measly demon? Strikes me we're still in a bind, he comes against us with everything."

"One *tzitzimihtl* is worth a thousand soldiers, hex or no. Her effect is . . . shattering."

"So you say."

Ixchel's grin vanished. "You require proof?"

Wouldn't have cared, once, Rook thought. *Not so long as I got what I wanted—Chess by my side, alive, and fixed to stay that way. But . . . I need to show them just how bad it is. Her, in all her glory.*

Damn, if he wasn't feeling his responsibilities. That never led anywhere healthy.

Deliberately: "Call me Doubting Thomas, but proof's always nice, yes. You offerin' any?"

"*Daughter.*"

The whisper was so quiet Rook half-thought he had only imagined it; Ixchel's lips had barely parted. In answer, though, Clo . . . or what had *been* Clo . . . *moved*, so fast she left a trail, stuttering from invisible to real and back again—a thousand poses, each scarring cornea and reality like a daguerreotype, acid-etched. First there, then *here*, slamming up nose-to-nose with complaint-happy Arkwright, who shrank from her eyeless leer, whimpering; head falling back, lips a-foam. Rook watched the hand he *almost* raised to fend her off wither, like wax in fire.

A frenzy of shell-bells tolling, ten thousand funerals strong—and then she started in on the poor sumbitch with all ten claws, finishing a fast half-second later. After which everyone got to watch the result fall back, to break apart at her feet: one dumb hex's worth of bloody bones, barely held together with gristle.

Clo blinked, and was back by Ixchel's side. "Your will be done, *mother*," she said, licking her gore-stained lips.

Now it was Ixchel's turn to smile. "Well," she asked Rook. "Are you satisfied?"

"Not hardly," Fennig replied.

The crowd swerved, almost as one, to scope out where they'd

probably forgotten he stood. In the murderous interim, he'd regained his feet and much of his former style—stood tall, hands braced on his cane, like he was about to pick a swordfight.

"So that's your deal, eh?" he asked. "A 'guardian' we can only trust to treat us all like her own personal coal-tender, somethin' she can chew up by the cupful, whenever her boiler gets low." Louder still, and as much to the crowd as to Ixchel: "'Cause that don't strike me as fair-dealing, if so: what did any of us ever swear the damn Oath for, if it weren't the promise of never gettin' fed on such-a-ways again? By *anyone*?"

The thing Ixchel'd made from Clo seemed to find this amusing. But Rook's Rainbow Lady puffed up with fresh menace, dragonfly cloak set a-buzz like an angry hive. "The Oath frees you from fear of each *other*, Henry Fennig," she said. "Yet never for one moment think it protects you from *me*, your goddess." She turned to the crowd, some of whom recoiled. "For *you*, whom I have folded in—given New Aztectlan as your home, your refuge—are all, to every last man, woman and child, *mine. By your own words.*"

"I'd beg to differ," Fennig shot back. "Was Hex City they swore to, these ones—most of 'em don't know what-all 'New Aztectlan' *is*."

"This is sophistry."

"Common sense, more like. A quality in short damn supply 'round here, as of late."

"Have a care, mortal man."

"Oh, I do, believe me. You should, too."

Been quite the while since anybody'd called Ixchel's guff to her face; Rook had to reckon that alone kept her frozen as Fennig crossed over, rolling up his sleeves. His cane he passed to Berta and Eulie, their tear-stained faces white with worry on his behalf, while those fine back-up specs of his he folded and gave the Rev himself, pressing them into the larger man's hand.

"Keep these for me, will ya?" he asked, for all the world as though he expected to survive whatever happened next.

Bemused, Rook stowed them in his vest pocket while Fennig continued blithely along his path to ruin, pausing just short of

Ixchel's reach. Clo he ignored, or tried to—instead, he met the Lady of Traps and Snares' empty gaze straight on, his naked eyes shedding light in a manner not unlike his dead wife's, if cooler.

"You know I can see through you too, right, Missus?" he asked her. "Which is how I come to learn that savin' the braggadocio, you ain't nothin' but a hex, same's any other—well-fed, ghosted up, but that's all. Talkin' up how you own this whole world, how you can make and remake it at will. . . . So why is it you ain't done that yet, exactly?"

"You dare to question *me*?"

"If I thought it'd do any good, sure. But since I know better, here's what I *will* say. My g'hals and me come up here with eyes open, hopin' that line you talked was only half a lie. And things went well, at first, but then I started seein' cracks, like it's given me to do—and lady, those cracks are *big*. Keep followin' this path you're on, all you'll do is drag yourself back down into Hell, plus the rest of us along with you . . . not that *you* care."

"Be silent, insect. If you would keep those two wives you still have, let alone your life, then—"

Fennig laughed, bitterly. "Oh, yeah. Go 'head, threaten me louder, so's everyone can hear. Do your worst, so's they see what you *really* pay your wages out in."

The cloak spasmed and eddied, a black rainbow waterspout, high as the wave she'd called to drown Bewelcome. "*Silence*, I said! You think to chide your betters, gutter-rat, bred and fed on garbage? You, who owe me *everything*—"

"Yeah? Well, at least *my* gutter always stood behind me, whenever the bulls started in to crackin' heads. I'm Five Points through and through, from cobbles t'curbs, and that'll always beat bein' a Mexican table-rapper's mascot tricked out in half-naked stargazer-meat all to hell." He folded his arms, bared his ill-set city dweller's teeth, stiff with rage. "The long and the short of it is, Missus, you promised but you didn't deliver, then made my son's mother into *that*, and let my son die to do it. Way I see it, ain't a single one of us owes *you* nothin'."

Ixchel stood a moment, while Clo grinned beside her. "Perhaps you think me weak enough to address with such disrespect," she said, at last, "since this vessel nears the end of its use, as any fool can see. But her successor awaits, and when I am reborn in her—"

Yet here she made yet another mistake, by looking directly at Marizol—at which point the girl's already terrified expression went up like lucifer-touched flashpaper, as all her nameless dread became horrid comprehension. "*Por amor de Dios, no!*" she screamed, broke from Rook's arms and flung herself on Berta and Eulie instead, rousing them from their grief-struck stupor. They grabbed her in a double hug, Eulie stroking Marizol's hair and murmuring to her, while Berta exchanged a glance with Fennig so penetrating Rook could've sworn he saw words swimming back and forth inside it.

Distracted by the effort of beckoning Marizol back, her tomb-rank voice willed almost sweet, Ixchel remained completely oblivious. "Come here, my heart's heart," she cooed. "I am not angry; you are a child, and cannot always see where the best way lies. Your parents will explain this when we are alone together, in ways you can understand."

"*Que no!* I will *not* do this thing! And if they seek to make me, to cast me off—then I cast *them* off!"

"Dear one, you know not what you say. Only wait, and I will—"

Fennig guffawed. "What, kiss it better? Looks like you forgot somethin' you told us from the start, Lady—how for a sacrifice t'take, the one gettin' done to's gotta *love* you, or choose to let you, any road. Good luck ever gettin' her to think of you *that* way, ever again."

"This is *your* fault."

"I should damn well hope so. But watch a minute—'cause I ain't done just yet." He flung up an arm at the remaining Missus Fennigs—sent a gush of power into them so thick, it jolted 'em upright like puppets. And hollered, as the light in his eyes went out: "Berta, Eulie. Take the girl, and *go!*"

No time to think yea or nay; might be this'd been exactly what Fennig and Berta were "jawing" over, while Marizol handed Ixchel her hat. But the three simply vanished with a *crack*, air collapsing to fill the space they'd occupied.

Ixchel's jade-chip parody of a face contorted; she turned on Fennig, hair wafting straight up, an inky nimbus. *"Bring them back, dog!"*

"Make me," Fennig snapped. "But ya can't, can ya? 'Cause that ain't what it says, in the fine print: '*Service* to the Suicide Moon,'—that's what you get, *all* you get, and welcome to it. Long as it ain't a direct rise against ya, or flat-out doin' something you told us *not* to, you got naught to say 'bout anything we do, Lady R.—no matter how much it . . . *inconveniences* you. My g'hals and me—we kept to the terms. You can suck us dry. But you can't *make* us do your will—or any other damn thing, neither."

Rook rumbled, down in his chest. "That's . . . very lawyerly of you, Henry. 'Obedience to her High Priest,' though, said priest being me—how 'bout that?"

The gangster shrugged. "Oh, that one holds," he admitted. "You could've stopped 'em 'fore they went, I have no doubt—stopped me from givin' the order, for that matter, if you'd known it was comin'. But . . ."

". . . I didn't. And now it's too late."

"Exactly." With a nod, Three-Fingered Hank stood up tall as Rainbow Lady Ixchel turned her dreadful eyes his way once more, blank and pitiless as her emblem the moon, if infinitely darker: a glare beneath which harder men than he had shivered, Rook included.

Still, truth to tell, Fennig wasn't even looking her way, keeping his own eyes trained instead square on the creature who'd once played triangle-point in his polyamorous affections—perhaps studying her for some recognition, however small, and getting none that Rook could perceive. Yet smiling slightly all the while, nonetheless.

"I put trust in you, Henry Fennig," Ixchel told him, slowly, "on my own consort's word; looked to you and your women as helpmeets, my strong right arm in battle just as one of them serves me yet. Tonight, however, you have gone against your queen, your goddess—risked not only the Machine, but the new world it brings on. Of all people but one, *you* should know best the penalty for such betrayal."

"True enough. Think about it this way, though: killing me, right here and now, over an 'offence' don't break none of your precious laws? That ain't justice, so much as tyranny—same kind we fought a war over, back in old King George's time. And *that* war, we *won*."

A ripple went through the crowd, gone almost before Ixchel could perceive it, let alone trace its source.

You don't even see what you're about to do here, do you, darlin'? thought Rook. *Teach 'em in one fell stroke what I've known all along—that you can't be trusted, not to keep your word, and not otherwise.*

"So get ready, Missus," Fennig finished. "Now everyone knows—I may be the first, but I damn sure won't be last."

Good epitaph, son.

Fennig met his eyes, his reply echoing straight inside Rook's skull. *Honoured, Reverend; you're a good man, even when you ain't. Now, don't forget those glazers of mine, will you? Believe it or not, it's worth your while.*

Ixchel didn't even have to give the order. Between one heartbeat and the next, Clo was back in Fennig's arms, like they'd never been separate. Except, of course, that this time her lips were peeled back to expose a shark's double row of teeth, bottom and top. Though her right hand cupped the nape of his neck, deceptively loving, her thorn-clawed left had already plunged to split his breastbone like a sunk rail spike, fingers cupped cruel 'round his beating heart.

Fennig coughed blood, arterial-bright and steaming. Rasped: "Love you, honey. Always will. This . . . ain't your fault."

"Yes it is," Clo replied, without a shred of remorse. And bit his face off first, a crunchy sweetmeat, before moving on to the rest.

AFTER NEAR EVERYONE ELSE had turned away but Ixchel, Rook (who'd forced himself to watch) and Clo (still intent on her pleasure, taking far longer with Fennig than she had with Arkwright, for reasons Rook didn't want to contemplate), Ixchel put a hand on her "daughter's" shoulder, pulling her gently free of what little was left.

"Enough," she told her, wiping blood from Clo's lower lip only to lick it off her finger, savouring the taste. "You are young yet, and though you do not tire, there is no reason not to pace yourself. Return to your chamber, to await my will."

"Yes, mother."

Taking Clo by the chin, Ixchel kissed her too-red mouth and stepped away, passing Rook by in the opposite direction. "I will expect you soon, my husband," she threw back, cloak humming in her wake, as if over-stimulated by tonight's amusements. "Do not keep me waiting."

He made her a leg, bowing low, which seemed acceptable. And hung back one minute longer, stroking the bulge Fennig's spectacles made through his vest cloth, feeling that residual pulse of energy under his fingertips as though the man was absent rather than excised: a patient, intimate resonance, like this fragile rig of wires and lenses carried just enough intelligence of its own to have stubborn faith he might one day return to reclaim them.

Fennig had to have known, or at least suspected, what Rook saw now: the specs were talisman as much as tool—mere contact conferred a stark fraction of Fennig's gift. Enough to look at the horrid ruin Ixchel had made of Clo Killeen . . . and realize it yet contained a last seed of the original.

Something that might even bloom again, one day.

CHAPTER NINE

NIGHT'S HOUSE, WITH ITS many chambers, its many occupants. Like the one located high on a hill overlooking Bewelcome where Chess Pargeter and "Reverend" Rook had once paused their horses, contemplating pre-emptive action 'gainst zealous young Sheriff Mesach Love, where two considerably less distinctive-looking men now stood in shadow, examining at a cautious distance the lamentable extent of Bewelcome's current devastation.

Both wore duster coats and sported neat-waxed walrus moustaches, one blond, the other dark. The dark one used a brass telescope to mark points of particular interest while the other rocked back and forth with hands dug deep in his pockets, all but toe-tapping to signal his impatience.

"I'll point out it's *your* intelligencer we wait on, Mister Geyer," the dark one said, without turning, "so whatever strategical quandary you find yourself enmeshed in, it's entirely of your own making. Actually, given how little faith you seem to have in this fellow, I'm driven to wonder why you thought to engage him, in the first place."

"Lack of options," ex-Pinkerton Agent Frank Geyer replied. "He was well-situated, well-disposed . . . and to be frank, George, he works cheap."

"Perfectly good qualities, in any spy," agreed the other man— ex-Agent George Thiel, of course, first official defector from their former mutual boss's increasingly dubious organization. "Pinkerton himself would approve."

"Not if he knew what we were doing with him, I don't think."

"And there's where I'd agree with you," a third voice called out, from the shadows, as its owner made his way up the hill's backside. This soon proved to be Fitz Hugh Ludlow, dandified clothes still mud-stiff from the fray. Reaching the hill's apex, he stooped and huffed for a moment before straightening, trotting out the same oily grin that'd so failed to ingratiate him to Ed Morrow. "But may I say how disheartening it is to hear yourself described with such unfortunate accuracy, 'specially by those who don't know you're on hand to listen in?"

"Where've you been, Ludlow?" Geyer demanded.

"Extricating myself from that matchstick-pile Sophy Love and company used to call a meeting house, for starters, after which I was forced to stop awhile and observe Reverend Rook and his cadre beating unholy hell out of her husband's unworthy successors."

Thiel turned, quirking an interested brow. "To what outcome?"

"Oh, bad all 'round, pretty much universally. Missus Love stood proud 'gainst the hexacious tide, only to get herself disintegrated. Reverend Catlin preached on God's supremacy while holding one of Doc Asbury's little machines, letting it suck in witchcraft 'til he blew his own hand off. Then Queen Rope herself appeared and tried to flood the town out, only for Chess Pargeter's ghost to rise up through the dirt, ass-naked but for a set of Red Weed underclothes, and put paid to her scheming. Can probably see the moat he made from here, you only squint hard enough." Ludlow paused for breath. "In short, an exciting evening had by all, well worth an entire yellow novel chapter to itself. And you, gentlemen?"

Geyer shook his head, as though to clear it. "Hold a moment . . . Sophronia Love is *dead*?"

Ludlow shrugged. "Impossible to tell, truly. I certainly saw her lose coherence in the face of that Paddy witch's onslaught. But this proves nothing; I've seen hexes transport folk from one point to another just as easily, with much the same result."

"She and her babe might be prisoners, then, inside Hex City's precincts," Thiel observed. "A useful idea, 'specially if we wanted to rouse Bewelcome's survivors for a rescue."

"True!" said Ludlow. "And what a narrative *that* would make for . . . saleable indeed, to all possible markets."

Geyer studied each for some hint of a joke, eyes widening with genuine discomfort when he didn't find any. "You two make my blood run cold," he said, at last.

Ludlow puffed up, finally insulted. "Sir, I follow my *calling*, from which you and Mister Thiel here benefit extraordinarily for very little bodily risk, while *I* put myself in the very thick of harm's way. Believe me, if I yearned to be called names, I'd've stayed in New York."

"Desperate times, Frank," Thiel replied, at the same time, without heat. "Desperate measures. We can't afford to be—"

"—what, *human*?"

"Over-nice, I was *going* to say. For the plain fact is, we need every advantage we can gain from here on out, putting our endgame together. What we do here we do for the very literal salvation of all mankind."

There was little to say in response, so no one tried, simply fell silent a spell, 'til Ludlow said, "Well, moving on to other things . . . as you know, Mister Pinkerton did not attend the meeting, for which I'm sure he'll be thankful, once Mister Morrow and Doctor Asbury debrief him on their return. He seldom leaves Camp Pink at all, these days, or so Mister Morrow has tried ably to keep from letting slip."

"And why's that, I wonder?" Thiel asked the wind. Beside him, Geyer snorted.

"Still semi-witched, I'd 'spect, from his dabblings in matters arcanistric. You only saw the start of it, George—that wound he took from Pargeter, how Asbury tried to treat it. He was worse when I met him on the Train, by far."

"Rumours to that effect, yes," Ludlow agreed. "They do say how the Professor's engineeringological victories have only made his particular . . . hungers all the easier to satisfy, as the Pinkertons' supply of collared hexes grows. But this latest miracle of his may well take the proverbial cake."

"Meaning?"

"Asbury gave Morrow bullets, Morrow shot 'em at the Rev— and they *took*. From what I could gather squatting behind a brake, everyone seemed pretty much equal horror-struck; Asbury too, now I think. But then, he's been looking unwell, in general."

"Tell me more about that," Thiel suggested.

Ludlow laughed and struck a pose, fair cracking his knuckles. "Oh, that's been coming on for some time now; going by tonight's brief appearance, the man looks almost on the verge of a collapse— dispirited, sirs, very dispirited, though not so much so that he's gone teetotal." He paused, ruminatorily. "Rather the opposite, really."

Geyer regarded him with scorn. "Never use a two-bit word when a five-dollar one's to hand, do you, Mister Ludlow?"

"Vocabulary's a tool *and* a hobby of mine, ex-Agent; fills in the blanks and keeps thing sharp, used judiciously. But believe you me, it's not as though I enjoy seeing one of the finest minds of our generation thus reduced, designing weapons for a second Civil War under the command of a near-madman, a hopeless hophead. It sets me all of a jargogle to think what Mister Asbury might whip up next."

"We should find a way to talk to him, Frank," Thiel said. "For months now I've tried to deconstruct that Manifold of yours, bend even a tenth of its powers to our side—but all to no avail. I'm but a humble 'tec with some Corps of Engineering experience left over from the War. Professor Asbury's brand of science is as far beyond mine as Nobel's Blasting Powder is to a tinderbox. And if he's finally reached the limits of his appetite for our old boss's more off-putting . . . shenanigans . . ."

Ludlow glanced from man to man. "I believe I begin to reckon what you have in mind, Mister Thiel—and as it just so happens, I can help. You see, though he chose not to attend the maybe-late Missus Love's little shindig, I received a secret communiqué from Mister

Pinkerton this very morning. He wants an interview, a general-at-the-front sort of deal, and believes I would be the perfect . . . now, what was the phrase he used? . . . 'chronicleer' to record his upcoming Campaign against the Hex for journalistic posterity. I'll need a bodyguard on my journey, of course, things being chancy as they are right now. Any volunteers?"

"Given the last time Pinkerton saw you, he called you out as a traitor—" Thiel began, to Geyer.

"Last time he saw *you*," Geyer pointed out, in return, "he ended up sending me to kill you—and the way he is these days, I doubt he'd even notice I was there, I took enough pains with my appearance. You're needed elsewhere anyways, to lead the Texican charge, if and when the Mexican attack occurs."

"*When*, not if."

"So if it's all the same, I believe I'll take my chances."

"Very well."

Ludlow clapped his hands. "Perfect. How I do love theatricals!"

Once again, both detectives considered him narrowly. "You do know you may see things you don't want to in that stronghold, Mister Ludlow," Thiel said, finally.

"Oh, don't worry yourself concerning the quality of *my* sleep, sir; I was caught downtown during the Draft Riots in '63. Which sanguinary event marks the very moment I discovered my gorge doesn't rise too easily, sad to say, when a good enough story's involved."

"I read the dispatches, in our Chicago office," Geyer replied. "But I've always wondered—was hexation involved?"

"Here and there, yes. New York's vastly diverse populace extends even to the hex-born—and since the gangs aren't exactly inclined to turn down any weapon falls to hand, they tend to use whoever turns hex under combat's excesses as heavy artillery, clearing the way for more natural incursion: hordes of immigrants and Nativists alike, all wielding bricks, bats, fists, knives, axes . . . but no pistols. Still, with the city a powder-keg always awaiting spark, we've never needed *hexation's* prompting when it comes to exercising our civic pastime, not within Gotham's precincts—or anywhere else human nature holds sway."

Above, the moon shone down like a dead man's eye full of secret glee, absorbing it all. No secrets in Night's house, after all. Not with everything that ill light touched transformed near-alchemically, the same way a spell renders metaphor real, into a spy for some hidden Enemy.

MILES AWAY, YANCEY CAME to shivering top to toe with her teeth too locked to chatter, tongue worried bloody. Though Yiska and her braves had laid her out already—piling all the rugs they had on top of her, high as they'd go—the chill of the Underneath still ran all through her, worse than before. Just how damn deep had she had to dive, in order to whisper upward directions in English Oona's slippery ear?

Not as deep as she might yet have to go, she suspected.

Even as she formed this thought, a pale palm appeared at either temple, briskly stroking heat into her. "You look ill, dead-speaker," Songbird observed, with a nasty touch of satisfaction. "The Ten Thousand Hells do not agree with you."

"D-don't think they were ... made t'appeal ... t'most," Yancey said, with effort. "'Sides, that . . . seemed like one Hell only, t'me. An' . . . more'n enough."

"Yes, you long-noses lack imagination, as a rule; I have observed this."

Yiska laid a gentle hand of her own on Songbird's shoulder. "*Ohé, bilagaana*, it gladdens me to see you returned safe, after such a long journey. Might it be you caught sight of our Enemy, while you were down there?"

Yancey tried to shake her head, and regretted it. "N'huh, no. Don't think so."

"You would know, if you had," Songbird said. "He is ... distinctive."

"I *do* know—met the sumbitch twice before, and not when he was all dressed up in Chess Pargeter's meat, either. How many times's it been for you?"

Songbird coloured, flush slight but noticeable. "Never you mind, innkeeper's daughter. He would have to be clumsy indeed to let either of us see him, if he did not wish to be seen."

"You speak the truth, for once," came Grandma's voice. "He is not to be underestimated, this Smoking Mirror." She moved out into the fire's light, earth shaking beneath her tread, then lowered herself down by slow degrees. "The tale of Tollan's Fall . . . have you heard it?"

"You know very well we have not, old—" But Songbird found herself pinned by Yiska's gaze, and amended whatever she might've been about to call the older hex. "Spinner."

"Be quiet, then, little ghost. Attend, for once. There is virtue in the past's lesson, always, for—since all gods repeat themselves, and most *Hataalii* likewise—it may give us some idea what he plans to do next."

The words of the story wove themselves out, echoing hexation-aided through bone and blood, in three languages at once. Exhausted, Yancey let her cold-burnt lids drift shut and saw vague shapes unspool behind them—squarish symbols wrought from contorted bodies, all fangs and feathers, tongues and bulging eyes. Ink-black, macaw-red writing scribed on whitewashed walls, so fresh it almost ran, while a steaming green jungle rose behind, and the unfamiliar din of insects.

Her place, she thought. *Lady Ixchel's dead world, the one she wants to swap ours for.*

"Tollan was chief city of the Tolteca," Grandma said, somehow not stumbling over the names, though they couldn't've come any more easy to whatever she used for a tongue than to Yancey's own. "A great nation which existed before the Mexica built their Empire, down where the sun meets the swamp. But their last king, Huemac, fell into evil ways, and was punished. It began when a *Hataalii* who called himself Toveyo appeared in front of the city, a beautiful man painted all over in green, and was invited inside.

"With sweet music and spells, Toveyo tempted Tollan's people to dance in their marketplace, making the song he played swirl faster and faster until it finally drove them into such a madness they rushed out through the city's gates, throwing themselves headlong into a canyon in the earth. As they fell, they bounced off the walls, breaking all their bones, and when they finally reached the bottom, their bodies turned to stone.

"Moments later, the mountains overlooking Tollan began to growl and belch flames, in which the city's priests saw figures making terrible gestures. Surely, they thought, the gods must be angry—and when Huemac ordered an offering to appease them, Toveyo was the first one seized. But when the priests bent his body over the altar stone and opened up his chest, they found he had no heart at all. His veins were also dry and empty, sending no precious blood spilling onto the temple's stones. Then a stench rose from the body, and though the priests and onlookers fled, an epidemic of foul wasting diseases followed.

"For choosing a man with neither the heart nor the blood that creatures such as She of the Ropes and Snares require as a sacrifice, Tollan was punished with crop-killing frosts and summer droughts, wild storms, floods. Huemac fled, leaving his illegitimate son in charge. Two armies of invaders were bought off with the last of the city's riches before the northern nomads known as the Sons of the Dog finally descended, at which point the first two armies turned back, and joined forces with them. For three years, the people of Tollan held them off with only a company of old men, boys and women, but eventually, the walls were breached. Tollan fell."

"So Toveyo got his will," Songbird said, examining her sheathless fingernails, while Yancey levered herself into a sitting position, each bout of shivering slightly less frantic. "He tricked Tollan into insulting their own gods, and those gods destroyed them. A victory for our kind."

Grandma shook her head. "No. For according to the Mexica, Toveyo was simply a face worn by the Smoking Mirror, Rainbow Lady's Ixchel's 'brother'—Night Wind Tezcatlipoca, Enemy of all, who loves to stir up chaos for its own sake: god of all *Hataalii*, all hexes. Who some say stands for nothing less than conflict as a means to change itself."

Songbird bristled. "He is not *my* god."

"Mine either," Yancey chimed in, surprised to find herself agreeing. And might be Grandma would've struck them both down in her rebuttal, had they not been interrupted.

"I should . . . hope not, Missus Kloves," said a new voice, hoarse and desert-dry. "For little as we see eye to eye in other ways—murderous revenge as . . . justice, for example—I'd never've took you for a . . . heathen idolater."

There, by the butte's foot, right where its shadow would've fallen in the day: that was where Sheriff Love's widow stood barefoot, her weeds ripped, long yellow hair unbound and heavy with dirt. Hoisted in her arms, she carried a good-sized baby boy who looked as though he'd been through similar straits, but was managing to sleep it off. Yancey felt her heart go foolishly soft at the very sight of his lumpy, boneless weight, mouth slack around one pudgy thumb.

"It *is* you, isn't it?" she asked, looking straight at Yancey, freckle-set brow furrowed. "I mean . . . haven't seen you since that . . . awful day. At Bewelcome."

When I blew your man's brains out, right in front of you? Yes ma'am, I recall it well. That was *me, and so's this.*

"How'd you get here, though, Missus Love, exactly?" she made herself say instead; polite, like they were taking tea. "Was it Reverend Rook sent you?"

Sophy Love shook her stately head, clutching her baby all the tighter. "No, one of that New York hex's three—women; the Irish one, I believe. Tell the truth, I could barely understand her! But I knew she wished harm on Gabe and me, so I called on the Lord to aid us. And then . . ."

She narrowed her eyes, as though she couldn't quite recall the specifics. But as she did, her son shifted in his slumber, gurgling—and beside her, Yancey felt Songbird suddenly stiffen and hiss, like a spooked cat. Felt something spike from her, and Grandma too: a pulling at the air, a pressure drop, as though before a storm. A hungry cry pitched almost too high to hear, so sharp it plucked even at her, and she wasn't a hex at all; Yiska, too, hand falling automatically to her tomahawk's grip.

They feel somebody, all of 'em, someone like them. Someone who could eat everything they have or be eaten, in turn. But . . . who?

That was when the baby—young Gabriel Love—jerked awake for good, seeking with barely focused gaze for a brace of rivals he couldn't possibly spot, even at this distance, and sent up what seemed like the ghost of the same squalling, thin as fine-chopped bones. All of an instant, then, Yancey could almost see what *they* saw, plain as Songbird's skin or Yiska's nose. Plain as the flare 'round Grandma's helmet-skull, lighting up her upturned bucket of a no-face, revealing her true nature to anyone.

"So sad," Sophy Love said to herself, completely unaware; she looked almost drunk, to Yancey's bar-bred eye—drunk on loss, on fatigue, on sorrow too long deferred, in favour of cold responsibility. "How I've hated you and prayed not to, for *so* long; foolish, really, for all the good it did me, either way. But now I see you again, you have my pity—to see any white woman so abandoned, fallen amongst savage witches."

"Wouldn't be so quick to insult them if I was you, ma'am," Yancey replied. "These ladies are powerful. They might yet be the ones to save your son's life."

"Is that a threat?"

Yancey almost laughed, hearing Songbird's mental speech yammering at her inner ear, at the same time—an endless reel of: *Kill him, while we can, before he strikes at us! Kill her!*

No, she thought. *But that is.*

Yiska *tsked*, out loud. "You disappoint me," she said—to Songbird, though Sophy Love no doubt heard it directed at her. "This is a chance we have, here . . . to do right even when doubted, to teach this *bilagaana* Book-babbler by example. Do not let your fear control you."

Songbird hissed again. And Grandma, stirring in her seat with the groan of a mountain settling, told her: "She is right, little ghost. The salt-man's wife knows no better."

Sophy's eyes went wide, for all the world as if she hadn't really *noticed* Grandma sitting there, 'til part of the butte itself took on life; her whole body recoiled a step, grip tightening on poor Gabe 'til her knuckles whitened. "My good Jesus," she said, with admirable calm. "You're . . . that other demon."

"No such thing. But you may call me that, if you wish."

Songbird threw her arms up, white braids swinging wide. "Enough coddling! We *must* defend ourselves, especially when our enemy knows nothing! I will do it, if you fear to—"

She thrust one hand out toward Gabe, fingers crooked like horns, knuckle sparking; Yancey seized it without thinking, only to scream when Songbird's conjured fire seared her palm. "Jesus Christ Almighty!"

"Loose me, dead-speaker!"

A familiar locust-chitter filled the air; Sophy Love whipped a shiny new version of Doctor Asbury's toy from her pocket, brandishing it Songbird's way. "Lay one hand upon him," she warned, "and I'll kill you where you stand, you Godforsaken creature."

But the Manifold's needle swung back toward Gabe, who was crying harder than ever—slid straight into the red, and stuck there.

And even as his own corona snapped and flared, Yancey heard Grandma say, for once without any real sort of judgement, though equally little sympathy: "Perhaps you should look to your own house, *bilagaana*. For as that thing you hold can tell you, *we* are not the only 'hexes' here."

Sophy Love looked down, caught breath balanced between love and revulsion, into her son's squalling face. Yancey didn't have to try to rifle through the woman's thoughts, now; hell, she was hard-pressed to keep 'em out. A dreadful black tide slopping up, transmuting that same maternal pull to bitterest gall: 1 Samuel, 15:53. *For rebellion is as the sin of witchcraft, and stubbornness is as iniquity and idolatry,* so *Because thou hast rejected the word of the LORD, he hath also rejected thee from being king.*

Oh, Gabriel—not you, of all people. How will you ever fulfil your father's legacy now? How could you even live among his own town's people—good, kind, Christian people—let alone rule them the way you were born to, knowing they'd think you the Devil's own cub?

Great and powerful God, why must you make only the most devoted of all your servants suffer so?

"Not my boy," Sophy Love murmured to herself. And sat down in a flump with her skirts pooled 'round her, face turned from the child she still hugged tight.

Yancey took three or four small steps toward the Widow; got down on her trousered knees in the dirt, her joints still stiff. And held out her arms for Bewelcome's former heir—exiled through no fault of his own to a desert worse than the one where Satan had tempted Christ, where stones could never be made bread, not even by the Word of God.

"I'll take him if you want, ma'am," she told Missus Love, softly as she could. "You just rest. And we'll talk it over later, in the morning."

Sophy said neither yea nor nay, but didn't put up much of a fight when Yancey lifted Gabe free and put him over one shoulder, patting his back 'til his wails trailed off into hiccups. Simply sat there slumped with her hair hanging down—mouth moving, perhaps in silent prayer—and looking at her hands, as though she wasn't quite sure whether or not she had the right to bury her face in them.

"I must get away from here," Songbird whispered, agitatedly, in Yiska's ear. "That boy knows nothing, he cannot control himself—"

"But you *can*, and set an example, doing so. Has he tried to feed on you, or the Spinner?"

"He *will*, as any of us would. He is . . . what he is!"

Grandma leaned in: "A *Hataalii*, yes, but untrained, unblooded; he took his mother away from that woman by instinct, instead of striking back himself. I feel no hunger in him, not as yet."

"*Ai-yaaah!* You pretend to great wisdom, as ever, but we Han have known of such things for centuries. Was it not we who first mapped the flow of *ch'i* through the body, as well as those points where it may escape, or be stolen? It is only because of *our* knowledge that *object* works at all."

On the horizon, further even than half-smitten Bewelcome itself, a foul star seemed to bloom. There was an awful noise; Yancey couldn't have named it if she'd tried. And out in the darkness, something else laughed long and loud, equally dreadful—as though amusement were its currency, and it accounted itself well-paid.

At the sound, Grandma's head swung 'round once more, spun on that boneless thing she called a neck 'til it all but made complete revolution, fast as wooden ribcage shutters snapping to over a bloody, beating heart.

"What has that thing the blackrobe Rook married done *now*?" she demanded, apparently of the universe itself.

SEVEN DIALS: FOUR

Our current world is Nahui-Ollin, the Earthquake Sun. It will shake itself apart one day, after which everything Quetzalcoatl stole will be returned to its rightful owner, Mictantecuhtli. The Seed of All will be re-buried at the bottom of a charnel pit, awaiting its next red watering. And then, eventually . . .

. . . everything will begin, once more, only to die, wither, be reborn. Again, again, again.

Endlessly.

We stole our bones from the gods of the Underworld, over and over— bones and flesh, our souls, our very selves. Which is why we will always try to keep them as long as we possibly can, no matter what the price, no matter how dreadful the reckoning.

No matter what, or who, it costs.

THEY WERE WELL OUT onto the bridge before he even realized what it was, and when he did, the understanding almost undid him. Chess had no worse a head for heights than anyone else raised up mostly at ground level, but *this* wasn't something mortal man was meant to look upon—a thread of black stone, less than a yard wide, stretching impossibly far into the distance without buttress or brace to prop it up, no rail to break your stumble, and sickeningly uneven underfoot. While below, an awful shifting ocean of fire spilled from horizon to horizon, its scorching light a sickly amalgam of pus-streaked blood and fever sweat.

It stank, too; a rip-throat stench, vile as any sulphur spring. Between those virulent tongues of flame, countless shapeless forms writhed while screams struck upward, so skull-splittingly loud the wall of noise hit almost as hard as the heat.

Hell—*true* Hell at long last, straight out of the Book itself. One a'them like Ash was always rabbiting on about, in between the Thou-Shalt-Not chorus.

Gehenna, Chess could almost hear Rook rumble, as he went reeling down the bridge after Oona. *Where the fearful, and unbelieving, and the abhominable, and murderers, and whoremongers, and sorcerers, and idolaters, and all liars, shall have their part in the lake which burneth with fire and brimstone . . . .* Revelation, *darlin'. No man can pretend he doesn't know his fate, he's only got ears to hear.*

Just shut up, you Goddamn man! Chess longed to scream, clinging precariously to his balance and his Ma's ghostly hand. But demanded instead: "The fuck's all *this*? What's a Bible-thumper's perdition doin' down this-a-way, lodged fast in the Enemy's own gullet?"

Ixchel's voice, cooing up through his gullet: ***Tezcatlipoca, who—Mictantecuhtli's claims to the title of Death's rulership aside—truly contains all those gone on, since he is the very Night the dead swim in . . .***

And you shut up too, you unhallowed bitch: shut up, shut up, shut up—

"'Ell should I know?" Oona yelled back. "Fings all run together down 'ere, if you ain't already noticed—I've seen men runnin' through the Dials what looked like bloody Swedes all got up for battle, or looked through mirrors an' seen places like them Chinks talks about—rooms full of knives and snakes, and whatnot. . . ."

She glanced back over her shoulder, like she expected to find 'em nipping at her heels—and shrieked out loud, face spread flat with sudden terror, when she saw what really *was*. The sight sent Chess whirling 'round to deliver the same sort of back-kick he'd used to fell Doc Glossing's corpse-doll, back in Mouth-of-Praise—'til he caught sight of what he was about to go toe-to-toe with, and thought better.

That giant black thing already reared up cavern-roof high, one limb drawn back as if to scythe his head clean off at the shoulders with its foot-long talons, swept its blow instead near a yard too high; its great leg, lifting forward for a further step, snagged on Chess's boot-heel, and folded. Released at last, Oona's fright-yell disappeared into the cacophony as the thing overbalanced, staggered too far to one side, and went over the edge. It spun as it fell, topmost portion dimming to a vague point, oval enough to form some sort of head; the blank where a face should have been, which turned to Chess's until for half an instant, it *was* a face. A human face, bloodstained and familiar, contorted into something no longer sane beneath its over-groomed crown of Bushwhacker locks, with the wreckage of an officer's grey shell-jacket flapping away on either side like dirty wings.

The name came up with an agonizing tug, yanked from his brain as if by hooks: *Saul Mobley.* Or—as Chess'd thought of him for half a year, before blowing out the back of his skull to escape his maddened death-charge plans, after which he'd never thought of him again— the Lieut.

So here's where you fetched up, Chess thought, viciously, *all mortar fire and smoke, worse by far than any earthly battlefield—you who wanted to fight on even after the War was lost, 'til all of us were dead, or crazy as yourself; almost got Rook and me hung, too, but not quite. Hope you relish it, you jackanapes motherfuck.*

If there was recognition in that hate-crazed gaze, however, Chess couldn't see it—the Lieut, or what little was left of him, was gone too fast anyhow, plunging into the inferno below. Chess stared after, a reckless mistake, as vertigo made him gasp. For an instant, the impulse to fling himself forward as well took hold, stomach seeming to float, bilious yet barely tethered, as if he'd already taken the final dive.

Then two small hands seized him by cheek and jaw, hauling his head back up for Oona to whack her forehead impatiently against his—a Bristol kiss, she'd called it, first time he'd run home with a split skull after having that same move demonstrated on him. And while no blood flowed, Chess's eyes teared up, nonetheless.

"Ow, *Christ*! Son of a mother—"

"Yeah, all that. Now stop sightseein', pull yer bloody trousers up, and *run*!"

He opened his mouth to complain again, but realized she was right—for that familiar rhythm was once more coming up from behind, shaking the bridge like a twanged guitar string. The Dead Posse itself, closing in like nightfall. Morbidly curious, he squinted, trying to tell features at this rancid-lit distance, even as Oona tried her best to haul his arm from its socket.

"What are you, deaf?" she yelled. "We ain't got time to ponder, boy—'oo knows but there's a door on the other side, and that already 'alfway shut? Let's *go*, you stupid little molly!"

Old habits, but it worked; Chess let the surge of anger pull him upright once more, and scarpered. This time he took the lead, dragging Oona headlong, holding his gaze steady on the path ahead as sweat stung his eyes, teeth clenched 'til they ached. Behind, the hammering was occasionally broken up by thuds and cries of squabbling collisions, along with a single horrific wail, by which Chess could only assume one of his spectral hunters—indistinguishable from the shadows they rode—had managed to throw itself over.

Eventually, a new black wall loomed up, stone pathway plunging straight into it through the tiniest of cracks, while Chess and Oona went careening along with it.

The transition from heat to cold was fierce as a blow. Snow slashed horizontally into their faces, so sharp the Seven Dials' chill rain seemed a friendly shower by comparison, and Chess and Oona stared down a zigzagging track onto a vast white plain. From where they stood they could see its centre, red and muddy, as great masses of fur-clad men hewed each other fiercely back and forth, armed with axe and sword and spear. Bodies fell, only to be dragged away by comrades and rise again, replacing their severed limbs as they did so; giant figures moved amongst the armies, some inhumanly handsome, others grossly trollish.

And off to the right, over the track's edge, yawned a black chasm at least as depthless as the lake of fire, breathing out a wind so freezing Chess could feel it sear his eyeballs. He knuckled them to bring tears, then blinked to keep 'em liquid. "Jesus *shit!*"

"Amen," Oona agreed, and lurched on, picking her way deftly down the track, bare toes already turning purplish-blue as they sank into the snow. Chess risked one quick glance back, and saw, the Dead Posse's black train negotiate the curve at full steam, right after them. Here too, though, their own fury was their undoing— yet another went slipping off into the dark, knocked sideways by its fellows' mindless rush, disappearing without a sound.

Chess snorted, calling out to Oona: "Give these clowns another half an hour and they'll end 'emselves, with no help from us whatsoever!"

"Uh huh. But no matter where they do 'appen t'fall, odds are they'll be back." She made as if to peer into the crevasse, but stopped herself just in time; gave a quick head shake instead, as if throwing something off. "Nothing ever really ends, *anywhere*. Wish I'd known, before'and."

"Sounds like you learned a thing or two out of the experience, if nothin' else."

"Yeah, sure. First off bein': don't never bloody die."

Chess snorted up another laugh at this, and she matched it— chattered it out between clenched teeth, which fed Chess's own hilarity in turn. Moments later, they were all but howling, holding each other up as they staggered along, when the path debouched onto the plain at the side of a giant upthrust spike of snow-crusted rock. Arms linked, they rounded it together—and drew up, slapped to silence by what they found waiting for 'em.

Somehow, the Dead Posse had outflanked them, waiting patient to be discovered. And as Chess let memory's tide pull his gaze from face to face, he found he did know them, after all—each and every one. Had he only thought he'd forgotten?

Hoped, perhaps.

There stood the Lieut, no worse for his abyssal plunge; next to him that flibbertigibbet Sadie from the Two Sisters, whose head he'd broke open for daring to drop a lure in Rook's lap, with her red-faced country beau not far behind, who'd caught up with Chess in Splitfoot Joe's only to get drilled twice before even clearing leather. The holes in the boy's chest were still open, leaking ichor so pale it had only a hint of pink left to it. Close by, almost two-score men in bluebelly do-up—white and otherwise—stood shot-riddled or torn by old Kees Hosteen's knife, scooped guts bulging their tattered shirts. The nameless Pink from 'Frisco who'd been Chess's first real kill kept 'em company, razor-cut throat-grin gaping wide—laid low in back-alley garbage with his gun took while Chess just lit the hell out, man's murder nothing but a ticket to get him shed of 'Frisco, and Oona along with it.

Other Pinks too, aplenty, like those three he'd shot on their knees after that first train job, 'fore Rook had slapped his gun away. Or former gang-brother Petrus Kavalier, done over the shoulder without even a glance, for the crime of merely raising a gun in horror at Rook's dark craft. A sprinkling of Injuns too, plus a scattering of "good citizens," men he'd thoughtlessly hoorawed past during some raid or other; gunslingers who'd ridden the exact same road, only to end it in front of his muzzles. Even that fool of a miner in the 'Frisco melodeon who wouldn't damn well give over on Rook, his Ma, *him*, 'til Chess gave him one back, between the eyes.

Too damn easy, Ed Morrow's voice told him, disapprovingly. *You knock 'em down and giggle over it, after.*

Over fifty, all told—maybe a hundred, if he wasn't flattering his own capacities somewhat. And all of 'em equally dead, cold in ways mere landscape couldn't explain, warmed only by hate-burnt eyes and wounds wisping steam.

My work, Chess thought. *Mine, and no one else's.*

Once, he'd've preened to own it, but now . . . now, it just made him tired. All of it. All of *them.* Man lived twenty years or more in this world, shouldn't he have something a bit better to show for it? Something more—permanent?

This is heresy, red boy, the Enemy told him, from nowhere, **degrading to your nature. Besides which, what can be more permanent**

than the grave . . . the split earth, Cipactli's open mouth, or all that comes after?

To avoid the temptation to even try to answer, Chess flicked his eyes back over the crowd, searching out faces from Bewelcome or Hoffstedt's Hoard—but found none, which bemused him. Only those who'd died at his own hand made up the Dead Posse roster, then, which had a bitter kind of sense to it, he supposed. This was the Enemy's territory, down here, and his way had nothing whatsoever to say about debts of conscience beyond the primal— blood for blood, too book-balancing cold for true revenge.

Christian Hell might be hot, after all, but Mictlan-Xibalba was cold as this place here. And *deep.*

Chess squeezed Oona's clutching hand, shrugged, and took up his pistoleer's pose, empty holsters notwithstanding. "Well," he said, "c'mon, then. Whoever got something to say can just go on and tell *me* 'fore we all die again of cold, or boredom."

The crowd parted. Three personages pushed to the forefront, all wearing the shredded remnants of Confederate greys; one in the middle was a bald-headed idjit, near Rook's size but flabbier. His smaller, equally ugly friends flanked him close. All three sported knife-slice neckties like that first Pink's, gone stiff grey-blue in this blizzardly weather; a rime set their lips glimmering, edges a-tremble with the force of their eager dog-panting. The big one expelled a wheezing sigh, half-strained through his brittle wound, like he'd been silent so long he didn't know which mouth was better for speaking.

"Might almost be worth it all . . . all this sufferin', here in the dark," he said, "just . . . t'pay you back, Pargeter."

"I don't misdoubt. But remind me, while we're at it: who the fuck are you meant to be to me, precisely?"

"Oh, you'll get it, you just try hard enough." Fists now, steady at the man's waist; he leaned forward, bringing his weight onto his toes like a pugilist. "We was soldiers together once, back in camp— you with your airs, swannin' 'round, like you could dictate to real-made men. Thought you'd trade me somethin' I didn't want for what I did, 'til I taught you better."

A preening wisp of a voice, shrunk now almost to nothing. Yet Chess could still catch an echo of what it might've been like once, full and mean, telling him: *Guess you're mine now, bitch.*

With that, the other shoe dropped; Chess felt a rib-crack weight across his back and a tearing in his nethers, recalled the world gone dim from both his eyes being so bruise-puffed they barely opened, throat sore from ill use, inside and out. And thought, like he'd snarled through it nonetheless, right at that very moment—

Not likely. 'Cause . . . I ain't no-damn-body's, motherfucker.

He spat again just to rid himself from the taste, and grinned.

"Why, Private Chilicothe," Chess named him. "You who played bad faith with my rules and never did pay me for the privilege, either, so I took my change out on your hide; you're right, now I *do* recall. 'Specially that part in the doc's tent, after—how sweet you looked lyin' there asleep, right 'fore I slit your throat and left you to piss yourself dyin'.'"

"Too scared to face me awake, that was all."

"Ha! You never *scared* me, you sumbitch, not even when you was hip-deep up in my business. Didn't leave that much've an impression."

Chilicothe's face shifted, lumpily; probably would've flushed, had he still had even a drop of blood to put toward the effort. "Pretend all you want, you little faggot bastard—I know better. Know damn well I *hurt* you, at least."

"For a minute or two, sure. But I've had worse."

Chilicothe's shade lashed out, no doubt expecting things to go the same as up top, him still having a good foot and a half on Chess's neat-made self. And Chess with no guns, plus no hexation to count on either, seeing how it seemed to vary in strength from spot to spot along this endless Hell-bound trudge.

But screw all that. For though he'd stopped looking to get into fist-fights the same day he'd realized he'd never make six feet, Chess'd be gang-fucked (again) if he wouldn't go down swinging.

Before he could make his move, however—duck in under the bastard's arm and hook him hard, maybe try to bust a rib, or just give him a good, swift punch to the nuts—Chess saw Oona come down on one knee, shoulders squared, rummaging through the snow. She came up with a sharp-splintered icicle roughly the size of some carved ivory Chinee dildo, and drove it straight into the back of Chilicothe's calf, deep enough to judder. Then twisted it 'til he howled, so hard Chess swore he could hear the flash-froze hamstring snap.

Chilicothe went down, face-first into Chess's fist. It was a good jab, right from the shoulder, and Chess felt the man's ghost-nose squish. The other two jumped to help, but Oona moved herself sidelong, hunching up to form a brake; one skipped over her like a thrown stone, went right into the other and carried him away down the hill in a flurry of thrashing limbs, snow-scree and bruises. Which left only Chilicothe behind, pinned as Chess stomped on him once, twice, whole chest coming down like a rotten wall, to where Chess thought he felt the fucker's wizened heart go *pop*, a mojo bag of vile intentions.

Chess spit down at him one more time, taking care to aim well. The result crackled mid-air and froze solid, falling dagger-style to embed itself a half-inch from the eye, then lodged and crusted over, bonding ice to skin. Chilicothe's mouth dropped open, too shocked to yelp, as Oona made her blackening feet once more.

"Better get while the goin's good, I'd fink," she suggested, throwing back her hair.

"Maybe I ain't finished yet."

"Suit your bloody self, then. But them rest over there won't wait forever."

Chess nodded, and bent down just a tad further, not deigning to hold himself out of Chilicothe's reach. "I never did scream, no matter how you tried to make me," he reminded him, voice flat. "'Member *that*? How it took all three of you to hold me down long enough, which only showed me what kind'a cowards you were, not to mention stick-stupid. And why? 'Cause you let me *live*, you shithead."

Up once more, then, back on his feet; he turned his scornful eyes to the rest as his grin widened. "But Christ knows I do like it rough, too, so if any of you dead fools feel up for a second go-round, let's get to it. I got nothin' but time to kill."

Chilicothe turned his face to the ground. But the rest of the mob shifted forward almost like one, closing in; Chess saw 'em coming and shifted stance, ready to once more take up nonexistent arms.

Well, there goes that *bright idea.*

Oona, by his side: "Just couldn't keep your bloody mouth shut, could ya?"

"Aw, Ma. Thought you'd've known me better'n that, by now."

As they got closer, however, Chess angled away, so's she wouldn't see his smirk fail. Last time things'd gotten this bad had been outside Splitfoot's, with Sheriff Mesach Love's Weed-puppets making a shambly forward-march on him, Ed, Yancey, Geyer—yet once a deathblow freed the last shreds of leftover soul, there had been no will in the Weed-things' eyes, no memory nor hatred. These revenants were equally dead, but every pair of eyes stayed stuck on him, brim-full with an aching need to punish.

On pure reflex, he slipped past, pushing Oona behind him with one hand. Lifted the other, *thinking* it wrapped in blue-white threads of lightning, concentrating harder than he had at anything since he first took up the gun—then yelped as a slap cracked 'cross the back of his head. "Jesus *shit*, woman!" he roared, catching hold of the hand she still held high. "The hell's this? Stop it!"

"You stupid bloody git," Oona yelled back, and Chess almost let go, in shock; were those actual tears in her eyes, rimming green with red? Cold truly must be getting to her. "Tryin' to play the 'ero, now an' 'ere? Get us *both* stuck, for good? What'd I always tell you, eh?"

"That'd be 'Save yerself, 'cause won't nobody else do it for ya,' I'd think," he mocked, vowels flat-mashing, Limejuicer style. Then pulled her hard back into his embrace, dipping to snarl, in one ear: "Yeah, well . . . I *ain't* you."

Around them, that bitter wind keened yet higher, sent snow-ghosts sifting through the crowd, tearing each from each; but a slight twist more and it broke upward into a shriek, unbearably pitched, as though the sky itself had torn. The light collapsed, grey as grave mould. And in its wake, a twister touched down, ripped straight from Chess's own memories—bomb-burst back-slap of Rook's gallows resurrection, sending all them manning the trap one way and those still waiting to swing the other. Its fury had crushed him facedown into the mud even as the Rev came up rocket-fast, hemp necktie still a-flap 'round his raw neck.

This one's funnel speared straight down, locking to earth 'round Chess and Oona: half trap and half shield, capping a perfect circle no more than a yard wide, while solid-turned air smacked outward in all directions.

In the real world, this was the kind of force would've torn men limb from limb, flung 'em hundreds of yards, to decorate the wrecked trees in scraps. Here, the Dead Posse mainly only lurched, ground backward, like mud-locked wagons hauled by straining men; a few busted free and rose up, splatting 'gainst the mountain's hide. But it was enough. A path had opened—several. Now, all they needed to figure was which one led where, and take it.

With a shrug, Chess banished the twister as though throwing off a mile-high coat fashioned from the Devil's own storm-blown hide, and bolted straight into its tail, yanking Oona along after him. *"Ma!"* he screamed, above the roar. "The Call, *where?* Which damn *way?*"

"Dunno . . . can't bloody *see*—!"

Chess broke into a tripping run, following the base of the rock wall bounding the plain; Oona fell once, with a squawk, then righted herself and hiked his coat immodestly, matching him as best she might. Though the cyclone had stripped snow from the earth, carving a black mud track, more snow cascaded down from the peaks above, throwing up plumes so blinding white Chess was forced to shield his eyes as he ducked through them. Too close behind for comfort, he could feel the Dead Posse's renewed pursuit in his boots, pounding up through the ground.

He almost missed the gap; *would* have missed it, in fact, if a hand hadn't thrust out from it at the last second, palm up-angled toward him, all but beckoning. *Grab hold*, its unseen owner seemed to say, though no voice spoke. *Grab hold, and see where* this *takes you.*

He grabbed fast, felt a moment's swooping relief when the hand proved at least as warm as his own, and did not resist as it pulled him into—through—the gap beyond, and Oona too.

Once past the barrier, Chess stumbled to his knees, cold stone firm under his palms and shins. The lack of wind was a Goddamn blessing. At his elbow, Oona wept in pain, cursing her feet for their slowness in resuming their normal colouration. Sounded like she would've stamped, if she hadn't figured that would probably hurt the more.

The floor beneath was flat, expert-laid, of smooth but unpolished granite. As his breath came back in gulps, Chess looked up and 'round, taking in yet another passageway. Like all the tunnels before, it stretched on into the distance to a vanishing point teasingly set just beyond his sight, but these walls, this roof and floor, looked *built*. A faint light, cheerless and dusty, trickled through high slits, giving off no sort of shade to indicate its source. Silence weighted the air.

In recessed alcoves set at intervals on each wall, men and women sat like stone—stiff and stock-staring off into the distance, at the floor, or their own folded hands. Might've been wax, but that Chess's keen sight detected the faintest movement at chest height. Unlike the crowds of Seven Dials, their getup covered every time and place Chess had ever known—serapes, dusters, flash check trousers, denim and silk gowns, nought at all—plus dozens he didn't, their skin, hair and eyes culled from every mix imaginable.

No ropes or chains to bind 'em fast, no dust to suggest how long they'd sat; only the figures, the corridor. The silence.

"Chess..." Oona whispered. And *Christ*, he thought, uncharitably. *Can I never have one damn minute to myself, a minute to stop and fucking pause?*

He turned, too exhausted even to sigh—and wound up looking straight into the face of the one person he'd genuinely never thought to find down here, in all his ramblings . . . but who else could it possibly be, really? Considering how recently he'd been thinking of him?

"Sheriff," Chess named him, finally. To which the man gave but a single bow, grave as ever, bones creaking. And though those little-girl pigtails of his swung back and forth with the motion, infinitely ridiculous, Chess felt absolutely no impulse to laugh.

"'Private' Pargeter," Mesach Love—dead twice-over and double-damned as well, if present circumstances were anything to go by—replied.

CHAPTER TEN

BY THE TIME BEWELCOME'S wounded and dead had been seen to, Ixchel's conjured floodwaters had subsided and the soldiers of the Thirteenth had hacked exit passages out through the Weed-walls which the Chess-Enemy had (oh *so* thoughtfully) left intact around the town, it was well past midnight. Ill-lit darkness and roads flooded fetlock-deep in mud cost their horses near an hour getting back to the camp—Morrow wound up tying a drink-exhausted Asbury to his mount, letting him sleep most of the way.

They passed the sentries at Camp Pink, many of whom still glared at Ed with suspicion, and found the plain canvas tent Pinkerton had assigned him near the camp's south edge. Morrow tipped the Professor into one of the empty cots without waking him, only pausing to strip off his own mud-caked boots before collapsing onto another. Before he closed his eyes, he realized the storm's dregs had finally cleared enough he could see the smoky lights of New Aztectlan's pyramid-temple glowing dimly through the open entry flap, far to the west—a dim line of arcane flame fringing the sky, just above its guard-woods' contorted shadows.

Sleep was fitful, broken by dreadful flashes of memory: Sophy Love vanishing in a burst of light, the Manifold exploding in Catlin's hand, Rook's stunned look as Morrow's shots went through his shields. The gleeful laughter of the thing wearing Chess Pargeter's flesh. Which last vision led, sure as rainfall, to other memories, and an uncomfortable state of half-arousal that had him longing for Yancey to visit his dreams once more—as much simply to *see* her as anything else, though whatever approximation of the other they might be able to manage long distance would've also been dearly appreciated.

But that particular benefice was not to be. Instead, the hand that fell on his shoulder next, shaking him awake, turned out to be broad, brown, callused—to belong to Private Jonas Carver. Who, to give him his due, looked profoundly ill-inclined to disturb Morrow's repose, though he obviously wasn't one to refuse orders.

"Sorry to roust you so soon, boss."

"Any man who guards my back 'gainst hexation gets to call me Ed, Private." Morrow pushed himself up and shoved his feet back into his boots, wincing as they squelched. "Pinkerton, is it? Command post?"

Carver shook his head. "Not right away—says we gotta meet somebody comin' in at the east perimeter, escort him to Command." As Morrow buttoned his duster up, Carver's eyes turned thoughtful. "Captain don't like him, but Mister Pink do sure seem to know how to run a unit. He ever serve on a front line?"

"Chief Union intelligencer, '61 and '62," Morrow confirmed, while Carver picked up the lantern he'd brought. They ducked back out into the chill night air, making their way past cookfire pits, tents and bivouacs toward the camp's east edge. "Helped guard Lincoln back in Baltimore, gettin' him to his inauguration—there was a hex involved, I hear. Which would explain a fair bit." He grimaced. "As for Captain Washford's opinion of the man . . . well, I'll tell you, Private—"

"Jonas, sir."

"—Jonas—" Morrow lowered his voice, prudently. "—I'd think him a damn sight bigger fool than any of us should be if he found himself *liking* Pinkerton, right now. But long as our boss's still giving sensible orders and the Captain knows how to take 'em, ain't nothing we have to worry on." Field dressing stations and triage tents had been put up on the camp's east side, right where the dawnward edge of the plain on which Hex City sat rose into scrubby foothills, to give them enough room from the rest of Camp Pink that those uninvolved in surgery and the like could ignore—if never entirely escape—its near-constant racket. Just beyond, at the end of a trail leading out of those hills, two horses stood; Morrow squinted up at their riders' faces as Carver lifted his lamp, and felt his squint become a scowl.

"Mister Ludlow," he said, without enthusiasm. "What exactly got you to ditch your comfy hotel bed in favour of a trip out *here*?"

Fitz Hugh Ludlow grinned, shrugging off lingering rain dampness by flapping his overcoat like a leathery set of wings. "Why, the story, Agent Morrow—the story, always! Your employer tells me we hover on the verge of victory and calls on me to scribe this history from an altogether new perspective, an opportunity I couldn't possibly pass up, not and still call myself a journalist. For as you're already well aware, we *are* making history here, are we not?" He turned that grin of his upon Carver, who did not return it. "Perhaps you'd also be persuaded to grant me an interview at some later date, Private? Tell my readers the day-to-day tale from behind the scene of freedom's ongoing struggle, on the lines of battle drawn between new world and old?"

Carver cast Morrow a narrow look, possibly unsure if he was being insulted, to which Morrow simply shrugged. To Ludlow Morrow said, coolly: "If you're here to see Pinkerton we might as well save ourselves any further jaw; I'm headed that way already, anyhow. But one way or t'other, I'll need identification from your friend here, 'fore he gets my safe-conduct—"

He broke off as the other man leaned into the lamplight, and it took all his effort to turn his initial surge of shocked delight into a mere one-cough throat-clearing.

"James Grey," Frank Geyer renamed himself, expressionlessly. He'd darkened his fair hair with some sort of medicamental slickum, combed it back and shaved off his moustache, which wouldn't fool anyone who knew him that took more than a second's look. But simple lack of expectation would probably keep anyone from actually doing so, long as Geyer avoided Pinkerton himself. "Mister Ludlow hired me as a guard, to see him safe 'cross the field. I'll render up my weapons, if that's obligatory. . . ."

Morrow hesitated, aware it would look suspicious not to accept. Then again, he didn't especially want to leave Geyer weaponless—not here, in what was now (to him) enemy territory.

Before a decision was forced either way, however, the silence broke: that ever-present low moan from the triage tents suddenly spiralled upward, without warning, into an agonized yowl—and a shirtless man (another of Washford's, Morrow could only assume, given his complexion) came staggering out into the night, eerie luminescence coating his high-yellow chest and back like paint but concentrating most brightly on the stumps of his arms, where the very skin bubbled alchemically. Some Paddy hex pressed into palliative care chased after him, arrayed in an oil-coat bloodstained near black that almost hid his collar's dim shine and yelling, as he did: "Come quick as ye can, for all love—we got ourselves another one!"

Hard upon both their heels came two more men dressed in the blue serge uniforms of Pinkerton's vaunted "hex-handlers"—themselves hexacious, similarly collared, who'd opted to serve out their process capturing, collaring and policing other magickals. They grabbed the escapee and wrestled him to his knees, but not before his force-grown scar-tissue had already begun to split like seeding fungus, thrusting out tendrils of whitish-green muscle which twined 'round one another, fused, and grew molluscine suckers all along their lengths.

Gaping at the sight of two uncontrollably flailing tentacles where his arms had once been, the first man twisted his head back to spit at his "doctor," snarling: "Now look what you gone an' done, you Goddamn potato-eater! Call yourself a medico? I ain't signed up for this!"

The triagist bridled. "Yeah?" he shouted back. "Well, I ain't signed up at *all*, nigger—so if yeh think yez can do any better, I go on and invite yez, yeh ungrateful black bastard!"

Carver had his gun out, automatically taking up stance in front of Ludlow, who had his pad out and pen already a-scribble, eagerly filing it all away. Morrow wasn't completely sure who Carver'd start shooting at first, it came down to that, but the distraction itself posed an all-but-perfect opportunity to give Geyer what he no doubt wanted most, right now.

"Tell me what you're here for, so I can let you get to it," Morrow ordered him, low, out the corner of his mouth.

"Asbury," was all Geyer replied, voice pitched at the self-same range.

Morrow gave the most minimal twitch of a nod and jerked his jaw sidelong. "My tent, back there, past the fire pit—got a big All-Seeing Eye on the flap, marked '25.' Hunker down when you get there; walk quick, but not too quick. Don't stop."

Geyer nodded, already in motion. "Agent," he said, and was gone, as the shouting match between the squabbling hexes—collared *and* new-flowered—erupted into the heat-shimmer flare of power battening on power. Even as Morrow recoiled, the monstrously warped Negro soldier grabbed both handlers with one tentacle each and began slamming them together, each impact producing a burst of St. Elmo's Fire and acrid lightning-smell. The ersatz medico tried to haul him off and got a vicious backlash 'cross the face for it, sending him spinning to the mud, magic-drawing metal collar he'd hauled from a pocket gone flying.

Carver swore with the despairing viciousness men used to mask grief, and shot his fellow soldier in the back of the knee; the man crumpled, howling, joint ruined. Before he could rise again the medico was on him, snapping the collar home. The new-made hex went limp, tentacles splayed out to either side like severed lengths of ship-cable.

Ludlow stared, agape, for once seeming to have completely forgotten his notes. "Good . . . God," he said presently. "Is this kind of happenstance *typical* of procedures, here?"

"Typical ain't a word we use much, hereabouts," Morrow replied. "Let's go, Mister Ludlow. Mister Pinkerton's got no love for waiting."

TRUDGING ON TOWARD the camp's centre, it belatedly occurred to Morrow how Geyer's mission here might be to poach Doctor Asbury's services and person completely; according to intelligence, his new partner Thiel had made no great secret of wanting to spoke Pinkerton's wheels however he could. But with so many Pinks (real and honorary) all crowded around—not to mention that brutal hangover the Professor had been assiduously courting, the last few days—he saw no possible way for Geyer to accomplish that goal, at least not now.

More likely Frank simply wanted a word with the doc, which might well be a more productive course; not only was Asbury's faith in Pinkerton near its lowest ebb, but his current state would render him an audience both captive and suggestible. By his own drunken testimony, the man was already more than half-convinced any value in his knowledge had been far outpaced by the damages wreaked by its abuses—and his appreciation of Asbury's undeniably effective hex-killer shells aside, Morrow was hard put to disagree. "Harnessing the power of hexation" lost a lot of its appeal, as a concept, when you daily saw the people producing said hex-force shoved headlong into those harnesses.

Inside the hastily erected log longhouse which served as Pinkerton's command post, the lamps were always on, supernaturally bright; Morrow shaded his eyes as he led Ludlow inside. A long oak table stretched out in the chamber's centre, covered with maps, reports, rosters, equipment lists and logbooks. A larger map, tacked to the wall, showed Hex City and Camp Pink faced off across the plain and Bewelcome in its southward valley, while scraps of coloured paper pinned here and there traced the patterns of troop movement. At the sight of an iron-bellied cookstove blazing with heat, Ludlow went for it with a moan of relief, rubbing his hands dry before the open grate.

From behind the inner door Morrow could hear voices: Pinkerton's Scots baritone plus a basso profundo he recognized as Captain Washford's, and a third whose timbre—for no obvious reason—raised Morrow's hackles. After a brief staring match with the two Pinks standing guard at the inner door, who finally moved far enough aside to let him gain access, he rapped on it twice, without announcing himself.

Pinkerton broke off. "Edward!" he called, with horrid jocularity. "Come in, come in—leave Mister Ludlow out there for the nonce, if ye would? Secure matters first!"

In some ways, Pinkerton's love of petty hex-tricks was worse than Reverend Rook's had ever been; never needing to ask who was at a closed door was only the mildest instance of such showing off. A symptom of his hexation's unnatural provenance, or merely how he would have always acted, given enough power? Morrow disliked to dwell on it. So he stepped inside, instead—only to stop and stare gawkishly as Ludlow had, minutes before.

The inner chamber, dark as the outer was bright, was lit only by an eerie grey-green fungal glow spilling from the spectral image hovering in mid-air before him: A clean-shaven man's head and shoulders, broad-nosed, with receding grey hair brushed back from high temples and eyes so deep-set they seemed mere pits. Below the elegantly cravated neck, the image trailed away into writhing streamers of mushroom-coloured smoke which led back to the gaped and drooling mouth of an old white-haired woman slumped unconscious in a chair; its fulgor illuminated Washford, standing at stiff attention, and Pinkerton, pacing back and forth.

Then—the image *moved*, eyes sliding sideways to Morrow, face frowning, like any living man's. Its lips shaped words; a fraction of a second later, the dim, muffled voice he'd heard before slid buzzing from the comatose woman's larynx. "Agent Edward Morrow? Former companion of Chess Pargeter, notorious outlaw and catamite?"

Morrow was bemused to realize he needed only a little effort to find his own voice. Perhaps he really was becoming inured, or at least simply too numb to shock further.

"Mister President," he said, managing a short nod.

"Mister Pinkerton tells me you've referred to me as a fool and a double-crosser, on previous occasions," said President Andrew Johnson's ectoplasmic factotum, its plummy North Carolina drawl rendering the harsh words oddly mild. "Well, I've been called far worse; there were rumblings of impeachment from the Judiciary, before this latest storm blew up. Let us agree, then, Mister Morrow, that if I raise no issue with your past choices, you shall raise none with mine—are we understood? Good," it finished, without waiting for an answer. "As it happens, you were right when you told Mister Pinkerton I wished no new war with Mexico. Sadly, the damned Carlotta colonists have stirred up vindictive sentiment at Emperor Maximilian's court, railing about the suffering Mexican inhabitants of this 'Hex City.' Backed by a faction of discontented Texican seceshes, there is daily clamour for another invasion of these States. This must be avoided at all costs."

"Of course, sir," said Morrow, not sure what other response to make.

"Glad you agree. Mister Pinkerton is of the opinion that the single best way to forestall the Hapsburg would be to simply destroy Hex City soon as may be, expelling or putting down its Mex-folk at the same time, thus depriving Maximilian of any 'mission of mercy' *casus belli*—"

"—and replacing it with a cause of true revenge," Washford interrupted, no longer able to hide the anger in his voice, "plus a populace even *more* ready to fight. Mister President, have we really sunk so low as to plan the eradication of a whole town of United States citizens, solely to toss some Spanish adventurer-tyrant a political bone?"

Again, the Presidential image—while still hanging stationary—slid its no-eyes over to Washford, whose presence it almost seemed to have forgotten.

"I do apologize for offending your fine sensibilities, Captain Washford," it said, after a moment's consideration. "Must admit, I hadn't thought you set quite so high a stake on the ideal of citizenship . . . until, of course, I recalled exactly how recently you and your men had attained that very state. Yet as you well know, with great gains come great debt, not to mention great responsibility. Your Brigade has served our mutual nation well, undeniably, and benefitted from that service. It would be *such* a shame to let all that fall by the wayside now, merely on a point of personal protocol—to violate your oath as a soldier and your honour as a gentleman by refusing a direct order from your Supreme Commander, thus potentially opening all the men under your command to a share in your own disgrace."

Morrow thought of young Private Carver in the room outside, whom the War had theoretically rendered free (by virtue of his uniform, and the authority it vested in him) to walk shoulder to shoulder with men of any other provenance—share a joke or take umbrage at a slight, carry weapons into battle and strike back if provoked, without fear of unjust retaliation. "Finally" free, he might have said, if asked—but was it really so? Or was that freedom merely momentary, doomed to vanish the moment their current struggle ceased, whether won or lost?

One way or the other, Morrow suspected, the Carlotta colonists couldn't be the only Americans, former or present, who found themselves tempted by the idea of the old order's return. Change was frightening, by nature . . . and for opportunists like Johnson, such basic human weakness was an all too easy thing to play on. As Washford himself, by his origins' nature, well knew.

"Yessir," Washford replied, brown face gone once more inscrutable. "I'll leave you two, then, shall I? Now I know how things are."

Pinkerton smiled. "Well, if you wish, Captain—but believe me, yuir input is always welcome."

"Oh, I believe it," Washford lied, barely glancing the big boss's way. "Fact is, though, we got a raft of things need doing over on my side of the camp, 'fore the next assault. You could keep me in the loop as to what you and the President decide is best, however, I'd be grateful."

"Ye'll be the first to know," Pinkerton assured him; "second, anyhow. Right after Mister Morrow here."

"Much obliged." Without so much as a glance back, Washford brushed past, shutting the door firmly behind him.

The Johnson-mask raised that portion of its manufactured forehead where its brows should lie. "That *is* one well-spoken nigger," it remarked. "Overreaching, certainly—but at least he knows his place, once it's shown him. And given his race's natural inclination to laziness and lack of self-governance, I'd rather weather a scooch of backtalk every now and then, if it gets me the sort of performance I understand he and his are capable of under fire. Cannon fodder of the highest possible grade, even for a passel of Cain's wayward children. . . . Still, it occurs to me casualties may mount high enough on the day of incursion to guarantee we don't have to worry over the dear Captain's moral qualms much longer, either way. Would you agree, Mister Pinkerton?"

"I'm almost sure of it, Mister President."

"Yes. Well . . . *make* sure, will you? There's a lad." Johnson glanced off to one side, at something not immediately present, and scowled in irritation. "And now, since I'm being told that if we continue much longer, the poor afflicted creature presenting your image on my end may suffer irreparable harm—let's finish, shall we?" Continuing, after Pinkerton's nod: "As I was saying before Captain Washford mounted his high horse, Maximilian's no fool—he wants another war no more than do I. But considering it was only Lady Rainbow's re-emergence which saved him from execution by the Juarez consort, his position is yet fragile enough that to assuage those factions, he has detached an expeditionary force northward; no bigger than a brigade, but small enough to cross New Mexico, reach Hex City and rescue its Mexes, faster than any larger force can intercept. Or so the Emperor hopes his courtiers will believe."

This last piece of information at least got Pinkerton to drop his aggravating smile. "The Texicans will join us in a moment," he claimed, "if Maximilian sends troops over their border wi'out askin' proper first. It's no' a serious consideration."

"Forgive me, sir, for failing to see how exactly that will improve our situation!" The ecto-likeness distorted, Johnson's features swelling and knotting the way clay does when flattened. "Do you think I am limited solely to what *you* tell me? Disabuse yourself of the notion, if so. Not all your former agents remain under your eyes, and I receive truly alarming reports of—*No!*" This went not to Pinkerton but off phantom stage left, a half-instant before "Johnson" suddenly evanesced into nothing; the old Spiritualist sucked in air with a huge gasp, convulsed and fell from her chair, spasming helpless on the floor.

"God's teeth," snarled Pinkerton, then wrenched the door open and beckoned his guards, who dragged the convulsing medium away. In their wake, Pinkerton slammed it shut once more and lit a lamp with a frustrated hex-flare—then rounded on Morrow. "You told me you spoke wi' Geyer back 'fore we began this siege, when neither of us knew he'd turned traitor—if that's even so, and you've no' played me false this entire time! But giving you the doubt's benefit, did aught he say betray his intent? Or Thiel's, the twice-perjured bastard?"

Morrow swallowed. "We . . . didn't talk much about it, but if you want my honest advice . . . I was him, I *would* head to meet up with the Mexes, since they're the closest purely humanish forces to ally with, I wanted t'take you down."

'Sides from Yiska and her crew, that is—Yiska, and Yancey, and whatever-the-hell that thing was ran off with Songbird, who ain't probably feeling too friendly toward you either, right about now.

"Why not the Texicans?" Pinkerton demanded.

"'Cause you'd see that coming, and there's no way you haven't already made overtures their way, anyhow. Might just as well sign up with Hex City and see how that shook down, I *wanted* to paint myself into a corner."

He watched the Agency's founder ponder this, and thought: *But at this point, I'd probably "ally" with Satan's left nut if I thought it'd take you down, you unreliable sumbitch. And depending where Chess's meat-suit ends up next, I may yet, in a fashion.*

Morrow could still remember how much he'd respected Pinkerton, once—how glad he'd been to wear the badge, to take up the case against Rook (and Chess) that'd led him this long and looping way. Recollection of that first private train-bound briefing, back when Asbury's theories on integrating hexes into society were fired with idealistic zeal rather than liquor, made him almost as sad as remembering the many ways Pinkerton's subsequent actions had contributed, since then, to thoroughly disabusing both Morrow and Asbury of those notions.

Could be his thoughts had run just a bit too loud for comfort, however. Pinkerton's eyes narrowed. Without warning, he grabbed Morrow's jaw, fingers digging deep. Morrow gasped as power smashed down upon him, sizzling against his skin and searing his mind, burrowing in with that horrible *shoving* grip as Pinkerton's will knotted itself with his, a fist in his soul.

For a moment, Morrow felt his mouth open to let everything spill forth, without exception. But a second later, the other man's mental grip shattered, slipping free—Morrow staggered back, only stopping himself from raising (and pumping) his eight-gauge with a vast, convulsive effort.

Pinkerton studied him, apparently a bit too closely concentrated on fine interior detail to notice how close he'd come to getting his head blown off. "*Verra* interesting indeed, Edward," he mused, the sheer speed of his anger's disappearance in itself disturbing. "That signature 'round your person, interfering with my investigations; since I know ye've not replaced your Manifold as yet, could it be ye've gone hex yourself, and not told me? Or struck up a bargain, mayhap, with *some* Power or other. . . ." He stopped, smiling. "Ah, though—I think, in fact, we both ken the name of one entity with whom ye had a most *intimate* relationship, before this conflict got quite underway. Do we not?"

Rook's words returned: *You've already seen how hard it is to hurt Chess. Stay close, and that'll be you, too.* But that whole "prophet of the Skinless Man" sham had served its ends and been done with, surely; whatever protection he'd been gifted on the overspill had to've died when Chess did, hadn't it? And yet—if *not*, as Pinkerton's just-proven inability to simply seize his mind and squeeze it for anything he wanted would seem to argue, then . . .

Maybe Chess—the real *Chess—is still alive, somewhere deep down. Inside the Enemy itself.*

To merely form the thought was almost enough to stop his breath. Still, he barely had time to consider it any further than a heartbeat, before a knock at the door interrupted them.

The new arrival proved to be Asbury, looking deeply, wretchedly miasmic. Geyer must still be lurking back in his tent, Morrow guessed, and tensed, hoping the Professor's thoughts wouldn't give anything away. Soon enough, however, it became clear that Pinkerton was clearly long-accustomed to paying as little attention to Asbury's interior workings as he could manage—a decision which one could only hope would eventually prove a profound mistake, on his part.

"Apologies for disturbing you, Doctor," said Pinkerton. "I presume from Ed here's manifest survival that your test went well, but thought I'd as lief confirm it in person, and privately. Were we successful, then?"

"Admirably so," Asbury admitted. "What third-mark Manifolds saw action performed optimally even when used foolishly, just as Reverend Rook himself proved unable to resist our new alloys. Yet, all this aside, I am unsure if the price paid was worth it." As Pinkerton raised a brow: "Missus Sophronia Love, sir, and her babe—both lost, victims of the Reverend's depredations. Without her to approve our methods, Bewelcome will be *far* less willing to provide us logistical support for the next advance, or otherwise. . . ."

Pinkerton snorted. "Though no man can question your genius, Doctor, your understanding of human psychology remains dearly deficient. A figurehead martyr does as well in rousing bellicosity as the Love woman would e'er have done her own self—and, better yet, lacks her disturbing tendency to argue." Collapsing into the same chair the medium had used, he tilted it back, smiling rakish over tented fingertips. "On t'other hand, I've good news for you, too— our distraction worked. The hex-train arrived while the Reverend's forces were engaged upon Bewelcome, laden down wi' the last of the supplies you need for that 'Land Ironclad' you designed. Should take but a day or so to finish the vehicle's assembly; arm its pieces with your anti-hexological shells, and we'll have an assault no amount of hexation can turn back." His eyes glittered at the image, hungrily.

"That *is* good news," said Asbury, looking as though he wanted to retch. "I can attend to that in the morn—wait. 'Distraction'?"

"Did ye think I'd only one purpose in mind for this attack?" Pinkerton spread his hands, grinning once more. "I knew Rook would move against Missus Love directly, sooner rather than later; this is a man used to congregations, knowing full well the value of a God-chose leader. Let slip news of a town meeting wi' all the leading citizens present, and I thought it likely he'd try for a decapitating strike—which would, in turn, open the way for our train. The opportunity to test your devices under fire was icing on that verra same cake."

Asbury straightened with effort. "Sir," he rasped, "I do not appreciate being treated so . . . disposably, exigencies of war notwithstanding—"

"All you need *appreciate* is *what I tell you*, ye daft old gaffer," Pinkerton snarled, all humour abruptly gone. "Now get back to your tent and rest, for I want your faculties clear for tomorrow's work—*entirely* clear, d'ye grasp my meaning? I smell so much as a wisp of gin on you, Professor, and I'll sober ye up *my* way, the which you'll not enjoy at all." He snapped his fingers, setting sparks a-crackle. "Now go."

The doctor stared at him one moment more, then left, without further word.

Morrow thought about how much he owed Chess Pargeter, and how little of that debt he'd been able to repay, thus far. At the same time, meanwhile, he thought about exactly how hard Chess would've laughed at the idea of anyone owing him anything, before pointing out that most of the danger he'd "saved" Morrow from had been danger Morrow'd only gotten into on account of travelling with Chess, in the first place. Hell, he could almost hear that little red-headed bitch-bastard's voice, a sharp hint of laughter between every word: *Why ex-agent Morrow, you sad sentimental; don't be an idjit, Ed.*

'Cause fine a ride as we might've took on each other, a time or two, we're neither of us so nice as to be worth gettin' killed over.

Pinkerton turned back, grin once more in place. "As for you, Ed—I'll see you off to *your* rest soon too, no fear. There's just one last . . . service . . . I require of ye tonight, beforehand."

Silence stretched out, uncomfortably unbroken, 'til Morrow made himself ask, finally: "And—that would be?"

CHAPTER ELEVEN

LED AT A QUICK CLIP by the man himself, Pinkerton, Ludlow, Carver and Morrow made their way past Camp Pink's primary fortifications: palisades, trench lines, reels of that strange new "barbed" wire with its diamond-shaped points, ordered wholesale from Ohio. For he always did have to be at the forefront of invention, did Mister Allan, even with hexation left entirely aside—and this was but one more innovation in the repertoire, same as the painstakingly compiled surveillance files, the "rogue's gallery" of photographic arrays, or the forays into long distance crime-cracking by telegraph and pony express. Hell, the man probably even considered Fitz Hugh Ludlow's presence just another arrow for the legend-building quiver, each wordy observation waiting to be tamed into yet another brick for the Agency's public façade.

What is it you're taking us out here to show him, exactly, "boss"? Morrow wondered. *And why in the Christ do you need me on hand, to do it?*

Of course, when stacked up against hexation's threat, most measures—those not devised by Doc Asbury, at any rate—seemed ridiculously inadequate; more make-work and reassurance than aught else, good for little except keeping everyone busy, between charges. But over these last months, Morrow had seen for himself that those hexes with strength enough to bypass the line were fewer and farther between than one might suppose. In fact, perfectly mundane shells and slugs could take even the strongest down, if combined with enough luck, speed and massed fire.

As Washford had noted, for all the sheer power Hex City's citizens boasted, almost none of them had any training in war, discipline under fire, or—most tellingly of all—practice working together. More than one sortie from New Aztectlan had failed when coordination broke down on the battlefield; the largest turned rout because one flank of hexes tried to lead a charge straight into the twelve-pounder Napoleons' teeth, disastrously overestimating their own ability to protect their line from case shot and canister shells. Indeed, the carnage of that one September afternoon taught such a sharp lesson that even if the truly dangerous-minded enemy captains—Rook himself, New York Hank, the mysterious Chink Pinkerton's intelligencers named merely as "Honourable"—managed to devise a counter-tactic, they wouldn't be able to find sufficient volunteers in their ranks willing to attempt it.

Then again, all of Camp Pink had spent days listening to the screams of men dying on *ceiba* tree spikes, or seen whole waves transfigured into sandstone, before being shattered by some casual power-lash from behind the City's seemingly impenetrable walls. And so the opposing forces had settled into standoff, striking and counter-striking in wary dashes, co-opting what sporadic reinforcements they could from hexes arriving in answer to the Call, and waiting for something to break. Yet stalemate notwithstanding, the air was so often filled with metallic blood-stink it simply didn't strike Morrow all that strange to be smelling it even now, even here, at one of the farthest-forward entrenchments.

Not until the four-foot-wide earthwork trough dug *behind* said marker hove into sight, at least. And when, just a moment later, he saw the gleam of torchlight reflected redly from the shifting liquid surface—realizing, as he did, just why the stink hung so thick here—Morrow found himself gulping back a twinge of nausea. Two hex-handlers sat on camp stools nearby, wearily wiping dark stains off their hands; at their feet, tarred wooden buckets lay tipped and stickily empty. Carver stared with horror at the result, Ludlow with avidity, clearly composing chapter titles in his mind: *Hex-Harried, American 'Tecs Driven to Emulate the Enemy's Methods of Sanguinary Sacrifice—Says Pinkerton: "We Will Fight Fire with Fire, and Blood with Blood!"*

"Read your report, Edward, whilst ye were napping," said Pinkerton, rubbing his hands briskly together. "Going by it, this Smoking Mirror of yuirs seems almost . . . dealable-with, may we say? More so than Lady Rainbow and her ilk, leastways."

"Not sure what dispatch *you* read, sir, but from my angle, that was hardly the gist of it."

"It rose against Rook's bitch directly, for once, and with witnesses aplenty—that's different, in itself. A clear indication that so long as it and we are both set on bringing her down, the creature's obviously more wi' us than against us."

Morrow all but goggled. "Well," he said, finally, "perhaps I failed to adequately describe the moment, then, if that's what you took away from it. But had you been present yourself—"

"'My enemy's enemy,' Ed . . . our single best choice of ally, really, given the selection. Classic tactics, in the Alexandrine mode."

"Again, I'm not half the scholar you are, sir, and don't pretend to be. But from my own experience, that maxim's only good advice if the enemy you're dealin' with isn't *the* Enemy."

"Nevertheless." Dismissing his arguments outright, Pinkerton indicated the trough with a theatrical sweep of one hand, offering Morrow a knife with the other. "Dinna be shy, Ed—gift us wi' your expertise. Summon the thing that wears yuir friend's shape, and let's see what it thinks of my ideas."

"And just how d'you suggest I—?" Morrow exhaled, gustily. "Aw, hell; all right."

For all had been abruptly made clear; much as he might want to believe otherwise, if Pinkerton had anything to say about it then this was *going* to happen, no matter what feeble objections Morrow might raise. Accepting the blade, therefore, he stepped to the trough's side and laid one wrist open with a quick cross-wise stroke, letting the resultant dark jet fall to mingle with what blood already lay there.

Had to be swinish, he thought, already a touch lightheaded, or horse; no way to get that volume of human blood shed without *someone* noticing, and challenging its necessity. Or so he hoped.

Pinkerton glanced to Carver and Ludlow, fixing them both. "To be clear, gents: this is to be a *negotiation*, no' any sort of attempt at a binding. Any man draws weapon once this begins, he'll be flogged."

"Absolutely," Ludlow agreed, without apparent qualm, or at least no wish to see his soft hide striped. But Carver merely stared back, obedience flecked with dismay; looked over at Morrow, brows hiked. As if to say: *I thought it was us* against *the Hex, not for it. Thought you at least was righteous, "Ed," even with unrighteousness aplenty all about....*

Just himself talking to himself, and Morrow knew it. Still, anger came surging up nonetheless, through mounting dizziness—and when he opened his mouth as though to snap at the younger man, what spilled out between his lips instead was a hiss-slur-click of unfamiliar Old Mex words, like he was some sort of human spirit-trumpet . . . *nahuatl*, the echo inside his skull named them. Blood-jet poetry drawn forth with the pulse of his own heart's juice, which all who were close enough to hear found they somehow understood:

O yohualli icahuacan teuctlin popoca ahuiltilon Dios ipalnemohuani: chimalli xochitl in cuecuepontimani in mahuiztli moteca molinian tlalticpac, ye nican ic xochimicohuayan in ixtlahuac itec a ohuaya ohuaya.

(At night rises up the smoke of the warriors, a delight to the Lord the Giver of Life; the shield-flower spreads abroad its leaves—marvellous deeds agitate the earth; here is the place of the fatal flowers of death, which bloom to cover the fields.)

Maca mahui noyollo ye oncan ixtlahuatl itic, noconele hua in itzimiquiliztli zan quinequin toyollo yaomiquiztla ohuaya.

(Let not my soul dread that open field; I earnestly desire the beginning of the slaughter, may your soul long for that murderous strife.)

In ma oc tonahuican antocnihuan ayiahuc, ma oc xonahuiacan antepilhuan in ixtlahuatl itec, y nemoaquihuic zan tictotlanehuia o a in chimalli xochitl in tlachinoll, ohuaya, ohuaya, ohuaya.

(Let us rejoice, dear friends, and may you rejoice, O children, both within the open field and going forth to it—let us revel amid the shield-flowers of the battle.)

"*Ohuaya,*" he repeated, bittersweet and thick, as through a mouthful of marigold-scented gore. "Huitzilopochtli, Tezcatlipoca, Xipe Totec, Quetzalcoatl: come one, come all, come now, come. *Ohuaya. Ohuaya. Ohuaya.*"

The invocation released Morrow, then, allowing him to stumble backward, cut wrist suddenly afire. Showing startling presence of mind, it was Ludlow who stepped up to knot a kerchief tightly over the gash, murmuring out the side of his mouth as he did: "Most uncanny, sir! The Apostles' gift of tongues, Hell-translated? If there is any way you might approximate some version of the original, er, Aztectlish for me, later—"

Here, thankfully, he broke off, eyes widening: the blood-filled trough's dense scum-skin had begun to bubble and steam, letting off a noise considerably thicker than that of boiling water—viscous, almost glutinous. Carver backed slowly away, clearly primed to draw, order or no. Pinkerton himself stepped to one side and, with no ceremony at all, grabbed one of the hex-handlers by the shoulder; the man stiffened, flailed and fell over to lie helpless, sucked near-dry in an instant, while blue-green light leaked out between Pinkerton's knuckles like marsh slime.

"Thought we were goin' to negotiate," said Morrow, dry-mouthed.

"Aye, and it's purest folly not to do so from strength, where ye can," said Pinkerton, not taking his eyes from the trench, while Morrow wished his mouth was wet enough to spit. *Should've thrown that damn knife into the trench and walked away,* he thought; *let him go fish for it, he wants this so—*

Just then, the blood exploded upward, splattering hot gore in all directions. It splashed off Pinkerton's shields like water from an oiled parasol, but Carver, Morrow, Ludlow and the hex-handlers, less protected, were all drenched instantly: blind, mildly scalded, repulsed beyond telling. Morrow choked and swiped his eyes clear, then felt an immediate urge to laugh hysterically at the look on Ludlow's face, gaping down at his ruined notebook. But when his gaze moved further, to the thing that now stood on the blood's surface like some awful Christ-parody, all idea of mirth died hard.

As in Bewelcome, the Enemy was naked but for a twining "suit" of Red Weed, still full of those bone-bits it'd picked up travelling through the earth—war trophies, decay-jewels, insults to dead and living alike. The vine's flowers hissed, extending their pistils like tiny tongues. His face still looked like Chess's, but stiff and set, as though worn like a mask, Xipe Totec-style; red hair, blue skin and green eyes all glowed with lightning, falling wispy from him as a mange-struck hound's shed fur. And behind him, on the earth, his shadow seemed to hump up far too large and black for his small form, moving with a sickening independence.

Yet the wry, contemptuous smile he . . . *it* . . . wore twisted unexpectedly in Morrow's gut, so like was it to one his lost friend might've come up with, under similar circumstances.

"Allan Pinkerton," the thing said, seeming to taste the name—only one, after all, to the many *it* bore, from Chess Pargeter to Night Wind, Smoking Mirror, We Are His Slaves, and so on. "We recall you. Speak."

Though Pinkerton had to moisten his lips, his voice came out laudably steady. "First off, I'd like tae thank ye for your actions in Bewelcome, which saved many innocent lives. Yuir generosity will no' soon be forgot—"

The Enemy gave a snort, and horked out a glob of blood at Pinkerton's feet, where the droplet sizzled and sprouted into a Weed-tendril, lashing upward to suck hungrily at Pinkerton's shields.

With a yelp, the Agency chief slammed his boot down, bursting it to spray, then turned his glare on the creature who'd spawned it, which sniffed disdainfully.

"I expect neither gratitude nor reverence from you, human man," it replied. "In fact, I suspect nothing you can offer would hold any interest for me at all, unless you prove otherwise. So speak the truth to me now, or say nothing."

Pinkerton scowled. "Verra well. Ye could not have failed to witness the demonstration of our new capacities, which we believe may suffice to destroy *any* foe of a hexological nature, no matter how powerful—*if*, that is, we can somehow get within sufficient proximity." He paused. "Am I correct to think that your interests lie merely in preserving the world as 'tis, rather than remaking—or ruling—it?"

"It is true I leave such meaningless occupations to others, as a rule. As for this world, Fifth in its line . . . why would I want it ended? Its disorder gives me great amusement."

"So you don't see there's any great call for a Sixth, eh?"

"What my sister wants is to fall back, not move forward—by her own admission, she wishes to restore the Fourth, height of our reign, which ended in floods and was remade from bones. But she fools herself. No system built on death can ever be maintained past its due time; her ambition is an impossibility. I have only to play my games, and wait for her defeat."

"You know what's happening inside Hex City, then—New Aztectlan, as they call it."

"At this very moment?" The Chess-thing shrugged. "I have some idea, but no. Does that disappoint you, Allan Pinkerton?"

"Somewhat. But I've found most deities disappoint, eventually."

The Enemy matched Pinkerton's wry grin with one of its own, slightly wider, displaying a row of black glass shark-teeth. "I have found the same," it replied. "And yet . . ." Here it nodded to a point further out into the desert, empty as a robbed socket. Blinked Chess's eyes, mildly.

Hell's it doin' now? Morrow barely had time to think, before something popped out of nowhere, high above. Two—no, make that three—somethings, falling fast.

The Enemy threw a hand up, casting Weed like sparks. Tendrils whipped 'round the lowermost body's arms and legs, breaking its fall, jolting out a high-pitched cry in piteous Spanish; the other two felt its tug and leaped away, legs threshing, like the air itself was water. One was a dark girl with Creole hair, her hazel eyes lash-fringed and liquid, while the other . . .

"Hell," Private Carver blurted out, "that's that gal from Bewelcome, ain't it? One who tried to smother me."

Morrow nodded. "One of Three-Fingered Hank's wives, yeah; I recall her. But—" *Why's she here, without him? Or that Irish colleen tried to blast Sophy Love, either?*

"Good questions, soldier," the Enemy noted, as though he'd spoke them aloud. "Shall we ask the lady to explain herself?"

Pinkerton cast Morrow a foul look, making him colour. "Well, I—"

The Weed cracked once more, snaring Berta Schemerhorne and her sister-wife (Eulalia Parr, the intelligencers' dispatches gave her name as), pulling them back down. At Pinkerton's finger-snap, the hex-handlers—the half-drained one recovered, or at least recovered enough—sprang forward, armed with hexation-deadening bridles spun from magnesium, to lasso and slap a set of temporary collars on 'em.

Reflexively, Carver moved to help, gun out; seemed to Morrow in retrospect that he almost seemed to think better of it, halfway into that first step, but no one could say the boy—'scuse me, free *man* of colour—wasn't game. And no matter how the women fought, without their power, they were just Eve's weak flesh: a double-helping of Adam's rib served rare, supposedly made for submission to God and man together.

Morrow had never particularly credited that teaching, really; it'd never described how his Ma and Pa got on, and he certainly didn't believe it now, after having palled 'round even briefly with the likes of Songbird and Yiska, let alone Yancey Colder Kloves. But he still sometimes caught these things resounding inside him, hearkening back to that part of him which'd once thought Chess's sort of outright daffodil patently incapable of beating a "real man" in battle, or that victory for non-hex over hex might be ensured by praying hard enough.

"Let *go*, damn you," Miss Berta snarled, while Miss Eulie and the third arrival, a big-eyed Mex girl-child, clung each to each, only pried loose with great effort on Carver's part. "We didn't come to fight! We came to damn well surrender!"

Pinkerton loomed above her as a half-dozen sentries rushed over, ringing the captives with rifle muzzles. "Oh, aye? And what would yuir man Fennig think of that, I wonder?"

"Nothing," Eulie said, softly. "Hank's dead—Clodagh too. Lady Rainbow killed him."

"Killed them both, the bitch, and after all he did for her, as well. Though, with Clo . . ." Berta shook her head, angry tears leaking free. ". . . hell, you'll see soon enough, I guess," she concluded, at last.

Pinkerton nodded to the child. "So who's this?

The girl gulped back her sobs. "*Marizol es mi nombre, jefe,*" she got out. "*Mi madre e padre*—mama, papa . . . they bring me to the City, to worship the Lady with them. I am not *bruja*, I swear it! I grow up in Huejuquilla, I am no one—I only wish to go home. Please . . ." As she slumped, Morrow knelt, circling her with one arm; she pressed herself into his side, shivering, with cold and fever mixed. "Please," she whispered. "I wish to go home."

Morrow looked to Pinkerton, who snorted in exasperation. "Sweet Christ, Edward, we've neither time nor men to spare on repatriations— how close do you think any State-uniformed man would get to the border, with the Hapsburg on the march? Still . . . belike the Bewelcomites could be persuaded to handle one more refugee." With a small but real smile: "She's no' much of an eater by the looks of her anyways."

Marizol blinked at Pinkerton, then flung herself over and grabbed him by the knees, sobs and rapid Spanish rendering her babble unintelligible. Pinkerton looked discomfited; Ludlow hid a smirk. Berta and Eulie exchanged looks of relief.

"She is thanking you for saving her," the Enemy explained, smirking.

Morrow's hackles abruptly went up.

"Saving her?" He asked, warily. "From what?"

Though he'd directed the question to the Enemy, it was Eulie who answered. "We'll tell you gladly, sir: the Lady, Ixchel—" She pronounced it *eetch-ell*, mangling the name unmercifully. "—is in bad straits indeed. That body she uses is rotting 'round her, so she's desperate for a new one, with poor Marizol her first choice."

Berta nodded. "It's true," she agreed. "Keep her from acquiring a new vessel, and your war's more than half-won."

Pinkerton's face went terrifyingly still. "Then you've just brought something the Lady wants *most* desperately right into me own camp," he replied, flatly. "What makes you think she'll not rend heaven and earth to get this little chit back?"

"Oh, there is no point to *that*." Again, the Enemy interjected, as if it found nothing more enjoyable than to be helpful. "My sister's great honour has already been openly rejected—cast back into her teeth, before all her subjects! For one must love a god to become the god's *ixiptla*, and this girl does *not* love my sister . . . nor, I think, will she ever."

"Easy enough to say," Pinkerton mused. "But Doc Asbury's spoke enough on the workings of this Oath, and claims it's no' *love* ye need—only consent, which ye can get in many ways. What assurances do I have that the Lady won't reach for this girl again, even here? That she won't rise up from the earth, say, seize *you* two and tell the girl if she doesnae cooperate, you'll be killed?"

Eulie gaped, while Berta sputtered. "I, I—don't think it *works* like that, Mister Pinkerton—"

Morrow cleared his throat, loudly. "Sir, we get her far enough away, fast enough, and she'll be safe. The Lady barely ever leaves the City—hasn't travelled beyond since it first went up, aside from the attack on Bewelcome, and she sure went home fast enough after *that*. Might well be she *can't* go any farther, or the Oath ties her to her seat of power, sure as it does all the others; she's got to know that if she leaves her folk for too long now, they'll lose all hope—and then *she's* lost. I'm telling you, sir, she won't risk it for one girl this late in the game, new vessel or no. She ain't that foolish."

Pinkerton returned Morrow's gaze, gave a slow, considering nod. "You make good sense, Edward." As Morrow let out his breath, however, Pinkerton went on: "But I'm no' sure I credit the Lady with *your* brand of logic. 'Sides which . . . I dinna see a point in taking the chance."

For the first time since the War, under fire, Morrow froze— so was therefore unable to do anything about it when, without changing expression, Pinkerton put his quick-drawn pistol's barrel against Marizol's forehead, and fired. The back of the girl's head blew out in a burst of bone, atomizing gore. Her eyes still wide, she let go and toppled limply back into the trough, splashing heavily, vanishing from sight.

Ludlow threw up his hands; Eulie collapsed in a dead faint; Berta shrieked like a gutted horse and flung herself against her restraints, twisting madly, while the hex-handlers forced her down onto her face. "*Marizol!*" she screamed into the cold earth, voice muffled. "*Marizol!*"

Only sheer numbness (another War-time legacy) kept Morrow from doubling over and retching in similar fashion. And from the greyish undertone to Carver's face, he saw, the Private felt much the same way.

The Enemy, on the other hand, closed its eyes, breathed deep and smiled—and God damn it all if this too wasn't a Chess-smile, recognizable from close-quarters inspection: blissful grin of satiation achieved, absinthe after long dryness, violence after long restraint or climax after celibacy.

Sacrifice received once more, however inadvert, or unasked. And accepted.

MORROW REMEMBERED LITTLE of the rest, though he vaguely recalled Carver taking charge of Berta and Eulie, shepherding them off to the stockade. A moment stood out peculiarly, tintype-stamped on his brain—Berta staring at Carver in dazed recognition, as if only now realizing how close she'd come to killing him, bare hours earlier. Nearby, Ludlow sat on the ground, once more examining his blood-drenched notebook, like a child does a broken toy.

The Enemy's words, too, he had somehow managed to file away, as it thanked Pinkerton for the life rendered up to it, and gave its counterproposal: *The day after the day after tomorrow, at sun's highest apex, I will stand before the walls of New Aztectlan— challenge my sister to leave her City and do me battle, god against god. If she dares not accept, even more loyalty and will to fight will be lost amongst her retinue; if she does, then surely you shall see, and seize, an opportunity. Whatever the result, your victory will be that much closer.*

"'God against god' . . . that suggests ye might lose," Pinkerton observed, so incautiously it made Morrow want to scream. "Mayhaps there's other reward in it for yuirself, though, hmmm? Something worth the risk?"

But the Enemy only laughed.

Avoidance of boredom is reward enough for me, Allan Pinkerton, it said, then sunk back into the trough, taking its bounty along with it—disappearing so utterly that nothing whatsoever remained in its wake, not even little Marizol's pathetic corpse.

Lying fully clothed on his cot yet again, Morrow stared up at his tent's canvas ceiling in silence, then closed his eyes and forced himself to breathe slowly, letting fatigue bear him down. He thought on Geyer, most likely still hidden in Asbury's tent; wondered how long it would take for Asbury to hear what had happened, and if that would finally be enough to drive him to flee with Geyer, after all. Then turned his mind to Yancey, knowing he had to dream of her if he could, for she needed to know what was happening—just how bad things already were, and would likely become.

And God, but he just needed to touch her, *be* with her—so much so he was almost afraid she would recoil, if she sensed that depth of need in him. The world grew fuzzy; his heartbeat slowed. His limbs were heavy. Soft darkness enshrouded him. Morrow went into it gladly, waiting for contact . . .

. . . only to open his eyes again but one second later, and find the Enemy in his bed.

"Christ," he said, disconsolate, "not *you* again."

It was like some bad parody of more memories than he liked to tally up: Chess Pargeter's face hanging over his, studying him while he slept; one deft little set of pistoleer's fingers tracing his body up and down, admiring it for handholds. As though he was just considering where best to clamber on and amuse himself a while, seeing what-all he could get away with before Morrow returned enough to his senses to object to the indignity.

"No one will miss your presence, soldier," the Enemy replied, coolly. "I only thought we should talk further, before my arrangement with your general comes to pass."

"Yeah, that was quite the bill of goods you sold him on. I'm takin' it things won't happen exactly the way you gave him t'understand they might, come mornin' after next."

"What he thinks is none of my concern, soldier. Though *I* take it you would prefer they go badly, rather than well, for a man who blinked not one eye before killing that child my sister covets, for the grand crime of being a potential inconvenience."

Morrow snorted. "Say it again, why don't you. And try to pretend like any of it means a damn thing, this time."

"For a man so lacking in power, you accord me very little respect. Is this wise?"

"Hard to tell, t'be frank. I mean, I do *fear* you, if that counts for anything—same way I would a wild dog, or one of them poisonous snakes." It almost felt like he was roaring drunk, this apparent freedom to insult something so powerful to its—Chess's—own visage. But here he willed himself sober, stringently, before he made choices he maybe wouldn't have time to regret; sat up straight and looked the Enemy in what passed for its eyes, only to watch it smirk back up, charmlessly.

"I know what you're doin'," Morrow told it. "Ain't anything new, you know. Our Devil plays *his* cards just the same."

It shook Chess's red curls at him. "Yet again, I *do not know this name*, soldier. However many times I hear it spoken, from however many of your kind, the concept makes no more sense to me than it did the first time."

"Yeah, well, I guess that kinda figures. Seein' that's just what we call the thing that passes close enough for *you*, as regards our own single-God creed."

"Your All-Father's rebel child, who lives under the earth and roasts dead souls on a fire pit, behaving in ways that would make my Lords One and Seven Death or Mictantecuhtli laugh? Yes, I have heard of him—how he tempts those not yet condemned to do ill by promising repayment, taking their afterlife as collateral. It is a pleasant fable."

"I can see how it'd strike you that way. Point is, whenever Satan wants to get things goin', he doesn't ever really put *himself* out at all, not like we think—just shows whoever he's after things that're are happening already, then steps back and lets 'em draw their own conclusions, so he can see what-all they'll do with the information."

"Ah. And this, you believe, was why I told my sister's secrets to your Mister Pinkerton . . . to find out what he was capable of, if he thought to gain some benefit."

"You saying I'm wrong?"

"Not entirely. But let me show you something now, without asking a fee in exchange, and then see what might follow, after."

Images flashed inside Morrow's head, quick and flat, yet sticky red-rendered: Pinkerton as one of those curlicued Old Mex stone images, dipped in blood and printed on a wall, acting out all sorts of secret mayhem—having fresh-turned hexes brought to his tent each night when the camp was too asleep to come looking and sucking 'em down like oysters, or making do with energy siphoned off those defeated by the hex-handlers instead; anything for a fix, just like the junkie he'd never stopped being. And all of this conducted under Asbury's auspices, with the ruined scientist's connivance, going along to get along, since Asbury sure as hell knew he couldn't hope to *stop* him.

Berta and Eulie, brought down like fleeing cattle, to be milked of their bounty at the boss-man's convenience. Or maybe done away with entirely once he was finished with 'em, like that child they'd tried so desperately hard to save, by bringing her all the way to their chief persecutor's camp—an object lesson in just how little Pinkerton cared for anybody outside of himself, these days, hexacious or not.

The "old complaint," all right, which Asbury'd claimed to be ministering to, and lied right to Morrow's face in doing so. *He ain't gettin' better*, Morrow thought, appalled. *Oh no.*

No indeed, soldier.

He's getting worse.

Yes. Something should be done. So ask yourself: is that opportunity I spoke of earlier to be his, while my sister and I come to blows? Or might it be someone else's . . . yours, perhaps?

"Shut your hole, you awful creature. I can't trust you no more'n the Fallen One, or any other demon."

Or Pinkerton, either. Better to trust yourself, then, and do as your conscience dictates, when the time comes . . . as I know you will.

"Think you know me that damn well, huh? I just might surprise you."

It gave him Chess's smirk again, and Morrow found himself gob-struck by the way that tiny flash of sharp black teeth travelled straightway to his groin, like a shock.

"Unlikely, I think," it replied. "Now come closer; let me show you something to remember me by, before I depart."

"Didn't think you creatures got itchy in that same way."

"Part of me *is* your red boy, soldier. And where he is now, he misses you—badly."

The offer tugged at him, just like it was supposed to. But how much of Chess really could be left, inside there? Any, at all? Didn't matter; regardless of how his gooseflesh might prick and his pants might tighten, Morrow wasn't anything like fool enough to feel like taking a chance on finding out.

"Well, tell him I miss him too, then," he said, finally, flushing to where his collar would've reached, had he been wearing one. "But not *that* bad."

"I could show you your woman, then—Mictlantecihuatl's handmaiden. Would you prefer that, as a gesture of *my* respect?"

"I'd *prefer* you not gesture my way at all, thanks. I'd prefer to sleep, alone."

"Will you tell her what passed here tonight, when you do?"

Morrow nodded. "If you ever let me."

"Good." Morrow looked at him. "And now you wonder what game I play, soldier? A long one, very long. So do not worry yourself; nothing you do, or think of doing, will inconvenience me much. What you want is what I want, after all."

"For now."

"For now, yes."

Riled, Morrow tried to turn away, but got caught by the wrist, and went rigid—there were things moving around inside the Enemy's hand that made him want to puke to feel, and when he checked, he thought he saw "Chess's" face ripple, like a mirage. Still, the Enemy—who truly seemed to take no insult at his disgust—merely laughed, and let him go.

It is decided, it "said." **You will march with your army to Hex City, and wait for my signal. My order.**

"Don't work for you," Morrow muttered, mutinous, into his own neck. While beside him, Chess Pargeter's mostly naked ghost raised a quizzical brow.

Oh no? Then for who, I wonder?

And was gone, leaving Morrow to wonder, too.

CHAPTER TWELVE

SUNSET POURED BLOOD across the snow-streaked desert, cold for all its brilliance. Half a mile to the northeast it struck dark bronze light off the western wall of what the shamanesses—human and inhuman—called *Tse Diyil*, that great slab-sided mound of rock thrust out up of the desert like God's fist punched up through oilcloth. It sparkled on the waters of the Chaco Wash, and stretched the shadow of the woman kneeling alone in the wasteland out behind her; her bent head gave it a distorted look, sending wraiths of darkness spiralling 'round with each shuddering breath.

For Sophronia Love, née Hartshorn, what little she'd experienced directly of the War herself had been enough to break her of the idea that meekness was an inherently blessed condition. She and Mesach had both seen enough of the Beast's face to know what needed to be done, and most efficiently minimize the chances of anything similar ever happening again. They would discuss it late at night or early in the morning, immediately before or after prayers, and sometimes during; the fact that they had been of one mind as well as one flesh—potentially—was what drew her to him, in the first place. Bewelcome had been their shared dream. Not the true New Jerusalem—they were neither of them so proud as to aspire *that* far—but a place for the faithful to live as they would, making a fresh start after the sins of war and civilization. To build lives in that they would not be ashamed to show their Saviour, when their time came.

Somehow, though, it had never occurred to Sophy how Mesach's time might come so much sooner than hers would. Or that the very duties they'd undertaken together would be the things which kept her behind, alone, unable to follow him until that burden was justly laid down. For whatever gifts God had given her to help meet those duties—even the outright miracle of her own rebirth, along with all Bewelcome's—they still could not undo the ache in her life that Mesach had left, bereft of his voice, his touch, his unwavering certainty.

Oh God, she missed him, her beautiful man.

One might think her time in the salt should have prepared her, but it hadn't—the passing year had seemed only a dream, the heartbeat between one drawn breath and the next, an upward-cast plea. She remembered folding Gabriel in, forming herself 'round him like a shield, then . . . nothing. The tumult had ceased instantaneously, leaving only absence and long darkness, without even a sense of time's movement to anchor her in its face, 'til that same timelessness had dissolved on the instant of her shattering re-entry into life, leaving not even a wrack of memory behind.

She had seen Mesach fall to Rook's and Pargeter's mingled devilry, been struck down herself—then come back, reunited for one shining instant, before losing him yet again to Yancey Kloves' bullet. And all of it *so* quickly that both days often seemed equally more nightmare than truth, lost in the black chasm which split her life in two pieces.

Thus far, that second life had been much less joyous than the first. She had buried herself in labour, overseeing Bewelcome's recovery, then integrating the town into Pinkerton's war against Hex City even while doing her best to keep Gabriel fed and healthy. True, his beauty (particularly as he grew, so sunny, so smart) provided some small annealment to her grief, but never anything near completely, and the secret hope which lay hidden beneath her maternal dedication—that she might one day become a casualty of war herself, liberated without guilt to thus rejoin her Mesach—was a shameful consolation.

And even so, it had still taken months before she could pass a single night without weeping, wrapping her head in blankets to keep her muffled sobs from waking Gabe.

God's strength was bottomless; that was what Mesach had preached, what she herself had seen proven, over and over. Yet what Sophy knew now, most dreadfully, was that hers was not— that when a second shattering blow cut her life apart again, her faith alone might not see her through the pain of rebuilding a third new one. And for the one soul she still truly loved, the only purpose left worth suffering for, to be *himself* the cause of that inevitable blow . . .

What did it say of her, that she was grateful another woman had her son—and that woman her own husband's murderer— because she feared being tempted to smother him, the first time an opportunity presented itself? That she could no longer give her baby the untainted love of days before, could barely stand even to *look* at him, because the forces he'd used to save them from death were drawn of the same darkness his sainted father had died fighting against?

Give him over to her, to them—his own kind. The words dinned in Sophy's head, barely recognizable as her own. *Then walk away into the desert, let the thirst and the cold take me, if some savage doesn't slay me for trespassing, first. It is the only answer. And I could still do it, I swear; I can do anything, for him. Maybe . . . it would be better, that way.*

"Perhaps, yes."

So quiet was this new voice that the start Sophy gave on realizing she'd actually heard it was far more muted than she would've expected it to be, had she been watching herself do so. She looked up, blinked watering eyes at the figure silhouetted against the sunset; it tilted its head her way like some watchful bird, apparently nothing but honestly curious.

"But could you, in truth, do such a thing?" it asked. "Are you really so desperate, salt-man's wife?"

I am interested, you see. For, even as your husband did—you interest me.

Sophy stood, shading her eyes, able to make out more of the thing only as her vision cleared. The fear which pierced her struck an oddly welcome note, driving home a simple truth: *No,* she thought, *I do not want to die, not yet. And not at* this *creature's hands.*

"Despair is an affront to the living God," she said out loud, voice hoarse, but unflinching.

The being who wore Chess Pargeter's mostly naked flesh gave a black-toothed smile, almost cruel as Pargeter's own. And for just a half-instant, she could hear him in her head once more, screaming into the sandstorm as Mesach went white, froze in place, began to crumble under the wind's incessant howl: *Yeah, go ahead on and cry, little boy—your Daddy ain't comin' home anytime soon, not now, not ever.*

That wasn't this man, though, for this wasn't a man, at all; not even the negotiable sort Pargeter claimed to be, with all his perverse appetites, his "love" that'd set Reverend Rook on her path, in the first place. You only had to look in its eyes the once, and not for long, to know that it had already far outstripped its Hell-bound original a thousandfold, in terms of being evil.

"This God of yours," this awful thing—"the Enemy," Missus Kloves and her savages had called it—mused, examining one claw-nailed hand, as though admiring the way the sunset painted it red. "Quetzalcoatl-Love spoke of him too, and frequently. What he said sometimes reminded me of the Duality Above All, first of our kind, who made this world—perhaps as a joke, or for some sort of wager with each other—and then retreated to the sky's palace, to let it work out its own damnation. But I have yet to hear one word thus far, for yea *or* nay, from that particular direction."

"Might be you're not fit to. *I* have."

"Ah. But then, your man 'knew' the same—did he not? And was mistaken, for what he heard was me. What makes you think otherwise?"

"Faith, monster. Faith."

Sophy folded her hands before her, a gesture this thing would be foolish indeed to read as demure. Fear she had, in plenty; she wouldn't bother to deny it, even if she could. But reverence, respect, or even the appearance of such? Not for something like this, ever, no matter how deeply it might cost her.

"You used my husband's pain against him," she told it, steadily. "Tempted him sure as any devil with what he most wanted, at the moment of his worst weakness. But know this: though you may have secured torment for *him* through lies and trickery, you nevertheless betrayed your own true nature, in the doing so. Which means, having already shown me what you are, you have nothing to offer . . . nothing I would accept, anyhow."

"Do not be so sure of that, salt-widow."

Though the Enemy took barely a step, it abruptly stood face to face with her, as if the space between them had briefly ceased to exist altogether. Sophy recoiled, tripped over her dress's fraying hem, and sat down hard. Before she could move further away, however, the Enemy had already dropped to one knee, other equal-taloned hand palm-spread over her breastbone; not gripping, so much, as simply holding her down, its strength effortless.

Then leaned in to murmur: "So I cannot bargain, then . . . not even with your life?"

Though the ground drew heat out straight through Sophy's back, quick as draining blood, her only answer was a weary sigh. To which the creature merely snorted, and took the prisoning hand away once more. "Yes, of course—you care nothing for that, expecting this Heaven of yours, no matter the way you may die in order to get there. A foolish question." It sat, hunkered low on its calves, offering no help as Sophy pushed herself back up. "Still, if you will take nothing for yourself, you may at least wish news of interest to your colleagues here," it nodded at the butte, "and at home. News of the War."

Sophy sat still, examining it closely, for—whether pagan god or demonic visitor—the single thing she knew for sure about it by now was that (like so many things in a man's shapes) it truly did love to hear itself talk.

Just as she'd suspected, she did not have long to wait.

"After much study, and my sister's example as my guide," the Enemy announced, "I decided it was past due time for me to take a hand in fate's design; really, I flatter myself to think I can do no worse. And so, on the night your son removed you from the battle, I chose to protect Bewelcome-town from Ixchel's wrath, raising walls of Weed to break her flood. Later, I told Allan Pinkerton that three nights hence—nightfall tomorrow, as you reckon time—I will challenge her to open battle, a test she can neither refuse nor accept, without vulnerability. If there is still any desire left in you to see justice done on what you call 'Hex City,' therefore, tomorrow night may be the best—and last—opportunity for that to be accomplished."

Sophy stared. "Why . . . would you care?"

The Enemy's grin widened. "Why not? It will be a great jest on someone, no matter who. Perhaps that is enough, for me."

Inside her head, meanwhile, its voice vised down yet further: resonant, bone-deep. Adding, *Or then again, perhaps you should consider it simply—providence.*

Above, the sun squeezed out, a shaken coal. And a second later, without noise or light, Sophy stood alone; the Enemy was gone, leaving not even mist behind. Night fell with desert speed to show the stars ablaze, diamond-hard and cold, in the sky above.

Sophy sat a few minutes more, lips moving. Praying, she hoped. Cursing, she suspected.

But the blood-din in her ears was far too loud for her to hear either way, and that, in itself, was occasion enough to give thanks, however hollow. So she waited until it dimmed, then regained her feet, and began trudging back northeast toward the butte.

ON THE CHILL NIGHT AIR, sound carried well, and far. Which was how Sophy came to hear the argument already in progress long before she crested the last sloping turn in the path 'round the butte that hid the war party's cave. The brave standing guard didn't make any sort of stab at greeting her at all, merely turning a pair of expressionless black eyes her way, a sight which might've unnerved her, once. But not just now, seeing her last conversation had been with something far more terrifying than either of them was ever likely to be, to the other.

So she simply nodded at him and passed by, skirts in hand. Kept on climbing, 'til at last she found her way to the small, smokeless fire 'round which the others sat gathered.

That ill-cobbled rock-creature—"Grandma," Yancey Kloves called her, a Hell-bound ghost recalled only momentarily from God's judgement by her feud with Lady Rainbow—squatted motionless at the cave's back like some ancient idol. Across from her, the heathen Chinee witch-girl sat blanket-wrapped and shivering, with only one slant eye peeping out from under a snowy fall of hair; an exhausted-looking Missus Kloves sat between with Gabe, trying unsuccessfully to soothe him, while he fussed and wriggled.

Doesn't know a thing about babies, Sophy found herself thinking, scornfully. And before she could reconsider, her arms were already out, fingers on one hand snapping impatiently. "Give him me," she heard herself tell Missus Kloves. "You change him already?"

"Half-hour back."

"Then he's hungry, so pass him over." At the other woman's look: "Really, ma'am, just what is it you think I'm likely to do to him, exactly? He's still my son, no matter his—*state*, and unless there's something going on here I'm not privy to, *you* won't be able to feed him. He can't even take mash, as yet."

Still, Missus Kloves hesitated. In the end, it was that Apache man-woman, The Night Has Passed—half-clad and rude in her breeches and shirtless vest, yet whose restless energy reminded Sophy, in a strange way, of Mesach himself—who leaned in and plucked Gabe from her, to plop him down into Sophy's grasp. "She talks sense, dead-speaker—for the first time in a full day and night, as well. I would listen, if only so we may return to what *we* speak of."

"Grandma" nodded, the move itself one dusty grunt, like the puff from a smallish rockslide, then shot a question in that shirr-clicking tongue of hers Missus Kloves' way. Who answered, in English, "Sure as I can be, given the limits of this particular method. And speaking of limits . . ." Here she gave another quick, furtive glance Sophy's way, before continuing: ". . . since not all of us have the—knack—I do for understanding you, Spinner, if Missus Love's going to sit in, then I'm sure she'd take it as a courtesy if you tried your best to use our own tongue."

"We would have no need for *courtesy* at all," Songbird muttered, "could she simply surpass her own blind fear of the *ch'i*'s effects, and allow us one simple translation spell."

Yiska—that was the other way her name might be said, Sophy now remembered—clicked tongue against teeth, warningly. "*Enough*, White Shell Girl. The salt-widow is our guest."

Petulant as the child she sometimes still looked like, Songbird complained: "Not *my* guest, or my hearth. Not *my* camp."

"Not if you do not wish it so. But seeing you have nowhere else to go, in safety—it would please me greatly, if you would stay."

Anyone else might have tried to touch her, then—but Yiska just stood there, allowing the Chinese witch to settle back, almost too slowly to be observed, against the shelter of one long leg. Once again, Sophy was struck by a reminder of Mesach, who had often chosen to deal with dissent the same way: step back and let the Spirit work on them how it might, leaving room for them to approach him again at their own pace. For *they came, every one whose heart stirred him up, and every one whom his spirit made willing, and they brought the LORD's offering to the work of the tabernacle of the congregation, and for all his service. . . .*

Exodus, 35:21.

"You can just go on and call me Missus Love, Miss Yiska, if you want," Sophy surprised herself once more by offering, as she felt Gabe latch on, swaddled snugly beneath the tail of her shawl. "Or . . . if you wish, even, by my given name, Sophronia."

At this, the squaw's already narrow eyes slitted further. "An interesting offer," she said, finally, "from the once-wife of a blackrobe *bilagaana*."

"My Mesach was a preacher, ma'am, not a priest. Our Church has no patience for Papistry."

From the shadows, "Grandma" spoke once more, and in response, Yiska peered closer at Sophy; Sophy sat still and straight, allowing it.

"So, then," Yiska said, at last. "I see that the Spinner is right: You are like me, marked for vision from the earth itself, and elsewhere. Bound to the *diyí*—what is the *bilagaana* word I want?" she demanded, of Missus Kloves, who shook her head.

"'Spirits'?" she suggested. Then, seeing Sophy grimace, at the very thought: "'Angels,' then; caretakers of creation, powers and principalities. The Holy Ghost."

"*Ohé*," Yiska said, approvingly. "You are bound to this Ghost by choice, sureness of belief, and thus it gives you protection from *Hataalii*, for good and bad. But it is caution you feel, respect, not fear. And such feeling is not a tool only, to take up or put away, like bow or spear." Though Yiska's eyes stayed intent on hers, somehow Sophy could tell that the words seemed meant for all to hear: a reproof for Songbird, a reminder to Yancey. And something else entirely—perhaps even both—for that rumbling *thing* whose insights she praised. "Guided, we may command, but only by obeying; we speak truth, but only having listened. Do you see?"

Oh, you are like him. He never cared much to lead for its own sake, either—only that people understood him true, saw what he saw.

And hadn't that been *why* people followed him in the first place? Wasn't that why Yiska's own men shed their blood so gladly, for her? Because only one who swore service to something beyond themselves could be worth serving, in turn?

Her eyes blurred. This time, Yiska did reach out, squeezing her arm softly as she swiped at them, reassuringly. To Missus Kloves, she said: "Tell Sophy Love your dream, dead-speaker."

Missus Kloves—Yancey—let her eyes drift shut. "Last few nights, I've been too wrung out studying on the Underneath to dream much of anything else at all," she began. "But when I lay down this evening, I finally dreamed of Edward Morrow, who told me things have changed. That his boss, Pinkerton, has found himself a dark new ally—"

"—that Enemy of all of ours? I know." A general look of

startlement whipped her way, from everywhere at once. "It came to me in the desert just now wearing Chess Pargeter's skin, told me it'd saved Bewelcome from Lady Rainbow's might, supposedly on my account, and was off to challenge her one on one, with Pinkerton for backup. Said this might be the last chance any of us had to see justice done."

Yancey stared. "But—why come out here to tell us personally, if he knew Ed would tell me—?" She stopped, then, answering her own question: "Because he knew Ed hadn't reached me yet, 'course; wanted to make *sure* we knew in time to act, if we could."

"What profit to him, though, if we do act?" Songbird asked. "Or cost, if we don't? Does he look to join with us, or use us? For we are toys to them, these gods—insects to be flicked away, if noticed." Glancing at Sophy: "Most of all, why tell *you*?"

Sophy girded herself, not allowing her own eyes to flick back down to Gabe, now thankfully asleep, toothless mouth yet a-work on her breast. "He knew I was in despair," she told them, unhesitating. "That I had it in mind to cut and run, just leave Gabe here with you, to live or die with those most like him. That I was putting my own words in the Lord's mouth, weak and prideful, and trying to tell myself what I dreamt on was His will, just because *I* wanted it so."

"And . . . he lied to you further? Tried to trick you, as he did your dead man?"

"No, he told me the truth. I don't know why; don't even know how I know he *wasn't* lying, when he did. I believed him, is all. I think he wants us there. That he's counting on it."

Songbird snorted. Yiska opened her mouth, then closed it, stumped. Above them, Grandma grated out something more, her crushed-rock voice bruising the air. Yancey blinked up at her, then translated for Sophy.

"She says it pleases the Enemy to dangle what you most want before you, so your own desires drive you into folly. Yet hearing this, she finds she believes you as well, much as she wants not to." Listening again: "Our task here's only half done, because we've been counting on Chess Pargeter's ghost to pull himself up single-handed . . .

save himself, and us as well. Since the Enemy needs us on that battleground, though, we need to make sure that happens." Yancey took a deep breath as Grandma finished. "Meet Chess halfway, and bring him out ourselves."

"How're you supposed to do that, Missus Kloves? You've got but two hexes to draw on, one a ghost—no offence, ma'am," Sophy offered, to "Grandma," who nodded again. "—and the three of us, you, me and Yiska here, whatever we are. Seems unlikely to me it's *God* he means for us to call upon, to raise those odds, but I can tell you this: I won't make heathen sacrifice, no matter if the sky itself begins to fall. So . . ."

"Grandma" leaned forward into this pause, horridly quick for all her decaying bulk, and spoke again, faster, clearer. Yancey listened.

"There's another hex in the mix, she points out," the girl told Sophy, at last. "And one more thing we could try, too . . . but only with your help."

This time, it was her eyes which went to Gabe's hidden form. And understanding fell at last on Sophy Love, like the proverbial tonne of rocks.

Unprompted, she put one hand to Gabe's dear, slack face, felt him relax beneath her too-long-withheld touch with a tiny, relieved sigh. Then her eyes blurred again, and she bent over him, touching his forehead to her own.

My boy, she thought. *My son, my Mesach's son; Lord, let this cup pass from me.*

But only if it be Your will.

"HE'S A BABY, barely knows his own name. He . . . won't understand one thing about what you want."

"No." Inexorable, despite this agreement: "But that's where *you* come in."

"Drawing upon the secret tongue shared only by mothers and infants?" Sophy shook her head. "Can we not at least wait 'til morning? Let him sleep?"

"Well, time's tight, ma'am, as you yourself just pointed out; we don't dare wait, really. Also—the Spinner says this should be done at night to have the best chance of working; the Crack gets wider in the dark, apparently, or some such. So, I'm sorry, more than you can know. But . . . no."

Sophy cradled Gabe, rocking him quietly, while she collected herself. "Will it hurt him?" she finally asked.

"Truth? I've no idea," said Yancey. "How could I? I've never tried anything like this before. You?"

While Sophy couldn't quite bring herself to laugh, she did manage a snort, at the absurdity. "Hardly." Then, shifting toward Yancey so they sat face to face on the cavern floor, with Gabriel sweetly asleep on Sophy's lap between them, she looked down at him, and sighed. "Very well. Let me wake him, first."

Gently, she eased him up in her arms 'til she could place her head beside his, coo softly in his ear, sleek his cheek with hers. He came awake slowly, goggle-blinking and dazed, as though trying to decide whether he was hungry or scared. Though still too young to smile a-purpose, his face relaxed at his mother's sound and smell. He yawned, widely.

Yancey, too, seemed unable to resist smiling down at him—but then placed one hand over his head, resting thumb and forefinger on both soft temples. As Gabe looked 'round in vague suspicion, she lifted the other to Sophy's forehead, pausing at the last instant, a question in her eyes. Sophy closed her own and nodded once, short and sharp. She felt Yancey's palm settle over her brow; it was surprisingly cool, and a little damp.

Long moments passed. The clamp of fear in her throat and chest eased off, though what replaced it was, illogically enough, irritation rather than relief. "Well?" Sophy demanded.

"I'm *trying*," said Yancey, equally impatient. "For yourself, Missus Love, you might try not to—" She stopped, let out a breath. "No. I can't tell you not to be afraid, when I am. Just . . . try not to be afraid of *me*."

Sophy opened her eyes and stared, so incredulous the girl coloured a little. Then asked, simply: "*How?*"

"Because—I'll swear you on a stack of Bibles, if we both survive and your boy likewise, then I'll go to Bewelcome after and put myself in your hands for you to execute, as a cold-blooded murderess." Nodding stiffly, as Sophy's jaw dropped: "Yes, I mean it. Bad doesn't wipe out bad, so I should answer for what I've done."

"My Mesach being the bad, I suppose?"

"You'll never believe me on that, I fear, but he was bad enough, to me. It doesn't matter, though. I mean it, all the same."

"Easily said. But how can I know?"

"Only one way to find out."

Sophy stared back, then closed her eyes again, with a huff. Loosened all the muscles she could by force of will alone, and prayed: *Lord God, help me know and do what is right. . . . Our Father, who art in heaven, hallowed be Thy name; Thy Kingdom come, Thy will be—*

There was no warning, and no transition. Simply the sudden feel of every voice in some million-strong choir broken at once into song, a single overwhelming note in twelve octaves, blotting out everything but pure, vibrating power. Even Gabe's sudden shriek of fear was only another note in that great song, mirrored by Sophy's own terror—and yes, she knew it now for nothing but truth, Yancey's as well. Three lives instantly laid open, decades of memory pouring torrential into each other, and all channelled through Gabriel's terrified conduit.

Oh Lord, Gabriel!

In an instant, the fear she felt was only for him. It made her brace herself, master the flood, wrap Gabriel's mind in hers; abandon all words and the ideas attached to them, shuck herself of everything pure expressions of love, conviction, protection.

I'm here, she sent, unable to think of anything else to "tell" him. *Always. Mama is always here.*

Experienced this way, there was dismayingly little to Gabriel's thoughts yet except the rawest of impulses: *Want; Hungry; New?; No!; Away!* And most terrifying of all, lurking there in the very background lay something dark and vast and dangerous, all possibilities rolled into each other at once, something Sophy could only think of as . . . *Wish*.

Distorted sensations, compiled through touch and taste as much as through sight or sound: her own grip; the taste of her milk; blissful smell of warm wool blankets; a half-formed thing that Sophy realized with a wrench was all Gabe could remember of Mesach's face. She twinned it with her own memory and sent it back to him, attaching her own love for Mesach and mirroring it with Gabriel's love for her. *Papa*, she willed him to hear. *Papa*.

The memory sharpened in Gabriel's mind, feeding Sophy a leap of joy, as: *Papa!* came back strong and clear.

And then, on that miracle's heels, a question—*Where?*

Sophy tried to think how to answer, but too late: the grief welling from her had already done so. And since nuance meant exactly nothing to Gabe, he felt the loss with all the force she did, unfiltered; he began to wail, full volume, inconsolable. She wept too, wholly unable to resist doing so, and saw that Yancey was crying as well: grief echoing to grief, a tear-stained lodestone.

Suddenly, caught unawares—and Sophy only kept these foreign memories from touching Gabe's mind with an agonizing wrench of effort—she was watching the massacre in Hoffstedt's Hoard from the thick of the carnage, while the thing that'd once been her husband wreaked monstrous vengeance in Pargeter's pursuit on a family and home which Experiance Colder had loved every bit as much as Sophy did Bewelcome, Gabe, Mesach himself. Then forward in time with a horrid jerk, to stand outside some shanty saloon (*Splitfoot Joe's*) where Mesach made the dead dance to his will, against all holiness and justice.

And then—*oh, God*—

Mesach's death once more, this time from Yancey's vantage point. But now Sophy could feel Yancey taking *her* bereavement in along with that one fraction of a second's useless, impermanent "triumph," recognizing just how deeply twinned Sophy's pain must be with her own.

The truth, and nothing but: hollow truth, awful truth. Under her mask of demureness, the other girl's steel will stood well-roused; she had meant every word of her offer to surrender, as ruthless with her own sins as she was with any other's.

Enough, Sophy thought, throat salt-clogged, willing the impulse over to Yancey. *Enough, enough, enough!*

It ended with the same suddenness as it'd begun. Sophy found herself back in the cave, eyes burning, nose thick. Yancey stared at her, face likewise swollen red, panting for breath. And Gabriel continued to scream, till Sophy instinctively reached out with her mind, soothing him.

Mama here, always, she repeated, soundlessly. *Mama stays. All's well. All's well.*

Gabriel stared up at her . . . and shaped what might be intended as a smile, clumsily. Grabbed for her finger with one hand, squeezing tight. From his mind came a wordless surge, a first *purposeful* sending: *MamaMamaMamaMeMyMineMamaMamaLove.*

Sophy bent her head again, trying desperately not to start crying again. Hearing behind her, as she did, some quizzical noise from "Grandma's" direction—absurdly quiet, a single rock shifting over sand.

On the outer edge of her perception, Yiska smiled, broadly. Murmured, approving: "And so, now we know. It works."

Songbird, meanwhile, stared at them all, equally amazed. For once, her look held neither superiority nor sour sullenness, but rather a kind of numb confusion like that felt by someone confronted by a mirage, unsure if what she saw was real.

And, should it finally be proved so, then something which looked almost like fear.

CHAPTER THIRTEEN

H<small>AVE MERCY UPON ME,</small> O LORD, <small>FOR</small> I <small>AM IN TROUBLE: MINE EYE IS</small> <small>CONSUMED WITH GRIEF, YEA, MY SOUL AND MY BELLY.</small>

F<small>OR MY LIFE IS SPENT WITH GRIEF, AND MY YEARS WITH SIGHING:</small> <small>MY STRENGTH FAILETH BECAUSE OF MINE INIQUITY, AND MY BONES ARE</small> <small>CONSUMED.</small>

I <small>WAS A REPROACH AMONG ALL MINE ENEMIES, BUT ESPECIALLY</small> <small>AMONG MY NEIGHBOURS, AND A FEAR TO MINE ACQUAINTANCE: THEY</small> <small>THAT DID SEE ME WITHOUT FLED FROM ME.</small>

I <small>AM FORGOTTEN AS A DEAD MAN OUT OF MIND:</small> I <small>AM LIKE A BROKEN</small> <small>VESSEL.</small>

Psalms, number 31, 9 to 12.

OVER HEX CITY, a moon the colour of bone rose high, overlooking everything beneath. The Lady who ruled it was asleep by now, Reverend Rook could only assume—either laid up in "their" bedchamber, damaged by the explosive force of Hank Fennig's passing, or busy playing with that creepish new toy of hers, the thing that'd once been Clodagh Killeen. Making it walk the floor with her, leaving its papery mane rustle and shell-bell rattle behind; using those empty blue lungfish eyes of its for lamps, for all he knew. Sending it out to spy on the battlefield or hang above Camp Pink like a miasma, searching always for any hint of where Marizol might be stowed away, so's it could swoop down to retrieve her.

Must be nice to have something you can rely on, Rook thought. Though granted, he himself'd known the feeling once, of course, and intimately.

But long ago, now. *So* long.

You will have your husband again, little king, and soon enough, Ixchel had told him, yet again, just before he finally took himself elsewhere. And this time, hadn't even bothered to answer out loud—why, when he knew damn well she heard whatsoever he was thinking? Just let the words bubble up through him, slow as frog song mud-drowned:

See, honey, you do keep on sayin' that. But—having seen that thing you claim is him up close, I'm just not sure whether I believe you, anymore. Or if I ever really did, for that matter.

This last was a sobering idea, when so many had already died in its service. Which was why Rook didn't really care to examine it overmuch, right at this very moment.

So here he was instead, back in the adobe hut where he'd once conjured Kees Hosteen and debated this War's exigencies with his Council, Fennig and Clo included, what now seemed like years ago. Lying back mother-naked on the heaped-up length of his own clothes and studying what little was visible of the ceiling in the lamps' flickering light, with two fingers shoved inside Sophy Love's Bible (snatched up almost without design in all the excitement, as the Hall went to matchsticks and the pre-torrent storm bore them all away, regardless) for a bookmark he didn't even need, given how the relevant passages were already playing 'emselves out in his head:

For I have heard the slander of many: fear was on every side: while they took counsel together against me, they devised to take away my life.

But I trusted in thee, O LORD: I said, Thou art my God.

. . . Let me not be ashamed, O LORD; for I have called upon thee: let the wicked be ashamed, and let them be silent in the grave. . . .

BLESSED BE THE LORD: FOR HE HATH SHEWED ME HIS MARVELLOUS KINDNESS IN A STRONG CITY.

31, 13, 22, and none of it damn well helped. Bibliomancy'd failed him, for what had to be the first time. Rook let the book fall, putting both hands over his eyes to block the world out with a double curtain of red-black flesh, and saw . . .

Ixchel, as ever, in her oldest form: that childish one with the high tits and her jade-chip mask, her shut lids marked like eyes, fixed and awful. Descending on him in a cloud, a boiling swarm of black rainbow-winged locusts, and saying, as she did: *Why do you hide from me, little king? Where do you think to go, to rid yourself of my presence? We are made one flesh, even by that Book you cling to, 'til death do us part . . . and, since that parting will never happen, long after.*

For as you know, there is no real death, for such as you and I.

No death the way he'd been taught to preach on it, certainly: a thousand torments with no hope of anything else once you passed through 'em, not even forgetfulness. Just watery cold and slimy stone, an endless raw-bones ball game played for worthless stakes. Sometimes he wondered why those old Mexes of hers had bothered staying alive at all, riding their nasty, brutish and short existences straight to the Machine's lip 'stead of hanging 'emselves outright, from the most convenient tree. But he guessed you did tend to dawdle, when you knew the road only went one way; if nothing else, the scenery must make for a welcome distraction.

And that's where I sent Chess, he knew. Down deep, down under, through awful pain, only to wait there for nothing but more—wait and watch, he could only suspect, while Tezcatlipoca strutted 'round using Chess's body for a chariot.

Yet he is there, still, in existence, no matter how far my brother may have buried him; we would feel it, were it not so. Which means he will return, eventually.

Rook shook his head. *Grandma, though—she told me that should never happen.* "For the dead to return unBalances the world."

A ghost should know better. For he is not *dead . . . and* she *is no god.*

Go back to that thing of yours and leave me alone, he thought at her, sure he could hear its skeletal rattle as he "spoke." *Give me an hour to myself, at least.*

Let you dream on the past, you mean, 'til your hand cramps? Very well: amuse yourself, then sleep, and be ready to do my bidding once more. For I own you, Asher Rook; your bed is made, just as you always tell yourself. You are mine now 'til Doomsday, in this world, and the next.

She laughed at him then, those old tinkling bone-bells. And eddied away into the ether once more, taking her insectile trappings with her.

It really was getting just like a marriage, 'tween her and him and Chess; the worst sort. Like he was hitched to two equally powerful people at once, one of whom barely tolerated him, while the other wanted to ride him down and eat his beating heart. And neither of 'em even bothered to laugh at his jokes, either.

Fact was, grief and guilt made for a heavy overcoat, 'specially when worn together—and Asher Elijah Rook had spent more time than he now cared to think on in their twinned embrace, muffled from the world with only his dreadful wife and Three-Fingered Hank for company. For far too long, he had felt as though things reached him only at a remove, as though each word spoke worked its way through three separate translations, familiar-unfamiliar.

By law, no mourning would be allowed for dead Mister Fennig, his previous good works in the city's service being all firmly set aside. Ixchel forbade even the smallest attempt at memorial, on grounds of treason; the sting of Hank's presence in her court, it seemed, would disappear even more completely than his denuded body had into the gaping maw of what used to be his triangle's point, the woman he'd loved and quarrelled with most fiercely, of all his ladies.

Yet still Rook couldn't sleep, here *or* there. Not with traces of Hank's mess still on the floor, and Ixchel telling Clodagh: *Search, daughter, cast yourself out upon the stars, into the empty places where my own eyes can no longer see—I must have a new body, and soon, if I am to meet my brother on the field. For he will challenge me, I know it . . . and I must meet him, when he does. No matter my state, I must come against him, with all my strength remaining—and in the end, I must win.*

I killed the only human being who ever loved me true for you, you horrid creature, Rook thought. *That, or to save him from myself. Only one I'll probably ever love, likewise, when all I ever wanted was the opposite, yet every move I made conspired to lay him low.*

Some things can't be undone, his father had told him, long time gone. *Some mistakes are irreparable, Asher. And the only way to pay for 'em is to take responsibility, accept punishment.*

He turned over, groaning, feeling Sophy Love's Bible nudge sharp 'gainst his side. And flipped it open at random, letting his finger-pads fall where they may; saw the words push up like scars, flower open, each sending out a single puff of poisonous black-silver print-pollen—*Isaiah* 13 again, 11 to 22, with some small transposition.

AND I WILL PUNISH THE WORLD FOR THEIR EVIL, AND THE WICKED FOR THEIR INIQUITY; AND I WILL CAUSE THE ARROGANCY OF THE PROUD TO CEASE, AND WILL LAY LOW THE HAUGHTINESS OF THE TERRIBLE.

THEREFORE I WILL SHAKE THE HEAVENS, AND THE EARTH SHALL REMOVE OUT OF HER PLACE, IN THE WRATH OF THE LORD OF HOSTS, AND IN THE DAY OF HIS FIERCE ANGER.

AND AS FOR THAT CITY, BABYLON THE PROUD . . . WILD BEASTS OF THE DESERT SHALL LIE THERE; AND THEIR HOUSES SHALL BE FULL OF DOLEFUL CREATURES; AND OWLS SHALL DWELL THERE, AND SATYRS SHALL DANCE THERE.

AND THE WILD BEASTS OF THE ISLANDS SHALL CRY IN THEIR DESOLATE HOUSES, AND DRAGONS IN THEIR PLEASANT PALACES: AND HER TIME IS NEAR TO COME, AND HER DAYS SHALL NOT BE PROLONGED.

"Tell me something I don't know," Rook ordered the damn thing, frowning. Seeing, as he did, the lamentable spectacle of Chess-but-not-Chess, rising up dry out of the sodden earth, wreathed in lightnings: his lips like clay, breath like dirt, Weed at his loins poking out all a-flower, while the markings all up and down his limbs shimmered like a heat wave. As bad as anything Rook had subjected himself to previously, yet still wearing that shape, that *Song of Solomon* mask which made him want to sing praises, rub his face in the dust, let the same bad parody of "Chess" bruise his naked heel against his head 'til all their quarrels finally fell away.

For *Behold, thou art fair, my beloved; yea, pleasant: also our bed is green.* Yet *By night on my bed I sought him who my soul loveth: I sought him, but I found him not.*

Since keeping his eyes shut changed nothing, he opened them, instead. And found, though his head rang, that the silence in this empty room was strangely restful. Here, he could pretend for a moment that the years had fallen away, or spun to a fate altogether different . . . a world without the War, or the gallows; without hexation, without Ixchel . . .

Without Chess.

He pressed the heels of his hands against his forehead again, cursing: no, not that. Never that. Or, by everyone's God but his, what had been the point of any of it?

But you never could really pretend despair was peace, not for very long.

And here, inevitably, memory finally welled up, just as Ixchel had mocked him it would. A scene from two scant years previous, when he and young Mister Pargeter were still poisonously entangled as heartworm through a dog's ticker—baking in bed together, holed up near the Border in some whorehouse whose accoutrements seemed to make Chess comfortable and uncomfortable in equal measure, and Rook itchy to amuse him out of his mulishness.

The details popped up in a glittering cloud, criminally fresh as ever. He saw them sharing tequila by the mouthful, saw himself dip to lap a bit more from the hollow of Chess's throat before turning him over and licking a careful trail down his sweat-shiny spine, then bury himself face-first at the musky source. Kissing him wetly open enough so's he could hook in a pair of fingers and scissor them half-viciously inside, preparing the way, while Chess just hiked his hips and purred out loud into the verminous pillows.

Moaning, as he did: *Oh Ash, Jesus fuck, enough with the niceties, already—have at it, make me Goddamn scream! Best be ready to do me through this damn mattress, you know what's good for you, 'cause I ain't fit to wait one minute more—*

You're what's good for me, you awful object.

Yeah? Then hurry up and get goin', you sumbitch, 'fore I just pop off entire and leave you to ride your hand alone, for once.

Why, Chess Pargeter! You been cheatin' on me, with yourself? A rap to the back of his skull, sharp enough to make his fist spark pleasantly. *Impatient little bastard.*

Three fingers now, well below both knuckles; Rook dipped his thumb lower, ran it quick 'cross Chess's swollen, gilt-furred balls, laughed out loud to see him pant and snarl. And felt that very noise jerk him up in turn, poking his own sensitive head out past the foreskin's tip like it was a gun and Chess's yearning hole the target, an inescapable challenge, near-impossible *not* to thrust himself inside. . . .

He set teeth on Chess's nape, nipping hard—made him gasp and squeal, then hump back, hump up, strong as some untamed bronco bent on stage-managing his own breaking. While Rook, in turn, found it was all he could do to just grab hold of either hip and enjoy the ride: deep-set, tall in the saddle but wholly at Chess's mercy, rather than the other way 'round. And well content to be so.

Hit it, Christ! Yes, there, riiiight fuckin' there, oh Lord Lord Lord—

He was touching himself now, in time to it, shamelessly—dipping low and then dragging up high once more, sweat-greasing his palm to pump out a bead or two of dew, then use that in turn to dig himself yet deeper. Yet feeling something crack wide inside him, as he did—dead flesh maggoted away to expose abraded tissue, exquisite as probing any unhealed wound.

One thing only you ever asked of me, darlin', he thought, *and I went on ahead and did different 'cause I knew better, like I always thought I did. Left you behind, then was surprised when you really* couldn't *be held responsible. And look at me now . . .*

Trapped between two gods, neither of 'em offering any sort of salvation worth the sacrifice. What he wouldn't do for just a hint of that still, small voice he'd once glimpsed inside Mesach Love's mind, or Sophy's bountiful Saviour! But such never had seen fit to show itself to faithless Asher Rook, no matter how long he prayed, or how hard. *Chess, I am . . . sorry, damnit, like I've never been. So sorry.*

Which is how, with one last, half-despairing grasp, he eventually found himself touching a whole new set of fingers entirely—five cold little digits, each tipped with an obsidian-flake nail, seemingly sprouting up through the tangle of his own belly-fur. Which knit irreparably with his while their owner murmured to him, gently, from somewhere over Rook's suddenly stiff shoulder: "Oh, how I know he would appreciate that apology, *mi conquistador*, were your red boy here to hear it! Though he would pretend otherwise, probably, and act accordingly."

The Rev turned his head just one tiny bit more, straining his neck muscles to their limits, and found himself eye to poison-green eye with the same thing that'd taken his measure at Bewelcome. There, however, it'd been far enough away to deny; here it was closer, very much so, flesh firm as Chess's own.

"You," he named it. "Enemy of All, right? We Are Your Slaves?"

"So I have been called, yes. And in my sweet sister's time I was K'awil, God K, who is also known as Bolon Dzacab, Serpent-legged and Powerful, He of the Nine Innumerable Maternal Generations." The creature smiled at him, showing those shiny black teeth. "But really, does it matter? Do you *wish* to be enslaved to me, Asher Rook? Or . . . to him whose meat I come wrapped in?"

Rook swallowed, dryly; felt his blood beat still all through the tenderest parts of him, every pulse a scrape, an implicit skinning.

"One thing you're not, though, is Chess—at all. Are you?"

"Not entirely. But thinking you might be able to swap me for him is as good a reason as any to want to see us all back underground, is it not? I offer you a chance here, priest-king—

only be ready to rise and I will lift you up further, if you swear to give me what *I* want."

"Which'd be?"

"Words with my sister, face to face. Time to put my argument."

"She don't respond too well to arguin', from my experience."

"Ah, but I have known her the longer, by far. Trust me in this. . . ."

"If nothing else?"

"I see we understand each other."

Rook pulled himself upright, pushing the Enemy's hand away, and tried to position his bedding so's to hide his only slightly flagging proof of interest—a move the thing all but snickered at. Still, it shifted back, crossing its legs like an Injun; folded palm against palm, primly, and allowed him time to collect himself.

"No offence," he said, "but I thought I was alone. How'd you get in here, anyhow?"

A shrug. "In your position, you are never alone, truly—here, most especially. As to the other, how can I be kept out? Like my sister, I came in through your dreams . . . an easy entrance, especially when you are hurt and disconsolate, reaching out for any shred of comfort your mind can conjure."

"That's all it took, huh?" Rook shook his head. "Best to keep my hands out of my pants from now on, then."

"Desire is a spell in itself, 'Reverend'—all wants are. But you cannot stop yourself from *wanting*, any more than you may choose to swear off breathing."

"Guess I can't, at that."

"It is indubitable. And so—let us skip ahead, ask and answer that most central of questions. What do *I* want? For you have been wondering, have you not?"

"Much as you were doing to distract me, yes."

"What I want is what *you* want, what your red boy wants. To see my sister fail."

"And how's that to be achieved? Seen that creature she made, yet?"

"The *tzitzimime* are not to be trifled with, yes. Like anything spawned from blood, however, they are difficult to control. Even one of them may be more risk than reward." It smiled, sidelong. "Besides which—I think you know something she does not, regarding this new 'daughter' of hers. What your maim-handed friend saw through his little clear mirrors, the ones he slipped you in that final fray, before his woman's shell ate him whole. Those *you* glanced through later on, just the once, when my sister was distracted by her victory."

Rook swallowed again. "Glasses, that's what we call those. 'Cause they're made of glass, this stuff we conjure out of sand and lime— cook it at high heat then blow it out, cool it, grind it so's you can see things clearer."

"I neither know nor care what 'glass' is, priest-king. Tell me what you saw, through your dead ally's eyes."

"I . . . saw . . . Clo, I thought. Still in there, under everything—the way Chess is in *you*, I only squint hard enough. And I thought I saw her looking back, too, almost as though . . ."

"As though some part of her were still the woman you knew, regardless of how my sister had remade her. As though, if you only found a way—she might be restored, and turn against the woman who killed her, killed her son, made her kill her man. Deformed her into this dreadful thing and laughed over it, then made *her* laugh, as well."

"You really hate Ixchel that much? Though she was your sister, or your wife."

"My sister, my wife, my mother, my all: my self. So no, little meat-thing, I do not hate *her*. How could I? Only we are left awake now, alone and alike—only us, in this whole mis-made world. But I cannot allow what she would see done. It is . . . foolish. Messy."

"Thought you liked chaos."

"Chaos is one thing. This—is idiocy."

"I ain't about to disagree."

"But what will you do about it? This is the question."

Rook pondered this, for what felt like a lamentably long time. And found it actually hurt him to admit, at last: "I can't work against her, you know."

The Enemy reached over, stroked his cheek with Chess's gun-roughened hand, almost sympathetically. "You will not have to."

THINK ON THAT OATH *of yours, priest-king,* the Enemy told him. *Its strictures, which once seemed so completely to my sister's benefit—were they really so? Might some lines be left to read between, some tiny chinks or "loopholes," as you call them, through which your own desires might yet crawl?*

Having heard it administered or administered it himself, a thousand times over, Rook did not even need to cast his mind back. Each phrase came easily to his tongue as a hot oil blister, blooming to flow between his lips.

Service I pledge to the Suicide Moon
Obedience to Her High Priest;
Fellowship to the City's children—
This I swear, on my own power's pain;
This I swear, to loss of blood and life,
That the Engine fail not to bring another World.

"Okay," he said, out loud; "I know it off by heart, as you can damn well see. What's your point?"

Think further, little king; remember your dead friend's words. It will suggest itself.

"'Service' pledged to the Suicide Moon," Rook began, carefully, "but 'obedience' to her priest—to *me*. So whatever I say, they have to do, on pain of the Blood Engine's maw. I could've ordered Berta and Eulie not to go, like Hank said; might be able to bring 'em back now if I knew where they were, or compel 'em to produce Marizol, likewise. But Ixchel'd need me to do it, and she wouldn't be able to *make* me do it, either."

"Nor would you, in turn, be constrained to tell her that she could," the Enemy added, softly. "Yet there is more."

Rook thought again, frowning hard. "That title of hers," he said, eventually. "Something . . . about that, isn't there?"

"Only one of many," the Enemy agreed. "And therein lies her trouble."

Hank Fennig up on the ramparts, staring down into the storm, gaze fixed on Ixchel's back: *She's got a hole, a plug stuck in it, like a cork.* Or telling him, back after that first uprising, the Mex shaman and his tied-together band: *But there's a crack in everything, y'see, Reverend. You just have to keep handy to find it, keep quiet* . . . and pay attention.

"Theophagy," Rook said. "She ate those other goddesses, way down in the Sunken Ball-Court: Ixtab-Yxtabay-Coyotlaxquhui-etcetera, and all that. But that's why she ain't really one thing nor the other now, isn't it? What with Ixtab the Rope being true Suicide Lady, and Ixchel herself just the Moon part. . . ."

"And Coyotlaxquhui, who Huitzilopochtli tore apart, being another kind of Moon entirely."

"Yeah, right. Not to mention that Filth-eater, or the Long Black Hair, or Mother Earth with her snake skirt, and her head like two other snakes kissing."

Now it was the Enemy who nodded, approvingly. "You recall them well for a steel hat, though your tongue stumbles over their true names."

"Listen up, Smoking Mirror: one of these days, one or the other of you needs to understand that *Americans are not Spaniards*. Hell, even Mexes ain't Spaniards, not completely."

Rook sighed. "Hank Fennig once told me the Oath was a true Patriot's creed—all hexes created equal. And that was something Ixchel never could grasp, being how she's unused to a world where people expect a two-way street—to get what you pay for, to keep what you earn. To her, she's the only one gets to give or take, so she don't have any call to account for any of it; we live and die at her sufferance, and she thinks we should be grateful to do so."

"A view so many of us share, yes. It became habit, which in turn became a weakness, by our end. And yet—it is so very hard to think clearly, little king, when drunk to the dregs on flowery wine."

"'The blood of men is sweet,' huh?"

"Exactly so."

Things sunk a level further, then, to where Rook no longer had to speak aloud at all; the truth of it came at him all at once, a kindled shoal of bottom-feeding trench fish coming on like lamps out of endless black, lit one after the other from their predecessor's flame. Slice by slice it presented itself, an unfurled pomander-orange stinking of secret wisdom, and the Enemy's Chess-eyes crinkled to see him cobble it back together—those cold fingers stroked at his forearm, raising gooseflesh.

Yes, priest-king; yes. Now say it, so I know you know.

"Them that took the Oath don't see things like she does, though, not in their hearts, where true hexation comes from. Which means... what they swore to never was *her*, per se, or me either. They swore to each other, to this place—Hex City. Only real power she has in this arrangement is as the City's protector, its occupying spirit. But she don't care about that, and she's shown it a hundred times over—by killing Hank over what she wreaked on Clo and her baby, most recently. Which means... they're freed from serving her at all, though they still gotta do what I say. Because—"

"—*you* care for them, for this place, and have proven it. Absolutely, *mi conquistador.* Much as you may wish otherwise, you have bound yourself to these people, their future. It has become a—religion of sorts, to you. Is that not the best of jokes?"

"They finally get wise and throw her out, though, then I go, too. Can't be High Priest for a goddess no one worships."

"Ah, true. But... would that not be best, really? For with both of you gone, alive or otherwise, the City could live still, every one of its citizens protected in their own mutual embrace; untroubled by hunger, no longer set to roam and rage across this world. You would have helped birth a paradise for your people, something unseen in *all* worlds, ever. A race of hexes neither outcasts nor victims nor gods, but men, women, children of great power, all bound willingly together for the common good."

America, Rook thought, *way it's s'posed to be, but ain't. Like what the War was fought for, but real. And all I have to do, to make it come true—is die for it.*

Or, at the very least . . . be willing to.

The Enemy clapped Chess's palms together. "Yes. Now say the rest, before you persuade yourself you have misunderstood."

Oh, for the Devil really is a lawyer, just like they say . . . and you really ain't Chess, no matter the resemblance, since Chess never would've had the perspicacity to notice the Oath's discrepancy—

But no, Chess would've seized fast on any escape clause he could, on his own behalf and Rook's too, without even consulting Rook first. Because he always *had* been the truly practical one, in their arrangement.

Pretty little red-headed Satan of a man. My sin and my salvation, just like I always wanted to be, for you. Just like I never could've managed to, even if I hadn't lied to myself at every step of the way, and you too, darlin'. You, too.

"Nothin' in the Oath that says that 'other world' the Engine brings on has to be the same one Ixchel dreams on, either," Rook said, at last, staring down at his empty hands like he thought he could read their creases.

"Not at all, no."

"It could be anything."

"It could."

"So, again, and having finally talked myself through all of this, 'til I'm 'bout to lose my Goddamn voice: what is it you want from me, that you can't get elsewhere? *Specify*."

Once more, it turned those eyes on him, and *Christ* if he didn't rouse in reply, shamefacedly.

"Were you a different man, Asher Rook, then I would tell you what I told this red boy's soldier, earlier tonight," the Enemy said. "To 'trust yourself and do as your conscience dictates, when the time comes.' But since you and I both know how unlikely it is you will listen to *that* most flaccid and decayed of organs, perhaps it is better for me to simply make you a promise, and take one in return: that if you agree to say what I tell you to whoever I tell you to say it to at the proper moment, then you will get what you want most."

"Chess back, I take it?"

"Once things are in their proper places, I will have no need of this body. I can feel your lover on the rise already, clawing his way up through the earth; should he reach me in time, I will be glad to step aside."

"And if he *don't* get here by then?"

"He has *you* on his side, does he not? You, the soldier and the soldier's woman, whose gift works best in graveyards, along with his own, not inconsiderable powers. So long as none of you allow this flesh to lie empty long enough to rot, I trust you to find some way."

"The hell kind of god *are* you?" Rook asked it, amazed.

"Not yours, obviously. Which is just as well, seeing you owe him so very much, and have paid him so very little."

Which was, if harsh, only true. And sounded all too familiar, to boot.

Restore the Balance, Grandma'd told him, which sounded like status quo regained. But where would going back to the way it'd always been leave Chess and him, anyways—or the rest of every other witch or wizard, inside Hex City or out, for that matter? Rook's mind went straight to the Council next, tallying his allies, and found he admired even the shakiest of them far more than he'd ever trusted himself. Might almost risk making the further error of thinking his own mistakes were worth it, to bring them all together. For what had been built in Hex City *had* to be preserved, even at the cost of his own power, of Chess, of himself.

So it wasn't really so much he might have to reconcile himself with dying, which at least was over quick enough, as it was that he might have to give away his own hexation, that very thing which made him *him*, and be fine with that. The same sacrifice he'd never yet been able to make, even for Chess's sweet-and-sour sake.

Finally do what I always should've, and trust a god to make it so, much as I know better: trust, hope, have faith, or at least pretend to. Do I really have a choice, either way?

He'd been silent a long time, he supposed, at this point. That would have to end.

"Fool me once," Rook said, out loud, to no one in particular. And gathered his strength.

NOW EVERYTHING WAS REDUCED to snatches, nothing more. He didn't even recall agreeing to this particular bargain, though he knew he must've, since next thing he knew, he had his hand wrist-deep in the Enemy's swinging rib-slats, feeling a hard, small something force itself into his palm. Rook drew out a jade ball, bright green on red, forearm suddenly bloody to the elbow; Tezcatlipoca folded Rook's fingers inward, smiling, and sealed the whole with a kiss that bloodied Chess's blue lips.

Swallow this, it told him. *It will act as an anchor, so that I may speak to you unheard, without my sister's eavesdropping.*

Thing was the size of a horse pastille, but Rook had no heart to complain—just choked the jade ball down, hoping it'd strangle him. And was unsurprised, when it didn't.

The Enemy nodded, and bent inward again, shifting into his lap. Told him, without moving that bloody mouth: *And now . . . what small reward I can give, to tide you over? Indulge yourself, Reverend—you know you want to.*

"Don't mind if I do," the Rev replied, hoarsely.

When I tried this with Ed Morrow, the red boy's soldier, he sent me on my way. Then I thought of you.

"How flattered should I be by that, exactly?"

Not at all. But you do wish me to stay, nevertheless.

Rook looked at it, carefully. This close, the thing he held looked less like Chess than it ever had . . . and yet. If this really *was* as good as he was likely to get, why stint himself?

"Been a bad year," he said, at last. And kissed the god of Night, Death and Magic, deeply.

LATER STILL, SKEWERED, Rook would feel his eyes roll back, borne away on a pain-pleasure flood centred in entirely unfamiliar regions; an only too-fitting crucifixion, offered up to seal the deal as half apology, half penance, with those too-calm eyes staring down at him, now gone all-black, amused to their impenetrable cores by the depths of his own self-hatred.

Ridiculous, really. Chess'd never required such of him, and wouldn't wanted it, if he'd offered. *Ride all damn day*, he'd said, once, in a flirtatious mood; *night comes, it's your turn in the saddle, and don't you think to spare me the whip, neither.* And how they'd driven each other, after that—right into the mattress, up against the wall, on every surface that'd bear the weight, and some that didn't. Had to pay extra for damages, after, but it was well worth the fee.

If you want it so badly, I have no objections, the Enemy would say, as he assumed position. *But in truth, no matter how I try, I will never understand you creatures. Why do you torment yourselves so, when life alone will do it for you, if you only wait long enough?*

While Rook bit his lip 'til it bled, huffed out a groan like Chess's nice-sized piece had cat-barbs going in and braced himself in vain 'gainst the even sharper backstroke, praying hurtful joy might soon turn to numbness, if not release. *Oh Jesus, hell if I know. Like the Roman Church and their confessional, putting absolution's sacrament in the hands of petty men—it's hubris pure and simple, sheerest impossibility. How can we possibly forgive each other? We can't even forgive ourselves.*

No hope for him, he knew that now. There never had been. Only the fall itself, the sheer and simple way one fell down—straight to Hell, no detours. And the dubious comfort of sharing your pain with whoever you might be able to grab tight enough hold of to drag there with you, along the way.

CHAPTER FOURTEEN

"'THANK YOU' SEEMS . . . markedly inadequate, in the face of what you just gave me," Sophy Love told Yancey Kloves, as they sat atop the butte, watching Grandma, Yiska and the braves preparing for their task: drawing Navaho signs on the rock, smudging a wide circle with aromatic smoke, singing atonal phrases into the wind. Torches on long poles surrounded a central fire in a ragged ring of flickering light. Though Gabriel had since managed—how like a man, or at least a baby!—to go back to sleep, Sophy could sense his dreaming thoughts yet, on the outermost edges of her brain; a not unpleasant mix of pressure and shadow-play, similar to being constantly aware of a nearby lantern's heat, even when its flue was shuttered.

"Least I could do," Yancey replied, looking wrung out. "Considering."

"Yes. But . . . it's a beginning."

"And I meant it, you know," she went on, not looking at Sophy or Gabe. "About surrendering."

Sophy drew a long breath, gathering her thoughts. The pain did seem more distant now, though that might well be due only to fatigue. But nevertheless, such an admission deserved honesty; she set herself to address it, if she could.

"Mesach . . ." she began, at last. "When he was in his right mind, I'm sure he knew—had to've known—that vengeance was the Lord's alone to take, not his. 'I will repay,' saieth our Creator."

"I've heard that."

"*Romans*, 12:19. It is a central tenet of our faith, and must be acknowledged, no matter the circumstances. So—in the end, just as Rook's and Pargeter's punishment was never truly his to administer—neither is yours mine. And while I appreciate the offer, I won't require it of you."

"Justice isn't vengeance, though, nor vice versa; forsaking one can't give you a free pass on the other. Can it?"

"No, Missus Kloves. Yet, to my mind . . . it's always the quick who stand in far more urgent need of justice than the dead."

For what did you accomplish, after all, she wondered, *by making Mesach pay the price he'd incurred—did you bring your loved ones back to life, the way Pargeter did mine? And what would I reap, exactly, were I to sow whole fields with your blood, madam—'sides from dragon's teeth and damnation, immediate regret in the short-term, risk to my eternal soul in the long—?*

Sophy sighed again. "All of which is to say . . . I won't honour Mesach's legacy by despairing of the Lord's Word and trying to substitute my own, elsewise the bloody wheel will never stop rolling. For though God *is* just, He is also merciful; another thing we too often forget, to our shame." She looked down at Gabe, frowning a bit in his sleep, and chucked him beneath the chin, gently. "Might be you'll answer for Mesach yet, Missus Kloves—but it won't be by my hand. There has to be forgiveness, somewhere."

As though urged to try and figure out where such a place might lie, they contemplated the star-bedecked horizon together awhile, 'til Yancey bowed her forehead against her knotted fists. With a start, Sophy realized the younger woman's shoulders were shaking. Uncertain what she might do to help, however, she carefully kept her gaze fixed outward, misdoubting Yancey could accept comfort from her just now—even had she had any in her to give, which she wasn't at all sure she did.

Silent moments passed, and presently Yancey's spine relaxed, her breath easing.

"Missus Love," she murmured, "if Reverend Rook had had half the faith you do, then . . ." Abruptly, she snorted. "But then, if my aunt had nuts she'd be my uncle, as Chess might've said . . . and did, on at least one occasion."

Sophy felt caught between shocked giggle and discomfited blush, to be reminded just how close Yancey was—in spirit, if not carnally—to that dangerous little man. "Back in Bewelcome, the Reverend promised me he'd keep Gabriel safe, if I surrendered to him," she said, for lack of any other response. "Even offered an oath to that effect. I thought it mere duplicity, at the time, but . . . could he have known Gabe was—what he was? Somehow?"

Yancey frowned, considering. "Seems unlikely," she said at last. "Not 'til after, I think, though he saw it in Chess before Chess turned; one could easily overlook in a child what seems obvious, in an adult." She spread her hands. "From what little I've seen, Asher Rook isn't to be trusted one inch, let alone further."

Sophy nodded slowly. "I suppose so . . . yet he did say something else to me. That 'When a hex breaks an oath, it means more than you know.' And Doctor Asbury claims it's an oath of some kind lets the Hex City folk work and live together—something they swear to that Lady of theirs, or the City, or each other."

"The Spinner once told the *bilagaana* blackrobe Rook of a binding of that kind."

Both women started; Yiska had come up behind them as they spoke, stealthy as ever, with Songbird in barefoot tow, blanket-wrap slid down to her shoulders to guard against the chill and her white hair seething in the cold wind.

"If two *Hataalii* wish to live together safely," Yiska continued, "there is a song by which they may bind their power into perfect balance, each feeding off each—but only if both agree to give up the *Hataalii* path completely, for fear of turning *Anaye*. And afterward, their power can never be divided. Break that oath, and one of the two *must* take it all, leaving the other dead."

Sophy grimaced. "I believe I can see why that arrangement held no appeal for Reverend Rook, prompting him to cobble together his own." Then, glancing from Yancey back to Yiska: "Still, whatever the strictures of Hex City's Oath, it clearly requires *no* sacrifice of power, and yet will work for any hex who swears it."

"Like that story of 'English' Oona's," said Yancey thoughtfully. At Sophy's blank look, she explained. "Chess's mother; I've been using her to reach Chess, down in Mictlan-Xibalba. She said somebody worked a binding on *her* which was kin to that 'song' of Grandma's, albeit more grotesque. He used it to trick his victims into giving up their power to him—sucked them dry, like the *wampyr* in my Ma's old folktales, then somehow fixed that link in place, so it stayed forever open but left them alive and leaking, a bucket with no bottom." Yancey scraped up a handful of sand in one fist, then spread her fingers and let it sift down into her other cupped hand. "Whatever they gathered, ever after, trickled instantly away. They couldn't hold any magic long enough to work even the simplest spell."

Songbird scoffed. "Impossible. Once fully flowered, no magician's reservoir of *ch'i* is so fragile as to be permanently punctured thus, short of death—" She stopped, mouth open. "—but when was this magic worked upon that red-haired whore, the man-killer's dam?"

"When she was giving birth to Chess," said Yancey steadily. "And—not coincidentally, I'm sure—right when her own hexation was coming awake, for good. Expression, Asbury calls it. The man who did it to her was Chess's own father, too."

"*Ai-yaaah.*" Songbird gripped her own elbows, shivering. "Three workers all linked by blood, with the mother in mid-bloom, fighting to survive her own babe's hunger . . . yes, perhaps only then could it be done. Devour the magic so forcefully as to destroy what holds it, without killing the holder, while the *ch'i* channels are open but not yet fully rooted. With but a little more skill, one might even make the transference permanent—the victim's power would flow perpetually *to the thief*, allowing him to draw on her *ch'i* as well as his own. The sorcerer who worked such a binding upon even a few victims, therefore, would be near-invincible. . . ."

"Might well be what he was trying for," said Yancey. "Though I didn't hear everything Oona said to Chess, this hex—'Columcille'— was some piece of work. Guess we can be thankful he either didn't succeed, or got killed 'fore he could do so more than once." Dismissing the matter with a shudder, she looked back to Yiska. "Whichever, what does seem so is that the common element here's consent, no matter the arrangement—that everyone has to swear to it willingly, make some sort of union."

"Like marriage," said Sophy. "*A man shall leave his father and mother and cleave unto his wife, and they become one flesh: Ephesians,* 5:31. What if—" She stopped, thunderstruck. "What if *that's* what the Oath does for the Hex City hexes? Makes all their separate power into one common pool, so they don't have to prey hexaciously on each other, 'cause once they swear the Oath, they *are* each other— spiritually united?"

Yancey and Yiska exchanged a startled look, as Songbird shook her head again. "I do not think any simple vow would suffice, a mere clerk's contract, even were it possible. Say a group of *mo-shu-shi* could, and *would*, bind all their *ch'i* freely into a shared reserve; certainly, they would feel no call to feed on any of their own. But neither would any of the circle be able to work *any* spell without the consent of *all* the rest, and how likely is that?"

Songbird turned to Yiska "Say you and two of your braves quarrelled over who would own a horse; would you consider it an acceptable solution to share the beast, but only so long as all three of you rode at once, all held the reins at once, so any disagreement over direction would send it in circles as you all pulled on those reins 'til the strongest won, or they snapped?"

"That would be one mightily large horse," Yiska noted, dryly.

"I understand the argument," Yancey replied. "Still, the New Aztectlan *Hataalii* don't seem quite so constricted, at least with regard to one another."

"But they *are* 'so constricted' with any regard to *her*—the Lady," Sophy broke in. "In Mister Ludlow's articles, his sources say not only does she feed freely on those hexes sacrificed to her in their usual devil-rites, but also upon those who break their laws, or defy her—that, by Hex City's reckoning, to do the latter *is* to risk the former." Unable to sit still, she rose and paced, adjusting Gabe to a more comfortable position as she worked her way through the idea. "If they're all bound primarily to her, and only secondarily to each other, that would make her the cornerstone of the whole City, hexaciously speaking. So were she to be destroyed, the entirety of the Oath would collapse, and . . ."

She trailed off, abruptly excited and sickened, as she saw where thorough pursuit of that logic-chain must—inevitably—lead.

"And hundreds of *Hataalii* in unnaturally close company, many already given up to the Witchery Way, would turn upon each other in an instant." For something so massive, Grandma could move with amazing quiet when she exerted herself; all eyes turned her way as the words rumbled through that motionless crack which served for her mouth, finishing Sophy's thought. "So *this* must be the Enemy's plan. For his cat's-paw Allan Pinkerton to tear her loose from this world, inevitably causing his own destruction, along with that of thousands more." The petrified bone-mask face grated as it turned, pinning Yiska now. "Well, then, granddaughter. If you still believe that Balance can and should be achieved for this City, then we must seek some other way to deal with her . . . and have only hours in which to find it."

"Yes," Sophy agreed—then stiffened, as something struck her. "Wait just a minute, uh . . . ma'am . . . how is it I can understand you, now? Has someone bespelled me after all, without my knowledge?"

The thing's huge head tilted, then gave a scrape of laughter. "Ask the dead-speaker—she who bound your thoughts together with your son's," it said, indicating Yancey. "Did you think such a communion would leave no marks? You hear what he hears, only that."

"Are our preparations then complete, Spinner?" asked Yiska.

"If the dead-speaker is ready to attempt another Call, then yes. Yet from what I gather, you may have already devised something to augment our efforts even further. . . ."

Yancey shot them a glance, like: *Didn't tell* me, *if so.*

Yiska gestured, dismissive. "A thought, no more—that it may

be possible to alter the peace-binding, so *Hataalii* might swear to *share* their power rather than merely balance it away. It would have strictures of its own, but it would allow a far safer conjunction, and could be dissolved without requiring death."

"Not necessarily, anyhow," Yancey chimed in. "God knows, if the plan's to boost my Call with hexation, I'd just as soon nobody be fighting to keep from killing each other while you're doing it."

Songbird backed away, upright and bristling. "Wait—do you truly consider attempting such a thing? Here, now? With *me*? I will not!" She glared at Grandma. "You, who so recently fed upon my *ch'i*, how long has it been since you were weak enough to be so taken— especially at the hands of some puling old man, who claimed to torture out of *kindness*?" She whirled to Sophy, who blinked, startled. "You have known this *Professor*, Joachim Asbury; perhaps you think him gentle, well-meaning, in his doddering foolishness? He tore away everything I am, and did it as a *gift*!" Her voice cracked. "'You are so young,' he said, when we lay there in the sand, my leg broken; 'I thought you might accept it, change more gently, become . . .' What? Some pitying *gweilo*'s maid-of-all-work?" Songbird shook her head, eyes wet with rage. "Idiot! I will not diminish, or allow myself to *be* diminished, let alone by one such as he. Or by you, either—any of you, however urgent your purpose."

"Calm yourself, White Shell Girl." Yiska told her, soothingly. "None here intend you harm."

"You have already *done* harm!" Songbird raged. "You came here to die in battle, like a warrior. *I* came against my will, vowing not to leave without my full power restored, and not to *die* at all."

Yiska sighed. "And yet earlier you mocked at Sophronia Love, for fearing to be touched by magic? You must set aside your own fear, which keeps you small. I will swear with you myself, if that will ease your mind."

"No," Grandma declared. "You are no *Hataalii*, not fully, with your weapons-love and your lack of study! That would be as useless as to swear with the dead-speaker—"

"Do you say my word is worthless, Spinner?" Yiska asked, not looking away from Songbird—and her voice, though calm, was dangerous.

"I *say* only that if we are to attempt this at all, it must be done between true *Hataalii*, not with medicine workers, or dead-speakers." With a groaning sound she rose to full height, towering over Songbird, so high Sophy somewhat fought down the urge to cringe back herself. "If you will not do this, ghost girl, seeing the child cannot, then we must risk the working unbound, and deal with what happens as it happens."

"'Scuse me, ladies."

Sophy had to admit she found an odd pleasure in the others' startlement, for though confounding expectations might win you no trust, it did at least command attention. But then again, truth could be its own compulsion—and God had put something in her head just now, plain as day. She couldn't fail to act on it.

"Was my understanding that if we can't retrieve Chess Pargeter's soul from its current limbo," she began, therefore, "our chances of thwarting Mister and 'Missus' Rook are much reduced—and that if they're not stopped, the whole land, the whole *world*, will be ruined or destroyed. That correct?" A nod from Yiska. "Then if Miz Songbird won't bond with you, Spinner . . ." For all her effort, here Sophy's voice broke, but she forced herself on. ". . . you can bond with Gabriel, through me. With Missus Kloves here to tutor, I'll show him what has to be done, and the Oath'll be made." She glanced back at Yancey, who had closed her mouth, grey eyes wide. "Why else was I bound to Gabe, if not for that?"

Given it was impossible to read Grandma's face or voice, Sophy had to wonder if the sympathy she thought she heard in the creature's next words—dim though it might ring—was nothing but her own imagination.

"Salt-man's wife," she rumbled, "your own beliefs say that to do this will damn your son's soul—and if your heart shares this opinion still, he will know it. Such things cannot be hidden, when a sharing reaches such depths. Being a baby, he will not understand—will feel only your doubt and fear and make it his own, perhaps even strike back at you, seeing it as a betrayal. Knowing all this, do you truly feel Gai-bree-ell—" Startling to hear one English name, however mangled, amidst all the transposed Indian. "—will be better off, for putting him to such risk?"

Sophy took a shivering breath, fighting for calm, and replied, slowly: "Seeing how I was always taught that merely to possess hexation at all was damnation irrevocable, then . . . if that's true, Gabe . . ."

. . . *is damned already.*

But no. She didn't believe that, and couldn't say it.

Instead—picking her way from word to word carefully—she said, ". . . at any rate, nothing we've talked of can do him any *more* harm. And if it's *not* true—if hexation is just a force like lightning, or bodily vitality—then all that matters is how it's used, not whether, and only the things one chooses to do with it can constitute resistance of Grace. For since all mortal men are born equally depraved, Gabe's best hope is to be with those who can most aptly teach him . . . 'specially if he can be made safe from their unholy hungers, as well as his own."

Cuddling him close, she watched him sleep for a moment. "So even if you *are* all damned," she added, voice kept low, "this makes you the ones best suited to teach us how Gabriel might escape that same fate—and if you are not, then Gabriel need not be, either. But whichever the case, there is no profit in fleeing the tests God demands of us."

A long silence passed, broken only by the crackling of the conjure-circle's fire, the faint susurrus of a wind smelling of smoke, ice, and chaparral. And when Grandma finally spoke again, it was in the quietest—most *human*—tone Sophy had ever heard from her, as yet.

"Almost, Sophronia Love," she said, "you persuade me to think better of *bilagaana*. Perhaps you *can* learn."

Sophy didn't know if she was meant to be complimented, or insulted.

"If this constitutes agreement, then let's about it," was all she said, in reply. And strode briskly into the circle, snapping over her shoulder, to Yancey, "Missus Kloves, you'd best oversee this procedure. Sooner it's complete, the sooner we can send you on your seeking-journey, and see what ensues."

"Wait, gods damn you! *Wait!*"

It was Songbird, chasing after Sophy now with the clumsiness of one unaccustomed to running; when she caught up, she was gasping, as though she'd never quite adjusted to no longer being able to levitate her way through life.

"If you are so set on gambling with your son's life—his *ch'i*, his soul—then do not bind him to *her* . . . to what she is now." She jabbed a finger angrily at Grandma, already a-trudge into the circle behind her, with Yiska and Yancey flanking. "She is a ghost with no flesh, a violation of *wu hsing*, an aberration of all Five Forces clinging to existence by will alone; there is nothing in her which may not come unravelled tomorrow, or the next day. And what then of any soul bound to hers?"

"Miss Yu, I really don't have time—"

Spasmodically quick, Songbird grabbed for Sophy's arm, startling her still; was this really the first time Sophy could ever recall the girl voluntarily touching *anyone*? It seemed entirely unpremeditated— even Grandma paused mid-step, possibly exhaling, though her state made that hard to reckon.

One way or the other, they all seemed equally surprised by what Songbird had to say next.

"If you *must* do this, then . . . it should be with me."

Not letting go of Sophy, she looked to Grandma, shoulders braced as if against imminent impact. But it was Yiska who answered, telling her mentor: "She is not wrong, Spinner."

The firelight showed a certain warmth dancing in her eyes, deeper than mere congratulation over Songbird's unselfishness; the Chinese hex flushed to see it, reaction painfully visible on her bleached skin. Behind them, Yancey coughed and covered her mouth, not quite able to hide a smirk whose implications Sophy— suddenly a bit red herself—found she did not quite wish to guess at.

"No. She is not." There was no anger in Grandma's reply, only a vast weariness. "And so, as Sophronia Love has said—let us begin with you, dead-speaker."

Yancey bowed, joining Songbird and Sophy by the fire, without protest.

"Ma'am," she said.

Taking Songbird's hand, she laid her other palm on Sophy's, cradling Gabe's head, and nodded at her. "You should wake him," she murmured. Nodding back, Sophy shifted Gabe's weight, planning to gently jostle him out of slumber—then paused.

Probing the new connections 'tween her mind and his, she gradually increased the intensity of her focus on Gabe, in no manner she could easily describe: As if her intention were a Dietz lamp, turning its oil-soaked wick steadily up until its bright blaze cut through all shadows. In her arms, Gabe yawned and blinked his eyes open, awareness quickening in reflex echo of hers. He smiled toothlessly, love pouring back into her, leavened a moment later by hunger—it had been some hours since he'd fed, she realized. *Soon*, she promised.

The promise was met by an imperious impatience that, in spite of everything, made her want to laugh. Gabe answered the thought with his own jolt of pleasure, gurgling.

Abruptly, two new presences intruded on their shared perception. Yancey's mind she recognized, its inner strength clear water over forged steel, while the other's . . . Sophy felt Gabe recoiling, and reached out to steady him, even as she forced herself not to retreat. The image that came fastest to mind was of a damaged locomotive, once mighty, now battered and leaking steam, limping along near the end of its fuel. Behind it dragged a carriage-train of memories, grindingly heavy for the shortness of Yu Ming-ch'in's life—a culture older than the Saviour Himself, calcified in pride and rigidity; a role laid out one hundred generations earlier, dooming her to be bred and born to be bought and sold. A fate-path once thought immoveable, now crazed with fractures like some frost-cracked granite block, and the helpless terror of not knowing what would replace it.

The moment all these things passed through Sophy's head,

a spark of fury flared up—Songbird's reflexive rejection of any attempt at pity, striking Sophy like a slap. Thrust back between her and Gabriel, Sophy took the blow without flinching, already feeling the strain as their separate magics roused to mutual, instinctive awareness. *Now*, she tried to send, a raw surge of urgency, nowhere so coherent as a *word.*

Must've been plain enough, though, for Yancey confirmed it by spinning a new thought-strand out toward Grandma, the ghost-hex only a squatting, shadowy bulk on the edge of this shared thought-space. Connection vibrated and pulsed in five directions at once, a harp-strung telegraph cable which sung high, almost painful, then broke.

There is fire between you, and it is by your choice that two fires shall become one which is both, where before, one would only have endured in the other's ash. Though obviously prompted by Grandma (Sophy could "hear" the Indian . . . *Diné* . . . words, lurking under the English equivalents their minds supplied), Yancey's part in this choir invisible wrapped them all, heavy with invocation. *You choose now to share a single fire, trust and understanding, a way of life. This fire will give you heat, warmth, food, and happiness. The new fire represents a new beginning, a new life. Let the fire endure for life, until* Tódilhil, *the Black Water Lake, separates you.*

Death do us part, Sophy thought. *Lord Almighty . . . this* is *like marriage.*

Do you choose to share your fire, and forever after forsake burning alone?

From Gabriel, only bewilderment: (*Share?*) Songbird too stayed still, body and mind unmoving, as if paralyzed.

After a moment, Yancey repeated the question. *Do you choose to share your fire, and forsake the solitary flame?*

Nothing. Nothing. And then—

Yes. A sharp, jagged burst, its meaning nonetheless clear, while something else—some long splash of force, searing to look upon—reached out from Songbird toward Gabe, then stopped bare inches from his face, trembling with effort. Make *him understand, Sophronia*

*Love; you are his mother, he yearns to obey you. I cannot hold back for
long. Make him answer, before I do as my nature urges.*

Now Sophy was the one frozen. For deep in Gabe's thoughts,
tangled with hers, she could feel his mind start on a horrifying slide
from fear and confusion to outright hunger, a deep, greedy, *brutish*
appetite wholly unlike anything any infant should be able to feel. He
began to struggle, reaching out for Songbird's power with his own, a
crackling white tendril that burned icily, stabbing Sophy from breast
to gut. If Gabriel touched Songbird's power in hunger, they were
lost, she knew—simply *knew*—and knew, as well, that there was no
real way to explain, not in any way Gabriel could comprehend.

Blindly, instinctively, she *seized* him, gripping his inchoate
voracity the same way she'd grab his wrist to stop him trying to
touch a candle: *No! Not safe. Hurt.* And then, though it tore her soul
in two to do it: *Like* this.

Sent pain in a burst, all her own worst memories distilled, and
"heard"—felt—him howl, at the touch of it. Then flooded him
with urgent love just a second later, until he yielded, unable even to
imagine resisting Mama on something she wanted so; swerved him
straight into Songbird's grip with his mind wide open, a friendship-
clutching hand rather than a bite-poised mouth. Thinking back, at
the same time, as though his skull were her very own puppet-head:
Yes, we agree, to everything. We swear to share the fire.

(*Yes.*)

Light burst over *Tse Diyil*, turning night briefly into day. The
detonation of commingling power knocked Sophy backward out of
mind-bond; she struck the ground with a horrified gasp. Christ's
name, she'd let go of Gabriel, dropped him! Furiously excoriating
herself, she struggled back to her feet—to find Gabriel floating
in mid-air, five feet off the ground, staring with wide eyes and a
delighted grin at Songbird, as if she was the most wonderful toy he
had ever seen.

Songbird hovered likewise, airborne, opposite him; her blanket
had fallen to the ground, revealing the tatters of the red silk gown
she'd arrived in. But that gown was mending itself even as Sophy

watched, spinning itself busily back into wholeness. She, too, wore a stunned smile, so unlike what Sophy knew as "her" that for a dazed moment, she wondered if this could really be the same girl. Some *other* albino Celestial, no doubt, come to take her place, and turn this whole affair into one giant jest.

A sphere of blazing golden-green radiance surrounded she and Gabe, pouring a spring morning's heat and light out onto the winter air. The conjure-fire had been blown apart, scattered to ash.

Gabriel laughed, and *flew* at Songbird; she caught him with perfect grace, naturally as Sophy herself, and let him sling his legs 'round her monkey-style. Not sure if this was dream or nightmare, Sophy saw that Songbird's fingertips were once more adorned in their former golden, talon-like sheaths, and that the power which glowed in her eyes was matched, hue for hue and force for force, in Gabriel's. Petulant girl; sweet, harmless infant; both were gone, for the nonce. The twinned thing before her was something alien, and hideously strong. . . .

As if sensing his mother's terror, however, Gabriel abruptly wriggled, turning in Songbird's arms 'til he saw where she stood, aghast—then leaped free, hurtling through the air to thud neatly into Sophy's arms. They closed 'round him automatically, trained to respond to his weight, and he giggled, squirming against her. Might've been any given night when his cries woke her, with him lying there infuriatingly happy, cheered by sight of her dragging herself half-asleep to his cradle.

"He *is* your son." Even Songbird's voice was different—calmer, more generous. She had drifted back down to ground a diplomatic few yards distant, hair eddying loose about silk-clad shoulders. "Though I cannot sense his mind as you do, the bond conveys— impressions, and this I know: he will never not be your son, Sophronia. He is simply . . . more than that, now."

At the sound of Songbird's voice, Gabe wriggled about again, grinning at his new friend; Songbird smiled back. Beyond her, Yancey stirred with a groan from the heap she'd been knocked into, pushing herself up on her elbows.

"It worked, then." Coming as it did in the union's wake, Yiska's voice sounded discordant, almost unfamiliar; Sophy winced, then wished she hadn't. But Songbird's smile didn't falter—instead, she revolved in place as on a spinning pedestal, arms spread, to show off the marvel of her restoration, and grinned yet wider when Yiska could not keep from gaping.

"*Ohé!*" She said, at last, admiringly. "You are a sight, in your glory—better than ever, to my mind. I rejoice, to see you like this again."

Once more, Sophy watched a blush tint Songbird's too-pale cheeks, bright and blotchy. "There are others to thank, for that," she replied, at last. "And I . . . will endeavour to do so."

Yiska grinned her approval. "Now you *are* learning, White Shell Girl."

That same spark, leaping between them, might've lead to something more, if not for what next intruded: a huge black thing which breached the darkness beyond the circle, hurtling itself at Yiska's back—glassy spike-ruff bristling, wolf jaws agape in a soundless snarl, and taloned ape-hands spread out to seize, rip, tear and gut. *Wolf? Bear?* Shock and disbelief slowed Sophy's heartbeat to agonized hammer blows. She saw Yiska twist, bringing up her spear even as Grandma heaved up a gout of power, but both were too slow, caught unprepared, too late.

Then: green-gold force lanced through the beast's ribcage, pinning it in mid-air. The thing writhed and flailed, shrieks so harsh and high they near dissolved into a buzz, like some mad, dying wasp. Yiska reeled back, leaned on her own spear-shaft, panting. Grandma's half-shaped hexing broke apart in her hands and dribbled, sizzling, all down her front, leaving smoking black tracks in its wake, though she appeared not to notice.

Numb, Sophy followed the line of power back to its source and saw Songbird, aloft once more with hand outstretched, holding the beast transfixed with a single pointing finger. She seemed as surprised as anyone else.

The green-gold aura surrounding her stretched to Gabe, wailing in Sophy's arms with rage and fright; abruptly, as this rose to one single angry shriek, the light flared and the beast exploded in a thunder-crack of shards that sifted the ground like coal-coloured snow. Startled, Songbird thudded down and turned to blink at Gabriel, who buried his face in Sophy's breast, still bawling. The green-gold light faded, leaving them all in the dark.

It hit Sophy how close they had all just come to dying. Her knees buckled; she was just barely able to turn the collapse into a clumsy seat-taking, Yancey Kloves' hand suddenly wedged 'neath one armpit to lever her down safely, though the cold ground's impact still rattled her spine. She gulped, shivering, hugging Gabe hard as felt safe to. It'd just been so *fast*—only now did she see Yiska's braves lunge into the circle, weapons drawn far too late, and useless, while shouted questions from the others skirled up too, as they came sprinting. Yiska's answers were curt, and sounded disappointed.

"Must've come through right at the moment the Oath took," Yancey managed, voice raw, staring into the dark. "Might even be the Oath itself *brought* it through—that the burst of power widened the Crack, or something like." Looking up, to Grandma: "We were all so ritual-took we'd have missed the Last Trump, probably . . . but I can't think how else it got by *you*."

"Do not flatter, Experiance Kloves. Even one so old as I does not always sense everything, immediately."

"Mmmm, and the eddies of the *ch'i* still swirl in disturbance," Songbird agreed, conjuring a marshlight sphere between her palms, illuminating her frown of concentration. "There may be more on the way, requiring vigilance from all. We have been undeservedly lucky."

"In more ways than one," Yiska murmured, smiling. To which Songbird looked down, unmistakably pleased, and Yancey grinned again.

For a moment, only—a wholly uncharitable one—Sophy's thoughts went back to Chess Pargeter and his Reverend, *Leviticus* 18:22, and everything similar. But . . . if whatever had grown up between these two ladies was somehow helping Songbird to find her place in the world, she felt unqualified to resent it; they already were unnatural, after all, to begin with. A bit more wouldn't hurt, probably.

Nothing 'gainst it in Holy Writ that I can cite to the contrary, either— not specifically.

Grandma said, "We must close this fissure, that much is clear. But how, even with the red boy's help?"

Songbird cleared her throat. "In Ch'in," she offered, "our doctors say that sometimes a wound must be unpicked, in order to heal cleanly."

Didn't mean much to Sophy, on the face of it—or the others, outside of those two. But Grandma nodded, slowly. "I see your meaning—it gives me an idea, though we will have to wait until the red boy comes back up to try it, for it will require all our strength. And so . . ."

Songbird nodded. "So."

She looked to Yancey, then. As, one by one, so did the rest of them.

Yes, Sophy realized. *Because—just like her part in the Oath, guiding Gabe through me, this is something only she, of all of us, can do.*

Yancey sighed, and nodded too. "Down again, then," she said, to herself. "Always down."

THEY HADN'T BOTHERED to re-light the conjure-fire, since the light pouring from Songbird and Gabe—along with the harsher white radiance of Grandma's unlocked power—cast all the luminance they could possibly need. Beyond it, forewarned, Yiska's warriors stood in a further circle, with spears, knives and bows at the ready. Yancey couldn't say she minded.

She sat cross-legged at the circle's centre with an ally at every compass-point, feeling their varying degrees of power weave around her like a bridled cyclone, pulling the lips of the Crack farther apart than they'd ever before reached. A feeling of thinness, insubstantiality, coiled in Yancey's gut; she had to breathe slow and even to steady herself, eyes tightly closed. On either side, the hexes blazed pyre-bright in her awareness, while Yiska and Sophy were blank spots, deep-rooted as rail spikes—different by faith, yet identically solid in their convictions. Yancey fixed each location in her mind, sensing their pull, the anchoring she counted on to call her home, if she happened to slip too deep.

Then, without ritual or hesitation—she was long past the need for either—she whooshed out her breath like a diver, and let go of the world.

That the plunge always felt "downward" was probably mere sophistry, since she'd never believed in the Underworld actually being *under* everything. But her dream-self, which thought in such terms, always held more power than her waking one, especially here.

Too quickly to reckon, Yancey's sense of the others shot upward and away, receding with blinding speed; a thundering wind and a sickening weightlessness engulfed her, as though she'd flung herself off some impossibly high cliff. The first time, hurtling abyss-ward, she'd screamed her throat raw. Now she only clenched her teeth and held focus, falling.

Within moments (or hours), she felt the track she'd worn on previous descents closing 'round her, a tunnel burrowing between worlds. The fall became a slide, at first smooth, then painfully bumpy, 'til her feet touched down on something like rock: black, ice-streaked, biting with cold. Yancey cupped her arms 'round herself, and shivered. This was farther down than she had ever gone, and she was dismayed to realize that—like a hawk stooping on prey, and missing—she had lost the bird's-eye sense of where Chess and Oona *were*, in the sprawling tapestry of deadlands. She'd come too close to the map, and could no longer read it.

The bleak, colourless terrain of the half-world spread out below her in all directions, falling away from the mountain peak on which she stood; above, the conduit connecting her to her body stretched upward, taut and humming. Reflexively, she touched Chess's guns, or their memory, to confirm they still hung at her belt. Thus reassured, she sprang downward from ledge to spire to boulder, each step only firm beneath her feet because she *willed* it so. In minutes, she stood on the plain, casting about.

Nothing.

All the curse words she'd ever learned from Chess and Ed came spilling out, under her breath. Neither time nor geography stayed steady here, once you got out beyond where things echoed the living world, and while she'd *known* that, she'd still unthinkingly assumed her talents would somehow account for it—clearly a mistake. The very idea that, after everything they'd sacrificed and accomplished, she would find herself stymied by a simple inability to *find* that contentious creature at the vital moment . . .

Typical, Goddamnit. Typical Chess.

Turning in a slow circle until the mountains were once again at her back, she squinted hard, and still found nothing. Should she wait, or walk? Waiting made more sense by the odds—if Chess made it to this place at all, he would eventually start to climb—but she could barely stand the thought of coming so far to do nothing but stand still.

Yet however she stretched out her time, it was limited. Granted, she never tired down here, but her flesh still bore the weariness, up above; if she pushed herself too far, she would get no warning before her body's collapse wrenched her back into a day-long blackout. And it might seem to take only minutes or days before Chess and Oona found their way here. That was, of course, even assuming they escaped the legions pursuing them, those maddened mobs of revenants she'd heard Chess call his Dead Posse. . . .

Yancey smiled, grimly. No, when it came down to sheer defiance, she somehow couldn't believe Chess Pargeter would ever let himself be beaten. Again, she touched the guns that had once been his, palms atop their stocks; so strange, to take comfort from such death-dealing implements. Yet no stranger than the man himself.

With no heartbeat in her ears or breath to plume in the air, it took her some moments to realize that the darkness some ways out was moving—a man-shaped shadow, pacing steadily toward her. In an instant, she had both guns out and cocked, with a speed Chess might have applauded. Her fear she pushed to one side, wasting no more thought on it. These guns were real only because her mind made them real, made them work—*would* make them work. No matter what, or who, this foe proved to be, either; it was of the dead, and it was given to her to *command* the dead.

Then enough of the alien starlight outlined it to make the figure's face visible. And Yancey straightened, grip slackening, 'til the guns almost fell unheeded from her hands.

"Uther," she whispered—tried to whisper, anyhow, as breathlessness made the name a mere mouthing. But the man who'd been her husband, if only for less than a day, clearly didn't need to hear his name to recognize it. He smiled, and opened his arms.

And she flung herself into them, straightaway, headlong. Childish as little Gabriel Love.

A bare parody of a true embrace, yet she clung fast anyhow, not wanting to face the truth of it yet, while every moment drove it deeper. Uther had held her before, even kissed her, though they had gone no further; she knew his smell, all the minor irregularities of a living man—scratch of his beard, sweat and stink, slight off-balance pressure of his left arm from an old knife-wound, ill-treated. Here with her now, he was solid and warm, yet she felt no pulse under her cheek. His chest did not move.

And as she slowly withdrew and looked up at him, even his face gave it away—the nascent crow's-feet at his eyes, the tan of the New Mexico sun, the scattered faint pockmarks of a childhood bout with chickenpox . . . gone. He had been remade but not reborn, smoothed into a perfection found only in death.

"Oh, God," she heard herself say, without meaning to. "I *did* love you, Uther. . . . I always will! But—"

Uther's reaction, however, was the last thing she'd expected; he threw his head back and laughed, then looked back down at her, still chuckling. "Oh, sweetheart, do you really think I need proof of your heart now, where we both are?" With a shrewdly raised eyebrow: "Or that it troubles me someone else could maybe make you happy . . . happier than I might've, even?"

Yancey would have flushed, if she could've, but Uther laughed again, and folded her back in. "Morrow's a good man, in the end," he told her. "Sometimes a little too prone to give in to lesser evils out of fear of greater ones, but you could do well with him, like he could, with you." As she stared: "Yes, we know. We see more than we can ever tell, Experiance. And though you've got a mighty strong sight in you, you'd better take care never to think you see everything there is to see."

"'We'?"

"Me, your father, your mother. Both said to say they love you, by the way."

Yancey blinked, swallowing. "They—couldn't be here?"

"They *are* here. It's just you can't . . ." Uther hesitated. "There aren't really words for it—has to do with you still being alive and all, only grasping one point in Time. And that was yóur *Pa's* attempt at an explanation!" He snorted. "Mala just gave me my marching orders and sent me on my way, to do what I can to help."

Yancey startled herself with a gulp of laughter. "Sounds like Ma," she admitted. "But—if you see it all, then you must know what I did—before the wedding, and after." Her throat hurt to say it. "I brought Chess there, and all that followed down on the Hoard, likewise. Did for Sheriff Love again, too, eventually; murdered him, right in front of his wife and child."

"Many have, honey." Uther sighed. "Can't say it didn't hurt to learn, either, or to watch. But I don't begrudge you none."

Yancey stepped back, breaking the contact. She didn't deserve even its shallow comfort. "Uther . . . I got you *killed*."

Uther shrugged. "Halfway, maybe—rest of it I did myself, and gladly. But that don't mean I'm unhappy you're still alive." More gently: "Stay that way, will you? We don't need you to think like you gotta hurry up and join us, seein' we're with you already. Always will be."

"I'll try," Yancey barely whispered.

"All I ask."

He took her into his arms again, and she let herself rest there for a while. *Did it always hurt, to be forgiven?* she wondered. But maybe that was why folks called God merciful *and* cruel. Some mercies hurt, and probably should, with an ache that was oddly pleasing.

"So you came to help," she said, presently. "How?"

Uther drew back a little, so's he could study her face. "You got a lot of clout in this place, honey; more than me, truth be told. But I got one thing you don't—time. I can take as long as you need to find the man you're looking for."

"Problem is, Uther, if he sees *you* comin', he'll think you're part of those huntin' him—one of those *he* did for, in a long and bloody line of such. That's why it's got to be me—somebody he knows, and trusts."

Uther stroked his chin. "Huh. Well, I think I might have another option, come to think." With a deadpan humour that fair made Yancey's heart turn over, for sheer familiarity: "Don't go nowhere, will you?"

And just as suddenly, she was alone again.

Yancey sank to the grey grass and buried her face in her palms, unsure whether to laugh or sob.

When she finally became aware of Uther standing before her again, she looked up—and leaped to her feet, mouth open at the sight of the man beside him. A man she'd only seen once, and only as a ghost, for the most fleeting of seconds through a third man's memories—but all the same, she knew him.

"Experiance Colder," said Uther, "this is—"

"Kloves," said Yancey, putting out her hand. "Yancey Kloves, Missus. We've never met, sir, but I know you through a mutual acquaintance . . . Chess Pargeter."

Kees Hosteen stiffened—then unlocked, a slow smile splitting his greying beard.

"Shouldn't surprise me, I guess," he replied. "Man does get around."

"True enough."

"So, what the hell's the little bastard gotten himself into this time?" Then, holding up a hand: "Actually, don't bother; take too long to explain anyway, I'm sure. Just tell me what I can do to help."

Yancey matched his smile, and did.

SEVEN DIALS: FIVE

Here at the bottom, in the underneath. The end of all things, and the beginning.

This is where the root grows down, snaking its way through layer upon layer, 'til it reaches at last the skull-seed of all life. And this is where the tree grows back up, accordingly—widdershins, counterclockwise, winding the world's watch the wrong way 'til its coils cry out, 'til time itself runs a path so crooked it crosses over itself. 'Til the blood-choked channel between the two breaks, at last, through that crust which separates life and death, sleep and waking, dream and reality.

After which, fuelled by burning bones and sweet decay alike, it stretches up impossibly high, reaching to scar the sky's very face: crack things apart, score them so badly they can never be mended, never return to what they were before, no matter what sacrifice is made. To birth a new world, whole, complete. Entire.

As though everything at once were commanding, or perhaps pleading: O you who die to live and live to die, gods and monsters—victims, killers, magicians of every world, together—kill yourselves, now, while you still can. Make the sun and moon come up, make it all afresh, anew. Start over, while you still can.

And do it now. Before it is too late.

THOUGH SHERIFF LOVE—Chess still couldn't think of the man without his former title, for all he doubted the dead got to hold onto such things—stretched up as lean and tall as ever in his familiar dusty black, the rest of the lawman's aspect was a strange cross-breed of the last two times Chess had seen him: hair caught back up in those two shortish ear-locks, parted severely and braided at the bottom, while his faith-hollowed face still bristled with that shaggy year's growth of beard Bewelcome's un-salting had gifted him, groomed only minimally (with fingers, perhaps), and honest-to-Christ *knotted* to keep it up out of his way.

What he looked most like was one of those old-time preachers whose Word Rook had liked to cite, back under the Lieut's command–Preparers of the Way sent out into the desert to await God's view-halloo, fed on honey and locusts, harassed by titty-shaking devils. Like those left behind in War-Heaven, however, Love bore the marks inflicted by his last go-out with lamentable clarity. That powder-burnt hole in his temple, for example, cracks starring out all 'round, with what rougher-yet damage the bullet had made coming out on the opposite side no doubt well-hid beneath his mane.

"Hadn't looked to see you here," Chess told him, studying for its traces—and vaguely recalling, as he did, how that might well have been the exact same thing he'd said to him when they'd met up at Yancey Kloves' wedding, all that time ago . . . or not *so* much, maybe. Hard to Goddamn tell, down here.

But the Sheriff didn't seem to notice. "Where else would you have thought to find me, 'Private'?" He answered. "Judgement, once met, is swift, and terrible; when released from the flesh, all men resolve to their proper places, and stay there long as the Lord deems fit. Though, that said . . ." He looked Chess up and down. ". . . you obviously haven't exactly resigned yourself to whatever fate He threw *your* way. Have you?"

Chess raised a brow. "You expected any different?"

"Given your nature? Not really, no."

"Huh. Very . . . Christian of you, I guess."

Nearby, Oona—frostbit feet miraculously returned to their

normal hue—straightened up, buttoning Chess's jacket closer about her, and tapped one hand impatiently on her still too-much-revealed thigh. "So 'oo's this, then?" she demanded, of Chess. "'Nother of your God-botherer fancy-men?"

Chess almost spat, at that. "*Hardly,*" he managed.

"Well, I'm not likely t'know, am I?"

"You sure ain't. So why don't you keep your mouth shut and let me get my bearings, after which we'll move on?"

Oona made a huffing noise, and tossed her red hair like a colt. The Sheriff, on the other hand, regarded her at first with interest, then outright startlement.

"Pargeter," he said, at last, "is . . . that a *woman?*"

"What gave it away?"

"I—hadn't known you to keep female company, is all, aside from Missus Kloves. And I know *she* isn't yet in our same situation."

"Yeah, and how'd that be, I wonder? No, wait, I got it . . . *God* told you."

Too much fun entirely, almost, to twit this great fool, now he'd recovered his vaunted reason and charitableness along with his salt-free skin. And yet—Chess had to admit it didn't bring quite the charge it once might've, under different circumstances. The stakes were just too high, too immediate, to be worth indulging himself over something so . . . petty.

"God doesn't speak to me," Love said, at last. "Not any more. Not—yet, anyhow."

To which Chess had no earthly idea *what* to reply, in all frankness. So they simply stood there a minute, glancing elsewhere, 'til Oona finally put in, "I'm 'is mother, in case you was wonderin'."

Again, Love gave half a moment's face-slapped double take, before rallying himself. "*Really,*" was all he replied.

Yeah, really. *Think I dropped out of the air full-made, preacher-man, or came up a-bloom from perdition's own root?*

The usual quick connective spark between those words buzzing 'round Chess's skull and his own sharp tongue, however, seemed to have gone fallow, making it lie surprisingly quiet in his mouth.

Indeed, he had to rouse it somewhat to simply say, in return: "Sheriff . . . I've been thinking on this a good long time. . . ."

"Do tell."

"Rook did you wrong at Bewelcome, and I helped. That-all at Hoffstedt's Hoard, though—that one's on you."

"I know it."

"But half of it's my fault, too. And *I* know it."

"Well. You do surprise me, Mister Pargeter."

"Nice to know it can be done."

And here, there occurred something utterly unexpected, something so strange in even this hundred-Hells world that Chess could only blink dumbly at it. Love looked away, shook his head . . . and *smiled*. A worn look, its bitterness muted only by long weariness, yet honest in its mirth as in its rue—and that mirth self-mocking, too. Then the smile died, and Love's eyes went bleak, looking off into the distance.

"Indeed," he agreed. "I've been humbled here, in many ways. So any startlement brought my way by you is nowhere near the worst."

Not much caring to think on Love's purgatorial tribulations, Chess cleared his throat, looking 'round. "So—where exactly is 'here,' anyway, if I might wrangle you away from your penitences for a moment or two? And while we're at it . . . don't suppose you know a back way out?"

"Are you two pursued?"

Chess snorted. "Always, Sheriff."

Love gave a nod, once more as grim as ever. "Others here have called this place the Anchorhold, after those Papist hermits who brick 'emselves into walls, to better serve God undistracted. Which fits, since from what I've gleaned, it's for those who need to contemplate their sins—to think on what they've done, before going on. As for how one leaves, however—" A shrug. "Might it be you've come bearing repentance in your heart for *your* crimes, Pargeter? All of them?"

"Fairly certain that'd take longer than we have to spare, even if I felt like tryin'."

"At least you're honest, in your fashion."

Beside them, Oona hooted softly; Chess shot her a glare.

"I looked for a way out of the 'Hold at first, and never found one," Love admitted. "Yet new souls do arrive—and some who were here when *I* arrived have gone, though none saw them go—"

Chess cut him off with an impatient wave. "Yeah, yeah, suffer, be purified, get saved," he spat. "No offence, Sheriff, but that's for them's been killed true and final. I still got a body up there, and I aim to get it back. And given who-all's holding its reins right now, I was kinda hopin' you'd have something a bit more helpful to offer me."

"Who would it be you think I share your antipathy for, exactly?"

"Old friend to us both, I'll wager *he'd* say; a certain big black motherfucker, got a mirror for a foot. Ring any fuckin' bells, Sheriff?"

Love closed his eyes, breathing hard. "Do you have any idea, Pargeter," he asked, after many moments, "how long I've prayed God to quench the hatred in my breast? And now you storm through, and blow all my heart's ashes back to Hellfire in a second. For that alone, I'd have you gone—back home, to another suffering gallery, even Heaven itself, little as you merit it. But to tell me that creature, that—"

"Enemy," supplied Chess.

"—that the Enemy still walks the world, using *your* flesh for his vessel? Where my Sophy and Gabriel dwell, and me powerless to help them . . . how can I forgive, or be forgiven, knowing *that*?"

"It's a conundrum, for certain."

Love shook his head. "You terrible little man," he said, without rancour. "Is there any one place you've ever appeared, where trouble hasn't followed?"

Now it was Chess's turn to look down, own head shaking in response. Because, Goddamnit—he didn't know.

The Anchorhold's air had been so quiet thus far, but for their voices, that the sound which next intruded—a splintering crack, as of ram-smashed stone—made them all start, even Love. Oona yelped in fright, reeling away; Chess spun, just in time to see the wall at his back bulge out, white-edged fractures webbed all across the dark granite. Before he could react, the rest collapsed, pouring down 'cross the floor like sand from a cracked hourglass. Cold white light spilled in, glittering with windblown snow so white it burned blackly, reflected off of Love's narrowed eyes.

Once again, Chilicothe was the first man to step through—lurching stiff-legged, punctured hamstring braced with the stock of his own useless rifle, strapped to fashion a crude splint. For all that the morbid lack of expression on his face did not change, Chess yet felt the lifeless gaze transfix him, a lamprey-like force locking on.

What is it you think you're fixing to do to me, you dead-ass motherfucker? Don't even recall your first name, if I ever knew it.

He drew in a slow illusion of breath, wondering in turn what tricks he had left to work which might throw the dead man back—'til, without warning, a long, tall back transposed between. Chess jolted awake once more, catching Oona by the arm; Love looked back over his shoulder, head jerking sideways to indicate a potential path of escape, even as he brought fists up pugilist-style.

"Go," the Sheriff ordered. "If this is truly not your time, Pargeter, then there may be an exit for you, and the lady—find it, while you can. These, on the other hand . . . being damned like myself, they hold no terrors for me. I doubt I can hold them for long, though, without aid."

"But—"

Love squinted down at him, fiercely. "No buts. Do you swear you'll oppose him, up top, with whatever might you can lay hand to? The Enemy?"

"He's mine as well as yours, and everybody's, so . . ."

"Don't equivocate, fornicator. Swear."

Oona was tugging at his arm once more, while Chilicothe grinned both their ways over Love's dusty shoulder. Around them, the retreating rows of devotees sat frozen as ever in their cabinets, seemingly unaware of what further hell might be about to rain down. Then again, Chess guessed, they were probably used to blocking such distractions out; so engrossed were they in chasing after their penance, they were determined to let nothing intrude. Love had been one of their number, but he'd broken his vows—put out a hand to help Chess, help Oona. Now he was back to square one, on their account.

"I swear," Chess told him, voice gone dry, as understanding of what Love had given up on his and Oona's behalf made *something* at his vision's limits pulse and throb. Feeling it deep-set, whatever *it* might be and no matter how little he wanted to; unable to ignore it, as he once would have, without thinking twice.

Because I've changed too, I s'pose. Little as I ever wanted to.

"Then *go*; take your dam. I will block their way, so long as God allows me."

Love spread his arms, and when he spoke again, his growl held a thunder beyond anything Ash Rook had ever produced. "How is the faithful city become an harlot! it was full of judgement; righteousness lodged in it; but now murderers!" More stone fell from the edges of the breach. Chilicothe leaned into the words as into a harsh wind; behind him, the rest of the Dead Posse screamed, imprecations dissolving into one frustrated wail, over which the blast of Love's voice lifted like a cyclone. "Therefore saieth the Lord, the Lord of hosts, the mighty One of Israel, 'Ah, I will ease me of mine adversaries, and avenge me of mine enemies'!"

Oona grabbed Chess's shoulder and shrieked something at him which he couldn't hear; didn't take much thought to guess the meaning, though. He nodded, scrambling back as Love threw the weight of his voice against the Posse, holding them out.

"*Are you not ashamed of these oaks ye have desired?*" Love bellowed at them, over the tumult. "*Are you not confounded by this, your chosen garden? Vengeance is God's alone, lost souls!*"

But despite initial balking, those set against him had rallied already, their din only growing louder, as they listened. So, turning tail—and God Almighty, was he ever getting sick of *that* particular manoeuvre—Chess broke into a lope, chasing after Oona while she scarpered up the passageway, away from the breach.

The 'Hold's corridor turned, crossed over another (equally endless, from what Chess could glimpse), then another, and so on. Every wall stood studded with alcoves, figures hung blind and motionless, faces abstract as masks, like those paintings on *arroyo* cave walls he'd rode under; the smooth-polished stone itself gave back their pursuers' racket, shaking each coffin-cabinet visibly, without ever once rousing those pinned inside.

As they chose turn after turn at random, none leading anywhere useful, Oona cursed. "Place is a *maze*, worse'n bloody Whitechapel! Christ, to get all this way and stopped *here*—"

"Some damn navigator you are! What happened, you lose track of that thread you been clingin' to all this time?"

"We're *in* it!" Oona screamed back, waving at the walls. "Woven into this 'ole place, it is—warp and woof! Can't even see a direction to it, now—like this 'ere ain't even part of the rest of things, like—"

She stopped; but the same thought had occurred to Chess, wildfire sparking from mind to mind: *Like maybe we're already outside.* Chess turned to the wall and, without even taking a second to think or doubt, punched it as hard as he could. It shattered under his fist, no more substantial than hollow plaster, powdering away— yet nothing emerged; no crack, nothing beyond. His hand sunk deeper on the next few punches, to wrist, to elbow, 'til he reared back, and started kicking.

Ankle. Calf. Fucking . . . *knee*, Goddamnit. Like sinking into custard, or quicksand.

Not enough.

"Gettin' closer—we want t'leg it, so's we don't end up trapped!" Oona yelled, from behind. "Come on, you bloody tosser! 'Ow many times you need t'go at it, 'fore you figure out you're done?"

"Speak for yourself, woman! I done enough running for today— don't aim to do more, if I can help it."

"Fine words. 'Cept you *can't*, can ya?"

Chess pivoted, locking eyes with her—green to green, equally sharp. "Well, if you want it to go faster, maybe you should put your *own* shoulder to the wheel, 'stead'a just standin' there yapping!"

Scoffing: "Oh, cert. As though *that'd* do anyfing—"

"Just *help* me, Ma, for the love of Christ Almighty! Thought you said you was a *hex*!"

He'd shouted it without forethought, almost in her face. And while the shame of showing such weakness swept him in a stove-blast, it still gave him a pleasurable little twist to see her wince, almost taken aback . . . hell, was that shame of a sort he saw echoing through *her* as well, disguised though it might be?

Whoever would've thought such a thing likely to happen, in Hell, or out of it?

I've asked you for so little, he thought, knowing it for simple truth. *Less and less, as time went on; nothin', after a point, if I could help it. And you—fact is, you* owe *me this. At the very least.*

"English" Oona shook her head, as if trying to block the knowledge out; raked her hair back with both hands, eyes shut, letting Chess's coat gap immodestly. Then hissed yet again, and shouldered her way in under his arm, knitting one hand in his: so small, yet so damn *strong*, too. Five fingers knit with five, to make a fist of ten.

"Let's do it, then," she said.

Two turns back, or maybe only one, the Dead Posse swept on, bellowing its hatred. But Chess Pargeter and his mother's ghost struck hard together, up to the shoulder, backs wrenching—threw their free hands up at the same time, clawed spade-like, to tear great chunks of apparently solid granite away like old sugar, collapsing a support column they hadn't known was there. The aftershock rippled from floor to ceiling; dusty plumes kicked up, making Chess's eyes water. And through that haze, that widening crevice, he became almost positive that—the more he blinked—he could almost glimpse a dim array of stars shining down.

"Keep goin'," he told her; Oona panted, and did. Once more. Twice. Dust like a storm. Feeling his own marrow shiver, arm all one ache, and knowing it must be twice as bad for her. The thought made him feel bad and good at once, like so much else.

A hoarse, hacking cough: "Don't see—"

"*I* can. Keep on."

"Bloody *am*, but *where*? I don't—"

"*Damnit*, Ma, stop arguing with me, and *keep ON!*"

So close, Jesus, behind *and* in front; he could almost feel that bastard Chilicothe's breath on his nape—cold-stinking, where once it'd been hot. And with that, the last of Chess's patience (never in great supply) snapped like a shot horse's legs. One step back, and he simply flung them both headlong at the wall, crashing their combined full body weights through it like some luckless pair of drunks through a saloon window. He felt her skull smack against something as they went—one of the displaced blocks, maybe.

Passing through one more membrane, they fell soft on cold earth, dry and thick with sere, sharp grass, then rolled twice and came up gasping—Oona with her hair all in disarray, a bruise big as his palm coming up on her forehead. With a wordless scream, she slapped him 'cross the face, hard enough to rattle his teeth; he shrugged the pain off, then glanced past her back the way they'd come, and laughed out loud.

"You son of a bitch!" she raved at him, all uncaring how she was mainly insulting herself. "Piss-poor spawn of a clap-rid Lime'ouse gin-doll!"

"So you've told me, yeah. Want to see something?"

"I'll give you 'somefing,' you bloody ball-less pillow-biter—"

"*Oona*, Christ. Turn 'round, 'fore you give yourself a conniption."

He could see her fairly strain not to, just to spite him. But temptation was far too strong—and when at last her head swung the way he'd indicated, he found himself at just the right angle to admire the way her jaw dropped.

Nothing there, no matter which way you looked: No wall, no rubble, no crack. Only empty air. Like none of it had ever even been.

The breach must've closed almost fast as they'd flown through it,. And maybe it was that realization which sent Oona wobbling back, forcing Chess to catch her—no great task, for she'd always been a tiny thing. He held her up a moment 'til her breathing slowed, faces pressed so uncomfortably close he could see her too-wide pupils start to contract once more, before carefully letting her back down again.

"Sorry for that," he found he'd somehow already let slip, before he could think better.

"Don't do it again," was all she said in return, eventually. "Not wivout you bloody well warn me, first."

"All right."

He stood still a moment, trying to decide as he did if he found this odd protective urge toward her welling up inside him gratifying, or infuriating. Might be she felt the same, though; she sure was quick enough to pull away, twitching his coat yet closer.

"Cold," she muttered, shuffling her bare feet.

"It is that," Chess agreed—and shivered, barely resisting the urge to hug himself. Wondering, as he did: *Where to now?*

The ice plain War-Heaven they'd passed through had been more frigid, but there, they'd been driven by fear and amazement, like cattle before dogs. Here, however—in the empty silence of this dry flatland, everything dusk-coloured for ash, or stone, or coal— their travels' exhaustion was suddenly that much harder to stave off, dull wind-chill leaching heat straight through the illusion of clothing. And for all the stars overhead were those Chess knew, their unnatural brightness and colourless light betrayed the truth. This was *not* the real world, still.

Jesus. How much further, exactly?

All directions looked alike, from where they stood. The grass was silver-grey, motionless even under a steady breeze, the soil it grew from black; Chess raised one hand to shade his eyes and scowled at his flesh's flinty hue, far too much like a (truly) dead man's for comfort.

"So now what?" he asked Oona, who shook her head.

"Still can't see the trail—can't see nothin' else, neither, for that matter. You?"

Shrugging, he squinted hard into that bleak wind, felt it draw phantom tears. 'Til, vision clearing, he finally caught sight of a slight variance in the general scheme of grey on black. Saw how, though the light in the distance had much the same washed-out pallor as everything else, its wavering movement identified it as—a *campfire*, by Christ, flames shimmering pearlescent and oily black by turns, coldly insubstantial. A second later, Chess could just make out the black silhouette of a man sitting just before it, and tensed as that same man—square-set, face hidden by darkness and distance alike, yet with something distinctly familiar to his whole bearing—twisted in his seat to look back at them.

Who . . . ?

He knew far too many of this underworld's denizens, it occurred to him, and not for the first time. Probably shouldn't've gotten so damn many people killed, while Up Top.

As if cued by that thought, the man raised one arm and swept it back and forth, impatiently, the gesture plainly beckoning—like he knew full well who Chess was, and wasn't too pleased by his tardiness.

Chess made a half-step forward, stumbling at first, then striding; Oona took off likewise, scrambling to keep up. "Where we goin'? 'Oo *is* that?"

"Friend, I think—close enough, anyhow. C'mon, woman."

"Sure? You ain't got all too many friends, from what I've observed. . . ."

"You should talk. C'mon!"

He grabbed for her hand, and she came—learning to trust him, for once, or could be she was just too damn tired to fight. And thus they pulled up fireside, where the man was already getting to his feet, turning his bearded face Chess's way, still seamed and burnt with weather that'd never touch him further. And grinning just a little bit, cheeks creasing further. "So *there* you are," he said. "Took long enough."

Kees Hosteen, as Chess didn't live or breathe.

THERE WAS NOTHING TO EAT, naturally—not even a pretence of coffee boiling on that smokeless fire, which barely gave off light, let alone heat. Yet Chess felt a sentimental rush of homeliness nonetheless, just to be once more sharing a hearth with the old Hollander, the only former Confederate fellow soldier he'd been proud to travel with, saving Ash Rook himself. Not to mention a man he'd twitted and teased unmercifully, extorting weaponage and such from in return for small intimacies—but someone he'd always been able to depend on, who'd always had his best interests at heart, even when Chess himself couldn't've named them if asked.

"I got you killed," Chess found himself telling him, again without really meaning to—and hell, what *was* this? Like his mouth had slipped its bridle, leaving no brake at all between thought and speech. But thankfully, Hosteen didn't seem to hold a grudge.

"Oh, as to that . . ." He shrugged. "Would've happened sometime anyhow, no matter what—wasn't none of us gonna see old age, not the way we carried on. Then again, you always did say you didn't expect to die any way but with a bullet . . . and look how *that* turned out."

Silence in his chest, as always—but keener this time, a side-slipped knife, twisted. Chess pressed one hand to his breastbone, as though to keep whatever might be left under there firmly in, and nodded. "What're you doing here, Kees?"

"Well, I *am* dead, but—chasin' after you, mostly. Like usual."

Chess snorted. "The hell for? Places I've been down here, you should be grateful you didn't catch me up 'til now." He glanced at Oona, then amended, before she could tell him to: "*Us* up."

"Yeah, I was wondering 'bout that. Care to introduce me?"

He gestured between Oona and their rescuer. "Oona, this is an old war buddy of mine, Kees Hosteen. Kees . . . this is 'English' Oona Pargeter. My mother."

Hosteen's jaw dropped; he looked Oona up and down. "Ho-lee shit," he blurted, then flushed. "Uh—sorry, ma'am, but—you're not—um, you don't look like, uh . . ."

"Like I'm dying of poppy-smoke underneath some Chink brothel?" finished Oona, acidly. "Not any more, I ain't."

"Well, I wasn't gonna—"

"Why not?" said Chess. "Go 'head, she's heard worse."

"You shut yer gob."

"Make me."

Hosteen looked back and forth between them, grey brows hiking. "Oh yeah," he said, at last. "I definitely see it now."

That seemed to defuse things, at least; Oona huffed, shrugged his coat closer and folded herself down into a cross-legged squat, while Chess gave a snort, and followed her.

"It was the Rev started it," Hosteen told him. "Had him a lock of my hair in a bottle, or some-such; called me up, sent me off t'spy on the Pinks. Leastways, he said that's all he wanted—asked me to look for you, too; tried to make out like it was just an afterthought, but . . ." He shook his head. "I did find you, once. Watched you for a bit." He paused. "Never could tell if you knew or not."

Chess grimaced, not sure what irked him more: the thought of Ash pretending not to care, or the thought of him *truly* not caring. "No. I . . . suspected it, but I never knew." A sharp, sidelong look: "How'd you get away, then?"

"You think I'm still on his leash?" Hosteen glowered at him.

"I think nothin' down here's what it seems, Kees, and I'm through with bein' the idjit never asks questions 'til it's too late."

Hosteen slumped, staring into the pale fire. "Hell, I can understand that. Truth is, he kept his word after all; broke the bottle and freed me, once I'd told him all I saw. Which I guess was how I ended up here."

"No Heaven for you either, huh?"

"Not yet."

"Don't tell me it was Rook sent you *this* time, too," Chess said.

"Naw, that'd be that *other* female of your acquaintance: Miss Experiance herself. Got hold of me like she did with your Ma, or so's I heard tell, though I don't think she ever spoke to her quite *so* direct."

Oona huffed again. "*Fought* there was somebody puttin' ideas in my 'ead! But seein' 'ow she never knew me, 'cept by whatever she gleaned from *you*—" a nod Chess's way "—then maybe that's what explains 'ow she went about it."

"Makes sense," Chess allowed.

"I'll take your word," Hosteen said. "Still and all, can't say it wasn't off-putting—she's hellish strong, that girl is, considerin' she ain't even a hex."

"I know it. So . . . why'd she send you, anyhow?"

A raised eyebrow: "You sayin' you *don't* need help?"

Again, it struck Chess that not so long previous, even if he'd known himself in such deep and desperate straits that only an offered hand would save him, he'd've thrown such a demand right back in the questioner's face, hard enough to break noses. So it was curious—continued to *be* curious—how he found himself more grateful than resentful that anyone gave enough of a damn to want to extricate him from this hole he'd dug for himself, let alone *two* people . . . both of whom he'd wronged, in their own ways, and one of whom wasn't even here, to boot.

"Don't think anybody's saying that," he told Hosteen, quietly. And saw the older man's shade smile, slight yet genuine. Felt it lift his missing heart's hollow like it'd been hooked.

"Okay, then. You two better come with me."

SEVEN DIALS: SIX

Worlds, like gods and babies, are born in blood; for this reason alone is the first dawn's light so blinding, the first drawn breath's cry such joy to hear—not that we may forget the agonies of their making, but that those agonies may be accepted, made worthwhile. Though life be bought with death, joy with sorrow and creation with destruction, yet they are life, joy, creation; if the price must always be paid, it is never paid for nothing. In the moment of birth, when Time awakes, all things are possible.

It is in the silence after dawn, as the light's sharpest edge slowly softens to day, that the weight of an altogether different price is felt: a price which terrifies not for what it demands, but for what it does not. For time, once awoken, cannot be stopped. And even newborn gods may know confusion and fear, look upon their fresh-forged world and think, as moments trickle irretrievably away: What now? What next?

And this, ofttimes, is fate's greatest cruelty: that for all creatures born of blood-watered earth, brought forth in that light, the infinite freedom between birth and death only reveals the most horrifying price of all.

Choice . . . and its consequences.

THEY WALKED CAREFULLY, picking their way 'cross a gathering litter of beach-smooth stones, while the oil fire fell behind. Oona turned her ankle once, and swore; Chess slipped an arm 'round her waist and braced her, playing human crutch, 'til she could limp on her own. And though neither of them thought to acknowledge—let alone thank—the other, it made for a moment of truce, warming in this cold wind.

"Missus Kloves said for me to tell you she can't see you plain, which is why she had to send me down," Hosteen told Chess. "Might be 'cause you ain't really dead as such, might not—but one way or t'other, she's been waiting on you a sight longer than I have, and things are gettin' hot. So she wants to point you out an exit, before you and your Ma here ramble all over the rest of Creation's underbelly."

"That'd've been bloody welcome, a few turns of the road back," Oona pointed out.

"And it's just as welcome now, Kees," Chess hastened to add, "thank you kindly. So—where next?"

Hosteen paused a moment, regarding Chess narrowly. "Don't think I've ever heard you say 'thanks' for nothin' before," he said.

Yeah, well, stick around. Might be I'll start apologizing again, and we'll both fall over.

"Two of you like some time alone, then?" Oona asked, waspish.

"Ma!"

"No, ma'am, I don't think so. But then again, I don't think you get to make those sorts of calls on his behalf—not anymore."

"Ah. So 'e's told you about our old . . . arrangement."

"Unfortunately, yes."

Chess cast her a side-eye, wondering if she at least had the grace to look shamed, but his angle was off—and as she stood there, face hidden behind her hair, he decided he didn't much care. Better to remember the way she'd acted over this journey, rather than dwell on old times.

My Ma, all right. Half of me, with the other quarter-or-so this Malcolm Devesstrin, whoever the hell he was; no better, and probably much worse. And the rest . . .

The rest was him: hex, pistoleer, sodomite. A flesh-bound god cast down, wrung out of god and flesh alike but alive, still, even here in death's grip. Alive, and free.

Nothin' she can do to me, now. Nothin' she ever could.

"Go on, Kees," Chess said, feeling an odd surge of affection toward them both. "Don't mind her."

The old Hollander sighed. "Missus Kloves says you're t'go far as you can, climb up 'til you can't see the top of things, and then she'll find you."

"We've already been climbing a while."

A shrug. "Well, I can only suppose there's more to go. But as to how much, damn if I know."

"That's . . . quite the riddle."

"All you got, though, ain't it? So I guess it'll have to do."

Once more, they walked on in silence, covering what seemed an interminable distance, 'til at last the way began to slope upward, first shallowly, then steeper. Dark peaks rose slowly, scoring the skyline ahead like teeth. The rocks grew craggier, crowding 'til they had no room to slip beneath either Chess's boot-soles or Oona's bleeding feet. Stepping wrong, she went down on one knee with a strangled groan, only to rise up again with Chess pulling on one wrist, Hosteen the other.

"Might be one of us should carry you," Hosteen said, to which she shook her head and spat, not ungratefully.

"I'm in me prime, son," she scoffed. "Back at the very 'eight of strength and 'ealth. Day I can't stomach a trawl like this, you can lay me out an' frow dirt in my face."

"You promise?" Chess muttered.

For his jibe, Oona punched him in the biceps, knuckles twisting painful—after which they laughed, long and loud, while Hosteen stood there amazed.

"Jesus," he said, at last. "You *two*."

Aw, you love it, Chess was about to say—*a mean little man and the bitch who made him; what's better entertainment than that?* Except it was that exact moment when the Dead Posse's tumult rose up again, ululating hoarse and rage-filled from one compass-edge to another, causing Hosteen himself to flatten 'gainst the rising cliff face like it was a battlefield trench wall. "Shit's *that*?" he hissed, feeling for his own no-longer-holstered gun.

Chess warned him silent with a headshake and a finger-corked *shush*, and was happy to see himself obeyed. He stared 'round, scanning what was left of the horizon, while Oona wrung his hand. "You see 'em?" she asked.

"Not yet . . . but they're comin'. I feel it."

"Me too, God piss on it," she said, softly.

Those furious phantom hoofbeats rising up through the "earth," rumbling like the Enemy's Fifth World gone to quake and ruin. Following the sound's echoes, Chess managed to sight in on what he thought might be their hunters, a blurred, shadow-black, vast roil of movement only barely perceptible by the shear and swirl of the dimly gleaming grass around it. And—something else as well, dragged twisting in their wake, a piece of snared prey scraped along the unforgiving terrain, twisting in its harness like a steer. Chess didn't need a clear view to know who *that* probably was.

"Think they got the Sheriff with 'em," he told Oona.

"What the 'ell *for*?"

"'Cause they ain't got us, and that's his fault, in their eyes. Now shut up, and let me—"

"Gettin' mighty tired of being told that, *boy*," Oona growled. "You were the one said t'*me*, 'You a 'ex, or ain'tcha?' Never occurred to you I could back you up? Or is that only for when you got no other choice?"

Chess drew breath to shout, only to be interrupted yet again, this time by Hosteen. "Chess, if she's anything like as strong as you were, or even the Rev—"

"She ain't," Chess snarled back. "But then again, down here, neither am I. Nothing Goddamn *takes* in this place." He kicked a rock in frustration, peevish. "Like goin' fist to fist with Love all over again—everything I threw at him, he just soaked up. How the hell do you beat something you can't hurt, Kees?"

"You never did like to deke around a fight, I recall. But we did it, sometimes, when the Lieut told us to—built blinds to hide in, took the bluebellies unawares. Ain't there no way to do something like that?"

"Shit, I dunno. The one time I did try a glamour, the whole thing backfired on Ed'n me."

"That's why you need me, then," Oona said. "'Cause if there's one thing I ever 'ad any knack for, it was glamour." As if to demonstrate the concept, she sidled up, toying with Chess's top shirt button, fair cooing in one ear: "'Less the 'igh and mighty Private Pargeter's too proud to take aid from 'is *mother*, that is. . . ."

So wrong, on every level. But Chess was used to her tricks, even if Hosteen wasn't. He caught her wrist and smiled back at her, their lips furling just alike, grim and charmless.

"Hell, I'll take it, all right," he replied. "But it ain't gonna be no one-way thoroughfare. I ask and you give, on damn command. Fair enough, Ma?"

"Fair enough."

If Ash Rook had been there, he'd've had a whole page of Holy Writ to trot out, quoting high and low 'til the dim air sparkled with hanging print, and reality itself warped to fit his words' likeness. For Chess, however—and Oona too, assuming she'd kept hold of her hexation long enough to develop such technique—the mechanics were far rougher, silent and deep, wrenched up from within like the bloody flux.

Acting on impulse, they found an accord so quickly it seemed choreographed: knit right hand to left, then threw opposite arms 'round Hosteen before the old Hollander could even think to extricate himself, and knit those ten clawed fingers like-a-wise. Over Hosteen's shoulder, Chess could already see dust kicking up in front of the Dead Posse like an evil cloud, rushing toward them with all the fell force of its transit. So he shut his eyes tight 'gainst the grit and laid his cheek to Oona's, beard-rough to reborn-smooth, folding tight together to poor Kees—while, at the very same time, the oldest tune he knew came pouring out through his mouth all unsummoned, a flood of bile and honey borne on somebody else's breath.

As they walked down to the water's brim,
Bow we down—

As they walked down to the water's brim,
Bow and balance to me;
As they walked down to the water's brim,
    the oldest pushed the youngest in.
For I'll be true to my love,
If my love will be true to me.

And here he heard Oona's voice in his ear again, murmuring, without her even opening her mouth. Saying: *My own Ma used to sing it different, though—in more of a country way, p'raps, 'stead'a the tune I always 'eard from those in the Clock-'ouse. Or maybe 'cause she died well content wiv what she 'ad, little as that might've been; us kids, 'er man, my useless Pa wiv 'is tricks, drinkin' all she worked for away at the week's end, and never fankin' 'er for the use of it, neither.*

Always wantin' t'make a silk purse from a sow's ear, was my Ma. Just like that 'arper in the song . . .

Her father's knight came riding by
And this maid's body chanced to spy.
Oh he took three locks of her yellow hair
And with them strung a bow so fair.
And what did he do with her breast-bone?
He made it a fiddle to play upon.
And what did he do with her veins so blue?
He made fiddle strings to play a tune.
And what did he do with her fingers slight?
He made little pegs to hold them tight.
And the only tune that the fiddle would play
Was oh, oh, the wind and rain—
And the only tune that the fiddle would play
Was oh, the dreadful wind and rain.

Make a corpse into music, a mermaid, a swan. Make your 'eart's desire into your own death. Make your sister's love into your husband. Make her grave your marriage bed.

Make—

—two men and an old/young woman into one more shadow on a heap of shadows, a blank spot blending into the outcropping, livid grey on grey. Nothing that would stand out far enough to be seen, even as the Dead Posse howled by and Hosteen trembled between them.

The Posse's train tore up and down, back and forth, with Love staggering headlong after at the point of a rope. Sometimes he tripped, fell and was pulled, scraping himself on the stony soil, only to rise up once more covered with fresh wounds, his mouth set; though they offered no quarter, he asked none. Sometimes Chess thought he saw his bitter lips move, as if he might be praying.

And that procession went on a while, far longer than Chess had thought it would—Chilicothe and the rest, the Lieut, the bluebellies; Sadie and her beau riding two to a mount, him firm-set, her hugging him side-saddle. Yet more followed after, like every man or woman killed within Chess's eyeshot these last three years was making up the bulk, called to follow after by the promise of whatever impermanent vengeance ghosts might wreak on ghosts.

Oona pressed closer still, so she could say—voice dropping to a cautious whisper, as she did—"Damn, son. You really 'ave killed a lot of men, just like you said. But *not* more'n I've fucked, as it 'appens."

Sliding back to their final living conversation, in the "hospital" under Selina Ah Toy's, as though all the intervening incidence counted for nothing.

Chess snorted, and shook his head. "Boast on, why don't you," he replied.

'Round and 'round, in and about and out once more, cutting patterns in the desolate waste with their hooves, 'til eventually the Posse drew to a shuddering stop, apparently stymied. The Lieut leaned to cut Love free and kick him sidelong in almost the same motion, while the rest looped back, turning their rides for the 'Hold, the crossroads, War-Heaven, Gehenna . . . anywhere but here.

You can walk back, preacher, Chess thought he heard the dead man say, into his high-muffled shell-coat's collar. *I'll count it as toll for slowing us down, since we might've caught him yet, were it not for your interference.*

Love stood up slow and dignified, re-ordering his bloody rags while the Posse gave one shared, heaving sigh and dispersed with a moan of hungry hate unfulfilled, leaving nothing behind but ache.

Turning his back on their trail—even the part of it he'd contributed to, just as it began to fade—Love said: "You may safely reveal yourselves now, I believe—Pargeter, ma'am. Since I can tell you're here."

"Funny, that," Chess replied, letting slip his mother's grip, so's to make himself take shape once more. "How *you* can but they couldn't, is what I mean."

"No great trick to it. It's like you said, before—"

"God told you?"

"Indirectly, yes, through simple intuition—God-given, like all other things. Yet I live . . . subsist, rather . . . in hope."

So easy to mock Love's ridiculous gimcrack faith, his sideshow humbleness. Once again, however, an unwanted sympathy scoured Chess's insides, making him feel small, raw. Almost as skin-bare as Love looked, at least for now.

"Well . . ." he said, at last, "fun as it's been, we'd better be movin' on. Good luck with your penitence, Sheriff."

He went to turn, only to see Love raise a hand, less in command than entreaty. "Wait but one moment more. I—there's something I'd say, if you'll hear it."

Chess scowled. "Like what?"

Love hesitated, studying the dirt below as though he hoped it'd give him clues, advice on how best to phrase what he so didn't want to say. "You've done wrong all your days, I know you won't deny it; that you take a certain perverse pride in the truth of it, even. But Mister Pargeter—Chess—your due fall's already done with, deservedly harsh, and sudden. Which means now you've been weighed, you have another chance, as I do." His nod took in Oona, even Hosteen, whom he seemed to recognize, perhaps from the first face-off at Bewelcome. "Remember what I told your Reverend, once? How grace is resistible, yet available for all? What I'm saying is, Chess—forgiveness isn't an impossibility, even for such as you. And much as you like a fight, perhaps it's time you ceased resisting."

Chess drew a long breath, oddly ragged; felt his own eyes slide to Oona, who stood there hugging herself again. "Does like to 'ear 'imself talk, don't 'e?" she asked, of no one in particular.

Chess shrugged. "They all do, the preachers. Or so's I've noticed."

"You may mock," Love told them. "But believe me when I say that God withholds nothing from the truly contrite, no matter who they may be."

"Even if what they 'be' goes against Bible itself, at least according to one particular part? 'Cause forgiven or not, I ain't never gonna lay down with a woman like I do with a man, Sheriff—be unnatural to my person, like it'd be unnatural to *you* to do the opposite, what with that gal of yours waiting for you."

"Sophy, you mean."

"Yeah, her. Granted, I used to think I hated all females, and that turned out t'be tripe—but I ain't about to change my habits now, even so. Not after all this."

"You already have, though, where it matters. I was *there*, at Bewelcome—saw first-hand how you saved me, my boy, my wife and all the rest, at the cost of your own skin. That you *are* capable of great good, no matter your inclinations . . . or how fervently you may claim the opposite, either."

"Oh, that was just for pique, to fox Rook's plans—to stick my dick in that infernal Machine of his wife's, and see what-all popped off."

"Yet you ended up doing the Lord's work nonetheless, if unintentionally; that counts for something."

"Does it?"

"Why would it not?" A pause, as Chess felt the exhaustion of the last few . . . days, hours, who the hell knew . . . wash up over him in a single flood, high enough to choke on. But the Sheriff went on, unabashed. "Though once I might have believed differently, I no longer consider your proclivities, your upbringing, the source of your *truly* sinful behaviour, since I know all too well that I too was guilty of real sin, before *and* after death—the sins of pride, of wrath, of despair. At the War's end, when I vowed to hammer my sword into ploughshares, but did not; when I judged myself fit to pass judgement on Reverend Rook and you, along with all your fellows; when I blamed you for your part in Bewelcome's fall, but took no responsibility for my own. Yet this is the charge God laid upon us all when first he gifted us free will, bittersweet fruit of that fateful Eden-tree, and I take it up happily now, in my time of need—bite down and swallow gladly, to its veriest dregs, regardless of the taste."

Jesus, Chess thought, *this really is some sermon. Too bad I ain't got a watch to set.*

The Sheriff went on, fervently unaware of his audience's growing restlessness. "I eat of the tree, and true knowledge at last is mine—I feel His grace falling down on us, like sunlight: even here, even me, even *you*. These others too, if they're amenable. All we ever have to do is accept it."

Oona was outright staring at him now, red brows knit; Chess wasn't sure if she was stuck between a gawp and snort, too dazed by Love's oddity to quite let loose with either. One way or the other, he didn't care to argue the point.

"Listen," he said, finally, "I do see that woman of yours, what d'you want me to tell her?"

"Tell her I've seen her already, in dreams. That I look to see her hereafter, once I've done my time."

"No reason to stay on in Hell if you don't need to, Sheriff."

Love shook his head, smiling. He was almost healed now—back to the way he'd been when they first found him. "Oh, but I do," he said, gently enough. "And besides—all places alike are Hell, without my Lord. Or Sophy."

He turned on his heel, then, and left them, retreating into the distance 'til he was only a line bisecting the horizon, a mere speck. Then gone, as though he'd never been at all.

Chess, Oona and Hosteen walked on, in the opposite direction.

THE CRAGS BECAME STEEPER, a mountain range, then one particular mountain, vertiginously high. Eventually, it all ran out—there was nowhere left to climb. Only a sawbacked ridge, flint-sharp, curving 'round a small dip of frost-cracked stone and pebbles just big enough for all three to stand in. Beyond, merely black sky, with one sharp spike of grey rock thrusting rudely starward.

"Now what?" Oona demanded.

Chess was Christ Almighty tired of shaking his head. "Wait?" He took a deep breath, trying to think. "Hey, Kees—considering how high up we are, why is it we ain't havin' any trouble breathin'?"

"We're dead," Oona reminded him. "Breathing's nought but a mind-trick any'ow, so what's 'at prove?"

"Proves what we should've kept *in* mind, all along—" Chess grabbed two spars of rock and hauled himself up, balancing precariously. "It's *all* tricks. Don't take nothin' for what it looks like." He licked one finger and held it up. "I got a breeze here, from the east—Kees, check the other side, see if it keeps goin'."

Hosteen's upward scramble took longer, but at length he balanced opposite Chess, testing the wind the same way. "I got it comin' in from the west." Looking to Oona: "Ma'am—if you don't mind?"

"Oh, for fuck's sake," Oona muttered—then wet her finger and simply stuck it straight up, reaching high as she could. "All right, I feel it. Comin' from . . ." She trailed off as she turned, tracing its path from south to north, 'til she ended up pointing straight *at* the spike itself.

"Not comin' from," said Chess, voice tight with excitement. "Goin' *to*." Swinging from spar to spar along the ridge 'til his boots were braced on the ridge, he wound up holding onto the spike with one hand. His other slid to where jagged point ran out—and beyond, curving 'round a column of pure blackness, hitherto invisible against the sky, that gave back the tactile sensation of rock.

And something more, now that he concentrated—a faint thrum, like he'd grabbed hold of a telegraph cable in mid-send; a feeling of *pulling*, as though the column had hold of him, too. His throat went dry, voice hoarse. "Think I found our next thread, Ma—the thread of all threads."

"Christ on churches." Oona tipped her head back, looking higher and higher, clearly seeing nothing. "We 'ave t'*climb* that?"

"We're hexes, woman; sure we can figure out some other means of locomotivating, we have to." Grinning, Chess looked to Hosteen. "You comin' too?"

Hosteen swallowed. "You know where that's goin'?"

"Not a clue. But I'm willin' to bet you don't want to stay here, any more'n we do."

"Ain't a question of 'want', so far as I can see. One way or t'other, though . . ." Carefully, Hosteen clambered down, dusting himself off. "I'm pretty sure this is far as I go." At Chess's double-take, he shrugged, almost sadly. "Got some time left yet t'do, Chess, and I know it. Like the Sheriff said."

"Aw, shit—" Covering up something he didn't want to think on too closely with anger, as ever, Chess jumped down. "Don't act like you believe some God-botherer's gasbagging *now*! I've *seen* the shit waits back down there. You ain't a bad enough man to deserve that."

"Wasn't that good a man, either." Hosteen glanced back to the head of the trail they'd just climbed. "I got blood and suffering on my hands too, you know. We all did. Any of us try to stop the Rev 'n' you, at Bewelcome? Did we say, 'No more!' afterward, or walk away?" He shook his own head, slowly. "In the end, we all gotta answer for what we done, no matter how much we might've thought we *had* t'do it, or didn't want to—'specially if we went on ahead and did it, anyways."

Chess wanted to punch something—Hosteen, the wall between worlds, he didn't know, as he somehow knew the older man could tell. But Hosteen regarded him still, unflinching.

"I shouldn't have . . . treated you the way I did," Chess said, at last. "You know. Triflin' with your affections, and suchlike."

Hosteen laughed. "Hell, I never minded too much! You were . . . precious to me, Chess Pargeter. More'n you know."

"If that's the best you had, Kees, then I'm sorry."

Hosteen shrugged once more. "I ain't."

Gently, he took Chess by the right hand, shaping its fingers 'round Oona's startled wrist before hoving in for a kiss, brief yet firm, smack dab on Chess's surprise-slack lips. His breath still tasted of tobacco, though Chess could only assume he hadn't smoked any since before his death. Funny how things clung, down here.

"You go on, the two of you," was all Hosteen said, his gravelly voice rougher than usual—and pushed them lightly on, "forward" becoming up, the invisible column above flowering iris-bright into a wormy, vertical tunnel, close as any closet. A current took hold, breaking Hosteen's grip; Oona gasped, hugging on monkey-tight, as the two of them lifted off.

So fast: a mere heartbeat, half a pulse more, and he couldn't even see Hosteen walk away. Something fiddled beneath his ribs, sharp and new, a painful poke.

"Seems there's a point t'givin' it away, after all," Oona said, shakily, into Chess's throat.

"Seems like. Maybe you should'a tried it, every once in a while."

A sudden, vertiginous rush, stomachs roiling, and their feet touched down once more; tunnel became path, similarly narrow, canted so steeply upward they had to half-climb, half-crawl. Oona disengaged, then started to slip, almost immediately—Chess scrambled backward, feeling for her hand again, and grabbed on hard, it being well dark enough no one else could catch him doing it.

"Don't let go!" she squeaked, breathless.

"I don't aim to," he said. And set his feet to the path once more, the long and windy way toward . . . who damn well knew?

GOOD GOD, IT SEEMED to drag on forever. Places, the "ceiling" and "floor" alike drew so close together they could barely move, except at the most painfully slow of paces—they wriggled like worms, chasing echoes. At first, these were simply a figure of speech, but as the journey wore on, they became more concrete: whispers yet too high to interpret, flittering like bats. Women's voices, Chess had no doubt.

Yancey?

There was something lonesome in all-but-knowing himself the last man left standing in his own entire world, misbegotten as he'd always been made to feel. Looking back, young Missus Yancey Kloves was the sole female he'd ever had much in common with, after a point—that same point when cute tyke became scrawny, redheaded bastard, with a later side dish of thief, thug, rowster and (of course) You Goddamned Preening Queerboy.

Babies die, Mister Pargeter. She wanted you dead, you would be.

Gal, you didn't know her, for which you should give thanks. . . .

But Chess hadn't either—not really. Simply well enough to imagine her capable of better, having seen her dole out a rough parody of such to any damn jack had the fawney, all the while wondering why none of that act (however ripe its falsity) could ever come *his* way, apparently. Why he didn't rate the lie's effort, not even if he'd been able to pay for it.

Oh, she'd pet me some when she was drunk enough, but otherwise . . . like I wasn't even there.

In the darkness, with what illusion of air they shared running thin, Chess found it increasingly hard to distinguish the bright, sharp young hex-to-be Oona he'd come to know since Seven Dials—a fair companion with more points of similarity than difference, her hair-trigger temper matching his own, albeit backed up with fists and whatnot rather than guns—from her past or future self, the greasy-haired harridan whose bony fists and poison tongue had crushed his childhood flat. And that old rage welled up acid, a carrion meal's afterbirth, to scald his stomach lining, fill his lungs with spume he longed to vomit.

Her hand twisted in his, nails digging deep, and he had to force down an urge to kick her where it counted 'til she blacked out—to slam her face-first in the dust and grind, 'til her fine new skin was grit-torn and seeping. Leave *her* behind, lost and lorn without recourse in an awful, empty universe, and see how she liked *that*.

Her voice in one ear, hoarse to grating, at exactly the worst time. "You don't 'ear that?"

"*What?*"

"Same bitch as before, I'll lay odds, frowin' more lines down like fish'ooks. Be nice if she could manage a bloody light, though, wouldn't it? Some sort'a *trail*, so's we didn't 'ave to nose 'round in the dark like bloody meal-worms."

Again, Chess's anger sparked, a well-worn flint struck along its deep-grooved edge. "We ain't privy to all that's happening, up there—might be she has her reasons. Might be she's working just as hard as us, for even less reward."

Oona snorted. "I knew doss-'ouse cows could knock what was lost outta a petitioner's own pocket, you asked 'em, so long as silver was involved. 'Oo is this 'Yancey' of yours, any'ow? What's 'er claim t'fame, exactly?"

"Dead-speaker, Goddamnit. You never did listen."

"I'm the only one *can* listen, sonny boy, 'cause for all your made-a-god airs, you still ain't worth nothin' for nothin' don't involve suckin' cock or shootin' other fools full'a 'oles. Tits on a bull, that's what you are—what you'll always be, now an' forever more, world wivout end. 'Specially so if you can't rouse yourself to *bloody break us free of this damn place.*"

"*You shut your trap*, you whore from Hell! I got more hexation in the tip of my faggot dick than you ever would've had if you lived to be a hundred-friggin'-ten, *Columcille* or no—"

But here the skirling whine of that voice—voices?—came swooping back around 'em yet again, interrupting, so painful-molten pitched he could almost see the angles it carved into the darkness. And all at once, Chess knew what Oona's plan was, if you could dignify it thus; the last act of a desperate woman in equally desperate straits, determined at least one of them should emerge from this choke-hold where they'd fetched up, only to lodge like they were caught in Time's own craw.

"Hell, you're tryin' to goad me, ain't ya? Like always. Get me riled enough to dump you here, thinking that'll make me kick my own ass up through however long's left to go. But . . . what happens to you then, Oona? Where do *you* end up, after I'm gone?"

And why should I care? Except how, stupidly—fucking moronically, to be exact—

He did, still. Same way as he always had.

Aw, fuck me.

A breath, through ragged teeth. His mother's ghost slumped to rest her forehead 'gainst his shirt, where her cold mouth made a small, wet imprint, about the size of a broke half-dollar.

"It workin'?" she asked, eventually, without much hope.

"Not as such."

She lay still there a moment, dead weight, like she was gathering her strength. And when she spoke again, a note rung in her voice he never remembered being there before—almost . . . maternal, he had to put a name to it.

"You gotta give me up, Chess. To move on."

"I don't 'gotta' do any damn thing I don't want to—you of all people should know that, by now."

"Then make yourself *want* to, you great git. 'Cause it's 'ow it's gotta be."

Chess hissed. "Says who?"

"Your Missus Kloves, is 'oo. Been sayin' it these last hours, or 'owever long, for all I knew you couldn't make it out. And all *I* didn't want to."

"Aw, that's horseshit. We bulled our way past enough of this crap together before—just have to push harder, is all. Don't let it divide and conquer. Ain't come all this Goddamn way dragging your dead ass behind me just to give up *now*, Goddamnit—"

"It *ain't* givin' up. It ain't. You just . . . Jesus! Why you always gotta be so bloody difficult?"

"Look who's talkin'."

Wanted to turn, so they could at least play at being able to see each other, but the rock wouldn't let him; all these tonnes of earth, these stones and dead things, these endless years of debris and garbage, pressing down unflinching 'til he felt his not-skin bruise, his not-bones bend and start to crack.

It'll squash me flat, is what it'll do, like a wheel-popped roadside toad. Christ, will there ever be an end to this, to us? Or is where we've gotten ourselves to yet more of Hell again, over and over, writ meaner and smaller every time?

Seemed like Oona felt it too, for she could barely draw a full breath before managing, her words thin: "That girl in New York, Mina Whittaker's 'er name . . . 'eard 'e give 'er a son too, before she did for 'im. Mose Whittaker, the Widowmaker's get. 'E'd be your brother, I s'pose, by 'alf measures at least."

"Why'd you tell me that?"

"Fought you might want to know. For after." Another strangled gasp. "Why . . . bloody . . . not?"

Sure. So now's when you let it slip, right when it won't net you anything to hold it back.

The scar along his jawline crawled as though it was on fire, tracing the path of her *yen hock*; he could almost remember the look in her eyes when she'd done it, lashing out like a one-clawed cat, trapped into one more move to make him change or run or both, anything but stay and die in that sty she knew would be her tomb. The tears he'd thought drug-addled rheum shone on her cheeks, colour feverish-high already: the germ ripening in her every cough, long before blood began to flow.

Best I could do for you, so I done it—I ain't proud. And don't tell me you wasn't glad enough to 'ave good reason to 'ate me, in the end.

"Guess I did ruin your life, in a way," he said, slowly, into a mouthful of dirt. "Though I still don't think you had t'let me."

"Fanks, ever so. What sort of apology d'you call that, then?"

"Better'n you rate, taken all in all. 'Less you disagree."

"No point to it. Is there?"

Not really, no.

Chess reached back, pinched arm straining 'til he thought it might crack its socket, and felt for what he hoped were her fingers. Nothing seemed where he'd left it; the tunnel might've been a hand's-width or a straw's span, some sort of hexacious illusion snaring them like tar while the walls stretched stars-high on either side. Was there even a floor?

Nail touched nail, the barest scratch of horn. Followed by something soft on the pad of his index . . . lips?

Don't do this to me, old woman.

Still, it rallied him, at least. With his last shred of effort, he ground out, before heaviness forced his mouth shut: "Ain't all that much forgiveness in me—you made sure of that. But what there is, you got. Now . . ."

. . . time to get off my damn back, for good and all. Go where you're goin'. Stay there.

"Oona Pargeter, I dismiss you," he said. And shut his eyes.

SHE FELL AWAY BEHIND HIM—tore a patch from him with her passing, hole linked to hole, momentarily open enough to let the dark on either side shine through. But he had no time to allow himself regret.

CHESS CAME UP PUNCHING, as if through a membrane, a bag, the same too-small, fetid and unspeakably hot channel which once let him loose on the world. Another audible snap, like bones baked in a fire—and then finally, *finally*—

—he was over that last stile, up through the world's crust, *out* at last. Crouched panting under a roiling marine sky, at the base of what he vaguely knew to be one of that old squaw Grandma's sacred places. A circle of people stood arrayed 'round him, to almost every quarter. Grandma herself in her bone-dust reliquary; that war-painted he-she Yiska, The Night Has Passed, with horse-jaw tomahawk upraised in one fist and that crimson-clad bitch-witch Songbird's pallid hand held gentle in the other. A scattering of men as well, withdrawn to a respectful distance, their bows held ready.

Beneath his feet, as he rose, something shifted unsteadily; he glanced down, just to confirm what it was—a crevasse big enough to thrust your hand into, cracked on either side like salt-stung dead man's lips—before cutting a hasty two-step and scrambling alongside, to much firmer ground.

"Mister Pargeter," a familiar voice cut in, from behind him, "welcome. Been waiting on you quite some time now—mighty glad to see you could accommodate, eventually, considering how hard it was to send you down directions."

Chess turned, braced for the sight of her already: small and slim, her dark hair braided in two long ropes ties with beaded leather, Injun-style. She wore almost the same rig he'd made for her out of her wedding-dress, save for those skin slippers she must've gotten raiding Yiska's wardrobe. Looked a bit more sunburnt, a tad older . . . but hell, that was all right.

She's alive, that's the important part—not drilled through the head by Mesach Love's woman, or swung like I thought she might be. And that's halfway more'n I can say, even now.

Speaking of whom, now: Christ, if that wasn't not-exactly-Missus Love herself standing back yet further, on Yancey's left hand. And holding that boy of hers in her arms as well, with hex-light spilling up from his forehead in a new-grown war bonnet, a guttering twenty-candle crown.

Biggest damn hen party he'd attended since leaving 'Frisco, one way or the other . . . and looking at Yancey Kloves, all Chess could think of to tell her was that he'd never in all his life seen anyone he was more glad to meet up with, Rook included.

But still, when he opened his mouth, the very first thing which fell out was—instead—

". . . where's Ed?"

BOOK THREE:
THE SIXTH WORLD

November 15, 1867
Month Fourteen, Day Eight House
Festival: Still Quecholli, or Treasured Feather

Day Calli (House) is governed by Tepeyollotl, Heart of the Mountain: Jaguar of Night, lord of echoes and earthquakes, so vast that the spots on his coat are said to represent the stars in the sky. Even though Tepeyollotl is a variant of Tezcatlipoca—sometimes called He Who Rules Us All, in his most threatening aspect—Calli is nevertheless considered a good day for rest, tranquility and family life, best spent cementing relationships of trust and mutual interest.

By the Mayan Long Count calendar, however, Day Eight Calli's primary influence is that of Mictlantecuhtli, Lord of the Dead—a terrible skeleton shown dressed in strips of bark paper, with bulging eyes and a gaping stomach through which the liver, home to the spirit, may be seen hanging. Associated with nighttime animals such as the owl, the bat and the spider, he is also the Fifth Lord of the Night, and ruler of both the tenth day ("Itzcuintli," or Dog) and the tenth month ("Tecpatl," or Stone Knife).

As befits the weapon used to carry out human sacrifices, Tecpatl symbolizes moments of grave ordeal, predestined trials and tribulations—good times to test one's character, yet bad times to rest on one's past reputation. Cutting through falsehood like its own blade, Tecpatl warns that the mind, like the spirit, must always be kept sharpened, so it can reach the very marrow of cosmic truth.

From the archives of the Western Union Company, Telegraph #67-8155, sent November 14, 1867, stamped as delivered same date:

WESTERN UNION

```
PDA FWDSTN NA-1 LONG PD=ALBUQ NM DEL 14 10:39PM
                                 [1867 NOV 14 11:22PM]
FITZ HUGH LUDLOW= :MR G THIEL=
URGENT EXPEDITE ARRIVAL STOP P HAS DETERMINED ON
DIRECT ATTACK UPON PRISM URGED BY NEW ALLY T-CAT
STOP I DEEM ALLY MOST DEEPLY UNTRUSTWORTHY STOP
MR GREY YET UNABLE TO ESCORT GOOD DOCTOR TO NEW
POSITION STOP ATTACK PLANNED FOR 15TH TOMORROW
STOP PRIVATE ACCESS TO CAMP TELEGRAPH LIMITED BUT
WILL DESTROY MESSAGE RECORD HERE STOP URGENT REPLY
SOONEST STOP MAINTAIN PROTOCOL STOP FHL
```

From the Western Union archives, Telegram #67-81594, sent November 15, no delivery stamp:

WESTERN UNION

```
ALBUQ NM LONG PD=PDA FWDSTN NA-1 DEL 15 01:14AM
EDITOR IN CHIEF= :FITZ HUGH LUDLOW=
MATERIAL UPDATES RECEIVED STOP REGRET IMPOSSIBLE
TO PROVIDE ADDITIONAL STAFF SUPPORT AT PRESENT STOP
REASON TO EXPECT LARGE PRESS CONTINGENT ARRIVING
FROM TWO REPUBLICS NEWSPAPER WITHIN 24 HRS STOP
OPERATIVES FROM LONE STAR GAZETTE DETACHED TO
PROVIDE BALANCE STOP EXPECT THEIR ARRIVAL SAME
TIMEFRAME STOP FACILITATE THEIR OPERATIONS HOWEVER
POSSIBLE STOP REITERATE TO GREY IMPORTANCE OF
ASSIGNMENT STOP GODSPEED FITZ STOP
```

Transcribed from the shorthand notes of Mister Fitz Hugh Ludlow, on the day of November 15th, 1867, at the site of New Aztectlan, New Mexico:

The cold light of a winter dawn creeps over the plain. Near half a mile south of where the Pinkerton forces and Captain Washford's have assembled before the bloody stone forest of the *ceiba* trees, I stand upon this rocky knoll, at the southward edge of the plain; its altitude, and the telescope obtained from Quartermaster Voormeis, grant me God's own view of this battle—a privilege of which your humble correspondent is most mindful! Yet dread grips me that before this day is out, I will wish I had never been afforded this opportunity. The most novel of human sciences stands opposed to the most ancient of un-Christian magics, and whatever the outcome of this conflict, it is a certainty that afterward, the world shall not be as it has been.

A path leads through the *ceiba* trees to New Aztectlan's entrance, though with my own eyes I have seen that path vanish in a heartbeat, to leave its travellers prisoned, and presently vivisected, by those malevolent obsidian growths. It is open now, showing the closed gates at their far end; human shapes line Hex City's walls above those gates. Toward the entrance to that pathway there marches a minuscule advance guard, less than a dozen people. But foolish is he who thinks this party is to be easily dismissed. For new-made "scientific" hex Mister Allan Pinkerton himself walks at its head, with the arcanistric genius Doctor Joachim Asbury at his right hand, supported by Agent Edward Morrow, once an undercover member of "Reverend" Asher Rook's own bandit gang. But most overwhelming a presence of all is the entity named Huitzilopochtli, incarnate in sodomite pistoleer Chess Pargeter's flesh, come to challenge his sister deity the Rainbow Lady Ixchel to a fateful, perhaps final, confrontation. With them they bring prisoners of war: trade offerings, warnings, or proofs of potency? We can only pray that the gambit is effective, whatever its reasoning.

The party has now stopped in the mouth of the pathway. The god-demon Huitzilopochtli advances now between those trees, and lifts his arms, green-clad in living vine—in God's Name, even I can hear his declamation, and at this mighty distance!

ED MORROW CAME TO SLOWLY, half-buried under what felt like a pile of corpses, many of 'em only partially intact, to the hellish accompaniment of screams and curses: Mexico City after the earthquake, this time writ even larger. Through half-slit eyes, he saw the parti-coloured sky above illuminated in obscure flashes, how the clouds above hung snarled and heavy as dye-soaked wool, green and grey and black—hinted-at sun just a bright, flat, colourless coin submerged inside that same darkening knot, while a moment later sheet lightning deformed the sky even as a genuine bolt ripped horizontally, thrashing uncoiled and light-bloody, a severed dragon's tail caught in mid-fall..

How did we get here? he wondered, horrified.

Sending his mind back, then, scraping out memory's bottom-most dregs. A mere half-hour before, the Enemy had stood in front of Hex City's walls, vine-armour knotted like veins across its blue skin and Chess's red curls standing up straight, a lightning-lifted crown. And called to its "sister" inside, in a voice both gentle yet impossible to ignore, so penetrative did its timbre seem to rumble for maybe a mile in every direction at once.

Ixchel, come out. Suicide Moon, Black Rainbow, Long Hair of Death; Filth-eater, Serpent-skirt, Lady of Ropes and Snares: arise, and face me as they did at Tollan. For now is the time of reckoning, my love . . . the time when this world we squat on must at last be saved or unmade, for good, and altogether . . .

Behind him, the aggregate mass of two armies stood clustered, poised at the ready: Washford's Battalion and Pinkerton's Agents, plus the ever-growing cadre of collared hex-handlers and their equal-collared hexes. To Morrow's right was Carver, pistol in one hand, spun magnesium double-tailed leash in the other; Eulie Parr stood with drooping head on left, while Berta Schemerhorne glowered unbroken on his right, and it afforded Morrow some odd sort of comfort to note that Carver seemed to find his dominant position over the two girls far more embarrassing than victorious.

Back of Morrow's left shoulder, meanwhile—ordered by Morrow himself, in a low voice, into that place of what little safety might be found—hunched Doctor Joachim Asbury, face sharp with full-sober misery and terror; Frank Geyer stood guard adjacent, in his James Grey guise, wearing what seemed to be one of Asbury's hex-nullifier bracelets clasped 'round his wrist. This'd puzzled Morrow greatly when first he'd noted it—Geyer was no hex—but once he'd seen how Pinkerton's power-addled gaze passed over Geyer as if he had never known him, he'd realized it might be more for disguise than restraint.

And ahead of them all, Pinkerton himself, standing only steps behind the Enemy, big hands knotting and unknotting as if already savouring the feel of Ixchel's flesh beneath his fingers. He'd doffed his civilian garb for the rudiments of a uniform, including a blue jacket with colonel's insignia, worn loose and open; the act had won him no affection from Washford's soldiers, but he seemed beyond caring. The air outlining him shimmered with power, and Morrow wondered sickly how many captive hexes had been sucked dry like oranges to bring his employer to this horrendous apex.

"Takin' her sweet time about it, isn't she?" Pinkerton demanded, of his Trickster "companion." Before adding, with an ostentatious guffaw: "Just like a woman!"

The Enemy shot him a black-on-black side-eye, unimpressed. *I would conduct myself more quietly, Pinkerton-creature, were I you,* it told him. *For she comes, even now.*

And oh, Jesus Christ Almighty, if she didn't, at that.

Rising up over Hex City's western walls, eddying high on that dragonfly cloak of hers, which seemed—denser than usual, a living veil, those faceted wings shielding what little could be glimpsed of a jade-scaled forehead, sunken eyes and tattooed cheeks, lips peeled back over vulpine teeth, the thorn-rope at her throat lying slack between those leathery horrors that had once been her vessel's fine, firm breasts. Beneath two sub-swarms of dragonflies that drooped like sleeves, her hands, fingers and wrists alike could be seen, if you squinted, to gleam with bone, much like the exposed tips of her doubly bare toes. Only her black flower of hair seemed intact, stiff and queenly, fresh braids high-piled 'round a knot of sharp stone knives.

On *her* right and left, meanwhile, came two more figures, hanging from the air like Juno enchained. The Rev was one, of course, recognizable even at this range—though now Morrow came to consider on it a moment, he did look *different*, somehow: stretched thin for such a massive brute, as though he'd been hollowed and restuffed, a mere shell of his former self. And the other—

My God, I do believe that is the wreck of Hank Fennig's last wife, just like her two "sisters" already said. Sorry for doubting you, ladies.

What sketchy breath he was able to draw at the sight of her seemed to burn like lye, or strangling mountaintop air. Like a mouthful of the same lime they'd thrown into the blood-pit, 'fore tossing the sandy earth it'd taken to carve it out back in and piling a bunch of rocks on top of that so she'd rest still, if not easy. The former Clodagh Killeen, shining skull-face set with corpse-lamp eyes and every other joint of her body lit up too, a star map of hellish constellations . . . just riding the sky as though it were sea while the sound of a million swelling rattlesnake bells tumbled to earth beneath her, pocking the dust like hail.

Jesus, Morrow thought again, while also sending up a brief prayer to anybody else who might be currently out there, listening. *And I thought the bitch who made her over this way was bad.*

Inclining her head, Ixchel stared down, and seemed to smile. *Brother. You are arrogant, as ever. I had expected you sooner.*

A shrug. *I needed time, to put things in place—and see what you have put in place, likewise.*

"Things." Like this . . . pretender you ally with, perhaps?

Pinkerton's face darkened. "I'll thank ye tae address me directly, ye high-nosed heathen hoor!" he called up, making fists yet harder, so's his knuckles spat sparks.

Be silent, was all Ixchel told him, without even deigning to look his way. *You are amongst your betters now, mud-toy. It does not behoove you to try and speak to me directly, any more so than it would a beetle to hold congress with jaguars.*

"Hah! The day such as 'Reverend' Asher Rook stands my equal, let alone my better, will be a cold one in Hell indeed."

But Hell is cold, Pinkerton-thing. As you would know, had you ever truly been there. She turned her eyes to him at last, so dark they almost seemed to cast their own negative light. *Still, if—not trusting my testimony—you wish to confirm it for yourself, I believe I might be persuaded to assist you.*

"I'd heard you rumoured beautiful, not so long ago," Pinkerton replied, grinning. "Right now, though, Lady, I must admit—I'm disinclined tae believe it."

I am not . . . at my best, no. But that will change.

"Oh, ye think? Once ye locate that little Mex girl of yuirs, mayhap?"

The Enemy cast another look, less annoyed than slyly amused, this time. *Be careful, Pinkerton,* it warned him; *be circumspect, if you can be. You tread unwisely.*

Pinkerton ignored this advice, however, as the creature had no doubt known all along that he would.

So, Ixchel said, gaze fixed on Pinkerton like she was trying to burn through all the layers of his skin at once. *You do have her.*

"I did. At one point."

Explain.

Pinkerton struck a pose, hands on hips. "'Twas these two who brought her to me, straight into my camp's heart—" He indicated the remaining Missuses Fennig, the motion bringing Eulie's head up at last, tears already a-sparkle in the corners of her eyes. "—which at first I thought was for mere negotiation, as a bargaining chip. But no; turns out they truly did only want to save her from you, and the awful fate ye'd condemned her to."

A sneer, difficult to distinguish, considering how skewed her lips already were. *And you jumped at the chance to "rescue" my sweet Marizol, vowed to me by her own parents as a love-offering—to play protector, hide her away somewhere, disguised perhaps behind your tinkerer's "hex-proof" trinkets—*

"Not as such, ma'am."

Then bring her forth! Restore her to me, now, and I may spare you . . . may.

"Can't do that, I'm afraid. For in the end, contemplating upon it, I realized that just as whatever did *you* good was nothing I wanted a hand in, neither did I wish tae run the risk of you taking her back, no matter what might occur later on. And so . . ."

Oh, just get the hell on *with it, you numbskull*, Morrow thought, annoyed with these theatrics. While Ixchel simply peered at Pinkerton, not even visibly angered by his ridiculous hubris.

What is it you are saying? she demanded.

But Pinkerton was revelling in his own stupid glory now, making the haze around him bunch and blur, almost dense as Ixchel's insect panoply. He took time to smooth his beard before calling up to her, gaily: "Yes, I've been somewhat remiss in no' makin' it clearer, havnae I? For which I apologize. But what I *mean* is . . . she's dead. Head-shot. Dead over a day, by my watch. And granted, Our Lord returned after three, good as new or better—but you, ye're nae Jesus Christ, is what I'm sayin'."

A slow, impassive blink was Ixchel's only reaction, revealing supernumerary false eyes mosaicked to their lids—but Morrow went cold all over, every hair erect and stinging. As memory winged past him, he heard Yancey's toneless voice asking, in that split-second before joy shattered to horror: *Sheriff Love?*

Signalling Carver and Geyer with a sidelong glance, he first gestured them back without moving—upper body held perfectly still—then eased backward himself 'til his shoulder bumped into Asbury's; at his nudge, the Professor yielded with a stumble, gawping bemusedly. By inch-fractions they withdrew, all Morrow's attention left concentrated on those three dreadful beings before them, muscles taut to a fare-thee-well hair trigger.

Then, unexpectedly, Morrow caught Reverend Rook's eyes— and in them the same tense dread plus something else, wholly unexpected: that amused arrogance the Rev had always affected, most 'specially to his enemies, was gone. Without changing expression, Rook *turned* slightly, still hanging in the air, looking past Morrow as if he wasn't there. The black book he'd held in one hand (Sophy Love's Bible, it jolted Morrow to see), a convenient page marked with a finger, had disappeared up his sleeve.

In that instant, Morrow knew what he had to do.

Ixchel screeched something in that rotten-flower dead tongue of hers, spraying stinking black blood like venom with the force of it, and flung herself down upon Pinkerton. The plunge was thunderstrike-quick; greenish-blue light exploded 'round both of them, as they—and the Enemy—disappeared, together. Morrow was already bringing his shotgun up, swinging it 'cross toward what had once been Clo; had he hesitated even a fraction of a second in choosing a target, he would have been too late, and almost was anyhow. Clo went hurtling straight at Carver, Eulie and Berta, who survived only because Carver sensibly flung the girls' leashes away, while simultaneously hurling himself backward. Clo's dagger-length bone claws came within an inch of tearing off the man's scalp 'fore Morrow's anti-hex shell slammed into her.

She screeched, spun in mid-air, crashed to the ground, bounced upright once more like a wolverine. A second shot caught her right between the breasts, smashing her backward. Clo reeled, gaping chest hole showing torn innards and broken bones, but the wound was already sealing. Hands flying, Morrow broke open the gun and slammed another two shells home, bracing himself to burn, as a fiery holocaust seemed to well up out of the horrid creature's eye sockets and mouth together.

Yet here, most welcome, Carver's pistol thundered instead, stitching smoking hole after smoking hole across Clo's front. She yowled and sprang away, blurring almost too fast to see over the ground, heading straight for the front lines. Carver stared after her, then let out a whoop, and began to reload.

"What you yelpin' over, you idjit?" cried Eulie, clambering to her feet. "She'll tear 'em apart!"

Carver chortled. "Two whole damn armies, miss? Think maybe you ain't counted those odds right! Ain't no way one woman, no matter how . . . I mean, she . . . can't . . ." But here he trailed off, jaw slack, too mazed with battle heat to register much beyond distant, dismayed shock. "Oh. Oh, sweet Jesus, no—"

Morrow took one second to check over his shoulder—yes, Rook too had vanished, far less obtrusively than his Lady—then turned back, heart heavy, to watch the catastrophe unfold.

The soldiers had obeyed their sergeants' orders with all their old precise professionalism: *Front line, aim! Second line, prep! Third line, load! Front line, FIRE!*—and a shockwave of lead ripped out across the empty plain, slowing Clo only for a second. Unfazed, the front line stepped back three paces; as the second line stepped forward into their place, knelt and aimed, Clo drew closer and closer: *Front line, FI—!*

Too late.

Clo opened her mouth. What came out was not sound, but light: a white-hot, triple-thick beam of white fire fed from mouth and empty eyes together that tore through the massed ranks like grapeshot crossed with sun focused through a jeweller's eye. Shrieks of agony erupted skyward, torrenting fountains of blood, severed limbs. Yet these war-hardened men might've stood fast nonetheless, even in the face of such carnage, if Clo had not then sprinted directly into the centre of the army—using that very same path of scorched flesh and earth as her guide-trail—and cut into them like a knife-bedecked whirlwind, slashing and stabbing faster and more accurately than any human.

No weapon touched her. Pistols and rifles went off to no effect, or felled hapless comrades. Geyer swayed on his feet, watching it; Asbury collapsed to all fours to empty his stomach. Berta and Eulie held each other up.

In mid-air, above the abruptly empty plain, Ixchel and Pinkerton reappeared with a thunderous *crack* of torn air, hands locked; they spiralled about each other, whirling down and down, and broke apart on landing with an impact Morrow felt in his very boots. Ixchel, still screaming—had she ever stopped?—vomited a gout of greasy black power straight onto Pinkerton's face, like a sluice-gate opened on a sewage pond; Morrow bit savagely on one knuckle, driving out nausea with pain, as he saw the force of the attack distort Ixchel's very skull, pushing jaws and nose plate forward 'til she seemed more ape than human. Her face's corpse-tight skin snapped and tore, peeling away from warped bone.

But Pinkerton didn't flinch; he opened his own mouth and *swallowed* the blast, sucked it greedily down like whisky. His body blurred, rippled, swelled, bulged; the seams of his coat and shirt burst, boots exploding off his feet. Skin marbled with fungus-like patches, he towered up 'til he was half again Ixchel's height, and roared.

Ixchel stumbled backward, face too ruined now to read. Yet her body, at last, betrayed the truth: this once-goddess was no longer the master of events. Pinkerton lunged forward and slammed both outsized fists down, pinning her to earth on her back with a massive, cartilaginous wrench. Just as he seized her throat, however, it was Pinkerton's turn to gag—Ixchel's own hand lashed up and *stretched*, palm and fingers splitting apart, peeling back, limp as a torn glove. Exposed bones, speared out long as bayonets, came punching through his shoulder at the juncture of neck and chest, drawing smoking blood to gout from the wound in thick jets.

Now Pinkerton himself bled power, and the bleeding was hot, fast, thick, continual, first in sparks, then arcs, then massive blue-green whiplashes which crackled back and forth between the two abominations, whirring in ever-accelerating circles. Ixchel would take and Pinkerton would grab back, desperately, only to lose whatever he'd grabbed once more, along with a fresh new gush. Meanwhile, as Clo continued to calmly decimate the boss's and America's armies alike, the very air began to howl and shriek, a funnel of dust and wind blossoming up skyward, turning vaguest dawn to endless night.

Morrow stood frozen, appalled, his shotgun drooping—utterly unable to think what (if anything) to do next.

From the shorthand notes of Fitz Hugh Ludlow:

Mister Pinkerton and Lady Ixchel strive immovably—most unnatural and monstrous forms—the very elements protest this horror, as a cyclone forms—the Enemy H has appeared! He speaks—by hexation, all can hear.

H: Dear sister. Once again, you craft your own doom.

P: Help me, you bastard!

H: But why?

P: What'd you bring me here for, if not that?

H: In truth, for distraction.

P: But—you said—

H: That I would stand with you when I called her out, yes— and I have. Did I say I would do more?

The Enemy laughs—and has vanished!—True treachery indeed!—The ghastly demon-girl begins her rout once more— oh, those poor, poor brave men—I see the hexes and their handlers coming to the fore—will their powers turn the tide?

THINGS SPED UP, just like at Mine Creek, at Marais des Cygnes, at Bewelcome. The hex-handlers thrust their charges forward by the necks, using those loop-and-pole arrangements they normally only hauled out for captures; the hexes, in turn, took one damn look at the slaughterhouse hay Clo and Ixchel were making with their magic-less brethren, and obviously thought better of that idea. A moment later, collars were being torn free bodily, regardless of how they might rip open fingers or throats in the prisoners' frenzied rush to die on their own terms, rather than in service to Pinkerton's craziness—concussive firecracker blasts of hexation went up and down again like signal flares, popping off heads and hands, 'til the handlers themselves also started to cut and run.

Morrow actually thought he could see one of 'em clearly mouth: *Fuck THIS shit!*, before turning tail and joining with the general scramble.

Ixchel whipped her tresses out to net a few stragglers, reeling them in, and sucked 'em mummy-dry in seconds like she was choking down shots back at Splitfoot Joe's, jacking her armament up any way she could. Which must've seemed a similarly bona fide idea to Pinkerton, for he too turned and cold-cocked the nearest deserter, who squealed like a pig sensing the knife as his former boss's much-altered shadow fell atop him: "Mister Pinkerton, I'm sorry, but you just can't expect a man to bear such rampant awfulness, not in all conscience—"

"I *can*, an' I *do*. An' if ye won't, then what damnable use are you t'me, except as fuel?"

"Oh Jesus, no! *No!*"

A dreadful alchemy seemed to overtake what remained of the Agency's founder, twisting his flesh to match his cannibal desires. He gaped wide, wider, widest of all—Christ Almighty, Morrow almost thought he heard the man's jaw-hinge muscles tear, his cheeks rip like cloth in a high wind. At last, his skull-top itself seemed to teeter on the ragged verge of separation, sheer violent jut of force-grown bone increasing his mouth's width and depth at least twice over. More than enough to fit a man's entire screaming face inside, it turned out.

Pinkerton bit down, a shark-toothed trap sprung shut, and set in to chew. The screaming stopped, then, eventually . . . but not fast enough, by far.

God, was all Morrow could think, numbly, over and over, as he watched and did nothing, because—what was there to do, exactly? *Goddamnit, God . . . come on already, old man, if you're comin'. Ain't this the sort of stuff you like to put a stop to? Or is Hell finally empty and all the devils here—just silence coming back, 'cause there's nothin' left out there to answer? Anything don't want to eat us, that is, or make us so's we crave to eat each other?*

A fair question, soldier, the Enemy's voice murmured, from behind him. *Yet I am here, nonetheless.*

Clinging on Morrow's shoulder, like any bad angel; Morrow didn't even bother turning his head to see. Simply shivered to feel that too-cold copy of Chess's deft little hand on his, reminding him—subtly, yet firmly—that he still held his weapon.

How many shells left, soldier?

"Takes two, one per barrel. I got 'em both."

You should use them, then.

That drew a weak sketch of a laugh. "On *who*?" Morrow managed.

Who do you think?

Morrow turned his eyes on Ixchel, hovering once more out of reach and range alike, pits where her eyes should lie already intent on Pinkerton's bent and heaving back, apparently too appetite-hypnotized to be aware of her threat—and Goddamn, but he really didn't know how that woman'd *ever* borne the sad chore of walking from place to place, back in the day. But then again, she probably hadn't had to do it for long.

Then back to Pinkerton, popped jaw crunching back and forth like a coyote cracking bones for marrow, blood greased back so far it'd dyed his sideburns cathouse red. 'Cept what he was actually chewing on had been a man's hollowed-out idea-pan, some poor bastard's entire life writ infinitesimal small on grey-pink loops of brain—same ones Pinkerton was shovelling down right as Morrow watched, licking his fingers for the last of it, while hexation sweated out like mercury through every pore.

How Morrow'd admired the man, once—truly, completely: a man of action, of application, far-seeing and inventive, carving a new path through a brave new world. But there was nothing of the personality he'd followed left at all, that he could see, no matter how hard he searched for it—only hunger, ape-stupid and degraded.

Yes, soldier. Remember what I told you? That time I spoke of when you must follow your own instincts, do as your conscience dictates . . . is now.

So I see, Morrow thought. And raised the gun, not giving himself time to think about it further, if only in faint hopes Pinkerton might not "overhear" him do so.

A man stuffed sausage-full with that much stolen witchery couldn't really fail to figure out when someone was plotting his doom, though, 'specially if they only stood a yard or so that-a-way; that disgusting object Pinkerton called a head jerked up, sniffing the air. And before he could turn, Morrow pulled both triggers at once and gave it to him, right in the back, hard enough he could see Pinkerton's naked spine glisten amongst the meat.

The hole opened was fearsome. So was what poured out, a flood of decay cut with arcane marsh-gas flame that turned the sand below all rotten black and crap-bucket brown, the sickening horn-dun yellow of a bled-out corpse's feet. Pinkerton shrank visibly as it escaped him, straining to catch the bulk in his cupped hands, only to have it scald them so bad their palms blistered up like slimy mittens. These he lifted Morrow's way, maybe in plea, or cut-off imprecation; it was impossible to tell either way, since the damage he'd done to his own speaking organs wasn't healing, leaving his unstrung tongue to flap useless in the rising wind.

The Enemy already seemed to've eddied away, like any good tempter. But Ixchel stared down still, grinning fit to bust, as though she'd seldom seen anything quite so sweet in all her long, hard un-life.

Daughter, she called, sweetly. *I see you at play and rejoice, for your pleasure gives me pleasure. Yet it seems I have need of you here.*

And the eager answer, resonant as a grave-struck gong, seemingly echoing back from everywhere at once: *I come, mother. I come.*

Though it was somewhat hard to tell, Morrow almost thought Pinkerton might've whimpered at the sound of it, for which Morrow certainly didn't blame him. Yet found he was running a tad low on sympathy, nonetheless.

Let's at least hope she makes it quick, was all he had time to think, before Clo swept in and tore Pinkerton in two, like paper. One half went this way, the other that, while the very best part of what was left inside him all went streaking up into Ixchel herself, who barely seemed to register its influx.

But then again, neither did Morrow, really. For that same instant must've been when whatever hit him next knocked him backward like a hundred haymakers, a blindsiding mortar burst, right into the corpse-tangle's raw and reeking briar patch heart.

SO HERE HE LAY, coming to by painfully slow degrees while someone tugged hard on what he gradually realized must be his broken arm, trying to extricate him from this hex-dug hole; Private Carver, calling his name and hauling, while what sounded like Ixchel and Clo wiping the field with the dregs of Pinkerton's forces raged somewhere behind. Barely able to resist screaming aloud, Morrow gritted out: "Please stop doin' that before I puke, Private—Jonas, I mean—"

Carver let go, sprang back. "Ed Morrow, that *is* you! You're awake?"

"Most definitely so, yeah."

"Oh, thank the Lord! Man, things are comin' fast as yellow-jack shit out here; I got these gals t'look after, and almost nobody left upright to help. After they all broke and run, things just got worse—don't even know where half them folks got to, Doc Asbury and the Captain included . . ." Here he stopped, peering closer. "What's wrong with your arm?"

"Broke, I think . . . that or so far out the socket it's like I can feel the damn ball movin' 'round loose in there . . ."

"Yeah? Well, it looks pretty awful, but might be the gals could take a look—"

"You trust 'em to?"

Another voice intruded, from further back—female, uptown New York—Berta? Calling out: "He doesn't have too much choice about it, Mister Morrow; lost his gun in the first rush, so we've been watchin' his back ever since. That's *after* he jimmied my collar free, of course . . ."

Another one—definitely Eulie, this time—chimed in. ". . . an' he was glad enough he did, when one of them dog-things with the hands jumped him. Sissy made short work of it, so when she was done, he popped mine off, too . . ."

But here she trailed away, voice dipping further, almost breaking. Perhaps recalling how there'd been a third person answered to that diminutive, once upon a time—someone whose shell still flew somewhere above, claw-handed and red to the elbow, seeking for further prey.

Morrow stopped to cough, long and heavily, Carver considerately glancing away 'til he was done. After which he then leaned in just as Morrow pulled himself up, and said: "Saw what happened, y'know . . . with Himself, back in the thick of it. What you did."

Face clammy, Morrow spat to clear his mouth before replying, carefully. "What was that, Jonas, exactly?"

Make or break time, and they knew it, 'specially since Morrow's injury made it highly unlikely he could fight back, if Carver decided he had to do anything about Pinkerton's untimely and highly unnatural demise.

But the younger man simply shrugged. "Nothin' I'd swear to, sir, in court or out of it. That's all I wanted to say."

Morrow felt welcome relief and a weird sort of sadness fall on him together to hear it, both genuinely grateful yet truly amazed that anyone he'd known such a powerfully brief time would advance him this high-blown level of trust. But then again, these *were* tumultuous days; Carver'd done much the same for Fennig's ladies already, and seen it returned fivefold. Might be he'd decided he might as well place his faith in whosoever it took his fancy to, for however short a time he might remain able to do so.

One way or the other, Morrow was glad to feel Eulie's light touch probe at his hurts, efficient as any "real" doctor. "This'll pain some," she told him. He nodded.

"Can't think but it wouldn't."

"All right, then. Just so's you know, and don't blame me."

"I wouldn't be, *uh!*, too likely to—*ohHOhhhh, that's some big fuckin' pile of*—"

"What-all'd I *tell* you, Mister Morrow? Pain hurts, that's just what it does; ain't no easy way 'round it, nice as it'd be if there was. Now, just hold on one tick more yet, and let me do what I gotta."

Something ran through him then, stem to stern, like the very hairs of his skin were all set afire at once; he fell back, slipping on offal. Felt his arm snap out, twist this way and that—*Jesus*, it seemed as though the movements must be earthshakingly huge, though he suspected they were anything but. At the same time, a violent shiver of arcane light buzzed blue all along his break, re-righting it. He could've told the exact moment his shoulder popped in, had that not been rendered fairly obvious by its precise coincidence with the second he began to vomit.

Sympathetic hands grasped his shoulders, one white-skinned and female, the other male and brown. "Just ride it out, Ed," Carver told him, in one ear, while Morrow hacked and shook.

Thanks for the advice, never in life would've occurred t'me to take that option, Morrow wanted to grump back soon as the pain-haze cleared, which was thankfully fast—but at that very same instant, he looked up once more to see Berta abruptly transfixed and staring even higher, tears streaming down her stately face.

"Oh God," she said, quiet, like she didn't even know her mouth was open. "Oh God, oh, Clo. What that damn woman *did* to you."

"Poor sissy," Eulie agreed, gripping Berta's hand tight. "But . . . ain't much we can do about it, I s'pect. So we best be movin' on, before . . ."

Too late for caution there, though.

Above, Clo and Ixchel orbited each other, a moon split in two, vomiting the last of Pinkerton's ill-gotten witchery back and forth between 'em like they were passing a bottle, while the Rev—back from wherever he'd disappeared off to, now the real fight was mainly over—danced attendance, picking off stragglers with nuggets of verse tossed like Ketchum Grenades. Here a AND IT CAME TO PASS . . . THAT JOSHUA . . . SAID UNTO THE CAPTAINS OF THE MEN OF WAR WHICH WENT WITH HIM, COME NEAR, PUT YOUR FEET UPON THE NECK OF THESE KINGS, there a AND DAVID WENT OUT, AND FOUGHT WITH THE PHILISTINES, AND SLEW THEM WITH A GREAT SLAUGHTER; AND THEY FLED FROM HIM. Which "they" sure did, like blast-frightened rabbits, and to no particularly good effect, either.

Clouds of dust, blasted sand and mist hung roiling along the plain's east edge, obscuring the way back to Camp Pink. Before it, a lone cavalryman in an officer's uniform—Washford, no doubt, even if it was impossible to pick out variations in backlit skin from this distance—galloped back and forth before the remnants of the Thirteenth, yelling orders, organizing its retreat. Morrow saw the skull-faced hag's eyes light up, tracking the rider's movements, and groaned to himself. Every instinct he had to attack, intervene, *distract* just for a moment warred hard against the helpless, hopeless knowledge of the exact uselessness of any such effort—not to mention just what a poor reward it would be for Carver, Berta and Eulie, getting 'em killed alongside him even after all this.

He drew breath to order the others away—and spasmed head to foot in a wriggling jolt, not painful this time but fire-streaked cold and thrilling; almost exactly like the icy ecstasy of spilling blood to empower Chess, another *nahuatl* epiphany boiling out of him. Except this one was . . . sharper, more controlled: a lasso tightening on his brain, rather than a gush spilling outward.

All of the above came in half an instant—joined, in the next, by a presence so startling it left no room even for joy.

Ed—it's Yancey! We found him, Ed; we got him! An image followed here, stamped on his brain like some instantaneous tintype: hollow, insubstantial, yet indisputably the face of the real Chess Pargeter, alive with whatever the Enemy so viciously lacked. *We're at Old Woman Butte, in Chaco Canyon*—a greyish flat-sided sandstone tower, rearing above the desert—*get here, soon as you can! Please, Ed. Pl—*

With a whipcrack of pain, the connection snapped; Morrow cried out, staggering back onto Carver's supporting arm again, as Berta and Eulie gaped. "Jesus, Ed!" Carver exclaimed. "The hell was *that*?"

"Message," Morrow gasped. "From—a friend." He paused, wondering how to explain, and lost his chance almost immediately—for just then, Eulie glanced up and shrieked, eyes bugging. Morrow and Carver whirled together to see Ixchel and Clo descending on them without much speed—why bother hurrying, with nowhere for the four to flee?

Briefly, Morrow wondered if they'd somehow sensed Yancey's calling, or if that coincidence was sheer fluke.

Didn't matter either way, he supposed, and shifted his grip to his empty shotgun's barrel, raising the stock like a club.

For a moment, he thought the *boom* that echoed out 'cross the plains was more thunder, another hexacious levinbolt called forth to fry them where they stood. But a second later, as the sadly familiar whistling roar of incoming mortar fire ripped across the sky, Morrow understood his own error.

"*Down!*" he yelled, grabbed Berta and dove face-first into the dirt, while Carver yanked Eulie down likewise. Above, Ixchel and Clo actually drew up, revolving one scant moment before the projectile struck. The shell burst between them with a flare of eldritch, oily light that painted both once-women in stark black silhouette, then shrouded them in colourless fire, evoking a single shared shriek of inhuman pain.

Ixchel plunged groundward like a dry leaf spit out of an autumn bonfire; Clo rocketed skyward instead, a day-born comet, fiercely trying to extinguish her fire against the wind.

Out of the dust-fog came an earthshaking roar, and the dust itself roiled apart to reveal something Morrow'd as yet only glimpsed in sketches and half-built frameworks: the newest version of Doctor Asbury's hex-powered "ghost-train," twice as massive, sporting three armed and armoured cars in a chain—a true Land Ironclad, slabbed in iron plates like *Merrimac* and *Monitor* alike, with gun-muzzles thrusting out on all sides. The foremost still smoked, evident source of the missile that had struck down the demon women—a "hex-mine," Asbury named it. Off the side of the foremost cab, Captain Washford clung to a steel bracket in the open air, sabre drawn and flashing in the murk.

At impossible speed, the arcanistric behemoth roared across the plain aimed for the fallen Moon-Lady, only to collide with Clo as she streaked down upon it out of the heavens, still ablaze like Lucifer: Struck the roof and bounced off, a stray firework scraping 'gainst stone, then arced smoothly 'round and came back down to land on all fours, clinging. With every star tattooed on her body manifesting seared pinholes of volcanic light, her clawed hands tore at the armour 'til battle-forged steel yielded to alien might—long strips peeled back same as hide would, torn edges glowing red with heat.

The ironclad began to weave back and forth, yet maintained speed toward Ixchel, the *ceiba* forest, the walls of New Aztectlan beyond. More shells burst forth, borne on tongues of fire; explosions inked in unnatural hues of green, blue and purple mushroomed up out of the *ceiba* trees, setting off chain reaction shockwaves which shattered row after row of those black monstrosities.

The push's up and running again, praise Christ, Morrow thought, frankly amazed. As all the while, left writhing on the ground directly in the Ironclad's path, Ixchel howled fit to burst—so loud it bruised the soul, shook the very dirt they stood on, and almost made it seem like she was about to pry the whole Crack's lips open using just her voice alone.

"Goddamn *yes!*" Carver yelled, dancing like a madman; Morrow didn't doubt but that he'd have drawn his gun and sprinted to join the attack, had Morrow not seized his arm at the last moment to haul him 'round. Carver glared at him, furiously. "We gotta help him, Ed, for love of all—that's the *Captain* out there!"

"Captain'll live or die on his own, with nought for us do about it—'cept fall alongside him, things go bad as they probably will!" Morrow yelled back. "What *we* gotta do get out of here, soon as we can—find a place, Old Woman Butte, in Chaco County . . ."

"Shit'd be the point of *that*, exactly?"

"'Cause Chess Pargeter is there, the *real* Chess Pargeter. And if anyone can set this all to rights . . . that'd be him."

"Don't know—" Carver started, mutinously. But froze a second later as Berta Schemerhorne grabbed him from behind, threading one arm through his quick as any needle, without even a by-your-leave. Her other hand was already twinned with Eulie's, knuckles locked, while Eulie herself slapped her free palm to Morrow's forehead.

"*I* do," Berta told Carver, firmly. Then, to Eulie: "You read 'im, sissy. I'll drive."

Aw, shit, Morrow thought, knowing what was coming. Then stiffened again, entranced once more, as the hex-girl sieved his memories with brutal speed, found Yancey's sending, flung a tendril of power out through the link itself to track its source. He heard Carver's gasp slide to a retch, poor bastard, and felt for him—with luck, they'd hopefully already be wherever they were going before his spasm had time to bring up more'n bile, though Morrow doubted he'd see that as much of a mercy.

Got a lot to learn 'bout hexes still, son, even after the last few days— but you will, believe me. 'Specially given who-all we're on our way to see.

Thought faded and skipped as time itself seemed to bend, a suture looped and violently pulled between now and yet-to-be. After which—with a *crack* of torn air, plus a flash of light-in-darkness that folded the world like a poorly-painted scrim—

—all four of them were gone.

From the shorthand notes of Fitz Hugh Ludlow:

As the she-demon rips open the Ironclad's roof, locks and cables part—the third car is released! It tumbles away, breaking up; passengers and demon-girl go flying—the remaining two cars roar on, Capt. Washford still yelling orders from his mounted perch to crush the fallen Lady—yet all in vain, for the first threat comes once more! Flung high out of the wreck, she lands upon the foremost car, resumes her ravaging—armour plating tears like sodden leather—but the Ironclad bears down still upon "goddess" Ixchel, felled and helpless yet, until—

Reverend Rook appears by his wife's side!—a blasphemy, and they are gone! Over the pit where the Lady fell, the Ironclad thunders too late—yet there is still the forest, and the City's walls—the guns continue firing—can the Ironclad still accomplish victory, before the she-demon guts it from within?

A great swathe of armour rips back—Washford vaults to the roof, sword in hand, and runs her through! Valiant fellow, a credit to his race—but NO! His blade snaps like green pine, she plunges both claws through his belly—he drives her and himself forward, off the car, down in front of it, to—their deaths? His, at least. Oh, poor Captain Washford!

Next: a shattering crash! Both Ironclad cars flip up and over, iron dice shook in a box—the Demon kneels, unmoved, where they made impact! To either side beyond her, the cars tumble and roll onward, ceiba trees smashed to dust, gaping paths of ruin—one reaches the City wall itself—IT EXPLODES! A pillar of hellish flame boils up to the sky, sickly-hued—Good God, the screaming can be heard from where I stand—

—but here hot shrapnel whined by Ludlow's ear fast enough to sting, slapping him back to himself just in time to realize his danger. No Pinkerton to shield him anymore, no Washford, either—he could not be behind the front line, since that existed no longer. His right hand ached, pencil death-gripped, its point worn almost to wood with the fury of his scribbling, while his other arm burned from holding telescope to eye. Yet even through tear-blurred vision, the last thing he saw through it stayed etched on his sight, a phantom forever threatening to turn real: that thing once known as Clodagh Killeen stalking back out onto the field of battle, hungry for yet more blood, a shard of Captain Washford's sabre still lodged deep in its midsection like a mis-set unicorn's horn.

Ludlow had scribed upon battlefields before, observing close-hand the hell which mere mortals, unassisted, could wreak upon each other; had, on occasion, pronounced—like many an "educated" fool—that Man needed no hexes, devils or angels guiding him to be capable of the greatest good *and* the greatest evil. As he looked out on this devastation below, however . . . carnage worse than any cannonade; foul-smelling smoke reaching skyward from the ruined plain; unnatural fires burning wild through the *ceiba* forest; the wrecks of the Ironclad's cars, still spitting sparks and smoke . . . and, worse than all, the lightning-eyed thing that moved through that ruin like a shark in chummed water, responsible for most of it, Ludlow realized, at last, what self-satisfied hubris his pronouncements had been. A foolish attempt to elevate, or perhaps denigrate, his own species—to place the average person on a level with *actual* gods and devils.

With a practised speed learned on those same aforementioned battlefields, Ludlow collapsed and stowed the telescope, then stuffed pad and pencil in his shoulder-bag to scramble down the knoll's backside. Cold, faintly damp scree skittered under his boots; he let himself slide down and came to a kneeling stop, then rabbited down the small arroyo below. If he remembered right, and his overwhelming terror hadn't got the absolute best of him, this let out into a small river valley that in turn debouched onto the winding path covering some-odd miles back to Bewelcome.

From a bank of scrub brush near the arroyo's far end, however, two strong hands shot up and yanked him hard down, into cover. Ludlow gave out with a choked yell—then relaxed as the owner of those hands came into view before him: Frank Geyer, mud-stained and dusty, but seemingly otherwise uninjured. Doctor Asbury crouched beside, miserable-looking, though at least his eyes were clear. In one hand, he held a small brass orb, a fob atop whirring as it slowly spun.

"Half-feared no one had made it out but myself," Ludlow whispered. "Did you see the end of it?"

Geyer shook his head. "No need to," he said. "Couldn't've gone well regardless, and I can only s'pose it didn't. Now stay still, and listen."

Ludlow frowned. Something seemed off about Geyer's voice; his own too, now he thought on it. As though they spoke in a stuffy, closed room—and the light 'round them lay far gloomier than it should, for what little cover they had.

"Sounds odd, don't it?" Geyer explained, noticing his reaction. "You can thank the Doc here for that—it's some sort of 'suppressor,' a hex-powered camouflage blind, for intelligence work. Upshot is, long's we keep quiet and don't move, he guarantees we won't be found, 'less some poor bastard trips right over us."

"'Found'? But who's there left to fear would—?" Ludlow began, then stopped. For something *was* approaching, from nearer than was comfortable and damned quick, to boot.

Though he'd previously thought the dim rumbling he'd been hearing some mere after-echo of the battle's chaos, now—as it grew ever louder, ever more rhythmic—he suddenly knew exactly where it was coming from, and cringed farther back under Asbury's tenuous magical cover. Again, Geyer signalled him to keep his mouth shut, and he obliged, gladly.

In silence, the three of them watched the long-predicted Mexican battalion's first outriders move past the arroyo mouth, mounting toward the plain. A sea of red, white and green Mexican flags, Habsburg's gold-crowned eagle and black griffins prominent in its centre, waved from bayonet blades atop rifles proudly held erect by red-coated cavalry officers; infantry in paler blue coats followed behind, fusiliers marching with rifles over shoulders. All the men wore broad-brimmed black hats, while a few of the officers sported tall beaver-helms good enough for any Beefeater in London.

Some of them were Carlotta colonists, Ludlow had no doubt—fled seceshes in favour of slavery, done up in their new country's finery. But from this distance Mex and American blended all together, and he didn't exactly feel like taking a closer look, just to find out which was which.

"No signs of damage," muttered Geyer. "With those Weed-walls up 'round Bewelcome, they probably just marched straight past. Langobard sure ain't got the gumption to try stopping them."

"Or the manpower, or the arms," Asbury pointed out. "Might they be here to reinforce Hex City, while retrieving their wayward citizens?"

"They're sure not ready for battle, with their pennants on parade." Geyer squinted, thinking. "Wonder if Maximilian sent a hex or two of his own, maybe, to negotiate the Mexes' release . . . could they see us, do you think, Professor? See whatever your device's giving off, anyhow?"

Asbury shook his head. "It is less a question of strength than of . . . frequency, rather, for lack of a better term; in this case, all the suppressor's stored hexacious energies are directed inward." He paused to give the fob another few twists, at which the whirring sped up again. "Though we would have to recharge it by siphoning hexation from another magickal source using my personal Manifold; so long as it runs, this field nullifies sound, warps most light around a certain radius, and entirely muffles all psycho-aetheric vibrations within. In other words, we simply register as being not here, or as good as."

Ludlow pursed his lips in a silent whistle. "Got a veritable magic shop in that bag of yours, don't you, Professor?"

Asbury looked almost ashamed. "Yes, well . . . if you tinker long enough, some advances are inevitable. But I must say—it does seem as though *everything* hexaciously powered is increasing in efficacy to a truly threatening degree, and that doesn't bode well." He bit his lip. "I do not much like to consider any future impact of the sheer aetheric destabilization these conflicts may have induced, Mister Ludlow. Indeed, I do not like to think on it at all."

It took more than an hour for the battalion—some thousand men or so, trailing followers and supply wagons—to finish moving by, after which Geyer made them wait another fifteen minutes, just to be safe. Then they set their feet to the path once more, muddying the Mexes' tracks with their own. Without asking, Ludlow slung Asbury's arm over his shoulders, ignoring the exhausted older man's halfhearted protests. "Where to now?" he asked. "Bewelcome?"

"Nope," said Geyer. "Gonna meet up with Mister Thiel . . . and the Texicans."

UPSIDE WAS ABOUT HOW Chess'd remembered it, from Down Under: full of discomfort and disarray, everything just that hair out of true—wind too cold, sun too bright, full to the gills with contrary motherfuckers who might slap you soon as kiss you, or shoot you without any kiss at all. Not to mention how there wasn't one person within eye's reach who hadn't fucked with him at least once, and not in the enjoyable way, either . . . his second good friend in all this lousy world Yancey Kloves, sad to say, very much included.

But for all that, even while he stood there squinting and shivering with the toll of his travels run through every part of him like a stain, he still felt as though he'd never seen anything so pretty as the same sun that pained him, the empty, windswept sky, the bone-coloured desert with its hidden varmints and disasters. That he'd never felt so Goddamn good in all his strange, short life as he did standing here weaponless and alone, barely able to recall what it was he thought he'd been doing when the Enemy'd tricked him into signing away his flesh and becoming yet another of that mirror-footed son-of-a-bitch's four faces. None of it seemed to matter, just for the moment; he felt naked and new, a colt licked to full trembling height, teetering on un-shod hooves that might one day take him . . . anywhere, really. Any-damn-where, at all.

Only wish Oona was here to share in it, he caught himself thinking, just for a moment. But he really *must've* been happy, for once—happy like he hadn't been since the bad old days, the simple days, measured out in bullets or blow-jobs—because he couldn't even bring himself to resent it.

One moment only, barely half a skipped beat of his missing heart. And then—it was all sent sideways, stretched and pinched and *twisting* in a way that made him want to bend double, claw at the dust 'til his fingertips split, unsure if he'd see blood or bone or what, exactly: just the awful spectacle of his own flesh crumbling away, maybe, like chalk, never to be resolved.

Oh God, oh God. Christ Almighty, not that I ever thought of You as such, 'cept to scream your name out in crisis and revel in the blasphemy . . .

So swift had all this passed that Yancey was only now replying to his first question, repeating: "'Where's Ed?' Might've hoped you'd be happy to see *me*, too, after all this while—though I s'pose time runs a bit different, down there."

Chess swallowed, or tried to; his mouth was so dry, he could barely taste his own teeth. "Yeah, it does, but . . . I am, really. It just . . . feels like . . ."

He felt himself droop and cursed it, but couldn't stop, wobbling on his pins like a chloral-drop drunk—saw her grey eyes widen as she took in the extent of his ruin and felt her seize onto him by both shoulders, holding him from collapse. Behind her, the others stepped closer, keen to help. "What's wrong with you?" she demanded. "Are you—hurt, somehow? What can I do?"

"Don't know," he managed. "An' . . . don't know that either, or that. I feel—oh, shit."

Now he really was ground-bound, bones gone all slippy, braced to hit with his eyes shut and maybe roll (or sprawl, at best), to minimize the damage. But a fresh grip intruded, keeping him upright: Yiska's mannish fingers, knitting fast with his own. Meantime, Songbird's gunpowder-flavoured Chinee magic twined 'round shoulder down elbow to wrist and right back up the same path on Chess's side, a dragon-scaled glove bolstering strength and channelling energy which warmed, probed, stung as it searched him for answers.

Yancey checked his sweaty forehead. "Why'd you ask about Ed?" she demanded. "Why right then—right now?"

"Dunno . . ."

"Well, *think*, Goddamnit. If you're not too sick to swear you're well enough to reason, so far's you're able."

"Screw *you*, Missus," he told her, with a surge of black temper, which at least made her smile. "Yeah, *there* you go," she said, with some affection. "Now spill it, 'fore you pass out."

"I just . . ." On instinct alone—hell, it'd worked so far—Chess rummaged down deep, cleared his mind as far as he could, and trusted the words to come on their own. Which is how he was surprised to hear himself saying, eventually—

"Ed—and you—you're the only things I feel . . . *tied* to, anymore—like I'd dust up and blow away, otherwise. Feel like I need him, is all—need you both, here, together. That make any sense?"

"More than you know, red boy," Grandma rumbled, from behind him. "But then, this is no great mystery, given you know so little."

"Oh, thanks for *that*, rock-pile," Chess snapped back, and quivered all over from inside to out, feeling horribly like he was going to puke, pass out . . . or fade clean the fuck away. For the first time since the War he recalled his past soldiery to mind—not the guns-and-killing part, but the code that made it okay to lean on a comrade when you knew you couldn't stand—and leaned on Yancey that way now, stifling his humiliation. Took deep breaths, for all he still didn't really feel a need to breathe, until the nauseating feeling that he might see the ground through his own boots at any second faded, if only by a touch.

"So what the hell *is* wrong with me?" he asked, to keep himself from looking down to check. "You gals botch the resurrection? Not to blame ya, if so; Rev himself never had the balls to try pulling *that* one off—"

"Chess," said Yancey, and he found himself shutting up—as surprised by his own vague shame as by her voice's steely command, not loud, but final.

"Resurrection is for dead things," Grandma replied, "and you are *not* a ghost; the Smoking Mirror repaired your flesh when he possessed it, so it lives yet, even without you inside it. If you had ever learned spirit-walking, or any *Hataalii* skills at all, then you would have some control over your current state. As it is, you have neither any place prepared in this world nor an empty vessel to return to. You must be anchored if you wish to remain here, especially while the Crack remains open." As Yancey, Songbird and Yiska exchanged looks, her voice became acid: "Do you doubt me? Who knows more of such things, amongst us?"

"Only you, Spinner," Yiska assured her.

"Well, then."

Chess scoffed. "Who was s'posed to tutor me in these skills of yours, exactly—Ash Rook? There's your answer on that one: fucker tried to kill me and this's the result, so everything I've learned since's been on the run, like always."

"Yes, and given how much damage you did while running, I would have expected you to know more, at the end of it. But it seems we are both fated to be disappointed."

Songbird grimaced, but when she spoke, her voice was calmer than Chess'd ever heard it before—enough so he'd've rubbed his eyes, if he hadn't somewhat feared that'd scrub 'em away like chalk marks. "This bickering is neither here nor there," she said, "and beneath us as well, even him. What must we *do*?"

"Let me think," Grandma growled.

"Yes, let us both," Yiska agreed. "For I think you already know—"

"Be *quiet*, granddaughter!"

"*No.*" Yiska stepped in front of Grandma. "The time for that is over, Spinner: decide, or do not. This is what you would tell *me.*"

The hulk stood there silent a long moment, looming over her, a landslide waiting to happen. "Very well, then, come here," it said, at last. "Let us speak on it further."

Their subsequent palaver—conducted quietly, in their own language—seemed to go on far longer than it had to. Luckily, Yancey's shoulder was small but warm, surprisingly hard with new-grown muscle. What'd they had her doing out here? Chess'd have to remember to ask, whenever they next got time for impractical conversation.

Even as he thought this, however, he felt that same ripple of unreality sift those approximations he was using for bones, frighting him with the idea that he might fall *through* her supporting grip at any moment. So he spat, and eked out: "Didn't mean to . . . horn in on your territory, gal. With Ed, and all."

"What?" She blushed like the flower-faced innocent she'd been, not so long back. "Oh, I think we're all three pretty equally entangled at this point, don't you? What with him your priest and me your priestess, I mean." Adding, lower: "Actually, I think might be that's why you got such a longing for him, all of a sudden. You need us both, to shore you up, just like before."

"By cuttin' on yourselves, you mean? I don't—" He grabbed himself by the mental scruff and shook, hard. "There's other ways," he said, finally.

"Like what?"

Chess snorted. "Oh, hell if I know, woman! Just seems like there's likely to be, and you'd know better'n me 'bout it anyhow, wouldn't you? Like every-damn-body."

Instead of snapping back in return, she smiled again. "Now, *this* is more like what I expected. That you'd roll out of Hell like you were getting out of bed, see me and scowl, and say: '*Took* you long enough.'"

'Chess managed a half-grin of his own, and agreed. "'Cause you did, that's for damn sure. But much as I couldn't see nor hear you down there, I already know the whyfore of *that*."

"In that Oona told you, you mean."

His brows knit. "Saw that, too, huh? Well, 'course you did . . . sent her to me in the first place, whispered advice in her ear. Two of you must've had some deep discussions, knowin' I couldn't listen in."

"We might've, at that. You jealous, Mister Pargeter?"

He suspected she was twitting him, and felt a strange stab of pride not only that he could identify such japery, but that it didn't make him want to punch anyone, when he did.

"A little, Missus Kloves," he said, at last. "But only that. She and me still ain't friends, as such."

Quite some change from the horned-up rake and ramblin' boy who'd put a bottle upside Sadie Whoever's head and left her to die on a dirty saloon floor, over the grand sin of flirting with "his" duplicitous hulk of a man. For a second, Chess almost wanted to slip back down into Hell and apologize to the poor little bitch, which rocked him back yet further, as though the "him" he'd always known was peeling away by degrees, shedding like skin. What could possibly be left underneath, after, when every bit of scar was finally gone?

"That's a sad story," Yancey told him, all humour suddenly gone from her voice. To which he shrugged, as best he could, and said: "It's a sad world."

Which, by God, they both well knew for nothing but truth.

But here were Grandma and that man-gal of hers stepping over now, finally done with their parlay. The rock-creature shook her massive-jawed head, with a noise like bones grinding, and told Yancey: "So, it is decided—you must bring your other half here, that soldier Morrow, if he yet lives. Then you and he will keep *this* one from losing sense of himself, until we get him to where he and the Smoking Mirror may confront each other."

Yancey sighed. "After which?" "

"They will fight, and this working will reach its end, one way or another." Grandma looked down on Chess, haughty as a thing with no eyes to narrow or nose to sneer through could be. "I hope you prove worth all this effort, red boy."

"Didn't think so already, why'd you bother bringin' me up at all?"

"Because we all have parts to play. I know it—and now, so do you. Do not fail."

Chess scowled. "I don't know you, woman. Might be you sure as hell don't know me."

"Ah, but I *do*, little killer. I have seen you through your man's eyes, and often. Your white man with a Book, cause of all this trouble, supposedly on *your* behalf. Because he could stand neither to lose you nor give up his magic, desiring to . . . what is your *bilagaana* phrase? 'Have his cake, and eat it'?"

"What's she talkin' 'bout?" Chess demanded, of Yiska.

She shrugged. "It is an old idea—that two *Hataalii* who wish to live together may do so, but only at the cost of their power. Rook might have done it before you ever had cause to know what you were, let alone what you might have been. But because he would not brook becoming less, he made you *more* . . . too much for Balance, unBalancing everything."

"Yeah, well—I never asked him to do any of that, Goddamnit. That was all his idea . . . his, and hers."

"Yes," Yiska agreed. "And she would have just done something else, the Lady of Snares and Traps, even had your Reverend refused her; this too is true, though my Grandmother is loath to admit it." Her eyes turned to Songbird, afloat and silk-shrouded, shimmering sweet in all her white-on-red finery, and Chess watched in surprise as a mere sight of that sharp-tongued harridan made Yiska's lips curve—let alone how Songbird's eyes dropped to see it, blanched cheekbones pinkening.

"Besides which," Yiska continued, softer, "I can sympathize with him, foolish though Asher Rook may have been, in the moment. I think we all can, being drawn most fiercely to our kind, like any other animal."

"Not to mention how we now know things were gonna change,

no matter who did what," Yancey put in, drawing a nod from Missus Love.

"Missus Kloves has it a'right," Sophy Love said, considering her boy, who was amusing himself by sucking on one paw and making dust-mites dance like fireflies 'round his own head, hexaciously lit up in a hundred different colours. "This vow of yours, Christian as it sounds in theory, was overturned long since by the Hex City Oath—and given what we achieved last night, Miss Yu and Gabriel stand living proof. No point in harrying Mister Pargeter over things he couldn't've known or things Rook claims he did to benefit him, rather than pursuing charges 'gainst him for all the bad he's done outright."

Which put her on his side, strangely enough, even after everything—or maybe not; hard to tell, even when they weren't discussing stuff that'd probably happened while he was still pulling himself up through Hell's asshole. The whole thing made Chess's skull ache, notwithstanding, though that was good too, in a way: proved he still *had* one, at least.

"You ladies just go on an' settle things amongst yourselves," he heard himself say, shakily, once more fighting to keep upright. "Don't . . . worry 'bout me. I'll juss wait it . . . out . . ."

Then he plunged forward, this time into Grandma's massive, lumpish arms, their sharp yet crumbly edges bruising him all over as she hoisted him. Telling him, inside his head: *Hush, fool. Take some of my strength, while the dead-speaker does what she must, with White Shell Girl and the salt-man's widow's help.*

Chess flopped in her grip like a fish, squirming 'til he fell back, betrayed by his own weakness—reduced to using harsh language, for lack of any better weapon. *Aw, save your "fool" you damn squaw-monster, 'specially since you never do put yourself out to learn folks' proper names, do ya? What is that, some sort'a Injun thing?*

A curl of alien laughter licked through him, excoriating even as it soothed—part of the service, possibly, since he did almost immediately feel a touch better. *You are a wonder,* Grandma admitted, reluctantly, while she rifled his mind with equally impolite "fingers," leaving nothing untouched. *Insulted by everything, always ready to fight; you revel in it, a beast in constant heat. No wonder the Enemy chose your shape to make War in, after the Lady sent you sowing death-in-life all along the Crack's length.*

Hey now, bitch, keep outta there! That stuff's private.

With a shoulder hitch, Grandma indicated the others, gathered back 'round that fire of theirs and raising a veritable storm of hexery as though they was spinning gold from straw in the old tale. Songbird and little Gabriel Love took centre place, with Yiska on one hand, Yancey the other, and everything going straight over into her like braided lightning. She was opening herself up, calling out to—Ed, he could only think, though he couldn't catch the words 'emselves, and felt a quick, silly surge of jealousy at the way the very idea of seeing Morrow enfleshed was making her flush.

Resign yourself, red boy, for nothing can be hidden now, Grandma told him, *not when you stand at the world's very turning pivot, as we all do—but you in particular, you Trickster-spawned trickster, most unreliable* Hataalii *of all. We stand between things. One world ends, almost certainly; this does not mean another will—or must—begin. You have blundered through this world rutting and killing, living and dying—doing only as you pleased and never counting the cost, to anyone. But now Balance itself hangs in the balance, so you must put away childish things, forever. You must be what you claim you are—a man—and act it, before it grows too late to matter.*

Something was gathering together while getting wider over there, even as they watched, bending the air like heat. Behind Yancey, or maybe in front of her—*around* her? Christ, but this shit was tricksy. His god-stints set aside, Chess truly didn't ever expect to understand magic, no matter how long he lived to keep on using it.

Maybe it just ain't in my nature, he thought, to which he "heard" Grandma snort.

And this is the worst of your folly, she replied. *You have only to think on my granddaughter, to see. Two-spirited like you, a born child of Begochiddy—and like you, too, she craves to ride and kill, to go where her heart pleases to take her, to* have *her way. Yet still she does her duty, for she at least knows to reckon her actions' cost to others. That you were raised without a tribe is a wound you did not ask to be given, but that you have never tried to* heal *that wound, or even wanted to try . . . this decision is yours to pay for or be repaid, in kind.*

Let me ask you this, Red Hair. Do you think the gods love, simply because they make? Do you think they must love what *they make?*

Chess shook his head, muzzily; felt her stone chest rake the side of his face, those uneven lumps she was using for tits all but drawing blood. *Not the gods I met. 'Sides which, love and me, we ain't exactly on good terms. I don't think nothin' "has" to love nothin', necessarily. And even if it does . . . that don't mean it won't hurt.*

Hmmm. Then, uneducated though you may be, you are smarter than that bilagaana *Reverend of yours, at least.*

He ain't my Reverend. Not anymore.

Yes, yes. Tell yourself that, if it helps.

Mutinous on his part, dismissive on hers—he felt like arguing it, but didn't have the strength. So fucking tapped out, an empty keg stuffed with nothing but the all-sorts dregs of a thousand previous hoorahs and just about to crack, no matter how sharply he drew on Grandma's bounty. Could feel how it was hurting her, too, but was frankly too exhausted to even enjoy it.

Is this it? he couldn't help but wonder. This? *Jesus.* Stupid Goddamn way to die . . . again.

Here something popped far off in the distance, mirrored by an ordnance-like boom in the foreground that made dust spray up 'tween him and Grandma and all the rest, a gigantic *huff*, like the entire world'd gasped for breath. And when it cleared, there was Ed Morrow's broad back with a darkie bluebelly and yet two more barefoot gals (hexes too, he could *smell* it on 'em) tight-arrayed all 'round, his long duster bloody and mud-smeared and tore down the back like ill-cut tails, so high you could see his suspenders.

By unintentional miracle, Ed himself had fetched up straight in front of Yancey, who was staring at him and grinning fit to bust, as though she'd gotten her Christmas present early. And Chess couldn't help but think he must be grinning back, since the next thing both of 'em did was to grab the other tight and go for each other mouth-first, so well-timed it was like they'd decided on it together as the best of all possible courses of action.

Well, that's that, Chess thought, feeling a touch grimmer than he'd expected to over the idea that whatever he'd had with Ed must be good and done with, given the evidence. At least 'til Ed pulled away at last, with reluctance, and looked around—for as their eyes met, the big Pinkerton man's all but gave out a flash of relief that would've been strong enough to knock Chess back a step, had he been standing.

"So you *are* here," Morrow said, grin not slackening a whit.

"Sure am," Chess answered, blinking a strange mist from his eyes. And levered himself up as Grandma let go, sliding to re-take his feet—only to be shocked when Morrow crossed the space between 'em with two long strides, caught him under both arms as though his weight was nothing (which, Christ knew, it might be) and swung Chess 'round child-high before planting a kiss almost as good as the one he'd given Yancey on him after all, all teeth and tongue, hugging him so hard he thought his chest might crack.

Once more, that scrim between them slid back, letting Morrow's ideas into Chess's head. *You Goddamned little creature*, he heard Ed think, incredulous. *Whoever would've thought I'd've missed you so much, so badly?*

Not me, I must admit, Chess thought back. *But I'm glad you did, all the same.*

Plucked and humming, Chess pushed back into it, determined to make the most of what was probably their last time together, even if Yancey was watching. But from the corner of his eye he saw her look on not too much appalled, if not exactly approving, while the two new hex-women and that black boy all kept their own eyes carefully elsewhere. Songbird studied her nail-sheaths, Sophy Love the skies; Yiska crossed her arms, and grinned too.

And Grandma simply waited it out, counting time. "If you are done with your greetings, soldier," she broke in, at last, "then there is work yet to be done. The red boy needs you, and your woman too. She will counsel you on your part, while the rest of us prepare."

Prepare for what? Chess wanted to ask, but that slump hit him one final time and he folded, this time onto Ed *and* Yancey, together. They knit their hands in his, hoisting in tandem to keep him at least half-aloft, and he was happy enough to let 'em.

". . . yes ma'am," he managed, finally, probably meaning it sarcastically, though the tone of his voice made it hard to tell. "Don't mind me." And slipped away.

ALMOST LITERALLY SLIPPED AWAY, he learned later on, after resurfacing.

"You came apart—dissolved, like sugar in water," Yancey told him, shuddering. "Just for a minute, thank God, 'fore Songbird and Grandma stepped in and—gathered you up, I s'pose, stuck you back together somehow, or what-have-you. But I swear, long as it lasted, it was like you were half *inside* us . . . me, anyways."

"No, me too," Morrow put in, with a shudder. "Goddamn disconcerting, I'll tell you what."

Chess squeezed his eyes tight, head still spinning. "Huh, don't say. Then I guess there was *somethin'* good about it, at least."

Which was worth it just to see Morrow get all pink around the ears, then grimace a bit in pain, squeezing his cut wrist into a pottery bowl Yiska'd scared up. On the other side, Yancey was doing much the same, stirring the result up with a murmur of *nahuatl* and a practical snap and flourish Chess didn't recall from the last couple of times he'd seen her do this same routine. Spilling blood in his name to root him to this world and trigger the power he drew from it, back at Bewelcome, back at Hoffstedt's Hoard—not that he wanted to think on that latter one too closely, even now.

"You're turned quite the little hexess now," he told her, hoping that counted as a compliment. And apparently it did, since she shrugged, but smiled doing it.

"Never that," she said. "Wouldn't get all too much if you fed off me, 'less you're doing it this way, remember? I'm just your priestess, like Ed here's your priest . . . and he won't be that for all too long either, probably, after we get that body of yours un-divinified again."

So crazed to be having this conversation, throwing 'round words like "god" in reference to himself, even after everything he'd already seen, or done: Chess Pargeter, whoreson and trigger-man, worth (on a good day) about as much as it cost to stock his gun or fill another man's bed. But then another thing struck him, odder yet, and cooled him to the core.

"'Body' . . ." he repeated. "So—if the Enemy's still got mine, then what the hell is *this* I'm ridin' 'round in?"

"A dream," offered Songbird, who'd been watching from the sidelines. Yiska nodded, and agreed: "The White Shell Girl has the right of it—you are spirit only, with nothing of the flesh about you at all, not blood nor bone nor breath."

"That don't help. What'm I made of, exactly?"

"Your own thoughts. So long as you believe you are, you are."

"So, in other words . . . if I really do fall asleep, I'm fucked."

Songbird snorted. "Look around you, English Oona's son; these are days of *wei-ch'i*, danger and opportunity both. How likely is it you will have time for that?"

Though Chess was damned if he knew, he opened his lips to answer nonetheless, only to have Yancey lay a finger 'cross them, stopping his mouth with worship-charged blood. The jolt hit him like a dose such as his Ma would've been proud to suck down, in her day—and when Ed tipped the rest of it up to his tongue, he drank greedily, feeling himself gain solidity with every fresh swallow. He shivered all down along his spine, curled his toes inside his boots and sent a dark red-green pulse back through 'em both as payment, sealing their wounds shut with new skin fine as corn silk.

Who says I don't pay my debts? Chess thought, semi-drunkenly. *Pay my way, at the least, when I'm asked to, or even if I ain't. And that's 'cause I don't want to owe nobody nothin', in this world or the next, if I can possibly help it.*

Grandma was starting in to jaw again, though, beckoning all parts of their odd little consort closer, so's they could formulate a plan of action. And though Chess didn't think it was likely she'd want his opinions on the matter, he drew up tall, blinking himself as awake as could be, under the circumstances—ready and willing to offer 'em, nonetheless.

"I have spoken with the dead northman's women," Grandma began, indicating those two hexes new-fled from Ixchel's City; "Glass-eyes Hank, the visioneer, as others called him. They tell me that neither expected to be able to do as they did in bringing *you*, soldier, and your fellow warrior—" She flipped a paw here at Carver, who looked damned uncomfortable indeed to find himself 'sconced up amongst such a freakish pack of circus-turns. "—from the battle's path. Not without their other sister-wife, at any rate."

"Clo," the lighter of the women offered. "She was always the strongest of us, 'sides from Hank himself; that's probably how the Lady was able to do . . . what she did, with her. Make her what she is now."

"And that'd be?" Chess asked.

"Bad," Morrow supplied. "Awful enough it'll take the whole lot of us to make a dent in that bitch's hide, and even then . . ." He shook his head. "Well, right now, I'm damn glad they were able to get you top-side again for better reasons than the usual—'cause ghost or no, you're just about the biggest gun we got."

Not that he wanted confirmation of Morrow's words, but flashes reached out from the big man nevertheless, whether Chess called 'em or no: a swooping, skull-faced creature with two fistfuls of razors, wigged in bells and wreathed in cold fire, tearing men seam from seam the way a hawk will mice; someone so horrifying that Ixchel was content to simply stand by as she did her will, picking her teeth. The idea that Chess, especially in his current state, could form any viable sort of opposition at all to such a creature would've seemed purely laughable, had it not been for the sadly hopeful look Ed was throwing his way—as though if Chess didn't suck as much blood as it took out of he and Yancey and step on up, even if he left 'em emptied in his wake, then everybody might as well either put up their hands and go home, or just shoot each other outright for good measure.

And how fucked are you, exactly, if that's so? Chess thought, stolen warmth deserting him somewhat, as his stomach thicked with cold. *How fucked are we* all, *for that matter?*

No point in asking, red boy, Grandma's pitiless mind-voice told him—and Yancey too, he suspected, from the way her eyes fell and her breath quickened, like she'd been caught peeping. *As I said, we stand at the crossroads—and these people, only, opt to fight with you, no matter the cost. Which is why they need as much hope as they can dream up for themselves.*

"There is a reason these women's powers have increased," Grandma said, aloud, before he could object, "and I think we all know it. In the wake of this morning's battle, the Crack has opened yet further, tearing Balance from balance, as threads cut crosswise destroy any fabric. It must be shut again before we have any hope of confronting the Mother of Hanged Men, let alone of defeating her—or the Enemy."

"And why do I think you already got some sort of plan in mind?" Morrow asked. But Yancey already had her brows knit, grey eyes all the paler for intent concentration.

"Songbird's wound-suturing," she said, at last. "We're gonna . . . what? Travel along the Crack itself, pouring in hexation like mortar, so we've already got the war half-fought by the time we arrive?"

Grandma inclined her "head," rock dust puffing quietly. "It will take all our effort," she confirmed. "My granddaughter will lead and guide, while the White Shell Girl and red boy unseam whatever infection keeps these lips from closing and lay down healing instead, as though spinning silk for a web—and though it is hardly in his nature to cure instead of kill, you will teach him, dead-speaker, even while shedding blood along with your soldier to keep him rooted here, until he can re-take what is his. Sophronia Love will do the same for her son, of course. And the others, Glass-eyes Hank's wives and this man who risked himself to free them—they will do their best to protect us on our journey, ending off whatever horrors slip through from Beneath." Turning, she addressed the rest once more, all at once: "Do I have your promises?"

Young Mister Carver exchanged a glance with the first witch-girl—*Berta*, something whispered behind Chess's eyes, in that way he'd finally brought himself to trust; other one was *Eulie*, casting her own eyes on Carver behind his back, unnoticed, and getting nothing but a squeeze on the hand from that "sister" of hers as reward. Yet he seemed to have made his mind up, all the same.

"Ma'am," he told Grandma, gruffly, touching hat and rifle-stock together, in an odd sort of improvised salute. "Don't know how much it'll help, me bein' only humanish—but given the stakes, I'll sure as hell do my best if I can't do any better, an' keep on 'til I can't do no more."

"You do us great honour, soldier," Yiska said, seeming to mean it. "A brave man is welcome always, no matter where he comes from."

Berta and Eulie turned Grandma's way. "Us too," Eulie said. "That's right, ain't it, sissy?"

"It is."

And so it went 'round the circle, faster and easier than Chess could ever in his life have suspected it would: Songbird (with a shrug for Yiska), Missus Love on her boy's behalf, Yancey and Ed, Yiska herself. By the time it came down to him, he felt almost guilty for hesitating—almost.

"What is it *you're* gonna be doin', meanwhile, while all this is goin' on?" he demanded, of his fellow not-ghost.

To which Grandma didn't quite shrug—her frame wouldn't support the movement required, he suspected—but answered, just the same: "Oh, one thing only, but without it . . . no plan, no hope, no chance at all. Better simply to lie down and let them walk on us. Ixchel, her demon and the Enemy, too."

So tell me, red boy, will you do your part or pout over some mistreatment while the rest die, along with all this world? Give me your vow as well, to stand with the others so long as they need you, and I will count myself well repaid for the sacrifice I am about to make.

Again, temper swept Chess up and down, pricking him all over: oddly pleasant, a tonic, raising his fever 'til he felt like he could ride bulls and throw cows. Making him snap back at her, if only inside his own head—

*Think I won't, you rattletrap? Well, maybe you ain't been payin'
attention: I'm Chess Pargeter, him who laid Mesach Love's town to waste
and brought it back, likewise; killed bluebellies, robbed trains and burned
homesteads groundward too, plenty times over, and that was long before
I even got myself hexified. So don't you dare think there's any damn thing
you name I can't do, I only put my mind to it.*

"Count me in," he told her, loud enough so's everyone in earshot
could hear. And saw her slab-face crinkle with just the slightest hint
of a smile, in return.

"Then I am answered. Yet now I must do something for which the
Old Drying Woman, this rock's protector, will be very angry with
me. And rightly so."

"Why?" Yiska asked, a hint of fear in her flat black eyes.

Grandma raised those four-fingered rakes she used for hands,
conjuring a flash between 'em might've made a blind man think
he could see once more. Replying, as everyone else cringed away:
"Because . . . of *this*."

ELSEWHERE, WHILE CLO STILL HARRIED the hex-train's
remains and Geyer, Asbury and Fitz Hugh Ludlow made their escape
from the Emperor's forces, Rook pulled Ixchel back up out of the
earth by her blood-fused topknot, and stood back a deferent pace
or two.

She spat mud, clearing her throat enough to snarl: *What did you
mean by this, little king? I gave no orders!*

Rook shrugged. "Sorry for that, ma'am; thought you might've not
wanted to be crushed, considering the difficulty you were already
expending to keep that body of yours intact. My mistake, and my
apologies." He glanced skyward. "But may I ask you to consider the
sun a moment? Most specifically, its position?"

Ixchel glared at him, but couldn't help a quick look, after which
she met his eyes with no less anger, but more uncertainty. *An hour
has passed? More? How have I lost this time?*

"I took you under the earth, Lady, to your sanctuary 'neath the
Temple," said Rook. "You were near gone as made no never-mind;

don't surprise me you didn't feel my sacrifices and supplications. Thought you might react better coming up where we went down."

He dared one more swift lick of power, murmuring an verse of Genesis he'd always liked—"THEN JACOB SAID UNTO HIS HOUSEHOLD, AND TO ALL THAT WERE WITH HIM . . . BE CLEAN."—and swept the mud and dirt from her in one warm caress of shimmering air, re-gathering the warmth into both hands only to offer it up, going on one knee, like it was the proposal they'd skipped altogether.

Eternal instinct, along with the brutal hunger of the moment, betrayed her. Within seconds she had seized the dully glowing mass and gulped it back, throat bulging like a bullfrog's.

Rook kept his head bent, carefully not thinking on the part of the verse he'd deliberately omitted: Therefore *Put away the strange gods that are among you.*

They had emerged before New Aztectlan's closed gates, *ceiba* forest wreckage stretching away to left and right. Rook signalled the sentries above, then turned to look back out over the plain. "If the scouts read things a'right, Lady, that Mex battalion should arrive 'fore sundown," he said. "They're still intent on playing coy, so might be I can convince them to stall an attack; depends on whether this *comandante* Delgado carries as big a stick as he claims to." He dusted his frock coat down by hand, not willing to draw more power, for risk of re-rousing Ixchel's appetite. "With your permission, I should go meet 'em alone, seeing how I've strength enough to meet treachery and clout enough to deal honestly—"

"No, husband," Ixchel interrupted; she'd recovered enough of herself that her voice sounded something like human once again, though sick-grating. "The *conquistador* soldiers can wait. There is another treachery to face, far closer to hand . . ."

Everything in Rook's guts froze up; he could *feel* the blood fall from his face. *Oh, shit,* was all he could think. Not now, not when the chance to act was so close! Besides which, he could have sworn she no longer had control enough to read him without him knowing it—

". . . that of my brother," she finished, at last.

Thank Christ.

Not looking back at Rook, she strode back into the City as its gates rumbled open. Which thankfully gave Rook a moment to master himself, before following.

He'd already sent word to the Council that all City-folk not directly involved in fighting take shelter, anyplace they could, and so far as he could see, that'd mostly held. But many—*too* many—were now emerging from their various hidey-holes to gawp down Main Avenue at the thing which'd forced itself up smack-dab centre in Temple Square, piercing that long, step-slatted black shadow like some foul bloom, spread sticky-wide and oozing with odd scent.

Not large, Rook saw, as he and Ixchel drew near, just a mound of Weed perhaps eight feet high and as many wide—verdant with new growth but slow-throbbing like some giant egg sac, fit to hatch any moment and pump out some fresh awfulness. Crimson flowers whirled, flared, folded all over, tiny mouths sucking hungrily with stamens and pistils alike fang-sharp at the hexation-rich air.

At the centre, the peak of its height, a tangle denser yet sketched a living, throne-like shape on which sat the Enemy, boneless-slouched as Chess himself might've, with one leg kicked over an arm of its living "chair" and its stolen head cocked on the opposite fist. It grinned down at them, slyly flirtatious.

"Took you long enough," it said.

Honourable Chu, Sal Followell and the Shoshone all faced the mound, aglow with power, though Rook smelled none of the acrid thunderbolt stink of witchery anger-loosed; not yet come to blows, then—simply skirmish-ready, even in the midst of battle. Meeting Chu's gaze, he nodded toward the busted-in wall, and saw that Celestial gentleman grimace in understanding. Lifting up airborne, he tapped his Injun partner on the shoulder as he did and waited for him to rise likewise, so they could hurtle back and fortify the breach before their newest enemies could take advantage.

Stepping into Chu's vacated place, Rook glared up at the second body-thieving god it'd been his misfortune to meet up with in as many years. "This your plan all along, then?" He demanded. "Draw us into a fight with the Pinks, make us spend our strength, wait 'til our defences were down so you could finally just up and walk in, ready to destroy us all?"

To this, however, the Smoking Mirror merely chuckled, raising one of Chess's red-gilt brows.

"Oh, Asher Rook," it told him, "if you have still so failed to grasp what I have in common with your beloved boy, the very thing which makes him *such* a perfect vessel, then perhaps you have never understood either of us, at all. For this is the truth: since, with both of us, intention always gives way to instinct, no action of ours ever can truly rise to the lofty level of something like a *plan*." Here it yawned, black shark teeth flashing, and added: "Besides which, as your minions here can tell you . . . I hardly *walked*."

"Thing come up through the ground, like a damn fever blister," Missus Followell cut in, angrily, "with Himself there riding it like his own personal cabriolet. And yeah, we all of us know *your* name, skin-changer, seein' there's one more like you told tales on in every place we hails from: coyote, crow, rabbit, spider, fox, whatever. But ain't a one of us gonna honour such as you by speakin' it, not 'less you *make* us."

Tezcatlipoca cut a parody of Chess's grin over at Ixchel—no cigar, yet well close enough to make Rook clench all over. "Such loyalty!" It complained. "How did you manage to win it, with so indifferent an investment? One more thing to credit that oh-so-able priest-king of yours with, perhaps."

A taunt, meant to draw ire, if not outright blood. Yet the Enemy's sister-mother-wife-and-all remained stock still, battered face showing not a hint of reaction—perhaps it *couldn't* move anymore, Rook thought, beyond the minimum needed for speech.

"Don't credit him alone!" Missus Followell snapped, fearless, without even a glance in Ixchel's direction. "This here's our place now, much as it is hers; we'll see you out of it yet, or die tryin', from the Rev on down. 'Cause that's what happens when hex can stand with hex, finally—and after thirty-odd years abloom, if anyone knows how that's worth bein' killed for, I'm her, believe you me."

"You almost speak as though *she* was of no consequence at all."

And . . . now those fierce eyes did drop, finally, as though Sal herself realized she'd maybe gone too far. For which Rook found himself surprisingly grateful.

"Wouldn't say that, no sir," she told her feet, choosing the words with care. "Without the Lady, there wouldn't be a City at all . . . we owe Her everything. That's why we keep the Oath, after all."

"Aaaah, yes. Your *Oath*."

Such a strange note in the creature's voice, neither mockery nor respect, but a strange amalgam of the two, with something else woven in beneath. A sort of yearning. Almost an envy.

Never had worshippers you didn't have to lie to, huh, Trickster? Though at least you compelled 'em with sweet words and pretty pictures personally, I'm sure, 'stead'a getting someone else to do that for you, like some others I might mention.

Over this same thought, however—as though summoned by even the implication of her name, let alone its mention—was where he at last heard Ixchel's voice intrude, hoarse yet clear, almost raw.

"'My' Oath is nothing new, brother . . . as you, like any of us, should know." Now it was her tone caught Rook off-guard, for she sounded almost as she had in those very first days, when she'd been nothing more than a voice in his head—all impassioned, seductive persuasion. "More than anything else, it is only the old agreement returned in new vestments. Sacrifice as sacrament, true devotion, instead of necessity. Though blood flows still for blood, power for power, the result is shared, sustainable. None *must* die, though they are glad enough to do so."

"As you are glad enough to let them, my love—of that, I am most certain."

Ixchel bowed her head, black cloud of hair falling only to drift upward once more, borne on a rising magical tide. "Surely. But *you* received your due share of *ixiptla*, gladly as any of us; *you*, too, flourished off the blood of those we now know to have been hexes-to-be, and like us all, worked wonders in return—preserving cities, renewing the land, shepherding the world through its seasons. Life for life, with pain the coin paid for existence. This has never changed and never will, since even the *conquistadors'* creed admits the same, with their White Christ dying to bring rebirth! And thus it is *we*, we two, who are the very . . . *gears* of this Machine of my husband's imaginings, its—*workings*, its . . . *motor. We* are the Blood Engine, ourselves." Struggling for proper words, she came as far forward as she could without setting foot onto the Weed, stretching one hand up. Her pithed voice broke, almost pleading, as if she wanted to weep.

"It is not too late," she told him. "Join me now, and all will be forgiven—we shall bring the Fourth World back or enter the Sixth, together. And it will be once more as it was, forever."

As her voice died away, a silence grew, hollowing Hex City's heart. Tezcatlipoca stared down at her; for once, his borrowed features wore no smile. Another clench of cold went through Rook— this thing was a liar, he had always known that. Might it change whatever passed for its mind, now, even on the very cusp? How rich a cosmic jape that would be: Chess's betrayer—himself—betrayed, in turn, by the inhabitant of Chess's stolen flesh.

"Oh, sister," the Enemy replied, almost in a whisper. "You *might* make it as it was, indeed, even now . . . but not forever. For just as nothing dead returns for long, nothing can last beyond its appointed time: not you, not me, not all our buried kin, drowned down there in darkness. Nothing."

"I do not—"

It sighed. "I know, I know. And still I will try to explain, much as I know it unlikely to help, before we do what we must.

"Listen. From First to Fourth, our worlds grew up around us—we were made and re-made *with* them, as *part* of them. All we ever were was a frightful tale, told so often and so well that all who heard, believed it—and we, ourselves, believed it so strongly that we *became* it. Of course we are the Blood Engine; that is what we were created to be, by the very mortals whose blood we drank to empower ourselves. Ghosts of dead magicians-to-be, grown so fat in turn on others' unexpressed magic that we warped the very world around us into our mirror, and looked to that mirror as 'proof' we were what we thought ourselves to be.

"So we gutted our people to glut ourselves, and grew so dependent on the Machine that when it collapsed—our weakened subjects shattered by the *conquistadors'* plagues, their guns and their greed, far swifter than we had ever imagined possible—most of us simply dissolved into oblivion. Which is as it should be. Because, as it has always been my role to proclaim, *all* things end."

Astonishingly, the Enemy's voice took on a note Rook had never heard before, from it *or* Chess: almost sympathetic. "Our time has gone, sister. What is to come will be different, taking place in a world much larger than ours ever was." It smiled. "I confess, I rather look forward to it."

Ixchel gaped up at him. "But doesn't it feel *right* to accept the tribute, brother? Doesn't it feel *good*?"

At that, Tezcatlipoca really did laugh, a hearty guffaw which threw its head back, making Rook's throat lock and his eyes burn— for that was *Chess's* laugh, pure and unalloyed, in all its nasty glee.

"Of course!" the Trickster-god declared, when its mirth had slackened enough to allow it. "Yet the mere fact that we *like* a thing doesn't make it the right choice. If it did, the world would run on fucking, and not precious victim-king-blood at all." And here the laughter ceased, as it whispered, eyes locked on hers: "Oh, but wait . . . perhaps it *does*."

A moment of silence, only one. Then Ixchel screamed, as much a bitter wail of grief as anything else; went charging up the Weed-slope, smashing the Enemy straight off its throne in a brute, inelegant tackle, strategy-stupid as any drink-addled groggery thug. They rolled over and down, coming to a tangled halt almost at Rook's feet. He goggled at the dustup, while behind him the City-folk hollered half in horror, half hysteria, like onlookers in any given saloon brawl he'd ever seen.

Ixchel got one leg between Tezcatlipoca's—Chess's—knees, and kicked him off, bodily. He cartwheeled through the air only to light down standing, conjuring something out of his palm with a fluid movement: long and thin, shining white, a scaled whip spun from congealed lightning ending in a snake's crack-jawed head. The creature writhed tail-end from the Enemy's hand, looped 'round its knuckles, blind skull splitting wide to reveal two layers of yellowed ivory fangs which dripped smoking liquid in time with its own teakettle hiss.

Rook braced for its next move, fingers popping with black and silver print, random words fizzing 'tween his nails like firework sparks: HE THE LORD DO NOT SAIETH WRATH END RUIN—

But before he could even consider striking, however, the Smoking Mirror had already lashed out, throwing that snake like a vaquero's rawhide—whipping an arc which sliced cleanly through Ixchel's vessel's neck as though every scale were diamond-edged, sending her head to bounce on the ground once, twice, 'til it fell over, eyes staring sidelong. The headless body dropped to its knees and held there, balanced, same as a coin fallen miraculously on edge.

Rook's legs folded under him, as if all his strength had simply decided *enough*, and shut itself off; he thudded to the ground beside Ixchel's popped-off skull, knees on fire, wondering if death was 'bout to seize him, too.

But not so much, no. For in the world they now shared, as already established, death did not mean as much as it otherwise might.

Instead, Ixchel's eyes rolled to meet his, dread stare strangling a half-born shriek in Rook's throat; she bit into her own lower lip and chewed, almost hard enough to sever it.

With black syrupy blood pouring down her chin, her impossible voice pounded into the Rev's head, rail spike deep: ***Fool! He thinks to show me weak—prove him wrong!***

Overcome by a dreamlike detachment, Rook somehow knew what to do without even asking—so he picked the head up by its tresses, coated his palm with blood and smeared it over the neck stump like caulking, then lofted it in a hexation-boosted throw toward the kneeling body, where it landed angled so as best to set vertebra to vertebra, neat as you please. While the smoking blood sealed together like boiling oil cut with molasses, Ixchel heaved herself to her feet, black-shrouded in counter-luminance.

Through jaws clenched so tight Rook thought they might have fused likewise, she grated out, "Not enough, brother. Not nearly enough."

The grin the Enemy gifted her with, in return, seemed to rock ground and sky at once: purest berserkery, without any of Chess's usual sense that no matter what, he *would* survive. This was a grimace which risked everything, at once utterly aware and utterly unafraid of mortality—its own, obviously, along with everyone else's.

Very well, then, sister, it replied. *We start over, though not in the way you mean.*

And as she blinked her slow, dead lids at him, not understanding, Rook saw the Weed around him begin to flex, to stir . . . to *grow*.

Too soon, Rook thought, desperately. *Christ Jesus Almighty blast other gods small and large alike, altogether! Too Goddamn soon, entirely.*

He slid a hand into one pocket, reaching for the token he'd hid there: just a dried spruce wand, nothing to look at, a mere peeled twig—but trigger, nonetheless, for the mightiest spell Rook'd yet devised, so powerful he'd had to work it in careful stages throughout the night while Ixchel slept, weaving it into the wards over the entire City and tying its activation to a single, simple physical event, for fear she'd sense its presence. Worthless, perhaps, depending—yet it was all he had. So he braced his thumb on the wand's middle and pushed, felt it bend . . .

Then froze, as did both undead gods and all their watchers, as a sharp and steely call stabbed into every mind within the City's walls. It had no words, only the simplest possible meaning—

Danger comes! Danger! To the East Gates!

A voiceless "voice" that carried the Honourable Chu's unmistakeable harsh tones. And simultaneous with it, something else: a vibrant pulse, so deep as to be felt more than heard, the lowest string of some Titan's harp plucked once and then again, each note just slightly louder. Sal Followell turned at its call, shoulders hunched and eyes wide to their whites, her fear freighted with an awful fatigue, thirty years' worth of disasters in the making: *What now, for all God's love? What next?*

"What . . . is *that*?" Ixchel rasped, echoing her, all unawares. And addressing the question neither to Rook nor any other human but to her fellow petty deity, with all the casual thoughtlessness of kin before strangers, as if their duel was already forgotten.

Rook, too intent to feel insulted, was already whipping back a reply to Chu, along the same channels: *Mexes here already, that it? Laying down fire, preparatory to attack?*

No. They are *here—but—*

A most curious sensation: Chu's mind went blank and grey, an empty sheet, as if sheer bewilderment precluded any coherent image. And almost simultaneously, the Enemy's next words wiped Rook's own mind equally blank, as it observed: *Aha, I see. Interesting, indeed. The Crack . . . is closing.*

Soft, and so awed that even the god's infuriating sly glee had faded; the lightning-snake danced forgotten on its wielder's palm, finally folding back inside once Tezcatlipoca remembered it the way a frog's tongue retracts.

Impossible! Ixchel burst out, to which the other only shrugged.

And yet, it replied, dryly. *Your yellow ancient sees it, from where he sits. Only wait long enough, look hard, and it will become clear to us all. Can you not feel the stitchery, rucking this crust beneath us like skin? Somewhere, someone—and I think we both know who—is sewing the grievous wound we gave this New World up.*

Against her will, Ixchel turned; Rook did the same, with everyone else soon following. Even as their attention shifted, meanwhile, the Enemy vanished in a thunderclap of collapsing air, only to instantly reappear as a speck perched upon the eastern wall itself—poised to peer down upon the tide of City-folk who were flooding that-a-way already, in response to Chu's call. With a silent curse, Rook released the trigger-wand, then offered that same hand to Sal, with the other threading Ixchel's cold fingers. A silent twist of will was all it took to send 'em hurtling over the crowd's heads as well, touching down at Chu's side atop the main Eastern gate.

A quick scan gave him the Mex battalion in mid-march, trailing southward from Bewelcome, though slowed somewhat by the wreckage remaining 'round hastily abandoned Camp Pink. Here and there, what wounded they found still living were being collected, hauled back to the medical supply wagons. But those thundering drumbeat vibrations continued rolling through the ground, and all movement quickly ceased. Even at this distance, Rook could hear faint yells and oaths, saw the soldiers reel back, pointing upward— breaking and running, some of 'em, at the simple advance of whatever massive *thing* was slowly heaving itself over the hilltops of the eastern horizon, its mere shadow so immense it spilled 'cross the dirt like a second night.

The hell? Rook wondered, agape. Then waited, already braced 'gainst the tidal wave to come, to find out.

AFTER LESS THAN half an hour's fast march from the battleground, Geyer had called halt in the middle of one of many narrow valleys winding through the eastern hills. How he knew their route Ludlow could never tell, since all this terrain looked alike to him, but was both grateful and relieved, having taken ever more of Doctor Asbury's weight as they marched; indeed, Ludlow was not entirely sure that the arcanologist was even conscious, at this point.

Within minutes, the first of the Texican outriders had spotted their position, and rode to meet them. These men's complete lack of any uniform, or consistency in gear, made Ludlow blink. A half dozen wore garb which ranged from Alamo buckskins to Mexican serapes, some going sombreroed and moccasined, others coonskin-capped and booted, while one sported a bloodstained grey Confederate officer's shell coat. Their arms and gear seemed equally potluck, including pistols and rifles and shotguns of a dozen different makes. The scouts' leader—a short, hawk-nosed ruffian who looked more than half-Mex, himself—introduced himself as Sergeant Juan Alvarez, then sent the fake secesh hotfoot back to the main force, before breaking out brandy and provisions to revive the weary travellers.

They debriefed as they ate, between chews, and Alvarez listened, expressionless. Ludlow found he truly couldn't tell if the man took their reports seriously, or was just waiting to see when they'd start to rave outright. Since Geyer had led by recounting the morning's events with due professional flatness, Ludlow'd strained to follow suit, deliberately leaching all trace of hyperbole from his own interpolations . . . yet the tale still spoke for itself, outrageous as ever. When they finished, Alvarez's only response was to stroke his moustache in ruminative silence.

"All this *brujeria*," he said abruptly. "None of it came *with* the Mexicans, *ay*? Just that Lady and her kin, who the earthquake loosed from Hell." Geyer and Ludlow looked first at each other then back to him, and nodded, almost in unison. Heartened, Alvarez turned next to Asbury, whose cheeks had finally regained some colour after a few long swigs. "And you, Doctor—what's left in your bag of tricks to help keep the *maleficios* off our backs, exactly, while we make for Hex City?"

Asbury blinked. "I—very little, sir," he admitted. "I have a Manifold, of course, to ward off active spells, and my aetheric screen for concealment, but nothing else . . . nothing functional, at any rate. Though if more were recovered from Pinkerton's leavings, I suppose I *could* try to—" Adding hastily, at the Sergeant's scowl: "But truly, I do not believe that will be necessary. The Emperor's stated goal is to 'liberate his people therein enslaved.' Any obstacle we pose to that objective is likelier, I think, to enjoy New Aztectlan's approval, rather than the reverse."

"Sounds good, but men don't always think clear in battle," Alvarez pointed out. "And for all I know, the *jefes* got secret orders to do some damn fool thing like turn us toward Hex City once we whup the Mexes, or even if we don't."

"Not this time, Sergeant," Geyer replied. "George Thiel knows the score, and he's no fool. He'll convince your Captain, just like we did you. Besides . . . strikes me if you thought we were complete lunatics, you wouldn't have wasted time on us at all, let alone served us private stock. Am I wrong?"

Alvarez fell to petting on his moustache again, like he thought if he only stroked it long enough, it might give him sage advice.

"Captain Farris and your Mister Thiel should be catching us up soon enough," he said, presently, "'long with the rest of the troops—and though we ain't got time to stop, we got spare horses. Man can listen and ride at the same time, you want to argue at me further."

Asbury's face fell, like Babylon. "No, please—must we go *back*? We are not a mile from the battlefield, even now! Mister Geyer I can understand, but Mister Ludlow and I can surely be of no further use to you, only burdening your quartermasters to no good purpose."

"Don't sell yourself short, Doc," Geyer said. "Risked myself plenty to get you out of Camp Pink intact—don't you think there might've been some point to the exercise, beyond simple human compassion?"

"Well, yes, certainly; I assumed as much. But . . ." Here the Professor trailed off, stared past Alvarez, blinking. "Sergeant—is that *your* man now, returning?"

Ludlow traced the glance, even as Alvarez shifted to confirm Asbury's reckoning. Yes, it was indeed Shell-coat, taking it at a gallop and waving his hat fiercely while he did, as if to drive them back, though his accompanying yells were still too distant for sense. But his horse-hooves' thunder kept on swelling, 'til Ludlow realized the vibration he "thought" he felt welling up through his boots was no fantasy. Behind, meanwhile, yet more horses carrying unfamiliar riders flooded into the valley in a torrent, scattering cold grey dust in their wake, and surged down the narrow path at a perilous angle—like they were too shit-scared *not* to risk dashing 'emselves to death on the arroyo's looming sides, veteran cavalry or no, alongside the threat of breaking their mounts' precious legs, in the bargain.

"Clear away!" Alvarez shouted, jumping straight up, jackrabbit-style; Geyer, Ludlow and Asbury obeyed with alacrity, scrambling out of the troops' way in flummoxed alarm, even as one of the few clearly uniformed men—a blue-jacketed lieutenant—pulled up to shout unintelligibly in Alvarez's ear while the rest of the Texican troop roiled past. Ludlow gaped, the beat beneath his feet increasing further, a dull volley of rhythmic hammer-blows: slow, strange, implacable. Louder, and louder, and *louder*—

"Holy Christ and all His Apostles plus sweet Saint Michael, too!" screamed Geyer, pointing back over Ludlow's shoulder, face gone white. Ludlow spun and promptly collapsed, knees instantaneously slack; Asbury blinked wetly up at the sight, eyes full of a similar horror, though leavened with an unremitting awe—a shock so intense, so monumental, it almost rang as joy.

The shape which reared up over the furthest visible hill and plunged down on one side of the valley was a gigantic black column furred with ship's-cable hairs and glinting with chitinous armour plates, towering what had to be close to threescore yards into the sky. It was followed seconds after by a second such pillar, equally massive, which hit ground on the defile's other side with the same sort of hissing, hydraulic-powered crash—then another on the left, another to the right—the speed with which arrangements moved was near-incomprehensible, for their multi-jointed size. Above, a vast black ovoid shape cut off the cold grey sunlight, drowning them in freezing shadow; a fifth and sixth column touched down, even as the first two lifted and reached forward again. High above, multiple sets of eye-spheres like obsidian boulders glittered in twin rows; mandibles the size of stalactites shone, flint-sharp and venom-sheened.

The dusty, musky *smell* of the thing rolled over them in a wave, strong enough to send Ludlow jackknifed over, retching up his recent refreshments. Beneath the creature, every horse in the valley screamed and reared together, slamming into one another in panic, sending their riders falling. Ludlow curled in on himself, arms over his head; what use dignity now? Surely this was the Apocalypse, and demon-monsters walked the Earth!

Welcome as grace in Hell, the sunlight fell free upon him once again as the gargantuan spider-beast moved on, too-many legs navigating the terrain's rises and drops faultlessly, better than any four-shod steed, and far, far faster. Its booming footsteps carried it almost straight along the same path Ludlow, Geyer and Asbury had come to get here—back toward New Aztectlan, quick and sure and dreadful. And much though he knew that evil place's inhabitants had all long since cut their teeth on horrors, Ludlow couldn't help but hope that even they might be taken aback, when *this* abomination finally hove in sight.

As Ludlow blinked after, however—wiping at his lips, then spitting one last bilious mouthful at his own feet—he finally perceived what threatened to shatter his sanity altogether. There were *people* clinging onto the creature's back; perhaps a dozen. Minuscule figures, only visible for their lightness against the spider's dark, but *there*.

Treating it, Good Lord, like it was some sort of *mount*. An island-sized elephant, without even the regulation howdah to keep them seated.

What sort of unholy sons of bitches . . . ?

At which point, peering yet closer, he made out that one of them might have red hair and a purple coat—and knew.

Geyer, whitened and dumbstruck, seemed to've seen it too. But Asbury simply stood there with tears rolling down his face, unable to distinguish spider from riders.

And quoted to himself, huskily, from *Job*—*"Gird up now thy loins like a man; for I will demand of thee, and answer thou me. Where wast thou, when I laid the foundations of the Earth? Declare, if thou hast understanding."*

ONLY A SECOND OR so after Grandma was done talking, Old Woman Butte shook itself under Chess's feet like a dreaming dog, so fierce it hurt even his semi-substantial flesh. He grabbed for Morrow's and Yancey's shoulders at once, too stunned to curse. Beneath the circle gathered atop the Butte, the ground turned black, empty as the Crack itself, though no one fell inside. Grandma stood unmoving, rock-paw hands still lifted to the sky; Chess looked up to see charcoal-coloured clouds corkscrewing around them, same way they had when the twister that'd been Ash Rook's first miracle blew up.

"We're *lifting!*" Carver hollered, petrified, wide eyes casting 'round in every direction. Chess glanced east, sized up the horizon and the sun's height with a marksman's instinctive sense of range, and saw the bluebelly was right—whatever the old Diné bitch had conjured, it was rising straight out of the Butte, bringing them along with it. The stuff they stood on no longer felt like stone, or even dirt—gone horridly soft, almost squelchy, like some overstuffed goose down mattress soaked in tar.

Morrow on his left hand, Yancey his right—they wrapped arms 'round him to get at each other, and damn, if he wasn't well content to let 'em. Songbird (typically) had taken to the air at the first sign of trouble, hovering nevertheless beside Yiska, as if tethered; Sophy Love clutched wailing Master Gabriel tight, straining not to stagger, while Berta and Eulie clung close to Carver in their turn, like schoolgirls in a rainstorm.

Higher and higher the curving black mound rose, its yielding surface hardening underfoot, cracking and splitting as it befurred itself with bristling hairs. Eight massive ropes of tarry black hex-matter shot out and downward, each bending up at the same time into a joint that rose above them. The great black blimp-bag contracted amidships, swelling into two sections like some fat saloon gal, corseted tight. Lightning flashed and flickered, painting them all with hissing, variegated lights.

And then, with a final thunderclap, the storm clouds broke at last, washed away. The winter sunlight poured down over them; with a groan, Chess squinted 'gainst it, feeling it stab straight through his head.

Songbird whispered something in Chink-jabber Chess couldn't spare the mojo to translate, though its sense was clear enough— finally, here was an event so crazed as to impress even her. Missus Love had given up trying to stand, and lay curled on her side, protecting Gabriel, saucer-eyed. Eulie and Berta dared a few cautious steps away from Carver, toward the edges of this living platform, but the moment they did the young Negro soldier almost collapsed.

He gawped 'cross at Morrow, who raised his eyebrows, as though to say: *Yeah, it's what you think it is, but what're we gonna do about it?*

Yet Carver stammered all the same, as if the words were being dragged out of him: "Ed, this . . . this is a . . . we're—we're on a giant . . ."

"A servant of *Na'ashjéii Asdzáá*, the Spider Who Weaves All, yes," cut in Yiska, not quite brusquely enough to mask her own astonishment. She turned to Grandma, who had not lowered her massive stone arms, and managed a laugh. "Spinner, this working of yours will live in the songs until the end of the Age! To summon a Weaver alone, without even a living body to command—I will write your song myself! I will . . ." She trailed off, smile fading. "Spinner?"

The great figure still had not moved: arms upheld, its flat stone face immobile. Suddenly, Chess saw clearly all the separate pieces of bone and granite that made "Grandma" up, as if he'd never grasped before just how patchwork a construction it really was. One fell from its place, soon followed by another, with a gritty, grinding noise, coming apart by degrees. Then, with a rending crash, Grandma's fossil-golem body collapsed, resolving into a mound of broken shards atop the titan arachnidan shell.

"Finished," Yiska said, to no one in particular. "As you knew you would be, after such effort. Oh, Grandmother mine: I will remember you, always. I, and all others who benefit from your sacrifice here, your re-Balancing."

Songbird goggled, far as her squinched eyes would let her. "We *needed* her!" she complained, finally.

"But we have you," Yiska pointed out, matter-of-fact as ever. "And Gabriel Love. And, best of all . . ."

As one, they swivelled to look at Chess, significantly. Prompting the man himself to mutter, in turn—or perhaps just to think, not that there was all that much distinction 'tween the two these days: *Great.*

Yiska knelt to rap on the spider's carapace, hard, like she was ordering up a hansom. "Follow the Crack," she told it. "To its end. To Hex City."

THE MAGIC THAT HELD UP the spider-titan's astonishing size ate the ground in mighty blurring leaps, moving so fast most of the riders had to flop down and grip the shell hairs death-tight to keep from flying off. The smeared-looking landscape shifted beneath them, wrenching at Chess's missing guts. He looked backward once, and saw ribbons of liquid light trailing out behind them from the creature's spinnerets, a cascade of red-gold and blue-green energies twining together as they stitched themselves into the earth. Behind the spider's eyes, Yiska, Sophy Love's babe and Songbird had wrapped themselves together, wove deep in their own power web, guiding this living shuttle as it knitted the world's tapestry back together.

A few minutes' watching was enough; Chess closed his own eyes, and held on grimly. He felt the closing Crack in every quarter, a boxcar door pressing him on all sides at once; every inch it narrowed made the world he clung to stabler, but also thinned away the raw hexation cloud feeding what scant substance he had left. So rather than lament, he set himself to the menial, painstaking work of drawing in every shred of it he could, a weaver's prentice sweeping scraps from the loom.

Miles passed in minutes, slowing as they closed in on the City, and the depth of the wound being healed grew by fathoms. Before Chess knew it, they were passing what had to be the Texican troop at speed, then onto the battlefield, where a hollering battalion of Mexes were just rushing the walls—the eastern gate, outside which Clo Killeen's mortal remains kept vigil, while Ixchel Rainbow and her Enemy watched from its already cracked ramparts. It was a sight which sent Chess's whole being humming with lightning-fed ire.

Two more magicians stood with his Enemy and Enemy's enemy alike, one Injun, one Chinee. The larger of whom turned now to the smaller, observing, "See—I *told* you it was spiders."

"Hmp," was all the Chinaman—"Honourable Chu," Chess's hex-sense named him—had to say, in return.

THOUGH FIRE-SCORCHED AND HALFWAY levelled, the defensive ring of black stone *ceiba* trees had one last trick to play, rearing back to vicious life soon as the colossal spider's legs touched down within 'em—lashing out with razor-edge branches to trap and score the chitinous limbs, making them spill viscous, steaming liquid. The spider gave a shriek like a ruptured boiler and slowed, staggering from side to side as it kicked its way free, only to be grappled once more; trees shattered glassily under its flailing limbs, widening the path of devastation. Morrow fisted a hand in the spider's hairs, the other gripping Yancey's so hard he'd have feared to hurt her, if her grip hadn't been so equally tight on his, and held on for dear life. For a moment, he saw himself rodeo-ing atop two huge broncos roped together, with laughter bubbling like vomit in his throat.

While the careening spider spun nearly all the way about, Morrow risked a look back at the battlefield, and gulped again. Taking advantage of the path being cleared for them, the Mexes were already racing for the breach—no lack of balls, this *comandante*, though perhaps an egregious lack of brains. Morrow opened his mouth to shout a warning, but found Yancey already there before him.

Yiska—company comin'! Her psychic shout spiked through both Morrow's temples, and he bit down on a yelp; judging by Yiska's wince, it hadn't been ticklesome for her, either. *Gotta get through that gate first, and fast!*

Yiska nodded, turning back to Songbird and Sophy Love. The three put their hands to the spider's shell, Gabriel's clasped in his mother's—and while no light or sound ensued, nothing Morrow could feel, Yancey abruptly shuddered head to toe, while Berta, Eulie and Carver yelled out as one. The spider wrenched itself 'round, ignoring its wounds, and cannoned straight at New Aztectlan's granite walls.

The forest, however, was still not quite defeated. Less than a score of yards away from impact, one of the largest *ceibas* of all physically tore itself out of the ground, cracking its trunk into twin obsidian scissor-blades and shearing off the spider's right foreleg at the lowest joint, with enough force to shatter itself. The spider lurched rightward into a sharp turn, stumbling parallel with the wall, ruined leg curling up useless as colourless mucus gushed out.

This violent and sudden dip brought Morrow level enough with those atop the walls to watch shock equal to his own race 'cross their faces—all but the Enemy, that was, who just gave an appreciative little nod.

Though Morrow wasn't sure if such things felt pain the way humans—or even animals—did, the spider did seem peeved to find itself thus crippled, for all it had seven other legs to work with. Which might be why it presented those horrible mandibles like a pair of ox-horns, and let loose with a spray of smoking poison all down Hex City's barricades. Hexes and small-folk alike jumped back, some with not quite enough alacrity to avoid being spattered; screams rose up, prompting the Lady to swear in Old Mex and "shout" over at Clo, who was presently engaged in playing hawk-on-doves with the first line of the Mexican charge—her mind-voice a desert wind whipped loud enough to dry everyone else's thoughts up in their skulls.

To me, daughter! I need your aid!

Mother, yes: I come again, and gladly, for there is little sport for me out here, with these puling men and horses. Give me epic blood to shed, I beg you.

Will ichor do?

Oh Jesus: and here she came, blazing the sky, fatal as any comet.

"*Agent Morrow!*" yelled Berta, scrabbling across the spider's back toward the edge while Carver and Eulie followed, both aghast. "I'll distract Clo, while you and Missus Kloves get Pargeter in place! As for the rest, you three—" she nodded at Yiska and her mates "—get in however you can, and find the Moon Court; Herself's probably got all her Mex-slaves there, charging her up. Eulie, I'm trusting you to guide 'em in."

Eulie nodded, eyes tearing. "I'll do it, honey. For you."

"For *all* of us, you mean. Hank, too. And what's left of Clo, likewise."

"Yes, sissy. I love—"

"Me too."

With a quick kiss to her "sister's" brow, she turned, crouching to leap—only to be hauled rudely back by the ankle, on her first attempt; Private Carver shouted into the wind, holding tight, perhaps trying to suggest alternatives. But Miss Berta, floating free above, only laughed.

"You're sweet, Private," she called back, loud enough so's all could hear—then dove in to kiss him too, a short, intense buss which set him on his heels, blinking. Adding: "If I can, I'll see you after!"

"And if you *can't?*"

"Then I won't."

Without anything further, then, she was gone over the side in a flap of petticoats, hurtling fast toward death or glory. Eulie dashed salt water from both cheeks, and told Morrow, voice strained near to breaking: "Best get goin', then, Goddamnit. Take him, her—"

"I heard, gal. Jonas! Keep this one safe."

Carver, still staring after Berta, drew himself up. "I aim to, Ed," he replied.

Yiska shouted commands in her own tongue, and as the spider hauled itself up—flung its entire massive bulk straight at the gate—Morrow took hold of Yancey, who took hold of Chess, who took hold of them both. The world thundered, roaring with the crash of fractured stone and splitting wood, screams of men and women, crack and gush of broken chitin.

As one, they closed their eyes, and jumped.

AND LET THIS BE *a lesson*, Fitz Hugh Ludlow thought, disjointedly, as he drew up his lathered, panting mount at the plain's edge. *There's some men don't need spit and polish to prove their discipline . . . or courage.*

Captain Charles Farris, with Thiel at his side, had rallied the Texican cavaliers more quickly than Ludlow would have believed before seeing it, bawling orders that got them into what seemed a mere semblance of a line—but one that never stumbled over itself, or slowed, even while following the spider's apocalyptically destructive trail. Sergeant Alvarez found mounts for Ludlow, Geyer and Asbury, giving none of them any chance to beg off before they too were caught up, swept along in the wake of far more expert riders; in what seemed like minutes, they were almost level with the creature's rearmost shadow. Clinging haphazardly to his horse's back, Ludlow strained to take notes in his mind even as he urged his steed to a gallop. None would ever believe his account, after all, if he could not tell it proper—but then again, this tangled cascade of events would probably defeat most readers, no matter how it was organized.

The arachnid behemoth, one leg foreshortened and useless, half-climbed, half-crushed the City's main gates, cracking the big wooden doors off their hinges in several pieces. Its legs flailed for a moment before several minuscule figures took to the air above—Ludlow thought he saw the blue tunic of the Chinaman named "Honourable," though he spotted neither Ixchel or Huitzilopochtli's nightmare figure—to fling lashes of power down on the spider's towering mass, blasting it so badly it slipped and belly-flopped atop the mound of collapsed rock. And then, as it staggered back, the death's angel shape of Clodagh Killeen fell burning out of the sky, straight for that narrow join where thorax met abdomen.

Half an instant before impact, a ribbon of light lassoed Killeen's ankle, just sudden enough to re-stave the star-demon's trajectory into the ground; she struck with a thud Ludlow swore he could feel where he sat, spurring old reflexes—he rummaged in his bag, hauled out his spyglass and opened it, almost jabbing one eye out in his haste. Back-tracing this latter hex-work back to its originator, he saw Missus Fennig Number Two, Berta Schemerhorne, drift sky-high over the spider, tapestries of shimmering air trailing from her fingers. Back down, and there was Killeen again, rising unhurt from the pit she'd carved on impact, fang-forested jaws yawning in hungry fury to pay blow for blow, hurt for hurt.

NO! Though Ludlow could see Ixchel nowhere, that voice—spectral, inhuman, enraged—was unmistakeable. *KILL THE BEAST! THIS ALONE MATTERS!*

Clo screeched in reply and changed course again, dropping back down onto the spider—then commenced ripping and shredding its back open with both clawed fists, efficiently as she'd torn wide Asbury's Ironclad. The spider reared, shrieking, and overbalanced; fell upturned with a terrifying *crunch*, all its legs flailing at the air at once.

But now it was Berta's turn to hawk-plunge, stooping on Clodagh like some crazed embroiderer set to undo all her life's stitchery in a night. She threw out hooks and nets, razor-edged, which sliced through Clo's shroud of flame to take off hands, lower legs, and in one strike chop off an arc of skull, as if opening a hard-boiled egg. Clo's only response was to slap her own amputated limbs back on, squashing them into place like potter's clay, seeming more inconvenienced than hurt. But Berta's spells kept coming all the same, tangling Clo up in knots of power, slowing her progress. The spider, forgotten, righted itself, and went stumbling for the wall again.

Suddenly, Ixchel burst into existence in the air above Berta, flinging a boulder-sized sphere of flame at her. Though Berta dodged, the missile erupted, flashing the sky scarlet; back-punched by the blast, Berta's spread-eagled form could be glimpsed hurtling away into the City itself with her burning hair trailing smoke, 'til she arced down to vanish amongst the buildings.

A second lash of hexacious might shredded the spell-webs entangling Clo, freeing the demon-girl to fall upon the spider again. Within seconds, she had bitten through and burrowed wholly *inside* the monstrous creature's shell, vanishing from sight. At the same time, Ixchel twisted in the air and disappeared into herself, likewise gone.

"Gonna stand there gawping all day?" Geyer's yell went off practically in his ear. Ludlow nearly screamed, dropping his spyglass, while the former Pink reined up beside him, Doctor Asbury gasping miserably behind. "C'mon, scrivener—wall's down. We need to get in there."

"What in hell *for*?" Ludlow shouted back.

"Stop American citizens dying, for a start! Not to mention if it *was* Chess Pargeter riding that beast, then Ed Morrow's surely here, too; Missus Kloves as well, I'd bet. So I'm not leaving friends to lay their lives down alone, 'specially if might be I could help." He gave Ludlow the stink-eye, cold and sidelong. "Now, you can be a man and stand with us, or you can be a vulture and hang back to make your living off the ruin—you decide."

Not waiting for a response, Geyer snapped his reins; with a whinny, his chestnut gelding plunged down the slope. Asbury shot Geyer a helpless shrug, then followed. Ludlow watched them go, clenching his fists.

Hell, he thought. *To be shamed into foolishness, and at my age.*

Swearing, he kicked his heels into his horse's sweat-lathered sides and rode after, leaving his dropped spyglass to gleam brassily in the dirt behind.

TOO GODDAMN FAMILIAR ENTIRELY, this queasy, weightless feeling of falling to earth in the grasp of something mostly air and wishing. Clutched to Chess by both arms, Yancey and Morrow touched down just inside the walls of New Aztectlan, hitting the ground just north of where a swathe of spider-bred rubble had crushed half a dozen adobe-bricked huts; the farthest still stood mostly intact, and Morrow lunged into it the instant his boots touched earth, dragging Yancey and Chess after him. He pulled them in and ducked down, eyes kept fixed on the hexes atop the walls, as they battered the spider back by degrees.

Any inclination Yancey might've had to carp about being manhandled vanished on making contact with the ground. The twisting cramp that knotted her stomach, pain-vise clamping her head simultaneously, dragged out a startled groan; Chess caught it, quick as ever, and scowled.

"Wondered how this place'd take you, you finally got here," he said. "Can you stand it?"

Yancey braced her hands on a fallen pile of bricks—they held her weight, but felt queerly thin to touch, like spun sugar—and fought to winch her shields back up. "Christ in Heaven, feels like if I jumped up too high, I'd fall straight through the ground coming down. Can't they sense how torn up it all is, here? How can they even breathe? There's . . . almost nothing *real* left. Anywhere." She cringed, as more screams and explosions echoed from outside.

"Feels like tryin' to swim a tub of molasses," Chess agreed, jaw clenched—then added, with a half-grin: "When I'm in over my head. And it's boiling."

"None of us got any Oath protecting us," Morrow suggested. "For me, that don't matter. You two, though . . ." He trailed off, clearly unable to think of any ending didn't make him unhappy. Chess moved forward to join him, hunkering down behind the pile of rubble, then rabbit-rising to squint over the top.

"Anyone see us?"

Morrow shook his head. "Think we got away with it. Not that that's gonna make a difference, in a minute." He slipped the knife from his belt. "If I'm getting to understand this shit at all, seems like the minute we start this, Herself'll know it—and her big brother, too. How much time are we gonna have before she shows up, to make her point about it?"

Yancey shrugged. "She can get to us pretty much instantly, wherever we are; don't expect it matters, aside from we're within the walls."

Chess nodded. "'Sides which, we *want* 'em to come, don't we? So I can put an end to this, if I can."

"Yeah, *if*," Morrow muttered. For which Chess couldn't blame him.

"We'll have as long's we have, Ed," he concluded. "Let's just get it damn well done."

Yancey nodded, and held out her wrist, matching Morrow's gaze with her own. From outside came another mighty crash—some other part of the walls going down? With a quick look, Morrow directed Chess to stand between them; Chess obeyed, gallows-grim, then watched as Morrow took Yancey's arm in his, a parody of hand-fasting, and laid her main veins open: a fiercer, more painful wound than any they'd dared before, liberating a gush of blood so strong it ate the fount of Yancey's strength almost instantly. It struck the earth under Chess's ghost-feet, pooled for a moment on the surface, before sinking in.

Next second, Ed had cut himself just as deep, the blood-stream doubling, rich red liquid puddling up until that whole same crimson store combined leapt upward, suffused itself throughout Chess's shadow-shape, deepening his colour and inflating him toward opacity: became the rich plum of his coat, the red of his hair. He flung out his arms and gasped, sucking in air, substance, power all together. Yancey felt that parasite hex-hunger of his latch on, draining them out with terrifying speed, pulsing gore-drops actually flying mid-air in all defiance of gravity's laws to enter him.

No prayers needed, this time: their sacrifice was free and willing, made right where the Crack in the world rendered all incantations meaningless. Within seconds, Chess had become almost solid, only the deep crimson flush of his skin betraying his fragile grasp on materiality; his body steamed in the cold air. As he opened his eyes, they glowed green as absinthe louched and lit.

At that precise moment, the roof blew off the hut, walls shattering outward—and Ixchel came descending, dragonfly cloak swarm-flapping to scour the sky. From below, simultaneously, the ground writhed and split, Weed spilling upward like maggots escaping a caved-in corpse; the Enemy stood atop, re-envisioned as Chess's blue-skinned reflection, naked but for barbaric graveyard ornamentation.

Staring at this pair, Yancey dimly knew she ought to be frightened—terrified, even. But . . . she was tired, so she folded gently to ground instead, which felt only slightly colder than she herself did. Reached for Ed's hand, feeling her slit tendons flap, her nicked bones grate uselessly together. Soon, she reassured herself, they would get up and run. In a second, perhaps . . . just after they'd rested only a scant tick, or two . . . .

Someone was shouting, but she couldn't tell who. Her eyes skewed sidelong, turned up, rolled 'til she could almost glimpse the dark inside her own skull. Then closed.

She was gone.

OUTSIDE THE CITY'S BREACHED wall, the spider lunged up in a titanic final spasm, rising to stand almost vertical, palps and mandibles stretching skyward. Red light bloomed in its eyes, brightened until—with a sodden explosion—all eight of 'em simply burst and Clo Killeen's immortal remains came rocketing up out of its forehead, scorched but triumphant, a penetrating stink of boiled mucus trailing her in a venomous cloud. She screamed in triumph, flipping dolphin-gleeful, then slid back down to spew gloating yet incomprehensible Irish jibber-jabber at the mortally wounded monster.

It was her undoing. The closest foreleg—whipping down, in a movement perhaps half spasm, half vengeance—caught her by the waist even as its owner tilted backward, describing a slow, dreadful, inexorable arc. Curling inward, the beast's immense bulk crashed down, smashing a second immense breach open in what was left of the wall before bursting open on impact like a piñata, spilling a vast tide of indistinct black, wriggling forms—were those guts? Organs? Or something . . . living?—both into and out of the City.

Over where the gates had once stood, the Honourable Chu and his Indian had rallied the last of the city's defenders, fighting to stave off the Emperor's soldiers as they attempted to force their way in. The hexes' supernatural might and desperation balanced the Mexes' guns and numbers, and Farris had taken advantage of the stalemate to rally his Texican cavalry into a wedge, hoping to take the Mexes in the back. But before they'd covered more than half the distance, the spider's death throes broke New Aztectlan's last inch of morale. Even at this distance, and without his spyglass, Ludlow could see the City's small-folk start to break and run.

Spurred by what they thought was victory, the Mexes whooped like Apache, pouring in over the wrecked gates after them—but a second later, when they got a close-up look at exactly what was flooding from the destroyed spider-beast's wreckage, their cries turned from revelry to panic.

"Hold the line!" screamed Captain Farris, waving his sabre for emphasis, too far back to see what the Mexes were cringing from.

"Hold the line, and ride them down! Ride, boys! For the Forty-Seventh!"

Geyer yodelled in answer, as did dozens of others, all around. Ludlow clung onto his horse and prayed.

Then the wedge closed with that foul, onrushing horde, and if Ludlow had had anything left in his stomach, he would have retched it up now. As if the giant spider had been nothing but a single titan womb on legs, the things it had released to scuttle in every direction around them were minuscule copies of itself—minuscule to their progenitor, but the size of Clydesdales to everyone else, except with twice the legs for twice the speed: spiders small enough to rope and ride, every bit as quick and vicious as the original.

Poor Captain Farris split one's head with a savage swing, only to be taken out of his saddle by another's leap, and brought down in a tangle; Ludlow watched his body swell with venom, skin separating at the joints, before the next row of horses came galloping over them both and foundered, screaming.

Gunfire rippled on all sides. Geyer blasted one spider away with a well-placed rifle shot, sending it flipping arse over thorax, ichor spewing, like it weighed no more than a tumbleweed. He dropped his muzzle to reload—and was immediately targeted by two more, who wasted a moment or so tussling with each other. Ludlow took advantage of the break to shoot one through what he could only think might be its brain pan with a gambler's derringer he kept up his sleeve, but the other reared back and spat a sticky web-string from its hindparts, snaring hand and gun fast. Then set in to pull, *hard*.

Oh God, shit on a shingle . . .

From behind Ludlow, however, a new voice suddenly intruded— no, not so much new, as unfamiliar. It was Asbury, sounding firm, awake, *adult* for almost the first time since he'd met the man—not the sad old drunk of the last few months, but that legendary figure he'd heard tell of back in New York, in San Francisco. The man whose eccentric brilliance and machinery it'd spawned had spent the last few years bent on the insane goal of turning magic into one more branch of science . . . and almost succeeded in that aim, give or take a few disasters.

"Hold still, Mister Ludlow," the Professor said, levelling his Manifold's latest iteration at Fitz Hugh's arm, the web, the spider beyond. "This will take a moment—and it *may* hurt."

Ludlow felt, more than heard, the magnesium-filament surge; the blue flash travelled from Manifold to him, using his very flesh and blood as a conductor, then down along the web itself, a living wire, to freeze the spider in its multiple tracks. A brief yet intense struggle ensued, Geyer and Ludlow both similarly transfixed— Geyer in amazement, Ludlow drawn rigid with discomfort and shock admixed.

And then—it was over. The spider bowed its awful head, mandibles clicking out a rhythm that mimicked the Manifold's own clockwork whirr, and rang for all the world like a signal of surrender. That same cone of dimness and silence Asbury had evoked in the desert fell over all three—four, if you counted their new "pet"—and shielded them from harm by erasing them from notice. Insects and combatants alike bypassed them as though they weren't even there, 'til the combined in- and out-rush thinned, and they were left alone once more.

Now treating the sticky rope which still connected it to Ludlow as a combination of leash and bridle, the spider knelt down further, a bison-sized camel. Geyer let out his breath, telling Asbury: "That's a neat damn trick, Professor. How'd you manage it?"

"More easily than you might suppose, Mister Geyer—the Manifold was constructed first to track and measure hexation, then to channel it. And what are these things made from, if not hexation-stuff itself . . . pure arcane impulse given shape through the Word, spell-directed, then taking on a kind of flesh which, can apparently outlast even removal from its originator?"

"Uh huh. Well, at any rate; thanks for that."

"You're very welcome, sir."

On either side of Hex City's ill-defended limits, Mexes and hexes made fierce battle, with Texican interference; the first wave of spiders were all either crushed or fled, leaving a perimeter of wounded men and leg-broke steeds behind, along with a slew of corpses, human and equine. Longer they were in the suddenly docile spider-thing's presence, meanwhile, the more violently Asbury and Geyer's horses kicked and squealed and snorted, like they'd had their noses rubbed in pepper. Geyer dismounted and let slip the reins, slapping its flank, not even turning to watch it flee.

Instead, he squinted down at their Manifold-hypnotized captive, as if making calculations in his mind which Ludlow frankly feared to hear voiced, before venturing, at last: "Seems tame enough, and I can't help but think it'd make good time, 'specially up walls. So, Doc, Mister Ludlow . . . how d'you think it'd take to being saddled?"

Distracted by his own thoughts, Ludlow couldn't keep track of Asbury's answer, though it seemed to be in the affirmative. Telling himself, instead, no matter what was decided on: *It is beyond my control now, all of it—has been, for quite some time. I preside here at the birth of hundred new things, recording them for posterity: truly, an age of terrible wonders!*

That'd more than do for a cut-line, anyhow.

IN THE MOON COURT, Ixchel's blood-cultists knelt naked in a spiral, all pseudo-Christian modesty discarded, praying for their Lady's triumph in a language none of 'em actually understood. The women passed stingray spines through earlobes, nipples, labia, shedding life-essence in drops, lactating a steady red stream; they thorn-roped their tongues, chanting words of blood, while their men pierced and re-pierced through frenums, urethrae, foreskins with volcanic glass shards, twisting to enlarge the holes in order to slip their own braids of *maguey*-fibre stuck with cactus through again and again, running their own flesh ragged. The overflow they dripped on the same sort of bark paper that demon who'd once been Clo now wore in her hair, then burned in a great stone bowl filled with incense, the chamber's centrepiece; the smoke went up slow and creepishly concentric, describing an almost symmetrical set of loops and coils, like a serpent couching to strike.

As repayment for their devotion, some smallish part of Ixchel must've been ensuring the wounds—which surely would have felled any lesser worshippers—kept on healing 'emselves perpetually, whatever else the rest of Her might be doing at any given time: hardly a kindness, really, at least not such as Eulalia Parr'd been raised to think of. But then, considering what she'd seen up above in their frantic duck-and-dash to reach this place, she really hadn't expected any better.

Between the rampaging Mexes and those horse-sized spider-things, Yiska, Songbird, Carver, Sophy and the terrified, barely manageable Gabriel had only just managed to get Eulie to the Temple's gate alive. She'd ordered them to flee the instant she crossed into this sanguinary edifice—"It's no place for any of you," she'd told them, overriding their protests. "Any not sworn to the Oath who goes in there, *they won't come out*. Ever."

Jonas had argued, of course: "Least let us guard the way out for ya!" he'd tried to insist. "Suppose things get even worse up here?"

Eulie had only laughed. "Private, things seem 'bout already as bad as they're ever likely to *get*." But really, she thought to herself, it probably wasn't a good idea to ever assume that, 'cause going by her recent experience, at least, things could *always* get worse.

So she squared her shoulders and stepped into the incense-choked, torchlit stone hall, gathering force 'round herself like a boiled-leather coat. Called out as she did, louder than anybody'd probably ever heard her speak, outside of Hank and the others: "Which of you were little miss Marizol's kin? Marizol, *mama y papa*? I got news you need to hear, 'fore you go any further."

A dozen eyes in as many shades of dark, black to brown to grey to blue, looked up at her, startled, as she crossed the hall—she "heard" their internal whispers clearly, for all her gutter-learned marketplace Spanish wasn't up to the task of exact translation: *Bruja! Cual es su nombre? Una de los Fennigs, los traidoras! Call Her, before we are distracted, La Madre, La Muerte Hermosa—*

"First one tries to call the Lady, I'll stop their throat for 'em, swear to Christ. *Ahora, rapidamente!* Any of y'all got a daughter named Marizol went missing a day or so gone, now's the time to speak up . . . c'mon, nobody? For *serious*?"

There was one second more of baffled silence, before a woman from the Court's left-most quarter ceased her labour and rose knees to toes, straightened gamely tall, still leaking from every which way.

"*Mi hija*," she said, slowly. "Marizol . . . she's my girl, *si*."

"Her you gave to the Lady, right? As her pet, her treat?"

From a worship-knot away, a man Eulie could only assume was probably Marizol's Pa tried to jerk himself up too and failed, sheer, raw weight of hardware through wounds tugging him back down again; he spat at her: "Marizol, *la Dama* call her *especial*! *Chosen*, like in old time—meant for better things. Like *una mujer San, la virgen de Guadalupe*."

"*Si*," Marizol's mother chimed in. "So we give, yes. Like we give *everything*. Because *la Dama* give back, jus' like she say, and never lie. Never."

Cries of ecstasy, of faith renewed, went up on every side— the cultists scourged 'emselves afresh, drawing yells, along with sanguinary tribute. And this time, Eulie could fair see the power as it came eddying out, in burning updraft ribbons. One of the longest and loudest-coloured fluttered up from Missus Marizol, the other from Mister, knotting together 'til they braided. It was enough to turn Eulie's stomach.

Without any notion of considering it beforehand, she leaned forward to deal Missus M. a rifle-shot slap 'cross her red-soaked chops.

"You fool dupes!" she hissed. "Know what your Lady *gave* Marizol, her *better thing*? A Goddamn grave, is what—like she gave my gal Clo, and my man Hank. Like she aims to give us all, hex or no. She sucks you dry and you thank her for it. Her, who runs up the tab and never pays for nothin'!"

She found herself shaking, and wondered a titch at the sheer outrage welling up inside her. Saw only poor Marizol, skull-cracked by that sumbitch Pinkerton's bullet, falling headlong into Saint Terra with no chance to wipe that silly, appeasing smile from her face. And laid overtop came Marizol's mother with one hand up to her cheek, tears starting at her eyes' corners, as though Eulie'd dealt her a hurt worse than any of the others she'd just spent God knew how many hours inflicting on herself.

How dare *you!* was what that wounded look cried out, so like Marizol's own; *how dare you tell me truth, 'stead of these pretty lies the Lady sells. How dare you show me it was me and her Pa drove her into yours and Berta's arms, sent her running for Camp Pink on faint hope of rescue, on the idea that a man should practise what he preaches. . . .*

This was almost as much ripe horse-crap, though, and Eulie well knew it; her own brand, or maybe even Hank's, who'd preferred to gamble his two remaining wives' freedom on the chance he could talk what'd become of the first one down, before she gutted him like a fish. For the plain truth was—and she could admit it now, at last, at the end of all things, without even resenting it—though he'd claimed to make 'em all the same pledge, it always had been Clo he'd loved best.

Sissy; oh, sissy. Think I'll say a prayer for you too, sometime soon— probably right as you're comin' to pull my head off, I had to start takin' bets.

Saw Marizol's Daddy staring daggers at her, then, like he'd pay big coin to jump over and throw a punch, he could only bring himself to work 'round the fact he'd just poked his pecker full of holes. So Eulie marshalled herself one last time and told the Moon Court at large, clear and cold as Christmas: "You're gonna kill yourselves for her, faster than slower, and the plain fact is, she don't even deserve it. And all I'm sayin' is maybe you need to think on that a bit, 'fore you end up like Marizol—like everybody else ever did what that old-as-Jesus bitch wanted, or didn't want, either."

"That's brave talk, all right, yella gal," came Sal Followell's no-nonsense voice, cutting in. "Problem is, though, *we're* the ones gonna have to try an' live with her, after this mess is done with."

Eulie turned to snap back, hands on hips—and faltered as she saw who was towering behind Sal in the doorway: the black-coated bulk of Reverend Rook himself, fingertips tented on his breast like a hanging judge already pondering sentence. He seemed more sorrowful than angry, but Eulie's heart quailed, nonetheless—Rook had always looked saddest just before wreaking his worst. And if she defied any order he gave, she'd bust her Oath wide, rendering herself helpless or dead within the minute.

"Chu and the Shoshone are shepherding folk into the Temple," Rook told Sal. "Should have the last of 'em in within minutes. Once they're inside, we can bring up the wards, and then it'll just be a matter of waiting 'em out 'til her Ladyship's strong enough to settle things—if her supply ain't been cut off in the meantime, that is."

Sal's mouth flattened to a hard line, once again addressing herself to Eulie. "See, you dumb little snip—? But no; I can't fault you none for tryin' what you felt you had to, after Hank and Clo. Still, and this is important . . ." She stepped forward and took Eulie firmly by the shoulders, like a mother hoping her gone-wanton daughter would see light without needing further correction. "There ain't *no* beating Her, not now, not ever—you try, you die. And even if you *could* win, *we* still all die! Go back to livin' like thieves and Gypsies, hidin' from each other and the world, with those of us who survive tearin' each other's hearts out just to sup on 'em." She shuddered in a breath, voice steadying again. "Them out there just got a little time 'fore they meet their fate—an' then it all begins again, Eulalia. Don't throw your life away when there ain't no need, or point."

Eulie glared at her. She'd always loved this mountain-stubborn old woman, bound fast to her in potential slavery by at least a quarter-blood, but the lump in her throat felt too hot by far to choke back. "So everything—Hank, Clo, their babe—it was all for nothing? Or worse, for *this*?" She swept a hand at the filthy, slaughterhouse-stinking Moon Court. "Those really the only choices we got, Sal? *Us*, who can do most any damn thing, now we got somewheres to stand together?"

Without warning, Sal's flinty eyes spilled tears, shocking as water from the rock. But even as she nodded, lips actually moving to shape the word *Yes*—

"Maybe not," Rook said instead, offhand, as though it was some interesting thought had only just occurred to him. He reached into his pocket, withdrew a small spruce twig, unornamented, at least not visibly. Which he took in both hands, without prayer, or fanfare . . . and snapped.

Time stopped.

MORROW HAD LOST COUNT of how often he'd skimmed death's edge and dodged away at the last second, these last few years—but splayed now on the cold ground, heart's blood pouring out into Chess so fast he could barely breathe, he had just enough strength left to realize that this might be the last time, if not quite enough left for fear. Only a dim awe, vague resignation . . . and a second later, the weirdly delighted urge to *laugh*, when Chess glared at the two inhuman Powers and roared, without preamble—

"Which one of you fucks got my heart?!"

Tezcatlipoca smiled and pointed to Ixchel, as though it'd seriously ever been in doubt.

Automatically, Morrow looked at the goddess as well, and felt a twinge of nausea. What a desperate joke it seemed, now, to think she could ever have been beautiful—swollen-jointed, leather-skinned, mask face torn askew. She seemed more animate rawhide than human. With a shock, he realized the hole he'd put in her head himself had reappeared, though nothing—not blood, nor foetor—trailed from it now. Long dry rips down her naked chest and belly showed sickening glimpses of yellowed ribs, shrivelled organs, dust-dry black veins.

And behind that exposed chest-lattice, something shadow-hidden, distending and collapsing with such force that it seemed as if whatever lay beneath the bone was fighting its captor as furiously as Chess himself would.

Ixchel, for her part, neither smiled or frowned, mouth froze in a paralytic's sneer, one corner furled to show her entire left-hand row of upper teeth. Only stared at Chess with a vivid hunger in her black eyes—the single part of her, really, that still seemed alive—before spreading her arms, as if to embrace him in welcome. He almost seemed to hesitate, at the sight.

No!

A bolt of terror galvanized Morrow; he managed to lift himself a bare inch, hurl a warning at Chess, sending it down the path of blood as the link flickered toward extinction.

No, damnit! Don't let her—

Here his strength gave out, thudding him back to the earth, but Chess glanced over at him—*into* him—and *winked*. Crouched. And hurled himself *backward*, slamming spine-first into Tezcatlipoca's chest, his body seeming to burst, exhaling a crimson cloud that billowed up 'round the god, penetrated him from every angle, pumping blue skin purple and red Weed even redder. Tezcatlipoca staggered, fell to his knees with the vines boiling and writhing 'round him, 'til gradually he began . . . to *laugh*.

Yeah, well, Morrow roused himself enough to think, dimly. *What else?*

Louder and louder this Fifth World's self-proclaimed Enemy guffawed, as if he finally understood the punch line of the best joke ever told. Then reared back up just as the swinging panels of his ribcage broke apart, two small, scar-knuckled fists punching them wide like saloon doors. Bare feet came next, kicking out through both blue-skinned thighs as if shrugging off garb made from sodden *papier-mâché*. The whole head split and moulted like a crab's shed shell, guffaws blended into a wordless yell of triumph, as Chess Pargeter—naked as the day of both birth and *re*-birth, before he thought to re-clothe himself in purple once more—lunged to his feet with red-gold lightning crackling from his eyes, a cowled halo drooping from shoulder blades to forearms like fiery wings, then trailing down 'round his fists in death-dealing frills.

"*Yeah!*" he announced. "*That's* better! 'Cause this here's *my* flesh and nobody else's, let alone some dead monkey-god's, no matter the size of his Smoking Mirror! There's one Chess Pargeter only, and I'm damn well him!"

With the same shimmying shudder Morrow'd seen him use on a gulp of absinthe, Chess shook the last shreds of Tezcatlipoca's blue skin from his body and met Ixchel's gape head-on, eyebrows sketching his curly red forelock.

"Oh, so what?" he asked her. "Didn't think I really meant to just pour a whole fresh bunch 'a blood-power into *you*, when I know that's all you drink? Come on. I ain't *that* dumb."

Ixchel blinked, or struggled to. *But . . . how . . . you are no variety of god, not anymore—only a ghost, fleshless, without root. How could you possibly unseat the Night Wind whose slaves we all are, one thing with four names, Father of Every Magic?*

Because I allowed him to, of course, a terrible voice said, behind her—the creature in question's own, freed at last from its human trumpet's confines, echoing unchecked like the black between stars. For there it was, humped back up with its skull-and-crossbones cape flapping free as it loomed over them all, one foot tucked under it and the other reflecting their shocked faces back at them, done over in shades of obsidian.

Well played, little brother, it told Chess, with a wink. And vanished from sight, before Ixchel could do much more than goggle.

Then Chess glanced back down, and grimaced at the damage Morrow and Yancey'd done themselves, glee dissipated by dismay. With one hand-flick, he sealed Morrow's wound; a second closed up Yancey's arm, stemming the tide.

Then came something Morrow truly didn't expect: Chess lifted his hands, flattened them into blades and brought them down, short and sharp, like an axeman cutting ship's line. Pain backlashed, hammering Morrow's head; too weak to move, he could only groan, realizing by the sudden *absence* in his mind just what Chess had to've done.

Why would you—?

Ixchel shook her head, slowly. "Fool," she rasped. "Twice fool, to cast away your last priests! How will you be renewed? How can you *live*, with no heart and no new form waiting in your cycle? When you exhaust the last of what you have now, you will die, surely as you should have in the Moon Room, when your lover cracked your breastbone."

Chess turned to face her. "S'pose that's about right," he agreed. "'Cause if my friends get to your Moon *Court*, like I'm bettin' they will any second, that's the exact state they said *you'd* be in. Not to mention how, since your friend and mine kept on sowin' all this time he's been wearin' me for pyjamas, I still got a whole shitload of Weed all 'cross this state to pull on. Lose your City and your Court along with it, though, and what've *you* got to draw on, exactly?"

There wasn't quite enough mobility left in Ixchel's face to show fear—but as she threw her head back to scream at the sky: *"Daughter! To me!"*—the terror which suffused that shout might've almost been the sweetest thing Morrow had ever heard.

For a half-second, anyhow. Until rubble-dropped Clo Killeen hurled the massive block of stone pinning her off and rose back up looking almost good as new, undead demon that she was, snarling loud enough Ed could hear her from where he lay.

Ah shit, was all he had time to think, then blacked out as well.

INSIDE HEX CITY, Mexes, Texicans and hexes were fighting equal-hard, carving out a truly hellish scene. The spider, once mounted, proved an odd ride indeed—broad-set and hairy in ways that rubbed painfully, ass-end canted up far higher than its front, almost like a living saddle. Geyer, who'd taken pride of place, used its own silk to navigate the thing along while Ludlow swapped his derringer for Geyer's rifle, blasting away at whatever blundered close enough to seem dangerous; perched on Ludlow's right hand, Asbury clutched his Manifold while wedged almost sidesaddle, eyes kept peeled for any less mundane threats.

This arrangement saw them safely into the main thoroughfare, where—once the crush increased so much that forward motion became impossible—Geyer urged their conveyance straight up the wall, jumping it literally from pillar to post, 'til they fetched at last within wrestling distance of a tall, flat-faced woman armed with gun and horse-jaw tomahawk. From her Wanted poster description, Ludlow recognized her as The Night Has Passed or Yiska, "Grandma's" chief lieutenant. Surely, her presence here meant that Missus Kloves couldn't be far behind, or Ed Morrow, for that matter.

"Pinkerton man," the squaw addressed Geyer, levelling her pistol at his head, even while Ludlow fought to draw similar bead on hers. "I remember you, from outside the Bone Channel, when we rode to Bewelcome. Come to finish what your master started?"

"Hardly. Would've thought you'd've heard already—Pinkerton's dead and there's another Agency waiting to take his place, run by my friend, George Thiel."

"Ah, then you must feel proud for him. Where is he now, I wonder?"

"Close enough, I'm sure. Though not close enough to stop you shooting me, you happen to take a mind to."

"No," she agreed. And though her barrel hadn't moved even an inch, Geyer nodded as well, nonetheless—civil, like they were taking tea together.

"You've no reason to trust me," he admitted, "or anyone else wears a government badge. But world's end aside, things do have to change, and I believe we all well know it, ma'am—or may I call you Yiska?"

"That is my name."

"Mine's Geyer. Frank."

"I know. Say your piece, Mister Geyer—I have other business, elsewhere."

Ludlow felt sweat sting his eyes. Beside him, Asbury's breathing seemed barely perceptible.

By God, I wish I had my tablet out, he thought, swallowing, and shifted his grip on the rifle, fingers damp.

"All right," Geyer said. "Your band—Missus Kloves, Miss Songbird and the rest—" At this last name, Asbury sat up a bit straighter, as though pricked. "You obviously had some scheme in mind, when you called *this* thing's Mama up"—and here he touched the spider between its rows of eyes, gentle but firm—"same as the rest've us had, when we came running. Hex City goes down today or we all fall in the attempt, witch, wizard or other. Your group holds representatives from several that've been equal ill-treated by men like me, depending on you to keep 'em safe. And all I can swear to you is that George Thiel and me ain't Pinkerton. No matter what the outcome, if we survive today and he ends up heading what's left of the boss's organization, from now on things'll be different."

Yiska gave him a long, cool look, then lowered the gun, though she kept it unholstered. Which frankly seemed nothing but wise to Ludlow, considering the circumstances.

"*If* we triumph," she told Geyer, at last, "then it will be because of hexes, and worse . . . Celestials like Yu Ming-ch'in, secret Jews like Yancey Kloves, two-spirits like the red boy and Bad Indians like me. Your friend and you would do well to remember that, after."

"We will. Anything else you can think of, might sweeten the pot on an alliance 'tween our two nations?"

"Hmmm. If you see another of those spiders, will you rope one for me?"

Geyer looked at Ludlow; Ludlow stared back, stumped. But to everyone's surprise, Asbury leaned forward and promised, with utter sincerity: "Madam . . . if you would be so kind as to provide us with an escort through this tumult, I believe Mister Geyer would be perfectly happy to give you *this* one."

Yiska grinned, widely. "You *are* a strange old man," she told him. "Just as the White Shell Girl says."

OUTSIDE, CLO TURNED, hair puffed, eyes blazing; Chess braced himself for her attack, making torch-bright fists. But just as she tensed to move, the entirety of Hex City itself rose up like a table-rapper, and not by stages. Its elevation was complete, immaculate, a dreadful miracle—one more, in half a year of the same. From the pyramidal Temple at its heart and its earth-clogged under-mesh of dungeon-passages to every building which remained intact, with Oath-bound hex and small-folk alike—plus a good many helpless invading soldiers—caught in the web between, the City lifted into the winds on a patchwork disk of dripping soil and hex-shaped stonework. Random men and women stood on glassy air, screaming as they stared down, watching the Earth fall away. Its shadow carved a hole in the sky.

And then, with a twist, a rip scored deep between worlds . . . New

Aztectlan was erased, completely. Winked out, a popped eye, leaving nothing behind but the hole where its foundations had lain. Scattered here and there amid the wreckage, lone soldiers and small groups stared 'round in appalled incomprehension, deprived of purpose and danger at once. And in their midst, coat slightly flapping on the sudden wind, ragged wings of some gigantic carrion crow—

—the Rev.

INSIDE THE MOON COURT, time stood still, as it had during the clash with Sheriff Love and Pinkerton at Bewelcome when Rook and Ixchel drew Chess "aside" to offer an alliance with his greatest enemies, rebirth and redemption bought at the price of Ed Morrow's blood. That meeting, in turn, was interrupted by Tezcatlipoca, string-puller extraordinaire, from which point things had gone . . . badly, to say the least. Yet Rook, who had been the one to work the trick directly—on Ixchel's instructions, but even so—still well-recalled its mechanics.

The challenge, this time 'round, had been to fashion and maintain the charm without his dread wife ever catching on to what he'd been up to; a calculated gamble, banking hard on her being distracted by her own decay, the cleverness of her gambit with Clo Killeen, her dreams of Chess's imminent return and the Enemy's threat alike. But then, Asher Rook had learned to account himself a fairly good schemer, well-versed in betrayal of every sort, particularly the most intimate. The kind that couldn't ever be paid back, except in flesh.

Only follow your own hungers, Tezcatlipoca had told him, through Chess's wicked lips. *If you agree to listen to me at the proper moment, to say what I tell you to whoever I tell you to say it to, then you will get what you want most.*

Well, here he stood on the precipice now, alone, with no still, small voice at all to follow, be it the Enemy's or . . . any other. And yet—when he allowed himself to consider it just a bit further, he found himself fairly certain he already knew *exactly* what it was that bad angel "friend" of his had wanted him to do, all along.

Rook let his head bow down, and felt a verse come on: *The book of the law shall not depart out of thy mouth . . . Be strong and of a good courage; be not afraid, neither be thou dismayed: for the LORD thy God is with thee, whithersoever thou goest. Joshua,* 8 to 9. The quote lay cold behind his teeth, robbed of all magic, good or bad. Simply dead and gritty, ashy-tasting, a spent fire—his very tongue rejected it. Or were those God's words which had rejected *him*, long since?

But God turns away no one, he told himself, mockingly. *Forgiveness for all so long as you own your sins, same's the old creed claims, even hypocrite Antinomians; yeah, right. Like Chess always said—if things weren't the same, they'd be different.*

But they ain't. And time's a-tickin', even here.

Flanked by Sal Followell and Eulie Parr, Rook opened up and cast wide while Ixchel's faithful pack of self-cannibalizers stared stupidly on, sending his word-thoughts into the head of every hex New Aztectlan held—all those linked by the Oath, bound in their mutual promise to obey his every command as Priest-King, that lawyer's loophole through which the Enemy had let in a wavering sliver of freedom-light just before it'd thrown him down and fucked him hard (admittedly, by his own invitation). And addressed his captive congregation out loud at the same time, in what he figured was like to be his very last sermon.

"Ladies and gents, I have a plan to save us all, and no time to explain it. Granted, you none of you have any earthly reason to believe a word I say; can't do much about that, unfortunately, not in the short space of time we've been given. Things bein' desperate as they are right now, though, I'll ask for but a single word alone, from each of you: no . . . or yes."

Eulie, softest of Fennig's three ladies, stared hard at him, as though trying to read something written on the insides of his eyes; Sal's own gaze seemed fit to bore holes, and damn sceptical, to boot. He could almost hear her gathering juice enough to spit.

Yet it was the younger woman who answered, in the end. Saying: "Hank always used to say you was better than you thought, Rev—so for me, it's yes."

Old Sal jolted a tad, at that—seemed as big a surprise to her as it was to Rook, frankly—but nodded, too. And the rest all followed astonishingly quickly, after that: Chu, the Shoshone, the blister-gals. Like watching a vote took long-distance, firefly flutter of signal-fires lit and doused, from wall to spider-, mortar-, train- and cavalry-damaged wall:

Yes. Yes. (No.) (Absolutely not.) (Screw you, Reverend.) Yes, yes, yes . . . (Yesyesyesyesyes)

Rook had the strange urge to weep, but tamped it down, hard.

"All right," he continued, instead. "Then as your king and Ixchel's High Priest, on the Oath itself, I order you to take the City and go—anywhere. Don't give me any details, just *go*, now. And for the Almighty's own love, don't look back."

Eulie blinked. "What about Her?"

"She's busy; probably won't even notice what's happenin', 'til you're already gone. If she does, I'll try to throw a spanner in it. Either way, nothin' you're doing's against *her*, so not a bit of it breaks your Oaths. Makes you completely safe from retribution, long's you don't come back 'til whatever happens next is done."

"And what about *you*?"

"Do you care?"

". . . somewhat."

"Aw, that's sweet." It hurt to say, and more to see Eulie back-set so, but the last thing he needed now was more stupid loyalty. "Well, consider it this way: I didn't bring her up, but I did help her stay. So when you think it over—" Rook folded his arms, his voice raw sand on chalk. "—I deserve just about anything I get."

A long silence, broken at last by dry-eyed, stone-steady Sal Followell.

"It's a fair-made point," she said. "Get gone."

THE PIT THE VANISHED CITY left behind was near a mile wide—shallow near its edges where Ixchel, Tezcatlipoca, the former Clodagh Killeen, and Chess stood with Morrow and Yancey Kloves sprawled out senseless beside 'em, deepening gradually toward the centre, then plunging into a lightless, bottomless hole at its very heart, from which air colder by far than the New Mexico winter wind still breathed. To get away from it, Rook willed himself forward, floating lightly over the wreckage of abandoned buildings toward his Lady and her foes; he took care not to meet Chess's eyes, or even acknowledge him. Not time for that. Not yet.

Ixchel took a stumbling step toward Rook, black eyes' sclerae gone finally yellow, cataracting over. It struck Rook that at last, she actually looked something like that broke-apart figure on the "smoking mirror" Songbird'd once given him, with its triangle dugs and dagger earrings. Shrunken up and clumsy, with nothing at all that Rook could recognize of poor dead Miz Adaluz left, but for maybe the skeleton that kept her upright.

"How . . ." she whispered. "Where—where did they . . . ?"

"Ma'am, in all honesty—I haven't the foggiest."

"They could not have done this without your permission. Not and expect to live." Now that she was using her lips to talk with again, her voice was neither the clear bell of the ghost-girl in his first visions nor Adaluz's rich huskiness—it was creaky, painful, the buzz of something ancient and desiccated, taking audible effort to raise its volume over her insect-cloak's chatter.

Rook nodded. "You'd think. But then again . . . maybe they all just got tired enough of your company to risk it, just the same."

Fury distorted Ixchel's skull bones and face-hide, making them groan and snap like warped wood; she raised her crooked fingers at him, protruding bones sharp as claws. "*You*—"

But here the air between them darkened, as Tezcatlipoca transposed himself, massive as a storm. Murmuring, in Ixchel's barely attached ear: *I believe you may have a more pressing problem to deal with, sister.*

Chess looked where the thing he'd had to evict from his flesh was pointing, and laughed outright.

"Seems like," he agreed. "'Cause—that bitch of yours? She don't look happy."

For it was true: something had shifted, not only inside Hex City but inside Clo's star-demon form, as well. And while everyone else stood transfixed by the spectacle of an entire fortress's unannounced departure, Clo had writhed in the throes of a very different sort of epiphany—the sudden release of everything Ixchel's curse had robbed from her. Now she was giving Ixchel full benefit of the same rage-mask face she'd shown so many others, earlier today. And though her eyes and joints still flared, blood-splattered jaws split by too many teeth and hair a mane of foulness with her hands poised for tearing, a spectral vulture's talons, she nevertheless looked much more like the buxom Irish lass Hank Fennig first introduced Rook to than she had for . . . hours, now. Hours, only.

Made sense, for all it wasn't like Rook'd calculated on it happening. Since Ixchel had pirated the whole City's power to bring Clo over as *tzitzimihtl*, it followed that when the City absented itself, that bond she'd fashioned would disappear right along with it. Most 'specially since (as proven, time and time again) magic's true "logic" was purely metaphorical: this for that, this into that, this as that. Professor Asbury—whom he'd glimpsed on his way down, bird-dogging the proceedings with a look on his face that said *Oh, if I only had my instruments!*—would probably explain it much better, Rook was sure; might even write a monograph on the subject, if they all survived the next few minutes.

Jesus, Rook thought. *What amazing Goddamn damage we've wreaked on this world, Herself and me, in such an amazingly Goddamn short time.*

"Why do you regard me thus, daughter?" Ixchel asked Clo, toneless.

Only to have her spit blood at her feet—her own and others', well-admixed. And snarl, in reply: "Ye pinch-faced hoor! You killed my babe, or good as . . . made me kill my *Hank*. You made me *eat* him."

"But that was only your new nature, asserting itself," Ixchel said. "The *tzitzimime* devour everything, as only befits sisters of the First Sacrificial Knife—they tidy the universe's leavings, ushering us all to our end, and these are Ending Times. Another world grows, and beckons; you have become one of the mechanisms which will take us there. A great honour! Can you not feel it, even now?"

Clo heaved a long sigh, packed full of every sort of sorrow. The sound swept through Rook, plucking at strings he'd thought gone dead; hell, even Chess seemed to feel it. Yet Ixchel stood like untouched as a stone in the midst of that flood, 'til Clo lifted her head once more, face scarred by her own tears, and whispered—in a voice that could have stripped not just paint but probably stone, as well—

". . . *yes.*"

An instant later, she had already swept by her unsuspecting maker in an all-blade storm, stripping one side of Lady Rainbow's defective vessel to the bone almost too fast to properly perceive; peeled her like a fruit and anatomized the rest, deeper than any textbook. The result was horror laid atop of horror—Ixchel threw up a hand only to watch the bones of it hurl free, no longer strung together by tendons, or even gristle. At the sight, her remaining eye fair started from its socket, while the raw hole on the other side matched it for roundness, if not for expressivity.

You **dare**—

Clo's rabid slaver-grin turned actual smile, just for that moment—full of snap, the way a young girl's should be, dead and damned or no.

"Oh, I do that," she returned, striking up a pose for the next go-'round. "Aim t'rob *you* of all you did me, if I can, though I doubt it's possible—not since you never loved no one in your whole existence, you gutter-trod rag of a Devil's saint. But if nothin' else, it'll do me some small good t'*try.*"

An exhalation, then: one breath between breaths, poisoning the air between 'em with decay's purest perfume. Rook knew it came from Ixchel without having to look—had sampled it himself a time or two, between engagements. From what he'd gathered, it meant she'd reached a decision.

And after all the trouble you went to! he thought, mouth curving bitter. *Woman—creature,* thing, *woman-shaped like you are—were I one tenth only of the man I used to think I was, might be I'd even pity you.*

Right there, within ten feet or three good strides, Chess stood once more corporeal and destruction-bent, watching carefully for his opportunity; Rook ached all over to touch him, just for the pleasure of getting slapped. Still, there'd be plenty of time for that later—since, at Chess's back, he could already see the Enemy lean in close (having shifted positions sometime within the last few seconds, like some sort of ink-shrouded octopus) to hiss some more advice its "little brother's" way. *Wait and see*, maybe. *This is your chance*, probably.

Kept close tabs on its game pieces, did the old Night Wind, especially while in play—and Rook had already done *his* duty. No need to send any more attention his way, when Chess made for a perfect substitute.

Gods or goddesses, you just can't trust 'em. Cheatin' Goddamn creatures.

And thus it was here, now: giving her trademark steam-whistle shriek, meanwhile, Clo came back in with everything she had, bound and determined to break the rest of her formerly beloved "mother" down for parts.

And Black Rainbow Ixchel, Mother of Hanged Men, Moon Lady, Gods-Eater, Long Black Hair of Death—six-in-one and a half-dozen of the other, risen up from Mictlan-Xibalba's clammy depths on will alone, to carve the world that'd forgot her back into her own reflection—

—struck down her own best handiwork with one black blast that left her crisped whole, an ash sculpture whose very momentum was enough to break it apart, irreparably, on the wind. A stinking fog hot with rageful pain crashed over them all, stabbing deep into nose and eyes yet clearing almost immediately, without ill effects. And when it did, there was nothing at all of Clo to be seen anymore, not even the smallest particle.

As might only be expected, such a lavish expenditure cost Ixchel dear. Rook saw the after-shock take her right in the stomach, the throat, the ribcage she'd grown extra-thick with more bones than any human needed, just to keep Chess's stolen heart from eating itself free and taking off running. She cracked open entirely all 'cross the boards, wounded side first, a seedpod spewing awful pollen—then twisted at the waist like someone was crumpling her, wringing her out from the inside.

Hamstrung, Ixchel fell to her knees, shattering one, and vomited, long and loud: not food, obviously, nor blood. Not even hex-stuff—this was something far worse. An endless, coring stream of *matter* that oozed and writhed, taking on shapes only to lose them again, like wax in a fire. The bulk of her hair fell forward, struck limp, only to be snared by this boiling mess; the seized locks shrivelled and split, changed, *degraded*.

With each fresh retch, Ixchel herself seemed to thin, all over—to lose heft, substance. Rook found he could glimpse the spine through her skin, that filmy imitation of clothing she wore worn away, leaving her naked. Then something else, in the dip between her stunted-wing shoulder blades—something familiar, though he himself had only ever heard it described by a dead man—a dapper young New York cynic who'd lived carefully opportunistic almost to the last, yet nevertheless somehow managed to die for love.

Cannibalism, theophagy . . . that'd be why she has a hole she can't fill, no-how and with nothin'. 'Cause takin' a bite out of them took a bite out of her.

Again, Rook found his eyes pulled over to Chess, like they were on strings. And watched the Enemy's mouth move, knowing in his heart what it was it must be saying.

AS I TOLD *your soldier and that man of yours likewise, little brother, so I now tell you—this is your moment. Do as your instincts tell you, and get what you want most.*

"Better be talkin' 'bout my heart, is all I'm gonna say."

Certainly I am. Yours, along with the hearts of many others, all kin to she and me. And you have only to do the work . . . reach in, reach deep, and . . . pull them out *of her.*

IT ALL CAME DOWN to instinct, for Chess, in the end—gunplay, love, magic, life itself, he'd blundered through them all on reflex and intuition, because (he'd always believed) when a second's hesitation got you dead, it was quicker and easier just to move on from your screw-ups than to waste time tryin' not to make 'em in the first place.

As Ed might have observed, though, if he'd been awake: *There's a word for a man won't take time to do a job right, 'cause he don't feel like owning up to it if he does it wrong.* And if the hell Rook and Chess had both made of their lives had taught Chess anything at all, it was that those weaknesses you *wouldn't* admit were the very things bound to get you, in the end.

Smoking Mirror's (never entirely well-meant) advice aside, therefore, when Chess took five quick running steps and leaped onto Ixchel, he hadn't *entirely* trusted instinct to guide him. He'd timed his assault not for the moment she'd lain most helpless but to catch her in the second she began to *rise* from that pool of greyish-black hex-vomitus, because he knew through long experience how *that* was the moment when a human body—something he wagered Ixchel had never quite remembered how to live in—was most off-balance. Must've been the right choice, after all, for he bowled her over easily, cutting her outraged cry off by driving her face back down into the dirt.

If she'd been mortal, or he'd still had Kees Hosteen's knife, he'd have punched her naked ribs at that point, 'til something gave or he got thrown off. But that instinct was pointless too, and he threw it aside. Even the now-familiar hex-hunger, that ravening vacuum in his gut which longed to batten on lamprey-like and *suck*, he denied, since trying to take her power that way would only open him up to her again. Instead, he brought his right fist back, then drove it—index knuckle extended slightly to concentrate all its force, along with his own hex-power, onto one point—straight down between her shoulder blades, just to the right of her spine.

The awful *crunch* his fist made as it penetrated almost made him want to retch himself. Skin and bone broke like sugar; when Chess yanked his hand out, a double palm-width of rib and hide flipped off along with it, bursting to dust the ground. The goddess wailed, a piteous, ear-scraping sound. But there was no mercy in Chess now, not even anger—only determination, ruthless and inexorable, to see this *done. Over* with.

He reached in, fingers blazing with hexation; grabbed something that felt like a handful of cobwebbed lace twined with sickeningly moist, hot sinew and hauled, with all his strength.

What came out was more heat-shimmer than substance, flickering in and out of being. Chess thought he saw a woman's face rippling in it, dead and still, a rope around its neck, while alien sigils whose meaning he understood all the same burned briefly into his eyes: *Ixtab, Rope Woman.* Then it dissolved, and was gone. Snake-quick, Chess dove in again, tore out another handful, producing a second ghost-cloud: *Chalchiuhtlicue, Jade Skirt,* this one named itself, shining green for one brief moment, before it fled likewise.

A third and a fourth: *Yxtabay, the Ensnarer; Tlazteotl, Defiler-Confessor,* and for a moment Chess's groin knotted with the lust of that horrendous *ménage* in Splitfoot Joe's. Snarling, he swept those clouds away too, with a phantasmal force-burst. Reaching down farther than it seemed Ixchel's body should allow him to, he found a final presence, and ripped it free; it coalesced into a swarm of dismembered limbs, a huge round pearlescently glowing face hovering above him. *Coyotlaxquhui, Bells of the Moon,* seemed to ring in silver notes in Chess's ears. Then gone, gone, gone. It took the sudden silence for Chess to realize Ixchel had been screaming throughout; with her quiet now, too exhausted to do anything but pant, he leaped up from her, suddenly revolted beyond words. For he had finally realized what those half-melted wraiths, those once-goddesses, had been throwing off like heat as they passed into long-overdue oblivion: what was left of their damn souls, just like those Weed-puppets Mesach Love had made out of various Hoffstedt's Hoarders, who'd welcomed their release at his, Yancey's and Ed's hands with similar spectral exhalations.

The resemblance, abhorrent as it was, buckled him at the waist; Chess retched, gave out with a clear spatter of bile—the Enemy hadn't needed food to sustain his flesh, it seemed—then spat and straightened, glowering down at Ixchel's feebly stirring form.

"Christ," he managed, disgusted. "You weren't even *you*, in the end, were you? One more big slumgullion lie. Like that meat-puppet of Doc Glossing's—roadkill in a halo, set to walking."

Then, standing over her, he lifted one boot to graze her face. He'd used a fair bit of power to open her up, but she'd lost more; if he only drove down hard enough, might be he could burst her head like glass. To make his point, he showed her a hand sheathed in fire, and said: *"Now give me back my heart."*

Weakened beyond belief, Ixchel rolled her head slowly to one side . . . and fixed on Rook, standing by idle, impassive. One leathery, bone-and-sinew arm stretched out toward him, words ringing skull-struck, yet audible to all three:

I command you, by the bond between us. Do not forget your Oath.

To which Rook shook his own head, unsurprised in the least. And smiled.

Chess wanted to retch yet again, so powerful was the sudden spasm of fresh desire that smile bred in him. And after everything, too—all the pain and ruin, brought upon not just him but the whole world. Christ! Shit, Rook didn't even look half so good as he once had: face lined, powerful neck loose-skinned and its stubble greying, stance indefinably broken. His very man-mountain hugeness seemed suddenly heavy, weary.

Then the hex-hunger stirred the base of his spine like a twisted knife, rendering him dry-mouthed, and Chess went abruptly cold. *Right*, he thought. *'Cause . . . that was always part of it, and I just never knew.*

How *much* of them had been this thing, though, always waiting between them, this slow-fused grenade primed for inevitable detonation? Chess had to believe at least part of it would have been real all the same; to think anything else was madness . . . but he couldn't *know*. Not all the way to the bone.

And then another hit still, like a smack from one of the Spider-Weaver's mighty legs: the idea that Rook must have felt the exact same way, on learning of their fate from Grandma, barring the bargain that bought safety at the price of impotence—felt this exact same rush of dread, realizing that no matter what you did, something you couldn't live without was doomed to pass away; that there was no certainty, no safety, not even in the most secret parts of your own heart. Whether that organ was present, it turned out, or not.

Oh, you Goddamned asshole, Chess raged silently, glaring at Rook. *Don't make me finally understand you now, after all of what's gone by—*

He hated Rook all the more fiercely, for losing him at least this one reason to hate him. And if some of the gut-wrenching want was mere brute power-appetite, as much or more was plain desire, not just for flesh's ravaging penetration but for everything which came before, around and after: peace; warmth; trust; affection . . . love.

Maybe just because he'd read Chess's face, Rook shook his head, gently. "Don't disappoint me now, darlin'," he said. "Been waiting a good long while to have this dance. So let's step up."

Chess drew in a shuddering breath, blew it back out. Rocked back on his heels, muscles drawing tight—ready to brawl, if not entirely willing.

"All right," he replied.

MORROW CAME UP GASPING, to find Yancey already awake, holding her head. In front of them, Chess and the Rev were going at each other with everything they had, with what he could only reckon were the shattered remains of Ixchel lying jackknifed to one side. Rook threw text at Chess, and Chess flipped it aside; where it hit it drew blood, but Chess seemed not to mind. Just bent himself into it like a wind, and kept on coming.

"You're no match for me, not one on one," Rook told him. "Not without that god-power goin' through you, or your heart returned, either—you're runnin' down already, darlin', like a watch. Can't you feel it?"

"Doesn't matter," Chess panted. "I'll do for you, then I'll do for her, just like I always said."

"How, with your black angel not doin' a damn thing on your behalf, anymore?" He glanced over where the Enemy's enormity coiled and eddied, grinning, biding its time—for what, Jesus and itself only knew. "You're a blunt instrument, Chess Pargeter. Never been a true sorcerer, for all you got hexation to spare. Not to mention how you don't know one trick I didn't teach you . . . and I didn't teach you shit."

Chess paused just a moment, face unreadable. "Oh no?" he asked, quietly.

Rook frowned, then roundhoused the smaller man right in the face, sending him staggering.

Chess spat blood and what looked like a piece of tooth, jaw immediately starting to bruise; the flame at his knuckles guttered, but didn't go out. Saying, without much surprise, once his mouth was again clear for use—"So that's how you want to play it, huh? *Big* man. And me without my Colts."

Rook shrugged and punched him again, knocking him back further: one time, two times, three, 'til Chess was panting at his feet with his ass in the dirt, Rook towering overtop. Looking down dismissive, to taunt: "Never told you to give 'em away to the only skirt ever took your fancy, did I? And now there's all your dreams of equality gone right down the drain, thrown out along with the bullets."

"Screw *you*, you God-botherin' bully."

"Uh huh, 'cause if we were settlin' this in bed, you *might* have a chance. But we ain't—it's on here, now, toe-to-toe, with me three times your size. And you *still* fight like a cathouse jade, son, just like your Momma showed you."

Chess's eyes narrowed. "Didn't seem to dislike it before, not all those times you had your dick up my ass. So don't you never call me 'son,' you house-sized shit-piece."

Yancey, hearing herself mentioned—however obliquely—had bolted upright, fumbling for the guns in question.

But as she went to raise one, without even looking her way first, Rook spat out a verse—For THEIR FEET RUN TO EVIL, AND MAKE HASTE TO SHED BLOOD—and sent it winging through the air to clip her 'cross the temple, slicing her scalp into a flap. Gore exploded free; she clapped a hand to stem it, yowling.

"You son of a bitch!" Morrow heard himself yell, feeling her pain like his own . . . could that be literally? With all the magic buzzing through the atmosphere, even mage-blind like he was, it was getting hard to tell. His own hand reached the stock of his shotgun, dropped in all the earlier excitement and half sand-buried, tightening on the grip, but hesitated; he suddenly found he couldn't remember whether he still had one of Asbury's hex-shells left, or not. Or whether, for that matter, the thing was loaded at all.

Chess kicked Rook high and hard, though not quite high enough to reach where he was aiming; Rook kicked back, catching him right in the stomach-pit, rolling him so's his ribs were at a good angle for further stomping. And then—

—things began to move fast and slow alike, the way they tended to, at the crux. It was like Morrow could see and hear it all, from every angle. How even as Rook pounded all the harder down on the man he'd once claimed to love so much he'd risk damnation to save him from harm, might be Chess was only letting him think he'd triumphed, fishing him in closer while gathering the last of his strength for some final assault. How there was something at the back of his head he was listening to: God, was that *Yancey*, playing through her pain to send him a blast of someone else's voice—some other dead person, a woman, whose hoarse, Limejuicer-tanged tones Morrow well knew from that dim pit under Songbird's long-demolished brothel?

'Ey, you idjit, it carped. *Is this what I put myself to all that trouble for, Down Under? You t'lie back an' take it, like the she-'e you told me you wouldn't never be?*

Chess, then, buckling under yet another hit and straining to get back upright: *Got another suggestion, old woman, I'd love to hear it. If not, then get back to wherever you landed—some fresh Hell if there's justice, Heaven if there ain't.*

Fink on what I told you, then, boy.

Christ, which part?

About Columcille—your Pa, that bastard. 'Is trick, and what it cost me. Remember that?

Though Morrow had no idea what she was on about, Chess sure

seemed to—wracked his brains, visibly, letting Rook get in a few more licks as he did, vicious enough to make Yancey wince, even with her own blood in her eyes.

The spell stops a person from usin' his own hexation, makes 'em same as everyone else again? Yeah, that'd be useful, right about now, and only what this fucker deserves, too—worst thing I could do to him, considering. But hell, you didn't even know how he done it!

"English" Oona didn't seem any more sympathetic in death than she'd been while alive, however, and Morrow could fair feel the curl of spite and temper, familiar as Chess's own. Lashing him with her barbed phantom tongue, while telling him—

You're 'is spawn, ain't ya, same as you're mine—and don't we both see the mark of me in every bloody part of you, no matter 'ow much you've worked t'deny it? Then there's gotta be some part of 'im in there too, you great flamin' molly . . . so get up an' dig 'ard, 'cause much as I know you like t'spend time on your knees, I somewhat doubt you crave t'die there—let alone for a third bloody time!

Chess coughed more spume, pink rather than red, which boded even worse—might be that last jab had broke a rib, even nicked a lung—and nodded, slightly. His hands were barely alight anymore, yet from where Morrow sat, it was as though some sort of flashpaper twist had ignited inside his brain pan; he braced himself as Rook hauled him up by the wrist, bone creaking awfully, other fist drawing back for a final knockout, a punch so hard it might well break Chess's neck.

He don't *know how to do it, whatever "it" is,* Morrow realized, horrified. *But he's sure gonna try.*

From Ixchel—back on her feet at last, if in no way steadily, half-dead remnants of her dragonfly cloak and her still limp fall of knotted hair doing nothing at all to hide her shame—came the order, fishwife-shrill: **Be done with him, I tell you, as you should when he first refused our offer. Finish! Do your duty, husband, as I command!**

"Don't make me do this, darlin'," the Rev pled with Chess, at the same exact moment, like he wasn't even listening to her.

While all at once, Morrow felt a great rush of wind, black and cold. Heard yet another voice—never anything like human, but familiar all the same—whisper, in the very smallest recess of his hex-staggered mind—

Now indeed, soldier . . . for just as these two dead women say, the moment has come once more, as it sometimes does. Luckily, I know you know the way already. So use that old man's toys, just as with Pinkerton; help my brother work his will. Let what we call magic and what you call science combine, and watch what results.

Morrow's finger found the shotgun's trigger; he knocked it back together with a fast upward jerk, barrel trained straight-centre of Rook's mammoth back, with no time for any sort of prayer. Just ready, aim—*fire*—

—and heard the hammers fall, with a feeble *click-click*, on empty chambers.

Yancey's face crumpled. Morrow felt the gut-punch of it, a rage he was too weak to give voice to. Even Tezcatlipoca seemed bemused for once, caught off-guard by something as simple as a lost count.

At the sound, the Rev barely glanced around, raising one eyebrow in the mildest of surprise, like: *Why, Ed Morrow—fancy meetin' you here.* Then shook his head, turned to Chess again, and drew his fist back once more.

A cordite-stink *crack* split the silence, pierced Rook's shields with a flare of light and gouged a burst of red from his broad back. He was thick enough it struck deep but didn't tear free, which Morrow guessed was good for Chess; still, he gasped out loud at the impact, watching smoke curl up from the barrel of Jonas Carver's pistol, shaking in his hands where he stood maybe ten yards distant. At Jonas's feet, the scorched and smoking form of Berta Schemerhorne huddled, leaned limply against him, half her clothes and most of her hair burnt away; her slow, harsh breaths were the very sound of pain.

Ah, said Tezcatlipoca, appreciatively nonchalant. *But then . . . he is a soldier, too.*

Grunting in shock and agony, Rook lost his balance and crashed full-force down into Chess's hard little arms, so surprisingly strong for his size. Again, it was as though Morrow saw past and present superimposed. Rook held fast in Chess's grip at the river after barely 'scaping Songbird's clutch, taking the judgement his lover passed then on his own arrogance like the bruising kiss it was meant as, and not resenting a single word.

"It's *you* makin' *me* do *this*," Chess told the Rev, simply, this time. And thrust his reignited hands up inside Rook's chest.

CONTRARY TO POPULAR BELIEF, seems instinct really does trump experience, far more often than many would like to admit, Chess was sure he recalled Rook telling him, at least the once. *That's been my observation thus far, at any rate—most 'specially whenever it comes to* you, *Private Pargeter.*

So maybe it *was* that blood-curse Oona's ghost had berated him into attempting to invoke, some phantom portion of the man he'd never known existed, yet somehow yearned for enough to choose himself an almost-double of to lay down his loyalty—his Goddamned, stupid *love*—for. Tall and strong and fickle, an educated bastard, full of fine words and passionate lies; kind of man you'd really think would know better, overall. Except for the fact that, in his heart of hearts, Ash Rook never had thought anyone else he met could ever prove one-tenth as smart as himself . . . or one-hundredth as ruthlessly deceitful, either.

This must be quite the double kick in the ass, then, Chess thought. *Shot in the back and stabbed in the front at once—hell, I could almost pity him, I was somebody else.*

Guided by forces that seemed as beyond his control as his own actions seemed unplanned, Chess felt his fingers plunge through muscle, bone, tissue, ether—groping blind 'til, with a wrench, they grasped the very outlines of that complicated, spiky thing he assumed might be whatever Rook considered his soul. One way or the other, it veritably oozed hexation, sparking-fine and savoury. Jesus, it was like Chess could taste it through his skin, so intensely did it make his mouth water and his guts convulse.

I can take this. I will. *Block off them valves, one by one—snap your connections so it all goes through you like water through a reed, a cracked flowerpot full of mud and shit. You'll never see the height of hexation you got right now again, you traitor, and you still* won't *die from it, not 'less I want you to. No, that's just what you'll have to live with from now 'til your own sorry end, the high price for what-all you done in her name, and mine.*

The answer came back to him then, rippling faint as a sigh up from under, with Rook's mouth and throat barely stirring around its passage.

Saying, simply, sadly—mere dimming snatches, trailing away into darkness—

Do it, then, darlin'. . . .

(*always knew I could count on*)

(*you*)

And hard on its heels, two far more complete ideas, fine-chewed over, as though Rook had been saving 'em a good long while. Like he'd rehearsed 'em many times in his head without ever really thinking he'd get the chance to speak either, aloud or otherwise.

For this will be my apology, the only one that could ever matter. The last and greatest gift I could possibly give you, here at the End of Days.

Chess's eyes went wide. Thinking, in his turn: *Oh no, nonono. You tower of crap, you do* not, *on any account, get to* LET *me.*

Too late, though. Because the very next heartbeat brought a rockslide of power, a fucking *avalanche*, pumping through him on a tide so high it set his hair standing straight. Rook's weight was nothing, less than nothing; he shoved him aside, not even pausing to see where he dropped, and strode straight for Ixchel, grabbing her by her remaining mane's thickest clump. Bent her back like a bow to holler, right in her rotting-meat face: "You give me up my heart, bitch, *right Goddamn now!* Come a heinous way, done a thousand bad deeds to get it, and *I AIN'T ABOUT TO ASK YOU TWICE!*"

For a split second, half a tick only, he almost felt her brace to spit his threats back at him, and take whatever come next.

But—***It is over, sister. You know it. I know it. So let it BE over.***

Please.

With those words, more sad than mocking, Chess felt the will go out of what was left of Ixchel Moon-Lady in a miasma, fetid-cold with deep regret.

As she replied, sadly: . . . *yes.*

Then added, to him—*So take it, you little monster. Take it all.*

Kissed him again, then, before he could think to stop her: bear-trap fanged and spring-hard, with just enough arcane force behind it to cough the thing he'd believed he wanted most back up into him through their fused mouths. Thrust it excruciatingly back inside his chest, with his wound as entry point; reward as rape, searing everything shut again in its wake, making him spasm 'til Chess fell back jackknifed in the dirt, hugging himself so hard he raised welts. Listening, lodged halfway between disgust and delight, as—slowly, unevenly, clogged with old blood and foulness, his heart, *his*, gods damn it all, themselves very much included—

His heart began, once more, to beat.

MORROW WAS HELPING YANCEY up when it happened: Chess's fall, Ixchel's rise. Her last desperate grab for Reverend Rook, still on his knees, as if in unconscious mimicry of the pose Chess himself had struck just before worm-turning their battle his way forever—remaining hand on his nape, the other's denuded stump thrust 'tween his jaws, prying them open like she meant to pull everything he had inside out of him by the tongue. Desperate for some final jolt to make a last stand with, and all unknowing that he was already sucked dry, forever.

Bent over his back monkey-style and snarling, as she did: *You rose against me, husband, as you swore never to do. You know the punishment.*

And the Rev, in return, plain as day: *Oh, I know, ma'am, believe me. I know.*

Even as Tezcatlipoca rushed to stop her, Ixchel reached deeper—deep enough to find Rook empty and, worse yet, cursed. Then realized, worse even than that, that the curse in question was already beginning to translate to her . . . to everything around her. Tezcatlipoca, as he laid a spectral paw on her shoulder. The very ground beneath their feet, that unsure spot where the Crack's seam had been left yet unpicked when Clo Killeen brought Grandma's suture-spinning spider down. Beneath them, the earth shivered and gave way—a sheer drop straight down into nothing, dark and cold and drear, all the way back to the Ball-Court, to Mictlan-Xibalba itself.

Ixchel fell, fast and hard: gone out of sight instantaneously, without last words of any sort. The cause of all their troubles removed forever in one swoop, with nothing—not a shadow, a rag or a bone or a hank of creepishly animate hair—left behind, to show she'd ever been there.

"Get back!" Morrow yelled as the schism widened, poised to yank Yancey's arm, but she—as ever—was already three steps ahead, pulling him with *her*. Carver scrambled backward as well, just as speedily, hoisting Berta Schemerhorne over his shoulder like a sack; they made the nearest ridge and turned to see Chess still teetering at the abyss's edge while the Enemy, poised at the pit's edge likewise and watching what little purchase he had crumble away, turned to him with one final eerie grin, a tip of his metaphorical hissing blue-flame "hat."

Well played, little brother, my sister's husband's husband! it said, with what truly did seem like genuine appreciation. *Oh, how I have enjoyed you—enjoyed being you, in fact. Though I know, sadly, that you do not feel the same.*

"Too Goddamn right, I don't," Chess managed, raising himself just a bit further into the air, Songbird-style; with a kick, he drove himself back from the pit's lip as though he was afraid it'd exert some sort of gravity on him, an invisible quicksand suck. One dangling boot-heel brushed against Reverend Rook's sleeve where he'd once more risen to waver at the very edge of the hole, bent in pain but doing nothing to assuage it, exhausted far beyond any concerns for his own welfare.

Yes. But now it is time to make an end to us at last, all three.

"The fuck you mean by that? Hey, *answer* me, you tricksy son of a—"

Chess was yelling at the air, however, by this time. Since, before he was halfway done, the god of Night and Blood and Magic had already jumped in, too . . . disappeared out of sight with a similar lack of protest, a weird sort of panache, as befitted a creature naturally bent on foxing the whole world around it.

Now only the hole remained. The hole, and Chess.

And Rook.

CHESS CROSSED HIS ARMS, heaved a sigh and half-turned, still aloft—studying Rook at an angle, obliquely, as though to distance himself until he felt able, at length, to offer up a begrudging hand.

"Long walk back to Bewelcome from here, if you ain't got the juice to open doors between places," he observed. "But I could get you there easy enough now, I guess, if I had to. And they'd probably have honest work to offer even *you*, considering the sorry state I hear you and yours left that crap-hole in."

Though nothing else changed in his stance, bowed as he was 'round that hot spear of pain in his back—Carver's bullet had probably bisected his shoulder blade, seeing his arm hung useless—Rook's eyes shifted to Chess's hovering figure, travelling sidelong and upward; gave him a look almost equally as long, as assessing. If Morrow could see them from this distance, he thought, he would probably find their quality strangely softened, now that the fierce halo of otherness that'd clung 'round the Rev from the moment they'd met was gone, never to return.

Certainly, in its wake, Rook himself could feel himself becoming nothing but a sad shadow of the man Chess had once known, back during the War . . . same one he'd taken a shine to, flirted with, killed over. Though God knew, he might well've done that last part anyhow, considering.

Chess, hung up from the heavens with his red hair a-glisten and his purple coat new-brushed, like it'd come right off the tailor's dummy; Chess, green eyes narrowed against a light they seemed to share. And Asher Rook in his comparative shabbiness, his remade *ordinariness*—merely human again, after so long a time as priest, king, consort to two gods at once.

What could there possibly be for him now that would ever compare to this hole at his feet, the one he had helped rip in the world, especially when that was closed over for good?

"No," Rook said, at length. "Not much call for a faithless preacher in a town that Word-ridden, even with their own minister laid up from havin' his hand blown off. I believe I'll have to decline."

Chess's brows lowered, brow wrinkling. "Don't be foolish."

A hoarse scratch of a laugh, the rope's passage yet worn rough along every note. "Oh, I'm long gone way past simple *folly*, darlin'— wouldn't you say? Still, I did save your soul from Hell, after all, like I promised . . . and you got to keep your hexation, to boot. Told you so."

"You didn't do a thing to get me out of Hell, you great ass, 'cept for puttin' me there in the first damn place. That was all me, with Yancey Kloves leading in front and my Ma kickin' my ass from behind. And now look at you!"

"Look at me," Rook agreed, smiling slightly, as if the idea of Chess being his destruction just warmed him through and through. "And look at *you*, too, Chess—oh, you are *something*, all right. Always were."

That's why I love you yet, darlin', in spite of everything—always will.

He saw Chess's gaze widen, then, like some sense of what Rook was contemplating had jolted itself through this hex-blind shell he now stood stranded in, encased away from the magic that should have lit his veins. As though they still knew each other so well, so intimately, they barely had to *speak* at all.

"You're the only thing here I'll miss, and that forever," Rook told him, stepping backward.

CHESS GRABBED FOR ROOK'S HAND, quick-draw fast; snatched the air so shy of his fingertips that he could feel their warmth. But Rook opened his wide, the span of it wider than all ten of Chess's neat pistoleer's fingers put together, and was gone. By the time Chess dived for the Crack as well, already folding itself shut over the whoosh of Rook's passage, he found himself caught fast in Ed Morrow's bear-hug grip with Yancey holding on almost as tight from the other side, as he kicked and flailed and screamed.

"Let go of me, fuckers! I could still—"

"Chess, you *can't*. It's too narrow, see? You'd never make it back up."

"I could blast it open, catch him 'fore he reaches where they're bound; Christ, I *know* the way, or close as! *Let me GO!*"

"Not gonna happen," said Morrow, hugging all the harder.

Yancey nodded. "'Sides which, you pop it again, what d'you think'll happen to the rest of us, given how much we already paid to get this thing closed? You really prepared to make everybody else suffer, in order to get your last chance at Rook?"

Chess cast her a glance full of all the venom he could muster, but she didn't shrink an inch. *It's like you don't even* know *me*, he thought, grinding his teeth—but nothing came out, no smart words, not even a San Fran gutter insult. Just an inarticulate groan ratcheting up to some sort of howl that dinned so bad in his own ears, he found himself trying to bash his head outright against the scar-rucked ground.

"Was the whole world you just stopped from ending, Chess. That was a good thing, wasn't it?" No reply, *no reply*. Simply Ed's voice continuing in his ear, gentler and far more understanding than he deserved: "Well, *wasn't* it?"

Followed by another voice still, faint and growing fainter, seeping up through the ground, into Chess's aching temples. Which whispered, in a tone so full of affection he truly believed he'd someday surely want to take comfort in its memory, during the awful moment of his own eventual death. *Impressed* me, *all right*, that one said. *But then, I always knew you had it in you.*

"You fuckin' liar," Chess whispered back, rolling his tear-stained face in the dust.

Not on this, Chess Pargeter. I told you . . . if one of us has to be damned, let it be me.

"*Liar*," Chess repeated, to no one, as Yancey and Morrow

405

exchanged a pair of similarly baffled glances. "Bastard, fool, fucking stupid *idjit*—I would've *took* damnation, always, if I knew you'd've been there with me!"

Ah, but darlin', I wouldn't be, since that's the institution's whole point, as I think you probably know. Hell's a prison fitted with nothin' but solitary cells, where each prisoner makes his way back to God alone, for however long and hard a time it takes.

He saw himself as if from a great height, and wondered at the ridiculousness of it: heartless, restless, wicked Chess Pargeter, left behind yet one more time with the heart he'd so long sought—at such terrible cost—finally regained, finally able to feel it *all* once more, only to lose what made feeling matter. Chess brought low, furious in his prideful anger, with nothing to do about it but roll in the dirt and shriek. Lost, bereft, utterly alone.

"I give it up!" He roared, in desperation—unsure who he might be talking to, exactly, if not the God he'd never quite believed in, for all he'd seen small-g gods aplenty. "*All* of it, *all* this happy horseshit! I give it up, I give it *back*, CHRIST—"

Too late by far, Chess; you can't. This is what you are. Wouldn't make any difference anyhow, even if you could.

"God damn you, Ash Rook! God DAMN YOU!"

Oh, I'm pretty sure He already has.

Those last words barely audible at all, a spray of consonants, petering off into silence.

With Ed and Yancey looking on, Chess gave yet one more coyote howl, then pulled his own ear-bob out and threw it down where the Crack used to be so hard it skittered 'cross what ridge of knit rock was left, leaving a trail of blood.

He tore at his own hair with both hands, utterly unheedful of any damage he might do himself, and cried out while he did it, like Rachel at Rama, "*Ohhhhhhhh*, that damn *MAN*! Lord God Almighty, Jesus Jesus *fuck*—what the hell'm I gonna do now, Ed, Yancey— *what*, for the love of Christ-shit-Jesus, without *him* to keep on runnin' after? What'm I gonna *do*?"

Hammering on the ground with bloody knuckles 'til Ed grappled even closer hold of him from one way, Yancey from the other, and held on 'til his yells stilled to sobs.

So that by the time Hex City came back—slowly but spectacularly, by degrees, kept aloft with nothing but the combined willpower of a hundred oath-linked hexes—they found the battle over, the world repaired. And Chess Pargeter—former god of Red Weed and War-Lightning—collapsed in the wreckage, weeping in Ed Morrow and Yancey Colder Kloves' arms, unashamed as a child.

THE NEXT DAY, Morrow and Yancey were gone, and Chess with them. But even had they been present to lend a hand, Frank Geyer thought New Aztectlan would still have required far more mending than its citizenry were currently feeling up to. The hex-folk in general, having gutted themselves to work their great translocation, had barely enough strength to keep breathing—not to mention that with the Crack sewn closed, they simply weren't like to regain their personal power anywhere near as quick as they'd become used to being able to.

Eventually, seeing how little there was left by way of real food and supplies, Jonas Carver—last survivor of the Thirteenth still present—volunteered the now-empty Camp Pink, pointing out that the quartermasters' tents were still well-stocked with all manner of usefulness: bandages, bottles of ether and surgical alcohol, provisions and water barrels, cots and blankets for the wounded, and so on. He, Fitz Hugh Ludlow, and Sal Followell organized the City's small-folk, leading them out to scavenge the campsite.

Meantime, *Comandante* Delgado of the Mexican Imperial Army cloistered himself with his countrymen, including those poor souls who'd been Ixchel's blood-cultists; Sophy Love, surprisingly, had joined in his crusade, ministering to men, women and children alike, treating wounds and counselling them on their bewildered loss. Geyer hadn't known she spoke Spanish, but when he realized she'd borne Gabe with her all throughout, much became clear. Nothing was yet decided, far as he could tell, but it spoke well for Delgado's common sense that even though he couldn't possibly have grasped everything which had happened, he saw no fault in ceasing to fight when no enemy remained worth continuing on with. If today's bloodshed did provide grounds for a true declaration of War some time in the future, therefore, it would not be at Delgado's exhortation.

"The Carlotta colonist soldiers demand repatriation," Sophy told Geyer, during a quiet break near noon. They sat at an outdoor trestle table brought back from Camp Pink, Gabe hungrily feeding at Sophy's breast. "Back to Texas, with never a care for what agreements they break; just like all men, my Mesach excepted. Those benighted worshippers of *Her*, though, have so little left to guide them in this world, I misdoubt they have any clear idea *where* to go." She paused. "Then again, Bewelcome is still on a new rail line, and has room for any who wish to stay."

"You do know everyone there thinks you're dead, ma'am."

"Yes, and telling them otherwise will be awkward. But it'll have to be done." She sighed, looked down at Gabe—who had fallen asleep, happily sated—and rebuttoned her dress, briskly. "Perhaps it's for the best we won't be staying."

"Ma'am?"

Sophy gave an impatient snort. "Our *Oath*, Mister Geyer. My son's bound to Miss Songbird for life, or as good as, so therefore I am too, through him. And with Miss Songbird, in turn, bound to that heathen shamaness, Yiska . . ." Geyer noted with interest that she'd said "heathen" far more as absent habit than with any real judgement. ". . . well, they do seem to prefer not to settle long in any one place, whatever its virtues."

Geyer hesitated, staring at the table-top. "Friend of mine told me one of his favourite jokes, once—he'd been a chaplain in the Union Army, back in the War," he said at last. "He said to me, 'Frank, do you know the one sure way to make God laugh?'" He paused until Sophy finally brought her gaze back to him, then finished: "'Tell Him your plans.'"

Sophy blinked, gave an odd, abrupt sound that seemed half sob, half laugh, and wiped her eyes.

"For *who knoweth the hour and the day*, indeed," she agreed.

As they sat there in companionable silence, meanwhile, Doctor Asbury bustled up, plunking himself down without waiting to be invited. In one hand, he held one of his Manifolds, a sheaf of scribble-covered paper in the other, which latter he brandished at Geyer as if it were a map to buried treasure, blue eyes alight with near-fanatical excitement.

"These measurements of the ambient *ch'i* confirm it! They match my calculations—not exactly, but so close as to preclude coincidence. Do you realize what this proves, Mister Geyer? That the relationship between magical energies is exactly that exhibited by Newtonian mathematics vis-à-vis gravity and mass! And this, in turn, only strengthens my primary hypothesis: that what we term hexation, 'magic,' must therefore operate not in antithesis to the laws of the physical universe, but in sympathy with them, even when it initially appears to *break* those same laws, completely!"

But Geyer had already stopped paying attention by the time he saw Thiel coming up behind Asbury, and stood to greet him. "George," he said. "See you managed to make Doctor Asbury's acquaintance without my help, after all."

Thiel waved a dismissive hand. "Best laid plans, Frank, just like you said to Missus Love; don't give it a thought." He sat down, giving Sophy a respectful nod, and gestured Geyer back to his seat. "I was lucky enough to encounter the Doctor while he took surveys of the City's, what would you say, magical geography? If his analyses prove correct—and so much of his work has, thus far—well, then . . . they open up some very interesting possibilities indeed, to say the least. For our nation, and the world."

"Pinkerton thought the same, you'll remember."

Thiel's face clouded. "Indeed. But that's why you'll need to be a part of it, Frank, from the very beginning—to act as my conscience, a true critic, a friend, rather than an underling. What the boss never had, in other words."

The rest of it lay between them, unspoken: *A check on me, if needed. To make sure things never go so far again.*

Glancing up once more, Thiel recognized yet another

approaching figure and stood, in reflex courtesy; Geyer mirrored him automatically, then saw why. It was Songbird, veiled in new-conjured red silk under an equally new-made parasol. Asbury, still intent on jotting the Manifold's numbers down in his notes, did not notice until Thiel cleared his throat.

"Lady Yu," he announced, loudly.

Asbury jerked, startled, and jumped to his feet. "Miss Songbird! Most humble apologies—I didn't, er, I was, well—"

"Old fool," Songbird called him, with something between annoyance and an odd sort of affection. "You wished me to make inquiries. Would you know their results, or not?"

". . . please."

"I have probed those hexes willing to allow it, studying the binding structure of their Oath, and found that the banishment of their Lady and the death of their High Priest has rendered it much simplified. Each hex of this City is now bound to every other, as safe from their hunger as they are from their own, and with the united power of the whole City to draw on." She held up an elegant white hand, correctly reading the alarm in Geyer's eyes, and added: "Subject, that is, to that whole's *consent*. Let any hex draw too much of the City's pooled might for his own ends, and any who objects may draw it back, undoing his efforts. Let Oathbound hexes quarrel, and their own Oath will prevent any true hexacious harm to one another—a mutual neutralization, like the Diné's *Hataalii* binding. Only those works on which all, or most, of the City-folk agree may be fed by them all at once, and even those will be greatly weakened if but a small portion actively contests them."

Asbury nodded, slowly. "United by common consent, yet self-limited by that consent's necessity—an elegant solution. And clear reason enough never to give the City-folk a common foe again."

"Threaten such an apparently perfect working demonstration model of true democracy," Thiel replied, "right when it's still in the process of being born? Why Professor, really; neither I nor Frank would dream of doing any such thing."

Asbury squinted at Thiel, as if trying to guess whether he was joking—but since the man had one of the best poker faces Geyer had ever encountered, he got little out of his efforts, and seemed to cotton on to that fact as quickly as one might assume a genius would.

So he turned back to Songbird instead, bowing stiffly. "I am . . . most grateful for your efforts, Miss Yu," he began. "And, on a more personal note—I must, once again, most humbly apologize the travails visited upon you at my hand, when I attempted to cleanse you of your power." Asbury paused to clear his throat, then went on. "It was wrong of me to presume to choose *for* you, however well-meaning I might have thought my own intentions, at the time. Having since reconsidered the results of those actions, I find that since I can offer no true excuse or justification for them I can only beg your forgiveness, most humbly—in full and certain knowledge, frankly, of how little I deserve to gain it."

Songbird blinked, seemingly taken aback. It occurred to Geyer that perhaps no one had ever attempted to apologize to her before, for any transgression. After a beat, however, she inclined her white-piled head, stiffly.

"I cannot say I suffered *over*much from your idiocy, when all is said and done," she admitted, at last. "Though I may, perhaps, have complained somewhat more than was properly due, at the time. . . ."

The laugh which burst out at this startled them all. Geyer spun to see Yiska, scuttling up from behind astride the great black "arachnorse" they'd turned over to her during the battle, already moving as easily with the eldritch mount as if she'd been born riding it.

"*'Somewhat more'*?" she repeated, guffawing, as she dismounted.

Songbird flushed, blotchily, and snapped: "Why were you so long on patrol? You risk yourself stupidly; think if those you lead were to lose you! If . . . what would *they* do, without you . . . ?"

But here she broke off again, flustered, while Yiska grinned down at her. "My White Shell Girl," the shamaness said, and kissed her, firmly. Songbird flailed at her a moment before relaxing into it, as Asbury blushed, and looked away; Sophy Love sighed and did likewise, looking more exasperated than repelled.

When they finally came up for air, Geyer cleared his throat and stepped forward, prompting Yiska to raise her eyebrows. "And what have *you* to say, Mister Former Agent Frank Geyer?" She asked.

"Well," said Geyer, "you may remember I spoke of my employer to you, during the battle—George Thiel? Thought it might be well you got to know each other, sooner rather than later."

He moved out of the way, letting Yiska and Thiel size each other up, and watched. After a moment, Thiel offered his hand. Yiska gave it a sceptical look, and folded her arms. "*Bilagaana* are not known for keeping their word," she said.

"No," Thiel agreed, "they aren't." His hand stayed extended, gaze steady. "But I am."

Yiska considered him for a long moment. Then, slowly, she reached out and grasped his forearm, ancient shorthand for: *I carry no concealed weapons, parleying in good faith. You?* Uninsulted, Thiel simply shifted his hand to grip hers the same way in return.

At last, Geyer allowed himself to smile.

AND THE NEXT MORNING, a new sun dawned.

EPILOGUE

December, 1867 to January, 1868
In and around New Mexico, and other environs
Festivals: Suspended

An agglomeration of yet more representative newspaper headlines filed by former San Francisco *Californian* correspondent Fitz Hugh Ludlow for his series *The Perambulatory 38th: Hexicas and Its Journeys Toward Statehood, in the Days After Allan Pinkerton's Defeat* (to be followed, once complete, by *The Sleepless Eye Re-Woken, or Pinkerton's Legacy: With George Thiel and his Agents from Sea to Sea, in Establishment of a Federally Funded Division of Experimental Arcanistry and Hex-Handling*).

December 7, 1867:

STILL IN THE WIND:
Of New Aztectlan, once "Hex City"
(Now the Independent Republic of *Hexicas*, So-Called)
There is Much Rumour, but No Sign—
In Bewelcome Township,
Mayor Langobard says:
"Thank the Lord, We Do Not Look To Hear From Them."

A TREE OF BONES

December 14, 1867:

FRENZY AT THE WHITE HOUSE!
Marshals Baffled as President Johnson
Receives Contact, in Person,
From a Witchy Coterie of Hex City's
all-Female Elected Emissaries:
Songbird Yu, Business-woman, late of San Francisco;
"The Night Has Passed," Navaho Woman Chief (Federally
Pardoned for Former Offences);
and *Mrs. Sophronia Love (Widow, un-Hexacious),*
Representing her Son, Gabriel.

December 20, 1867:

"A SPECIAL CASE":
New Territorial Declaration and Constitution
Drafted for Hexicas
To Be Entered Into by Mutual Agreement—
Annexation Impossible, President Johnson Admits,
"Since the Territory in Question cannot
be Tracked, or Even Entered,
Without Express Permission from Its Inhabitants."
Spokeswoman Mrs. Love Maintains "All Hexicans
Consider Themselves U.S. Citizens,"
Even Though some have Sought Refuge from
American Laws or Mores.
"We Embrace All, Refuse None, Hex or No."

December 25, 1867:

FIRST HEXICAN NOEL!
Christmas Festivities to be Held Throughout the City-State,
Though Attendance of Religious Component is Hardly Mandatory.
Yr. Humble Correspondent, for One, Will be There.

And from various January, 1868, editions of Bewelcome Township, New Mexico's *Daily Letter*—

HEXICAS GLIMPSED OVER OWN RUINS
Tourists Making Pilgrimage to the Crater
Where this Devil-City Once Sat
Report "Great Light & Show, Fiery Clouds & Odd Noises"—
Say Hexes Alighted to Accept a Party of Varying Indians,
Mennonites, Freed Slaves & Coolies
Before Transporting them Inside & Making Off.
Reverend Oren Catlin Petitions Thiel Agency,
on Behalf of Frightened Congregation:
"Can Nothing be Done About Such Intrusions?"
GEORGE THIEL'S ANSWER TO REVEREND CATLIN, VIA POST:
Pres. Johnson's Instructions on Matter Clear Indeed—
"Hexicas, as Sovereign Area, is To Be Left Alone."

SUSPECT HEXATION?
Whether in Yourself or Others,
This Former Scourge may now be Converted
to a Badge of Honour
Earned in Governmental Service:
Therefore, if Seeking Registration or Forced Expression
through Asbury's Proven Process,
Citizens are urged to Contact their local
Thiel Agency Field Office at Once.

OUR NEW NEIGHBOURS
In Wake of Hexicas' Relocation and the
Rainbow Lady's Toppling,
Those Mexican Blood-cultists not Repatriated Across Border
Have Opted to Stay, Buy Farms, Work Land.
Claim Mrs. Love Told Them: "My Husband's Town is
Home to any Who Wish Solace."
Rev. Catlin: "Can They Be Called True Christians?"

A TREE OF BONES

A Vote Taken at Nazarene Hall to Resolve this Issue
Would Seem to Prove Yes:
<u>Yeas win over Nays, 47 to 13.</u>

WEEDING COTILLION
Science Confirms It: Red Weed Keeps Our Lands Arable!
All Those Wishing to Contribute to our Moat's Feed and Care
Are Therefore Directed to Assemble and Donate.
Cotillion Begins at Sun-down, with Prayers
(Rev. Catlin, Presiding);
Medicos in Attendance to Treat Wounds;
Food, Drink and Dancing to Follow.

FINE ARACHNORSES, NEW-BROKE
An Assortment of these Inestimable Creatures, Locally Bred,
Are Now Available for Purchase at Luffy's Stables:
Since All Survived the Season, they are Tough & Active—
Good Spinners, Faster Than Horses, Very Cheap.
In Interest of Public Safety, Mister Luffy Cautions that
only Seasoned Riders Need Apply,
and "Remember to Feed them Much Sugar, Often, or Face Mutiny."
(Those Unhappy with their Mounts should Note that the
U.S. Army is now Paying Top Dollar
for Arachnorses and Riders with Night Travel & Climbing
Experience, to be part of new Spider Cavalry Units.)

Telegram transcript, sent from the desk of Frank Geyer to George
Thiel, Yuma City, Arizona:

GREAT NEWS STOP MIXTURE OF ASBURY'S SCALE
MEASUREMENTS AND AUTOMATIC VIEWING HAS FINALLY
LOCATED OUR FRIENDS STOP INTELLIGENCE CONFIRMS MAP
COORDINATES STOP NO REPLY NECESSARY STOP MEET NEW
MEXICO PREPARED TO RIDE STOP

ED MORROW WAS DRAWING WATER when the riders appeared: a mixed posse of former Pinks, plus some of Washford's remaining men—not Carver, of course, who'd taken his honourable discharge and elected to go with Berta and Eulie when Hex City migrated once more. But Morrow thought he recognized most of them, even if he couldn't necessarily put names to faces.

"Want me to cover 'em?" Yancey asked, stepping up beside him, soft as a cat in those beaded hide slippers Yiska had parting-gifted her with. Her hair'd begun to grow back white 'round the scar left from Reverend Rook's last wound-strike to her scalp, creating a lightning bolt effect that made her seem all entirely too piratical-rakish for such a tiny slip of a thing, and she stood with her coat-flaps twitched back and both guns exposed, hand just beginning to hover 'bout the one on her right hip—a pose which, once struck, minded him so strongly of Chess Morrow fair felt it rise in his throat, like a lump.

"No," he said, "don't think that'll be necessary. Look who's in front."

The rest stood back, keeping a "polite" distance just far enough to render all parties equally safe from weapons fire, as once-Agent Frank Geyer and a smaller, greyer man Morrow could only assume must be the fabled George Thiel came cantering down. Geyer looked older himself, fresh marks of war still lingering from top to toe, an ache Morrow could well identify with. Thiel, slightly more distanced as he'd been from that crazy final rout, seemed more intact, yet far less easy to read.

"Mister Morrow," he began, without preamble, "don't believe we've ever been introduced, though Frank here speaks highly of you—you and Missus Kloves, both." A nod, in Yancey's general direction: "Ma'am."

Yancey nodded back. "You'd be Mister Thiel, I reckon. Him Pinkerton wanted killed on grounds of disloyalty, back when."

"I would."

"Uh huh. And seeing you've apparently since been elevated to his old job, I'm not too surprised."

Thiel flushed slightly. "That . . . was never my intent, ma'am. Was the President himself who put this charge upon me in the Hex City debacle's wake, making it all but impossible to refuse."

"Oh, yes. Still, it's not as though either of you *got* anything out of not doing so, 'sides from control over the most powerful new branch of government since taxes were first levied."

Now it was Geyer's turn to colour. "Missus Kloves! I beg you, if only for our old acquaintance's sake—"

"I don't recall that acquaintanceship having ever netted me much overall, Mister Geyer, beyond the rare thrill of being placed in harm's way again and yet again. So no, neither of you are Allan Pinkerton, that's true—but by God, I'd only hope you didn't aspire to be. What is it brings you here, exactly?"

"As you say, we work for the government, ma'am. Which, in turn, makes our motivation sadly difficult to explain to *non-governmental*—"

"Hadn't noticed Ed garnering any battlefield commissions lately," Yancey pointed out, "which puts him and me on pretty much common ground, as mere civilians . . . so from that angle, whatever you can't tell me you can't tell either of us, and vice versa."

"Yancey," Morrow interjected, warningly, but she just rolled her eyes, and rightly so. For what was he likely to do about it, anyhow?

I'm wrapped right 'round this tough little woman's finger, close as any wedding band, he thought, without regret; *closer, even. Tied tight as I ever was to Chess, too, though far more comfortably . . . and for most've the same reasons.*

All of the above, yes. And damnable pleased, in the end, to still be alive enough to be so.

"Well, gentlemen, since you don't actually seem inclined to threaten my . . . partner and me, I believe I'll leave you to it—though this isn't as large a ranch as some, I'm sure there's honest work yet needs to be done. Shovelling manure, perhaps."

As she sauntered away, Thiel raised his eyebrows, and whistled. "That's some lady you've yoked yourself to there, Morrow. I'd want to stay on her good side, if I was you."

"Still should, if you're smart. Now—since I believe you two probably have a piece to say, you might want to go ahead and say it."

Geyer nodded. Asking, without further preamble: "Have you seen Chess Pargeter?"

"Since Hex City removed itself from mortal ken? Or since he brought us here?"

"So, all this *was* his work," Thiel said.

"Who else?" Morrow wondered, logically. "I'm a simple non-magickal, and Yancey's skills don't run to fashioning her wants out of thin air. What *is* a bit creepish, though, is how fast you found us."

"Surely you didn't think you'd stay undetected."

"Hoped so, but frankly? No. What drew your eyes?"

"The fact this place didn't exist, and then it did—that alone argued hexation. But that it appeared paperwork and all made me believe perhaps Missus Kloves was also involved in the planning stages, if not in their execution."

Morrow leaned back against the well's adobe brick lip, feeling his old hurts begin to pain. "Chess accounts himself her friend as much as he's mine, so . . . might be. Tell you straight out, I ain't privy to all they get up to."

Chimes alerted them to Yancey as she came back 'round the other side of the house, brushing up against the wind-caller hung above its porch. She didn't wave while she passed by, just shut the door on them, decisively.

"Do you know where he went?" Thiel demanded, undistracted.

"Nope."

"Would you tell us, if you did?"

"Am I constrained to answer?"

"Not sure how we'd constrain you, exactly, without force—which, by the by, we're unlikely to use, you being a hero of the barely averted Second Schism, and all."

"Then no."

Geyer smiled, slightly. "That's what I told him."

"Yes, yes," Thiel replied, a touch tetchily, "and on more than one occasion, which is why I now owe you at least five dollars."

"Only five?"

"Very well, then. Make it ten."

They seemed quite the team, Morrow thought—easy in their back-and-forth, the way he and Chess had once been, at least during those initial days after Tampico, and he, Chess and Yancey still could be, as proven. Platonic camaraderie infused with just a hint of former intimacies on his part, a certain basic overlap of powers on hers.

MORROW CAST HIS MIND BACK, recalling what it'd been like to watch Chess pull this farm up whole and entire out of the Painted Desert's hide, like he was unwrapping a buried present, while Yancey hung over his shoulder from behind, whispering directions in his ear: Husbanding it solely from dirt and imagination, sticking floor to frame to walls to roof, while the soil all 'round gave up its salt and let loose with a stream of fresh water, allowing all manner of small green things to commence to grow. Most wonderfully of all, Chess hadn't appeared to resent her interference—had seemed to relish it, actually. As though he was so damn sick of thinking for himself, just for the nonce, he genuinely craved the idea of taking orders.

Knowing himself superfluous, Morrow had made sure to just stand back with his arms crossed, thinking that as the "normal" person in this equation, he basically had shit-all nothing to bring to the table. And expecting to hear Chess thinking back: *Well,* that *ain't exactly true . . .*

But no—Chess was concentrated still on the house, tongue caught between his teeth, and Morrow felt a bit sad that maybe there was no spark left between 'em anymore; sad, followed by conflicted. What if Yancey heard, and got jealous? Jealous of what, though?

Really not all that much, ever, mutually satisfying fits of revelry aside—not when compared with Chess and the Rev's operatically poisonous entanglement, its abyssal deeps and hypoxic heights, the bitter fruits sown and reaped. Which left a sting of its own, an unexpected wound, a lack that Morrow had never expected.

This display of creative power came hard on the heels of five days of complete sloth, an addled and sullen silence, during which Morrow and Yancey did little but keep close yet quiet, allowing Chess to suffer through his version of mourning undisturbed, if not alone. He sat with boots off and cross-legged, unwarily shirtless, squinting down where part of the Crack had lain while the sun beat him red—and though his tears had long since dried, a constant storm of dust rose and fell like civilizations in the hollow his stare carved before him: Restless, virulent, boiling.

Sometimes Morrow thought he could glimpse visions in that pit, peering at it over Chess's freckled shoulder, or almost so. The black corpse-whip of Lady Ixchel's hair, eddying over exposed bone; the gargantuan creep of Grandma's spider; Hex City scarring the sky, a six-walled stone tumour. The too-calm face of Reverend Rook caught in mid-air, still falling.

So it went, until the morning Morrow woke to find Chess standing by his bed-roll with arms crossed, barefoot yet, but his fair flesh no longer quite as dangerously flushed.

"Thanks," was all he could apparently think to say, finally.

Morrow rubbed sleep from his eyes. "No problem," he offered. "Uh . . . care for a spot of coffee?"

"If all you got on offer's the same shit I smelled cookin' this last week, then no."

A moment later, Yancey came yawning out of the tent they'd raised and stopped short, one eyebrow kiting, to register Chess up and about once more, none the worse for wear.

"Well," she said, "I'll go hunt us up some meat."

"I'd help, you wanted," Chess offered—and wasn't *that* a surprise? Almost as much as the way he'd put it, quick and plain-spoke, without any sort of sting to the tail. "Ain't had to eat for some long time, but . . ."

He spread his hands, a net of sparks flickering briefly from fingertip to fingertip, laced and trailing, at which Yancey just nodded, grown sadly used to the everyday miraculous.

"Might be you could cast a charm, bring the lizards a bit faster? Much obliged, if so."

"All right."

An hour after, arrayed 'round the fire Morrow had laid in their absence, they'd eaten stew in silence before Chess finally wiped his mouth on one cuff and said: "Well, seems those Hex City females want me on that council of theirs—sure ain't ceased to bother me with layin' out offer on offer for any sort of position might be to my liking, anyhow, this whole time."

"I didn't—" Morrow started to reply, then stopped, as Chess tapped one temple: *Of course, right. In* there.

"That'd be mainly Yiska, I'd think," Yancey observed. "Not Songbird, even now."

Chess shook his head, almost smiling. "You're right enough on that one." His lip twisted further, flattening into something more grim. "Don't matter much either way, though—I ain't 'bout to lock myself up in some flying castle and run myself ragged strivin' for the betterment of hex-kind, just 'cause them and me share some sort of kinship; never been sentimental that way, or any. Hell, if blood meant anything at all t'me, I'd be far more like to run off New York way and find that gal Oona said killed my Pa, if only to stand her a drink and shake her damn hand."

"But you ain't gonna do that either, I take it," Morrow concluded. "So—"

"What *are* you going to do, exactly?" Yancey inquired, with a touch of that old coolly practical hotelier's savvy Morrow remembered from their first encounter with her, back in the Horde.

"Build y'all a house, I thought, for starters, and carve out a patch of good land 'round here too, for you 'n' Ed to play your games on. As a small token of my appreciation."

"Again, much obliged. Then what?"

"Christ on a three-dollar cross! You're damn hard to please, missy; anyone ever tell you that?"

"Oh, one or two. Though far less than the choir who've told *you* the same, I'd reckon."

They locked glares a long moment, anger-lit green to mock-mild grey, before both snorted and looked away once more, caught on the mutual ragged edge of laughter. And in the aftermath of his conjuring, stew re-heated, Chess told Morrow: "Can't put it off any longer, Ed; my ride's almost here. Come morning, you won't see me for some long time—but then again," he nodded at Yancey, "*this* one can probably fill you in on all my bad deeds now and then, what with those dreams of hers. And I don't doubt we'll meet again, eventually."

Again, Morrow felt that hollow clutch in his stomach-pit, impossible to deny or explain. "Seems likely, yeah," he replied. "So . . ."

". . . so."

They stood there a moment, both glancing elsewhere, studying the rocks and dirt (and fresh grass, sod, bare beginnings of a garden, that tree Yancey'd placed for shade over by the well) as though either thought they might be likely to offer advice on how best to continue. Yancey herself hung back by the fire, leaving them room enough for whatever demonstrations they felt were appropriate in her presence, though Morrow had the odd feeling that even if she absented herself entirely she'd probably be able to "hear" them anyhow, no matter what distance she might take herself off to.

Once upon a time—and not so long past, either—Chess might've tried to kiss him goodbye; once upon a time, Morrow would've let him, or even kissed him first like he had at Grandma's camp, back by Old Woman Butte. But for reasons he wasn't quite sure of, that seemed impossible, now . . . and it seemed as if each knew it.

"Was thinking I might make myself useful, believe it or not," Chess told him, left hand habit-braced on that same side's empty holster. "Put myself to work extirpating the Weed where it runs rampant and ain't being fed, since it was grown for my benefit, or hunting down whatever weird objects might've been left behind— orphaned out of Mictlan-Xibalba, y'know, when I finally got the Crack closed for good. Then again, I'll bet there's a parcel of hexes new-made out there, once the dust died down; might track them down too, while I'm at it. Stop 'em from harassing simple folks or eating each other, then tell 'em how they got a place to go if they want to, where they won't have to do either."

Here he trailed away, as though slightly embarrassed to listen to his own pretensions to redemption, the laughable idea that Chess damn Pargeter should ever want to do a lick of good here and there, in between the usual range of shooting, riding and fucking. That at the grand old age of twenty-six or so, after watching his first and only love fall into Hell's maw and staving off at least one apocalypse thereby, he might've actually *changed* a bit—gotten older, if not substantially wiser. Grown up, if only a bit.

"That sounds good, Chess," was all Morrow could think to say, while the sorrow of Chess's losses pricked at his heart. "Both things, I mean. All of it."

"Yeah? Well, good. Sounds plumb crazy when *I* say it, to be frank, so if you don't think it is, then maybe . . ."

Chess let himself trail away, then, and smiled. Not a grin, whether gleeful or fierce or bitter; not a snarl disguised, either. Just *there*, a simple play of muscles, innocent enough to wound. The smile of a far less complicated man, one who hadn't died twice, or been twice reborn. One who'd never been any sort of a god.

"Never had no daddy, as you know," he said, at last, "and nobody ever told me to call him by that name, either, 'less he had coin to spend. But I'm fine with that, for I did have friends, in the end; one false as Confederate dollars, and one true-damn-blue."

Morrow swallowed. "I hope I know which was the camp I fell in."

"Well, damn, Ed . . . by this time, *I'd* hope you did, too."

And suddenly Yancey was there as well, having made her way across from the cook-pit without either of them noticing, as good a fake Injun as ever wore moccasins. Laying her hand on Chess's arm, friendly and just a bit possessive, to say: "I'd hope I might've made for a third, Mister Pargeter, man or no."

Chess hissed through his teeth. "Woman, please. You know you do."

A horse took him away before dawn—Morrow'd feared it might be one of those small(ish)-sized spiders, but apparently, Chess hadn't been feeling all *that* adventurous. One way or the other, by the time Yancey woke he was long gone, and she and Morrow sat together to watch the sun come up over their new homestead: hexation's bounty, payment perhaps for being the two people in all of Chess Pargeter's life who'd only given, never taken. Or just two pals, Goddamnit.

Later, freed from the restraint they'd felt in Chess's presence, they finally consummated their affections for what had to be— strange as it was to say it—the very first time, at least in the flesh. And held each other afterward, close and tight, until they slept.

BUT NOW, THIEL'S VOICE brought Morrow back to the matter at hand.

"Am I right in assuming Mister Pargeter *was* offered a place at Hexicas' pyramid-head, but gave it up untried—preferring to stand alone, as ever?"

"Well, he sure ain't there now, so I'd think that part's pretty public knowledge."

"Yet he's still a power to be reckoned with, even stripped of his former godhood."

"Nothin' you could do to stop him, he turned against you. Nothin' *I* could do to stop him either, in point of fact, if that was your grand plan—like I said, I don't know where he is, to begin with. And like Yancey already intimated . . ."

". . . neither of you'd feel all too much obliged to pull his reins, even assuming you could," Geyer filled in, with another glance at Thiel.

"That's right."

"Hmmm," Thiel said, with no particular emphasis, and no hint of what he might mean by it, either.

Geyer glanced at him, then back at Morrow. "Remember what Pinkerton always feared, Ed?" He asked. "That if hexes could combine, they'd rule the world in a decade?"

"Sure, like everyone did. But the Hexicans don't strike me like that's their aim—not this generation, anyhow. And again, you sure couldn't stand in their way, they decided otherwise."

"But your friend Mister Pargeter might," Thiel pointed out.

"Might. If you could find him, and he wanted to."

"Can I count on your support, in that area?"

Morrow snorted. "Support—so I can steer him around, point him where you want him? How likely you think *that* is to work out, exactly? Doc Asbury's gimmicks ain't the be-all and end-all, sirs. If you go against Hexicas, you'll find that out. Same thing if you go against Chess Pargeter, likewise."

"Oh, undoubtedly," Thiel replied, coolly. "But then again, if you continue to tame Mister Pargeter the way you have already, you and Missus Kloves—gently alter his nature with this highly laudable mixture of true affection and morally improving example—then perhaps we'll never have to."

God damn, this was a perceptive fellow; Morrow was almost afraid to tell him any more, knowing it'd be filed away somewhere for reference. Which Geyer seemed to figure out pretty quick, as his next words indicated.

"What George's maybe trying to say is . . . you and Mister Pargeter—and Missus Kloves too, with all her woes—have mainly known the West thus far in its raw state," he explained, "unrefined; a work in progress. But things will have to change, for that progress to continue. Things are *already* changing."

"And this would be the part where you ask me which side of that change I want to end up on, right? Whether I want to go the way of the buffalo, or stake my claim to Manifest Destiny?" At Geyer's look: "Yeah, that's right, sir: I read a paper or two, now and then."

"The question stands," Thiel said.

"Then I s'pose my answer would be: good luck with all that. I'm well out of this tussle, considering I worked two years without pay to set it up, let alone to bring it to bed. You want to talk to Chess, chase him down; see if he'll stand still for it."

"Will he?"

"He just might, you come at him on a good day. 'Cause, see—*he's* changed, too."

Geyer nodded. "That's what I'd heard. Saw evidence of, too, outside Hex City."

"That's as well," Thiel replied. "Because you're right, of course, Mister Morrow: I don't really expect our hexacious brethren will be rejoining the Union anytime soon. But I *can* foresee a time—sooner, rather than later—when Hexicas finds it useful to send emissaries our way, same as any other sovereign nation. Hell, even Vatican City receives petitioners. And I can even see a day when your young Mister Pargeter might consent to be their chief ambassador, once he's been off on his own in the world a while—lived a few more years alone under the shadow of his own infamous name, 'til he's had the rougher edges either knocked off him, or just smoothed over a tad. Daniel Boone himself ended up a state representative, after all."

"'Til the speculators did for him?" Morrow shook his head, smiling. "You don't know Chess all too well, Mister Thiel, that's for sure."

"Not yet. But I hope to."

NEXT MORNING ON, Yancey woke early, as was her wont—emerging headlong from a dream, a distinct vision of Chess in the future, small as ever though not quite so slim, his beard tamed and groomed into Satanic points, more silver than red. Saw him strutting down the aisle at some big to-do in a city as far from New Mexico as Boston had been from Hoffstedt's Hoard, when her parents first set out on their emigrants' journey. A voice announced him, flat-vowelled and hoity, clearly Eastern: *The Representative from Hex City, Sheriff Chess Pargeter, and his . . . companion.* And though who *that* was she couldn't see, somehow she knew it wasn't Ed, which (even in her sleep) made her quite uncharitably glad.

A moment later, however, she rolled over to realize the bed was empty—thought he might've gone to the jakes at first, 'til she caught him hoisting his already packed saddlebags by the back door. He froze when he saw her, ridiculously shamefaced for such a big man, 'specially one who'd already come intact through Hex War, fire, flood and rout, not to mention tussling with her *and* Chess, in his time.

"I'm not impressed," she told him, hands on hips.

He sighed. Replying: "Wouldn't expect you to be, overmuch."

"Wanted to warn Chess 'bout those jackasses, is that it? 'Cause you could've got *me* to do it, easy enough; that's the nice part about having a dead-speaker for your woman. Means you don't have to do almost anything in person, not unless you want to."

Morrow looked down, one hand ruffling the back of his neck uncomfortably, as though he had some sort of cud he'd been chewing over caught in his throat.

"Well," he began, at last, "I guess I just thought . . . Sheriff Love bein' dead—again, and all—that . . . you'd want to settle down, build yourself a life, do . . . womanly stuff."

"You did," she replied, flatly.

"Well, yeah. Don't you?"

Chess's voice in her head, then, like always—like he just couldn't help himself, present or not. Observing: *Oh, all men really are fools, just like my Ma always used to say.*

She felt the sudden sting of tears as she looked at this fool she'd roped herself to, studying him hard, wondering at the fact it'd taken them this long to find a place where they weren't of a complete accord anymore. Just what happened when you stopped meeting in dreams and tried living side by side, she supposed, in the frail and fragile meat, with all its pleasures and complaints; when you moved from intention into reality, and found yourself abruptly saddled with all the mistakes and complications human beings were heir to, by simple flaw of design.

Yancey sniffed. Then managed, at last, schooling her thick voice hard in how best not to tremble, "No, Ed. That must've been some other female you were thinking of."

Morrow gazed back with those fine hazel eyes of his, for all the world like he didn't know what to make of her, and it made her want to weep even harder. She remembered what that Agent, Mister Thiel, had said, just before riding away: *Things have changed, Mister Morrow; you'd agree with that evaluation, surely.* To which Ed had frowned just like was doing now, and answered: *For now, all right.*

Yes, absolutely. But far more likely . . . for ever.

Her face felt hot, tight; though she knew she was probably flushing all over, she couldn't break their stare, even for an instant. It seemed vitally important, as though if she did, she'd lose him forever—*And I don't want to, you idiot, can't you see, without me having to tell you? I want* this, *not some Goddamned dead dream of respectable matronage I left behind in the Hoard, with Uther's and my Pa's corpses. I want* you.

"What-all do we even know about each other, really?" He asked her, sadly.

"I know you're as good a man as any I've ever met, and that's better than I could hope for."

"Marshall Kloves included?"

For all it made her feel terrible, in honesty's name, she had to nod.

"Him I could've got to love, eventually—he was banking on it, and I do believe that's true. But it wasn't to be." She continued, with difficulty: "You . . . could probably learn to love me too, though, you just gave enough time to it. That's if you don't feel the same way I do, just right now."

"Oh, honey, I'm so sorry."

"Sorry you don't? Or sorry you can't?"

"*Sorry* you think I'd even have to try, seein' how I love you so hard right this very minute, it's like my Goddamn heart's 'bout to stop."

Then she was in his arms, and she *was* crying, almost as hard as Chess had, after Rook's fall. But it was all right, it'd have to be. Everything was all right, now.

In this whole sad, hex-broken world, they—at least—had each other.

A MONTH SINCE Hex City's downfall, and in that whole time, Chess hadn't used his powers once—just rode through the Painted Desert like anybody else, quiet and careful, 'til he finally reached some dirt-scratch town on the Texican border. Dry Well, he thought the sign at the trading post had read, which fit. There he unwrapped the ear-bob he'd retrieved from that seam where the Crack closed over, still crusted with blood, and threw it down on the countertop. "How much?" he asked, voice tight and small, as though his mouth were full of sand.

The shop-keep barely glanced up from assessing it; didn't seem to register his torn lobe or the spattering of bullet holes 'cross his jacket, now so badly neglect-faded it looked halfway back to Confederate grey. Didn't seem to recognize him at *all*, or only as yet another penniless drifter, of whom these streets did seem well-choked. "We don't lack for turquoise 'round here, but gold's scarce," he said. "Give ya five."

"It's worth twice that."

"Then go back where you got it, sell it there. Five."

"Eight, and I'm bein' over-nice."

"Five or four-fifty, makes no never-mind to me. Keep arguin' and it's four-fifty, *plus* I call the Marshals. Your choice."

Chess raised a brow, feeling: *You cheat everybody comes in here, motherfuck, or am I just special?* prick at his tongue, like that broken knife blade one of his Ma's roistering biddies used to carry hid in her mouth, back when Oona'd still had enough to splash out she could account herself flush with "friends." But for once, he took a perverse sort of pride in *not* indulging himself.

"Five, then," he said. "Any place to stay close by, with food on the premises?"

"You want good, or cheap?"

Chess spread his hands out. "I'm like you see, and I still need to buy new gear."

"That'd be cheap—try Widow Maysie's, end of the street." As he counted out the cash, his nude eye flicked toward the hitching post, greedy. "Could prob'ly do better, you was willin' to sell that horse of yours."

"I don't aim to stay too long."

"Suit yourself, then."

And again, his former self's voice slid forward to snap, in his scarred ear: *Goddamn if I won't 'cause I always do, you stupid old shit-kicker.* Familiar yet irrelevant as the carping of a ghost, too foolish to know he should fall over and get himself buried.

The Widow had three rooms empty and a gaggle of kids running her ragged, but turned suddenly nice as pie when Chess proved he was willing to pay extra for solitude—laid out fresh sheets, made him up a plate of beans with salt pork, even lent him her dead man's shave-kit, after he asked where to find a barber. "That man's no good, sir," she told him. "A dago from parts East; calls himself a leech, but I seen him leave gut-shot men lead-poisoned, and still take cash money for it. Do better to do it yourself, and save the expense."

Save it for you, *you mean,* Chess heard Chess-that-was whisper, his bile already dimming, a mosquito's hum. And returned to himself abruptly, falling straightway into a silence-pocket that argued she might've been talking a while yet, without his participation— just staring down and panting slightly, blood all a-hammer while considering on nothing much, the way some badly shocked troops'd done in battle's wake, during the War. "Soldier's heart," the medicos had called it, or "nostalgia." Yet another of those old Greek terms the Rev'd known so well how to explain, in between his Bible-blather, his Shakespearian discourses.

A surfeit of memory, Chess—not good memory, either, even as it engages us to all else's exclusion. For "nostalgia" means "our pain," you see.

"Sir, are you well? Are you all—"

Fine enough, you idjit, given. Better by far, after a while, without your yammering laid in on top of the rest of it.

But: "Ma'am," he managed, finally, doing what he thought might be a passable Ed Morrow imitation, "that's . . . kind advice, I'm sure. Thank you for it."

"Why, you're most welcome. Room's at the hall's end—you take as long as you need, make yourself presentable. I'll boil water for washing."

"Ma'am," he repeated, dipping his head like a play-actor. And stumbled past, nose suddenly salt-stuffed and eyes a-sting, too dim to negotiate except by touch alone.

It took him far longer than he'd thought it would to do for the beard he'd worn almost since he bid San Francisco farewell, hacking and scraping for what seemed like hours 'til the skin showed through, though at least he didn't cut himself too badly. After, he examined his face in the dull tin mirror and was surprised to realize the scar 'neath his jawline barely showed at all, except from odd angles.

Otherwise, he looked thinner, older, burnt 'cross the nose and tanned darker than he'd ever seen himself before. A slight lightening at either temple, uneven on each side, dimmed his hair's red from flame to afterglow. An outright thread of grey wove through one gilt brow, making it fork, then hike quizzically.

Maybe no one would take me for Chess Pargeter after all, he thought, for one breathless moment—frozen while a paralyzing wave of something swept up through him, strong but nameless, almost impossible to decode. Hope? Horror? Regret?

Regret, hell.

No, he was himself still, no matter what: small-made and slim, face like a scowling fox, harder by far than he seemed at a distance. Though the embers might burn low and crusted, they remained hot; something would blow on 'em soon enough, making 'em flare and pop. And then?

Well. *Then*, he supposed, they'd just have to see. Him too, along with everybody else.

Chess plunged his hands back into the washbasin, made one more grooming circuit, wiping away what was left of his whiskers. Then slung his ruined jacket back on, and went out in search of drink.

Nearest thing in Dry Well to a saloon was a combination eatery and melodeon in which a three-piece band sawed away at their fiddles, and two indifferent-looking skirted creatures moped wherever they thought they could show 'emselves off to best advantage. One bit got you a shot and dinner, a plate heaped with sowbelly, and the three Bs—biscuits, bacon, beef—with wild onions as a side dish, against the scurvy. There was a card game in one corner, a hot topical discussion in the other: Pinkerton's legacy, that new outfit Geyer and that other ex-agent had cobbled together out of old Allan's leavings. Doc Asbury they had working hard, making reparation, parsing his Manifolds from weapons back to tools—

something Songbird would be glad to hear of, Chess supposed, for all the harm the old man had done her, in his misguided attempts to defang hexation at its individual roots rather than its ultimately unknowable source.

How he might convey that information to her, on the other hand, he had no idea. Nor why he might want to try.

You may speak to us at your convenience, red boy, that man-squaw Yiska's voice murmured at his inner ear, the very same instant this thought framed itself—for she too seemed more powerful, perhaps augmented by dead Grandma's legacy, now she'd passed beyond the veil Chess didn't plan to penetrate again anytime soonish. *We welcome your intelligence. There is a place amongst us held open for you, always.*

And why would I want that? he ached to cry out, even aloud, for all around him to wonder at. *I ain't none of yours, like you ain't none of mine. Only person left on this damn earth I belong to is—*

—Ed, maybe, when all was said and done. Maybe even Yancey Colder Kloves, who might one day consent to set her weeds aside and be Missus Morrow. But aside from them . . .

Two women he'd hated in this rambling, violent life of his, a whore and a goddess, and he couldn't even say he hated the first anymore, or not quite so much as he had. While for all his affections bent Ed's way, frolic-wise and other-, there remained one man alone he'd ever loved, thus far. Loved and hated both, in almost equal measure.

The hurt of it crept up and down like sickness, but never went away; a self-refreshing void, set right where that hollow his heart filled once more used to gape. As though his own pulse, so long absent, were nothing but a hammer pounding one new nail for every beat into his own flesh, forever wrenching the same wound open.

All things pass, still, red boy. All things move on. Even him. Even you.

He didn't want the advice, necessarily, for all he knew it was probably good. Yet he couldn't deny there were parts of him—larger parts than ever before—which wished to Mictlan-Xibalba's lowest deeps it might, eventually, prove true.

Over by the trio, an altercation was rising, argument sliding fast to incipient brawl. A long-legged young man sat scowling with a guitar slung over his chair-back, mariachi-style, while three other cowboy bravos poked at him. "Sing for us, Alarid!" one demanded, jeeringly.

"Don't think I will."

"Aw, c'mon, we're all waitin'. I know just the song, too: *Oh, Charlie's neat and Charlie's sweet, and Charlie, he's a dandy . . . and every time we chance t'meet, he gives me sugar candy . . .*"

The lanky sumbitch in question—his first name being Charles, Chess could only assume—narrowed his eyes, which were bright blue fringed with lashes so dark and thick they looked like he'd smeared on what the San Fran ladies called fireplace kohl. His hair, too, was black as a coalhouse cat, unruly, with one long lock falling like a kiss-curl; some Mex in his complexion, the arrogant furl of his grandee's lip. This was the sort of young buck annoyed those 'round him simply by existing, and didn't seem to've figured yet that that should make him pull his head *in*, rather than jut it out all the prouder.

"'Sweet'," he repeated. "Problem is, though—I'm savin' *my* candy for better men than you, Sam Holger. Not that I'd ever thought you *wanted* it before, as such . . ."

Holger turned first red, then white, choking hard on an in-drawn breath, like it was fire-water. "You . . . faggot motherfucker, you," he began, spluttering, "always puttin' on your Goddamn airs and graces—"

"Better airs and graces than cowflop-stink, and ten pounds of stupid in a five-pound sack."

"That's pretty big talk, for a pole-smokin' queerboy," Holger's right-hand pal put in.

"Well, I *am* big, or so I've been told." As if to prove it, not-so-sweet Charlie unfolded himself, attaining a height from which he could stare down on almost every man there. "'Sides which, you don't have to be tall to raise all sorts of hell, even on the invert side of things. Y'all never heard of Chess Pargeter?"

Right-hand guffawed while left-hand snorted, and Sam Holger just shook his head. "Oh, so," he said, sneering. "Got yourself somewhat've a crush, I 'spect, from them songs and penny novels. But you ain't no Chess Pargeter, Charlie Alarid."

Chess could see where this was headed. Holger he took for a bully, but blooded. Charlie, too proud to back down, read all over as being as yet unversed in how best to make others do the same. It felt familiar enough to time, a song Chess could hum in his sleep. Why should he get involved?

'Cause the boy seems to idolize you, fool—and he's not bad to look on, either. Though on t'other hand, it was *thinking with your dick got you into . . . everything, in the first place.*

Aw hell, he thought, once again.

Downing the rest of his shot, therefore, Chess kicked his own chair back deliberately, making it ring 'gainst the floor—and when the rest of 'em jumped, heads turning, he rose too: not so high as Charlie, yet with a tad more martial emphasis. Commenting, as he did: "No, he sure ain't. *I* am, though."

Right-hand and left- scoffed again, like they was wound-up clockwork with only the one trick. "The hell you say!" right-hand blurted. "Am what?" Holger demanded, at almost the same time.

"Chess Pargeter, ass-wipe. Did I stutter?"

All three gave him a hard stare, followed by a snort.

Left-hand: "What, 'cause you're red-headed and runtish?"

Holger nodded. "You ain't neither! Just some sad-sack don't even have a gun on his belt, stickin' his nose in where it don't belong—'sides which, even if you *was* him, word is that whoremaster Rook's been cast down, and all his old gods along with him. There ain't no hexes left, now they took their city and gone . . . so if you got left behind, what sort'a hex could you even be?"

"There ain't even such a thing as *hexation* no more, is what *I* heard," put in right-hand, crossing his arms.

Chess felt himself boggle. "What idjit told you *that*?"

"Hell," the fool replied, "I don't recall—read it in the papers, I s'pose. It's known."

Now it was Chess's turn to snort, then snap his fingers. Without fanfare, he was suddenly *him* once more: imperially regaled from tip to toe, boots shone, spurs gleaming—his red hair silver-touched but sleek, pomaded. All finery replaced but the ear-bob, his Colts . . . and the beard.

"That a fact?" He asked, mildly enough.

Holger swallowed, visibly. His pals turned pale. And Charlie Alarid, previously the sole fierce Spartan in this whole five-horse crap-hole—he clapped his hands together, happy as a kid on Christmas, and laughed right out loud.

"*Told* ya," was all he said.

The place seemed dimmer than before. Or was it just how Chess shone brighter, casting everyone 'round him into shadow? Not that he could help it, any more'n they could.

"I . . . ain't afraid of you," Holger lied, queasily, licking his lips. To which Chess simply shook his head.

"Boy," he said, though the man in question probably had five years on him, "you need to listen, and listen good—there's no way this goes well, for anybody but me. Walk away and you live, with a story to drink on. Make me kill you, what's that? Stampin' on an anthill just for fun, conduct unbecoming. You 'n' yours ain't worth the juice it'd cost me to set you afire, let alone the piss it'd take to put you out."

Sounded fair enough as he said it, but how was he to know, without Morrow there to translate? Still, even as he turned his back, he suspected it wasn't going to work. And indeed, a second later, Holger's first bullet came pocking over his shoulder, shattering a lamp behind the bar—but the second bounced straight off in a heat-haze ripple, ricocheting back through the webbing between Holger's gun-hand thumb and forefinger. Holger squalled, cradling his maimed hand. As his weapon hit the floor, meanwhile, Mister right-hand reputation-debunker and their left-hand pal alike were left stunned, unsure whether to help, flee or just stand steady, hoping Chess wouldn't notice they were still there.

"Now," Chess said, turning back, "just think a little, and you'll see exactly how foolish a move that was. 'Cause me, I've been a damn *god* most've this last year, like Rainbow Bitch Ixchel-that-was and the rest—got hexation comin' out my eyeballs, so much I don't hardly know what-all to do with it, which is why I oft-times don't choose to. But even was I 'only' plain Chess Pargeter once more, you'd still be the stupidest motherfucker alive to talk at me that-a-way . . . and you wouldn't be *that* for long."

He nodded at Holger. "Once upon a time, I'd've told you to come back when you'd trained left-handed, try it again. Here's the difference a war makes, though—right this instant, I'm more inclined t'be merciful than not, since I've been travelling with good people a while. So . . ."

Here he stepped forward as Holger stumbled back, caught hold of him by the wrist and laid his opposite hand to his sweaty forehead, willing reparative sleep all through him. Holger folded up, wounds already knitting, to clunk skull-first back onto the floor at Chess's feet; Chess stepped away while the fool's friends lunged to catch him, wiping both palms of him like Pilate.

". . . take *that*, clear out, and leave me be," he concluded. "I'm drinkin', and I don't care to be disturbed."

Everyone mostly took care not to do so, after—looked anywheres else, all but whistling. Chess sat and was served, though the barkeep kept on forgetting to charge him. He took it first as his due, then eventually sighed, shook what coin he had left 'til it had multiplied itself threefold, and left it by his up-turned glass.

Halfway down the street, he noticed young master Alarid still drifting vaguely after him, hands in his pockets and guitar dangling, and stopped to fix him with a cold eye. "Already saved your ass once tonight," Chess pointed out, "so you can stop starin' at me like I'm 'bout to grant you wishes."

Charlie shrugged, not even pretending to be shamed. "Made *my* dreams come true when you showed Sam Holger and them how queer can go hand in hand with tough sumbitch, so . . . maybe I just want to thank you, is all."

"Okay, then—you're welcome. Now move on."

"I'd heard you was prickly."

"Oh, I am that. But I s'pose now you'll tell me how you like 'em that way, right?"

Charlie smiled, as if to say: *Pricks're good*. And suddenly, it was all Chess could do not to snicker.

Been so long since he'd flirted with anyone out of more than spite—a restless urge to mess with men's minds, along with everything else—that he could barely remember what it felt like, let alone whether the result'd be worth the effort.

What'm I gonna do with you? he thought, letting his eyes roam up and down, and Charlie—obviously well-able to tell what Chess was considering—shot him a hot look under lowered lashes in return, as though he believed he could suggest some options.

"Don't think just 'cause we share the same tastes that makes me your patron saint," Chess told the kid, at last. "I ain't lived through . . . all I did just to tour the West in search of fellow mis-mades, or save fools of any persuasion from their own mouths."

"I *told* you I'm grateful, Mister Pargeter. Don't want no more'n that."

"So you say."

"Well . . . might be I'd like to buy you breakfast, you was amenable, 'fore you ride off yonder."

"Who says I'm leavin'?"

Now it was Charlie's turn to hike a brow. "Who'd want to *stay* here, he didn't have to?"

A good question, and one which came into even clearer relief when Chess saw the Widow waiting for him in her doorway, youngest child braced dozing between her and him like a shield.

"Don't *do* nothin' in my house, Mister Pargeter," she asked him, "if you'd be so kind. Please."

Nothin' like magic, or nothin' like ridin' young Charles here 'til he pops? Chess thought, sourly. But he tipped his hat and agreed to her terms, which seemed to disappoint Charlie somewhat. *That ain't the Chess Pargeter I heard tell of!*

Chess shrugged. *Probably not*, he thought.

Must've got over his dismay by morning, however, since he turned up back at the same not-quite-a-saloon done up twice as elaborate as the night before, like he was trying to show Chess who could shout "Lock up your sons!" the loudest.

"Don't see Sam Holger," Chess noted, glancing 'round, as he tucked into his eggs.

Charlie shook his head, coaxing a rippling run from his instrument, far prettier than most pauses. "Naw, don't expect him to show his face for some time yet; he'll want to make sure everybody who was there when you laid him low is elsewhere, so nobody's 'round to cry lie on him when he starts in to claimin' he kicked your ass."

"So let him."

"Couldn't live with myself, if I did."

"So you'll risk getting killed over nothing, instead? Believe me, kid, Holger's the exact type someone like you should keep away from, they want to stay upright—sort who won't learn his lesson no matter how many times it's repeated, or how hard."

"Aw, he's full of wind, is all. Been after me since we was knee-high, for reasons don't stand lookin' at. What duds I wear, what songs I play: be sort of funny, it wasn't so damn sad."

"That ain't the sort of joke you laugh at, not 'less you got a gun to back your taste in humour up. 'Course, you bein' somewhat of a fop probably doesn't help, either." Adding, gently, as Charlie stared up at him in utter confusion: "A clothes-horse, a dandy, like they said . . . fashionable beyond the proper bounds of sense, is what that means."

"You get *all* your clothes store-made, or so I heard."

"Don't get 'em *made* at all, anymore—but yes, I used to. Still, you'll note I ain't the one of us wearin' orange cowhide pants with brass buttons all up and down 'em, or a shirt embroidered with roses."

Charlie shrugged. "Thought it'd suit me better to stand out as much as I can, since I don't have no hope of bein' passed over."

"Now that, I understand. But if you're gonna spend your whole life pickin' fights, you need to know how to end 'em, not just start 'em."

"You could teach me, I guess. If you wanted to."

"If I wanted to, sure. You sayin' I should?"

"I ain't qualified to know what you should or shouldn't, Mister Pargeter. Just . . ."

Just I'm the only other queer you ever met, let alone the only hex, Chess thought, suddenly exhausted, though it was hardly gone ten in the morning. *Just like you look at me like I'm Jesus, like I could multiply fishes and turn water into wine—and Goddamn if I couldn't, either. Goddamn if I couldn't do any damn thing I want, even now.*

It was a heavy burden, all this possibility. He didn't remember ever feeling that way before, but maybe that was what coming back from the dead—twice, with different results both times—did for a fellow.

"Paradin' 'round town dressed like that, let alone the rest, your Ma and Pa must've hated you somethin' fierce," Chess said, at last.

"By the end? I somewhat think they did. Named me after a king, though—Charlemagne, first of France: 'Charles the big.' Guess they hoped it'd fit."

"Good thing you grew into it."

That made Charlie preen a bit, which prompted Chess to crack another smile. But the next turn in their dance made it all slide side-a-ways, when Charlie asked: "You was . . . *with* Reverend Rook, is what I heard."

"From them songs, and such? Sure was, and famous for it."

"Dead, too, for some of that same time . . . that's the other rumour."

"That too, yeah. Twice over."

"And then—you came back. Why?"

Didn't care to stay prone, he thought, but didn't say. "'Cause I still had work needed doin'," he averred, instead.

"To kill him, then. For . . . killin' you?"

"That was *her* idea," Chess heard himself snap. After a moment, with difficulty: "Ash Rook didn't need *me* to get himself killed. No more'n—"

I needed him to get killed, myself.

Truth was, as Chess only just now understood he already well knew, if it hadn't gone the way it did, it'd've gone one of a hundred others. Chess had been moving toward fatality all his life, all unknowing of the cost. The moment when his inborn payload finally exploded, destroying everything 'round him sure as double canister shot.

A bomb, a plague, one more slice of walking doom. One more hex in a world that hated hexes, all the more so whenever they managed not to hate each other, or themselves.

But now there was Hexicas, at least. And that, too, was Ash Rook's work, along with all the rest.

"Wanted him dead, that's true 'nough—a thousand times over, and more," Chess concluded, his own voice so low, so rough, he barely recognized it. "But even that he took pride in deprivin' me of, by the end. Judged himself by his bad Book's standard, found himself wanting and passed sentence, 'fore I had a chance to do more'n curse him over it. For Asher Goddamn Rook never could stand to be outdone by anyone, at anything."

Something on his cheek now, warm enough, but not wet: Charlie Alarid's big hand, cupping his cheek and half his chin. One guitar string-callused thumb, tracing the track where tears would go, if only there were any left to shed.

"I'm sorry," the kid said, and seemed to mean it. Chess shook his head.

"No need," he replied. "I'm sorry enough for the both of us."

The barkeep, gazing studiously elsewhere, let out a dry little prompting cough: *Time, gentlemen. Please.* Which made Chess hiss a bit, but only a bit; more for show than anything else, and not much for that, either. He rose, Charlie following like a too-long shadow, and stalked over, as the barkeep recoiled.

"Get a lot of trouble like last night in here?" Chess demanded, placing one fist on the countertop.

"Uh . . . somewhat, I s'pose." Jaw wobbly as a turkey-neck, the man stole a squint at Charlie, adding: "Mainly when Mister Alarid's about, truth to tell."

"You do know how he ain't the only bent creature in this world, though, right?" Chess asked. "Or me, neither?" As the man shifted even further back, visibly uncomfortable, Chess leaned in, confiding: "Hell, there's even ladies like *ladies*, if you could credit it. Or them who take what's given, without pledging any sort'a allegiance at all—all manner of strange creatures, roamin' 'round out there in the dark! And any given one of 'em might sometime want a drink, a plate or to just set a while, without some drunken moron runnin' their mouth."

"Uh, I . . . don't know nothin' on any of that, Mister Pargeter. I just . . ."

"Run a bar, yeah. Need the custom, no matter who brings it. So I'm gonna make sure no fool like Sam Holger ruins your prospects on that score, ever again. Now, how'd that be?"

". . . good, I guess . . ."

"All right, then. Stand back."

Using one lit finger to carve with, Chess doodled what looked like one of Songbird's Chinee sigils on the wall behind, big enough to bake pies on. "This'll be my eye when I'm gone," he told the barkeep, hoping the idea sounded more likely than not. "What it sees, I see; show it something I don't like, and I'll be back. You probably don't want that, I'm thinkin'."

"No sir, Mister Pargeter."

Emerging into the noonday sun, Chess turned to unhitch his horse, and found another animal tied up next to it: a stallion, black as Charlie Alarid's hair and almost as stupidly big, already rigged out for hard travel.

"This'd be yours, I expect," Chess said, as the kid stepped up behind him.

"Told you I was leavin'."

"You did say something of the sort." Chess swung up onto his own ride, popping the rope free with one hand, then shaking it to atoms with the other; he could call it back anytime he wanted, and it'd interfere with the reins. As Charlie mounted up as well, Chess touched the horse with a single spur, nudging it to turn, telling him:

"Hope you don't think travelling in the same direction means we're *together*, as such."

Charlie laughed, a music-touched sound, rhythmic as his own fretwork. "We'll see. That thing you did in there, though—it actually work?"

"Hell, no; I ain't got the sort of time to spend monitoring them that's bound to hate our likes, let alone the inclination. Nice design, though, ain't it?"

"It is."

"Scary, too. That ought'a do somethin', if only for a little while."

"I somewhat think *you* were the scary part, Mister Pargeter. But Bud should recall the threat a good long time, if nothin' else."

They made good time back to that sign Chess had passed coming through, where Charlie reined in a moment, casting a side-eye back toward town—thinking on his folks, perhaps, and how he might not ever see them again. Time was, just the basic implication anyone could have kin they didn't wish dead would've made Chess want to bash their stupid brains in, but not now. Another change.

Yet once again, Ed Morrow came into his mind; big Ed sweating beneath him on that first night at Splitfoot Joe's, eyes gone wide and white as a half-broke horse's, while Chess fisted their hands together and slid down his length with a holler, sure nothing on earth mattered as much but that too-happy place where the two of 'em would end up in just *one—hump—more*. *'Cause I don't care to think on it no more, and you're gonna get me so's I can't*, without a shred of regard for the other party's feelings. Like every other time he'd pulled that same trick on so many other men, none of whose faces he could even vaguely recall, let alone their names . . . all but Rook, and Ed.

Poor old Kees Hosteen, too, who'd cleft to him in the face of mocking indifference, only to die for his partiality just as surely as Chillicothe and his pals, or the Lieut, or that Pink Chess'd had his first gun off. Or all of Bewelcome township, for the grand sin of insulting Chess's taste in bed-partners; all of Hoffstedt's Hoard like-a-wise, excepting Yancey and Geyer, for the equal-grand sin of siding with Chess against Bewelcome's own Sheriff Love, when that crusty gentleman came calling.

Sit there eyein' me up like you never saw nothing prettier, Chess thought, his own gaze straying automatically back to Charlie's own sizable form, wrapped in bad fashion thought it might be. *If you knew me at all beyond my fame, you wouldn't want to come anywhere near, for fear of being pulled down like undertow. Or then again, maybe you still would; maybe you'd just come running the faster, dick in hand. 'Cause from what I've seen, you somewhat like things dangerous.*

"That smile for me, Mister Pargeter?" Charlie called over; Chess hissed again, and shook his head. *Incorrigible,* that was the word he'd heard the Rev use, way back when—when he'd still thought Rook a good man to the core, an up-stood man-mountain set adrift 'mongst killers and rogues, with his thread-worn Bible quotes and his odd ideas about . . . everything, really. Before he'd finally found out better.

Only now did it occur to Chess, though, that there was probably always at least a shred of that man left in Asher Rook, deep down— had to've been, seeing what things came to, in their final throes. Same shred that'd dug itself inside Chess somewheres dark and set in to breed, eventually producing the person who'd kept on shocking himself with his own capacity for self-sacrifice. For that might be credited to Rook as well, along with Ed, and Yancey. And Chess himself, too, in the end.

Even me.

"Think a lot on yourself, don't you, Mister Alarid?" Chess asked the man in question.

"Aw, why so formal? You could always call me Charlie. And me, I could call you—"

"Gettin' a bit ahead of the game, ain't you?"

"You tell me."

"Oh, I will," Chess said, coolly. And turned his horse toward the sun, so the glare would block the fact that he couldn't quite stop himself from smiling, yet again.

HELL REALLY WAS MURKY, like the Bard had claimed; that was one funny thing, amongst so many. Though the fact that it resembled Asher Rook's earliest dreams so little was also fairly amusing, for certain values of same: a dry, sere, awful place for all its deep darkness, like the inside of an oven never quite brought to full heat, and different from Mictlan-Xibalba's clammy climes as lava was from dirt.

Not the same, and not a dream, either. Forever, too, or so the rumours claimed. He was prepared to believe it.

In the end, heat aside, Rook's Hell had proven less the classic Baptist endless cook-kettle he'd always heard about than that Bead-rattler Saint Theresa's vision of a place of absence where God turned His face away, weeping on sinners' betrayal, and the sinners suffered thereby, as much as for any other reason. But being him, God's face—one he'd never seen, any more than he'd heard His voice, no matter how much of His Word he'd back-spouted to his own venal ends—wasn't the one which he found himself fixed on most.

All places bordered each other, down here. He felt them pluck at the edges of this private Inferno, begging pride of place. The Ball-Court, where Ixchel and her smoky brother lay coiled 'round each other, sunk back into torpor, plus a thousand thousand other places sown all 'round the globe, equally terror-wonderful. Where Anansi and Suu Pwa the Dust Devil, Crow and Rabbit and Sedna, Tiamat and Marduk, the Old Sow Who Eats her Farrow had devolved into an equally primal morass, along with pagan martyrs and Christian saints alike—Hypatia and Catherine, both of Alexandria; witches and possessees, witch-hunters and exorcists, workers dark or light, all trading in the same mythic substance. All of whom had begun as human, once upon a time; most of whom had been sacrificed to some idea of the divine and became divine in turn, at least temporarily. All of them, quite probably, hexes.

But who will worship at my *shrine,* Rook could only wonder, trapped here in his cell, *now even Chess doesn't think on me anymore? Who will remember I lived, let alone died—or how, or why? Who for? In service of what?*

Now he had space to be truly honest with himself, Rook could finally admit he'd already figured how the real reason he could never preach effectively on a forgiving God was that on some level, he knew himself both unforgiven, and unforgivable. But *one* deity had loved him, at least, for a little while—and it was the mere idea of Chess being happy again, someday, which was occasionally enough to make him feel happiness's twice-removed ghost, in return.

Rook remembered a fight, early on. How they'd looked at each other after, aching to grab hold and wrestle, to rip and tear 'til somebody was back on top and both of 'em were satisfied. 'Til Rook had finally said, with what he thought was fairly good imitation of cool insouciance: *So here we are, Private—stuck together, one flesh, like any man and . . . man. Friends?*

To which Chess took a deep breath, moving forward, 'til he was well within Rook's reach. Staring up at him, hotly, as he said—*We ain't ever been* friends, *Ash Rook.*

Would've been nice if he could've had Chess kneel next to him as he died, if only to hold his hand, make it not hurt and watch as he went into that great night, submerged, a stone through dark fathoms. Hell, maybe to read to him from that Bible he'd given up in Ixchel's service, which would've emptied itself out accordingly. Rook could almost see it now, leaning his forehead 'gainst the cookhot wall, 'til it frankly hurt too much to do anymore. How the words would've floated up and disappeared into air, going out like sparks, leaving the pages bare.

But that wasn't how it was to be, no. He'd seen to *that* himself.

Live a long time, Chess, he'd told him, once, when in his cups enough to grow maudlin. *I don't look to see you anymore 'fore I need to, if that. Repent, if you can—*

Fuck that, fool; won't get rid of me that *easy, 'specially not if I catch you tryin'. You'll see me again, no matter where you think you're goin'.*

Maybe. But—not soon, darlin'. Please.

Once a whenever, something he took for his turnkey came eddying in to hammer nails into all his softest places, then twist them; it was dreadful, formless, smelling of wet ash and covered in spikes, with too many mouths and not enough tongues to form much speech at all. In the beginning he'd railed at it, then begged it, then flattered it, then fallen silent. Now Rook asked it questions, hoping to trick it into contradicting itself. Could be its information, wasn't any better than his own, but the game did keep him thinking, if nothing else. Kept him dreaming, ensconced down here in the Devil's shit-pit, with nothing to do but regret.

"Is Chess alive yet?"

No.

"Will I ever get out of here?"

No.

"Is there mercy, ever, even for such as I?"

No.

"Uh huh. So tell me this, Beelzebub—ain't it true what I heard, that same as faithless preachers, all devils are liars?"

A long, long pause. Then, at last—with some reluctance—

. . . no.

So, yes. Yes to Chess still upright, burning back and forth across the wild world, bright and hot as any flame. Yes to repentance, to redemption, if only after long suffering—and now that he was forewarned, perhaps foolishly, he began to believe he might yet be able to take whatever else this place might have to dish out to him.

Not soon, the poor portion which was left of "Reverend" Asher Elijah Rook thought, giving himself over to his punishments, *but maybe someday, darlin'—someday. Which makes us both right, in a way; now, ain't that something?*

So, closing what he thought were his eyes, he leaned back on his bed of pain, opening himself up wide to well-deserved agony. . . .

And settled in to wait.

THE END

ABOUT THE AUTHOR

Born in London, England and raised in Toronto, Canada, Gemma Files has been an award-winning horror writer for over twenty years, as well as a film critic, screenwriter and teacher. She has published two collections of short work: *Kissing Carrion* (2003) and *The Worm in Every Heart* (2004), both from Wildside Press. She has also written two chapbooks of poetry. Her first novel, *A Book Of Tongues*: Volume One of the Hexslinger Series, won the 2010 Black Quill award for "Best Small Press Chill" (Editors' and Readers' Choice) from *DarkScribe Magazine*, and was also nominated for a Bram Stoker Award for Best First Novel. Its sequel, *A Rope of Thorns* (2011), along with this book, complete a trilogy which is really one narrative broken into three instalments. For her next trick, she looks forward to writing something different.

Learn more about Gemma Files at her official website, *musicatmidnight-gfiles.blogspot.com*, or more than you probably want to know at her blog, *handful_ofdust.livejournal.com*.

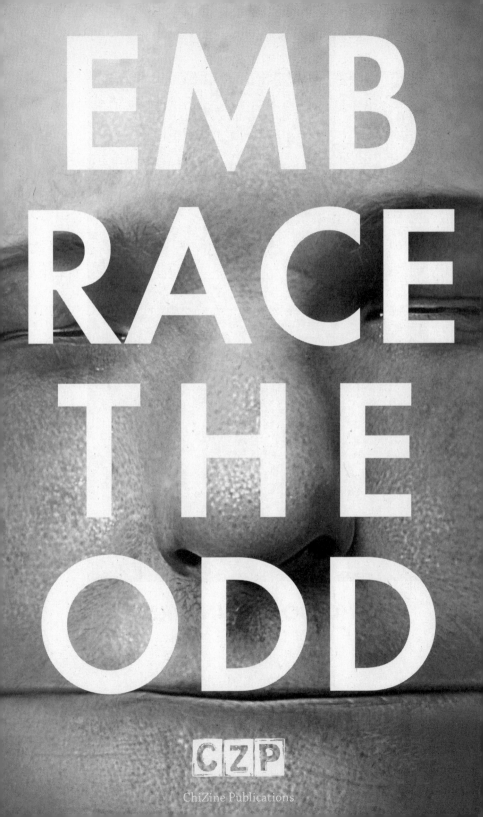

EMB
RACE
THE
ODD

CZP

ChiZine Publications

SHOEBOX TRAIN WRECK

JOHN MANTOOTH

AVAILABLE MARCH 2012
FROM CHIZINE PUBLICATIONS

978-1-926851-54-9

THE STEEL SERAGLIO

MIKE CAREY, LINDA CAREY & LOUISE CAREY

AVAILABLE MARCH 2O12
FROM CHIZINE PUBLICATIONS

978-1-926851-53-2

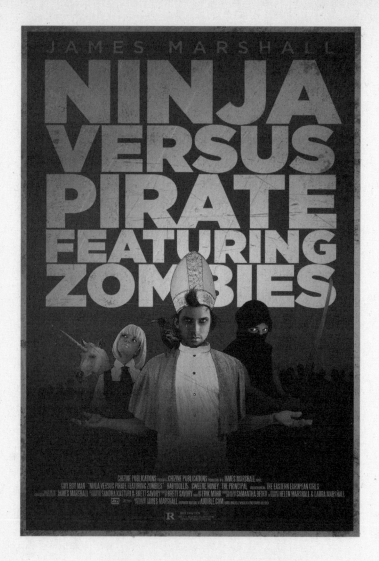

NINJA VERSUS PIRATE
FEATURING ZOMBIES

JAMES MARSHALL

AVAILABLE MAY 2012
FROM CHIZINE PUBLICATIONS

978-1-926851-58-7

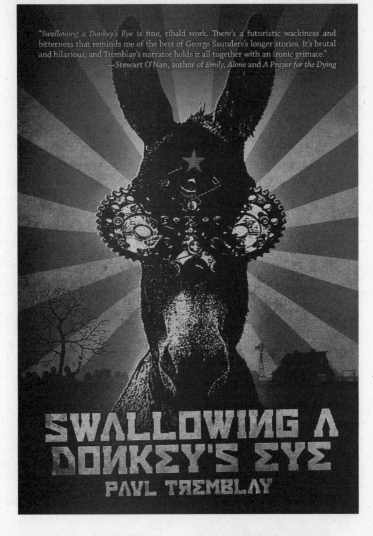

BULLETTIME

NICK MAMATAS

AVAILABLE AUGUST 2012
FROM CHIZINE PUBLICATIONS

978-1-926851-71-6

978-1-926851-35-8

TONE MILAZZO

**PICKING UP
THE GHOST**

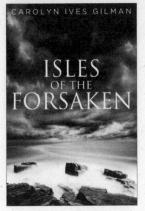

978-1-926851-43-3

CAROLYN IVES GILMAN

**ISLES OF
THE FORSAKEN**

978-1-926851-44-0

TIM PRATT

BRIARPATCH

978-1-926851-43-3

CAITLIN SWEET

THE PATTERN SCARS

978-1-926851-46-4

TERESA MILBRODT

BEARDED WOMEN

978-1-926851-45-7

MICHAEL ROWE

ENTER, NIGHT

CHIZINEPUB.COM   CZP

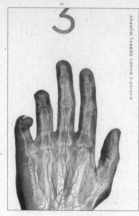

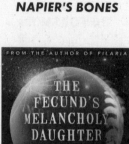

978-0-9813746-6-6

GORD ZAJAC

MAJOR KARNAGE

978-0-9813746-8-0

ROBERT BOYCZUK

NEXUS: ASCENSION

978-1-926851-00-6

CRAIG DAVIDSON

SARAH COURT

978-1-926851-06-8

PAUL TREMBLAY

**IN THE
MEAN TIME**

978-1-926851-02-0

HALLI VILLEGAS

**THE HAIR WREATH
AND OTHER STORIES**

978-1-926851-04-4

TONY BURGESS

**PEOPLE LIVE STILL
IN CASHTOWN
CORNERS**

978-0-9812978-9-7

TIM LEBBON

THE THIEF OF BROKEN TOYS

978-0-9812978-8-0

PHILIP NUTMAN

CITIES OF NIGHT

978-0-9812978-7-3

SIMON LOGAN

KATJA FROM THE PUNK BAND

978-0-9812978-6-6

GEMMA FILES

A BOOK OF TONGUES

978-0-9812978-5-9

DOUGLAS SMITH

CHIMERASCOPE

978-0-9812978-4-2

NICHOLAS KAUFMANN

CHASING THE DRAGON

978-0-9809410-9-8

ROBERT J. WIERSEMA

**THE WORLD MORE
FULL OF WEEPING**

978-0-9812978-2-8

CLAUDE LALUMIÈRE

**OBJECTS OF
WORSHIP**

978-0-9809410-7-4

DANIEL A. RABUZZI

THE CHOIR BOATS

978-0-9809410-5-0

AVIE TIDHAR AND NIR YANIV

**THE TEL AVIV
DOSSIER**

978-0-9809410-3-6

ROBERT BOYCZUK

**HORROR STORY
AND OTHER
HORROR STORIES**

978-0-9812978-3-5

DAVID NICKLE

**MONSTROUS
AFFECTIONS**

978-0-9809410-1-2

BRENT HAYWARD

FILARIA

"CHIZINE PUBLICATIONS REPRESENTS SOMETHING WHICH IS COMMON IN THE MUSIC INDUSTRY BUT SADLY RARER WITHIN THE PUBLISHING INDUSTRY: THAT A CLEVER INDEPENDENT CAN RUN RINGS ROUND THE MAJORS IN TERMS OF STYLE AND CONTENT."

–MARTIN LEWIS, *SF SITE*